CLAIMING THE DRAKOS HEIR

JENNIFER FAYE

THE COWBOY'S SECRET FAMILY

JUDY DUARTE

MILLS & BOON

First Published in Great Britain 2019
by Mills & Boon, an imprint of HarperCollinsPublishers,
1 London Bridge Street, London, SE1 9GF

Claiming The Drakos Heir © 2019 Jennifer F. Stroka
The Cowboy's Secret Family © 2019 Judy Duarte

ISBN: 978-0-263-27245-1

0619

MIX
Paper from
responsible sources
FSC **FSC® C007454**
www.fsc.org

This book is produced from independently certified FSC™ paper to ensure responsible forest management.

For more information visit: www.harpercollins.co.uk/green

Printed and bound in Spain
by CPI, Barcelona

Award-winning author **Jennifer Faye** pens fun, heart-warming, contemporary romances, filled with rugged cowboys, sexy billionaires and enchanting royalty. Internationally published, with books translated into nine languages, she is a two-times winner of the *RT Book Reviews* Reviewers' Choice Award. She has also won the CataRomance Reviewers' Choice Award, been named a TOP PICK author, and has been nominated for numerous other awards.

Since 2002, *USA TODAY* bestselling author **Judy Duarte** has written over forty books for Mills & Boon, earned two RITA® Award nominations, won two Maggie Awards and received a National Readers' Choice Award. When she's not cooped up in her writing cave, she enjoys travelling with her husband and spending quality time with her grandchildren. You can learn more about Judy and her books on her website, judyduarte. com, or at Facebook.com/judyduartenovelist

CLAIMING THE DRAKOS HEIR

JENNIFER FAYE

CHAPTER ONE

TODAY WAS THE WEDDING.

And nothing was going to go wrong.

Popi Costas assured herself that all would be well on this gorgeous autumn day. After all, she'd gone over every detail at least a dozen times. This was the most important wedding that she'd ever planned—even topping the royal wedding they'd hosted earlier that year.

This was the last wedding on Infinity Island before the groom, Xander, brought in work crews to give the private Greek island a much-needed facelift. In fact, they'd been having all the residents pack up their things so they could be put into storage while the renovations took place.

In the meantime, Popi planned to visit with her parents until the work on the island was complete. And after all the misery they'd faced that summer, they all needed some happiness. She could barely believe two months had passed since her adopted sister and brother-in-law had been alive in one breath...

And gone in the next.

How had it all gone so wrong? Popi had asked herself that question countless times. And she'd never come up with a sufficient answer. All she knew was what she'd been told—her sister and brother-in-law had died in a boating accident.

Something had triggered an explosion and no one had escaped the blazing inferno in the middle of the sea. It felt as though a piece of Popi had died along with them. If only she'd have said something... Done something...

She halted her thoughts. Today was about her best

friend, Lea, getting married to the love of her life. If two people ever belonged together, it was the two of them—

Knock-knock.

Popi lowered the curling iron she'd been using to put elegant barrel rolls in her long hair. With only half her hair curled, she really didn't need any interruptions right now. If it was Lea, she would let herself inside. So it had to be someone else. Maybe if she ignored her unwanted guest, they would go away. Yes, that sounded like a good plan.

Popi sectioned off more hair and rolled it onto the iron. She needed to get to the reception as soon as possible to make sure everything was in place. Even though she'd just been there less than two hours ago and gone over the plans with the staff for the umpteenth time, she still worried something would go astray.

She didn't know why she was so nervous. She planned weddings for a living—big ones, small ones, traditional, original and everything in between. But this wedding was for her dearest friend. And Popi needed it to go off without a hitch.

Just then the baby kicked. Being almost nine months pregnant with her niece or nephew added a whole new level of turbulent emotions to the situation. When she'd agreed to be the surrogate for her sister, she never imagined life could be so cruel and at the same time provide such a precious blessing—a little piece of her sister lived on.

Popi placed a protective hand over her abdomen. "Don't worry, little one. I will make sure you are safe and loved."

Popi unrolled the iron. She never considered becoming a parent while she was still in her twenties, but there was no way she would turn her back on her sister's baby. Though she tried to put on a brave face, on the inside she was worried about being a good parent. She'd been reading parenting books but would it be enough?

Her life was about to change in so many ways, as the baby was due in a couple of weeks. Not long at all—

Knock-knock. Knock-knock.

So much for ignoring them.

"Anyone home?" A male voice called out through the open window.

Who could that be?

Popi wasn't expecting anyone. Everyone she knew was getting ready for the wedding. And then the thought of something going wrong with the wedding had her rushing out of the bathroom in her fluffy, short pink robe that barely fit over her baby bump and with a large portion of her hair pulled up in a big orange clip.

Popi swung the door open. Her gaze took in the man's scruffy but sexy appearance. From his longish hair to the thick scruff trailing along his dark, tanned jawline—his slack jaw, as though he'd opened his mouth to say something but totally forgot what it was he'd been meaning to say.

His casual white shirt and cargo shorts let her know he wasn't one of the wedding guests. Nor did he work on the island, as she knew everyone. That meant he must have been hired to help with the island renovations. But what was he doing here today?

When her gaze returned to his face, she noticed his rounded eyes were blue—not just blue, but a light blue that caught and held her attention. But his gaze wasn't meeting hers. In fact, his gaze was aimed southward.

His Adam's apple bobbed. "You're pregnant."

She stifled a laugh at his obvious discomfort. Had this man never seen a pregnant woman before? Or was she so large now that it bordered on the obscene?

Popi pressed a hand to the small of her back, trying to ease the ache. "You win the gold star for the day. I am indeed pregnant. Very pregnant." And then realizing that by putting her hand behind her back that her fuzzy robe was straining to cover all her amplified curves, she immediately lowered her arm to her side.

Was it just her or did the man look distinctly pale? Not like he hadn't seen any sun recently, because he most definitely had a better tan than her, but rather his face had drained of its color.

Struggling not to squirm under his bold stare, she asked, "What can I do for you?"

He cleared his throat and raised his gaze until those dreamy blue eyes finally stared into her own. "Are you Popi?"

"I am."

"I don't know if you were expecting me—"

"I wasn't." The movers weren't scheduled to arrive until tomorrow to transfer her belongings to storage. "Today is a really bad day for me." It was the worst day for a surprise. Her focus was supposed to be on Lea, not anything else. But apparently this very strong, very handsome stranger hadn't gotten the message.

He had broad shoulders and his shirt clung to his muscled chest, while the short sleeves wrapped snuggly around his bulging biceps. One arm had a tattoo of a map of the world overlaid with a compass. From the looks of this man, he didn't believe in spending much time indoors. And the sun gods had blessed him with strength and the most amazing tan that accentuated the lines of his muscles.

Popi swallowed hard. Maybe she'd been too focused on her problems lately to notice what was around her. Or else it was the pregnancy hormones. But this guy looked good enough to serve up on the top of a wedding cake.

Realizing she was once again staring, Popi lifted her gaze, finding she had to crane her neck to meet his gaze. "You're early."

"Early?"

"Yes. You aren't supposed to be here until tomorrow. I have a wedding today." But it wouldn't hurt to get a move on the work, since she hadn't finished packing, and she wanted to get to the mainland and her parents' house by tomorrow evening.

Confusion reflected in his eyes. "I didn't know about any wedding. No one mentioned it." Then his brows lifted. "Are you getting married?"

She couldn't help but laugh. Her irritation with him drained away. "Not a chance. It's my best friend's wedding and I'm coordinating it."

"Oh." He looked caught off guard and unsure what to say or do next.

"No worries." She stepped back. "Come on in. You can move all the boxes out of the guest room and stack them here in the living room. They'll be ready for pickup in the morning."

"You want them moved now?"

"Yes."

The man's face creased with worry lines, but she didn't have time to answer whatever questions he had. How many questions could there be to move boxes from one room to the next?

She checked the time on her watch. "I have to hurry."

"But—"

"I can't answer questions now. If it's too much for you, you'll have to come back tomorrow." She turned for the master suite. No moving man, no matter how hot she found him, was going to hold her up. She had a bride waiting for her.

CHAPTER TWO

WHAT JUST HAPPENED?

Apollo Drakos stood slack-jawed as the woman sashayed down the hallway, but to be honest her sashay was more like a waddle. A cute waddle, but still a waddle all the same.

How could she still be pregnant?

His attorney had assured him the baby was born, though no one had been able to tell him if it was a boy or girl. Not that it mattered to him. Either way, he was still claiming his niece or nephew.

The attorney had gone on to inform him that Miss Costas would have a strong case to gain full custody of the baby, as well as control over the child's inheritance. The attorney even seemed to think that with Miss Costas being adopted and not the child's biological aunt, it wouldn't be enough to sway the judge from giving her custody. But did Popi really want to take on that responsibility? Or was she doing it out of necessity?

Apollo knew he had no one to blame for this mess but himself. While Popi had been here, helping to make his brother and sister-in-law's dream of a family into a reality, he'd been off on another adventure—avoiding the fact that he was the unwanted son, the outcast. But he'd come here as soon as he'd heard. That had to count for something, didn't it?

But how was this going to work now that he knew Popi was still pregnant? Although it did look as though she was going to give birth soon. Not that he was an expert on pregnant women. Yet all of her was thin except for her stomach. It was very round indeed. Funnily enough, from behind you couldn't even tell she was pregnant. However, the cute little waddle did give it away.

It wasn't until now—seeing Popi round with a baby—that he realized how much she'd done for his brother and sister-in-law. Not everyone would step up and offer to carry someone else's baby—certainly not him, if that were even a possibility.

Gathering himself, Apollo pressed his lips together in a firm line. Who exactly did this woman think he was? And where was she moving to with his brother's baby?

The baby belonged at the Drakos estate, which was situated just outside Athens. It was a place Apollo rarely visited. Though the vast estate was aesthetically beautiful, it held many dark memories. When Apollo was a kid, it felt more like a prison he so desperately wanted to escape. While his older brother, Nile, had been cast as the "good son," Apollo had been labelled "worthless" by their father.

Apollo slammed the door on the bad memories. But no matter how many times he turned his back on the past, the door would eventually creak open once more. He'd heard it said that you can't outrun the past. He should know—he'd been trying for years and it was still just a blink away.

He needed to concentrate on the here and now. Everything was such an utter mess. If only he'd have come home when his brother had asked…

But being away on a two-month hiking expedition in the Himalayas, he'd been out of contact with the entire world—including his older brother, Nile. At the time, Apollo found it so freeing. A chance to let go of the ghosts of the past and embrace the present. At the time, he'd had no idea how much that freedom would cost him.

When he'd returned to civilization, he'd been unconscious, injured and alone. By the time he'd been able to speak on the phone, he'd had no one to call about his accident because his brother had been furious with him during their final phone conversation. After surgery and therapy for his broken leg, a private investigator had tracked him down at the hospital. It was then that he'd received the worst news of his life.

His big, strong, protective brother was dead.

Apollo's footloose and carefree life had come to an end in that moment.

All of the things that he'd put off—all of the words that he'd hesitated to say to Nile—the overdue apology, the thank-you, the *I love you, brother*—the chance to say any of it had slipped through his fingers. His brother would never know what he meant to him—how much he longed to mend their relationship.

In that moment, Apollo had never felt so alone in his life.

And then in the next breath, the investigator had informed him that he had a niece or nephew. Apollo's heart had leapt. There was another Drakos in this world. He wasn't alone.

He had one last chance to make it up to his brother for cutting loose and leaving home all those years ago. He'd let Nile deal with all the Drakos' business and their father. But on one sunny afternoon, his brother's life had been cut incredibly short, as was his sister-in-law's.

A boating accident. Who dies while boating?

It seemed unreal. So implausible. And yet the sharp pain of loss was quite real. And to add salt to the wound, it had happened almost two months ago. His brother and sister-in-law had been laid to rest and Apollo hadn't been there for any of it because no one knew where he was... except his brother.

He'd once again let down Nile. But that wouldn't happen again. He was on Infinity Island to retrieve his niece or nephew…even if it meant he had to wait for its very precious arrival.

Apollo's thoughts turned back to Popi. He knew she'd been through a lot—he knew better than anyone. How would she react when she learned he was there for the baby?

Maybe she'd filed for custody of the baby because she didn't think he'd want to take responsibility for the baby. Maybe once he explained things to her, she'd realize the baby belonged with him, where the child would be groomed to take over the Drakos empire. Could it really be that simple? Would Popi hand the baby over to him like she'd been planning to do with his brother and her sister?

Apollo thought about following her to the back of the bungalow and reasoning with her. But then he recalled that little pink robe. He swallowed hard. Did she realize it barely covered her? It was so tantalizing, hinting at the curvy goodness that lay beneath. But the robe never really revealed anything scandalous. It was more the knowledge that she didn't have a thing on underneath that turned his blood red-hot.

He tugged on his shirt collar. It was a bit warm out, even with the sea breeze. His mind was still replaying the images of Popi. He'd gotten a good view of her shapely legs. They were long and smooth. His mouth grew dry. Why did this woman have to be so good-looking? It was a distraction that he didn't need or want.

His back teeth ground together. He had to get past the superficial. His purpose for coming to the island couldn't be forgotten. If he stayed focused, he would soon forget about Popi's finer assets. At least he hoped so.

Apollo walked back out the front door. He started down the steps with no particular destination in mind. He didn't even know anything about this island, except that the woman who was carrying his last living relative lived here.

He came to a stop and turned. Why was he walking away? Maybe because that's what he'd been doing his whole life. But no more.

Apollo returned to the porch and took a seat in one of the two wicker chairs. They looked stiff and uninviting, but once he was seated, he found them surprisingly comfortable. He lounged back and decided to learn more about Infinity Island. He pulled out his phone and typed the name into the search engine.

He was surprised by the large number of articles written about the island. In his limited experience with women, he knew it may take Popi quite some time to get ready. He settled back in the chair, pulled up the first article about this "wedding" island and started to read.

To his surprise there was a picture of Popi, smiling at the camera. She was arm and arm with another woman. He wondered if this was today's bride. The caption beneath the photo said that the other woman was the owner, while Popi was the wedding planner.

Apollo inwardly groaned. This woman believed in hearts, flowers and happily-ever-afters. Those were things he'd purposely avoided all his adult life. What exactly had he gotten himself into? Maybe he should have let his army of attorneys handle it. But he didn't want to put either of them through a long, drawn-out legal battle. They'd already been through so much—especially Popi.

And so he kept reading about the island. The more he knew, the easier it would be to reason with her, should it come to that. After all, the heir to the Drakos fortune couldn't be raised in a hut on some small, out-of-the-way island…

A movement out of the corner of his eye had him glancing up. In a whirl of coral gauzy material, and with long brown curls bouncing, Popi walked swiftly away from the bungalow. Apparently she hadn't noticed him sitting off to the side.

He got to his feet and slipped the phone in his pocket, but in just that small amount of time she'd darted down a path. The problem was there were a lot of paths, and he wasn't sure which one she'd gone down. How could a very pregnant woman move so quickly?

He knew she was busy with the wedding, but after it was over, perhaps at the reception, he could grab a moment of her time. He just wanted her to know he was here now. She didn't have to go through the remainder of this pregnancy alone.

CHAPTER THREE

SHE DIDN'T NEED any more complications.

Popi made a mental note to let the supervisor in charge of the move know about the man showing up at her bungalow on the wrong day. And on top of it, the man hadn't done anything she'd instructed him to do. In fact, the man had done absolutely nothing. He better not even try to charge time for today. She wouldn't stand for it.

Popi headed straight for the Hideaway Café. She refused to let herself get utterly distracted by that man—no matter how sexy he was with those mesmerizing blue eyes and that intriguing tattoo on his bicep. She halted her thoughts. She had a very important wedding today. Everything else would have to wait until another time—including the mystery man.

Popi came to a stop on the patio of the café. This was Lea's dream wedding spot. It had the most awesome view of the bay, but as beautiful as the view was, it wasn't Popi's vision for saying "I do." Whenever she got married, she loved the idea of a lush garden. Intimate and yet with hundreds of colorful blooms in every shade imaginable.

Popi paused to take in the view. She'd worked closely with Lea to plan this wedding down to the finest detail. Lea had told her not to push so hard, but Popi needed to focus on the wedding. Working was her way of dealing with the loss of her sister. The work kept her grounded when everything around her felt as though it was spinning out of control.

All the outdoor white tables with their colorful umbrellas had been removed to make room for rows of white folding chairs. Lea had opted for wildflowers, which included locally grown orchids. Popi hadn't been sure about the idea, but now seeing them in arrangements throughout the venue, she had to admit it looked stunning.

There was little more than an hour until the wedding—time that would be needed to get the bride ready. Though Lea had moved to the island little more than a year ago, she was embracing the Greek culture, and the older women on the island had filled Lea's head with all the wedding traditions. Lea was excited to merge some of the old ways with some of her own traditions. It would make for a beautiful wedding.

After inspecting the venue preparations, Popi took off for Lea's bungalow. Thankfully there was a golf cart at the offices. She planned to acquire it, as her feet were getting tired and the event hadn't even begun. Carrying around an extra human was taxing.

She placed a hand on her aching lower back. "Not that I'd have it any other way. We'll make your parents proud."

She sat in the cart and then set off down the familiar path. One of the first Greek traditions they'd dealt with was setting the wedding date. When the elders on the island had heard the wedding was to be in August, they immediately spoke up. They advised that if the wedding must be in August, then the first two weeks of the month should be avoided at all costs, as they were reserved for religious reasons.

Neither Lea nor Popi were very religious, but, they reasoned, why tempt fate and the ire of the elders? As such, they planned the wedding for the last weekend in the month. Everyone seemed pleased with the decision, as Xander had arranged for a cruise ship to take everyone from the island for a Mediterranean cruise right after the reception.

The plan was, while they were all off on a two-week

cruise, followed by temporary lodgings in Athens, the island would undergo extensive renovations. When the citizens were allowed to return to their bungalows, everything would be updated and the crews would be out of their way. It was quite an amazing gift from the bridegroom to his new extended family.

A couple of minutes later, Popi pulled to a stop in front of Lea's bungalow. The bridegroom wasn't there. He was bunking with the island's handyman, Joseph, until the wedding. In the time Xander had been on the island, the older man had taken him under his wing, like a father would do.

When Popi entered the bungalow, she was surprised to find so many women rushing around. But she didn't see Lea among them. And then her name was called. She glanced around, finding Lea waving her to the guest room.

Popi made her way to Lea. Once inside the room, she closed the door. "What are you doing in here instead of your room?"

Lea rolled her eyes. "The elders are so caught up in the wedding. They think my soon-to-be husband is in line to be a saint for all he's doing for them that they don't want to jinx anything."

"Do I dare ask what that means?"

"They're preparing the marital bed… Um…what did they call it? Oh, yes, *to krevati*."

"What?" She'd heard of the tradition but she'd never heard of anyone actually doing it. "You mean like with the rose petals, ribbons and money?"

"And rice. Don't forget the rice. They've been here cleaning and putting fresh linens on the bed. I had to talk them out of rolling an infant on the bed. I told them we didn't need any help in the fertility department." Lea ran a loving hand over her own expanding midsection.

Popi burst out laughing. "Definitely not. But they could have just rolled you around on the bed."

"Don't give them any ideas." Lea shook her head. "So I've been hiding in here."

"You don't have time to hide. It isn't long until you say 'I do.' I'll just go get some makeup and I'll be right back."

Popi was the maid of honor, or *koumbara*, and it was her responsibility to see that the bride was ready on time. The rest of the bridal party soon showed up, including Lea's assistant and her soon to be sister-in-law, Stasia. Because an odd number of attendants was good luck. And three attendants were the best.

Together they worked until Lea was all done up with her long hair pulled up with just a few strategically placed curly wisps of hair softening her face. A wreath of fresh flowers was clipped into place.

Popi stepped back and took in Lea's dress. It was truly breathtaking. White tiers of Chantilly lace, tulle and ribbons adorned her. There was a V-shaped neckline with delicate straps over her shoulders and satin ribbon wrapped around her waist. She truly looked like a Greek goddess.

"You're perfect," Popi announced. And the other young women readily agreed.

"Not quite." Lea slipped off her white heels.

"What are you doing?" Popi frowned. "Is it your shoes? Is something wrong with them?"

Lea shook her head. "Does someone have a pen?"

"I do." Stasia pulled a fine black marker from her purse.

Popi watched as Lea wrote the names of her bridal party on the bottom of her shoes. Lea had written her name first, before Popi could tell her not to do it. It was another Greek tradition that the names of the single ladies be written on the bottom of the bride's shoes. The names that are worn off by the end of the evening will soon be married. Popi was certain that her name would still be there, because there was no chance she was getting married anytime soon.

She already had her hands more than full with the little bundle of joy inside her.

As though the baby sensed her thoughts, it kicked. Once. Twice. And the last kick was swifter than the others, sending Popi bending over. She pressed a hand to the area where she'd been kicked.

"Are you okay?" Lea asked, concern written all over her face, as well as the other ladies.

Popi drew in a deep, soothing breath and straightened. "Yeah. I think I have a footballer in there."

"Oh." Lea smiled.

"Don't smile," Popi said. "Your time is coming."

Lea continued to smile as she pressed a hand to her baby bump. "It'll all be worth it in the end."

Popi smiled. "You just keep telling yourself that when the baby starts tap-dancing on your bladder."

Lea's smile dimmed. "I hadn't thought of that."

Knock-knock.

Popi went to the door and opened it a crack. On the other side was the photographer. After glancing around to make sure the coast was clear of the groom, Popi admitted the photographer. It was almost time to head to the Hideaway.

After today, their lives were going to change dramatically. Her friend would be married, with a baby created from that love already on the way. It didn't get any better than that. Popi was so happy for her—for all of them.

Sometimes Popi wondered if the baby she was carrying would feel like they'd missed out on something by not having a father. But then again, they most certainly would feel cheated by never knowing either of their biological parents. A sadness filled Popi. If only she could change the past.

She recalled her last conversation with her sister. Neither suspected it would be the last time they spoke. And the conversation had gone totally sideways.

Popi blamed herself for the heated exchange...for Andrina and Nile being on that boat at that particular time... for them needlessly dying. Popi's throat tightened. Her breath caught in her lungs. If only she'd said something different—if she'd had more patience—then they'd both still be alive. If that conversation had gone differently, her sister and brother-in-law would be here, anxiously awaiting the arrival of their first child. She was positive of it.

The photographer bumped into her, jarring her from the emotional black hole that threatened to swallow her whole. The man turned to her. "Sorry. Would you mind helping the bride with her hair so I can get a few photos?"

Not trusting her voice, Popi nodded.

Today was not the time to contemplate her sister's death. Today was about smiles, hopes and good tidings. Popi choked down all her worries and smiled. Lea deserved nothing but happiness on her big day.

He didn't want to be here.

But on this small island, places to wait for Popi were limited. And the wedding appeared to be taking place in a common area of the village.

Apollo found himself standing off to the side. No one seemed to make a big deal of him being there. They acted as though he was just another wedding guest. Some even shook his hand and greeted him.

Up until now, Apollo had done nothing but make one mistake after the next since the day he was born. He thought he'd have time to fix things—to change his ways. After all, he was young. There was plenty of time to make up for the past, but then suddenly out of nowhere he'd been blindsided when time had run out for Nile and his wife, Andrina. And now he owed it to his brother not to mess things up where the baby was concerned.

As he thought of Nile, the breath hitched in Apollo's

throat. It wasn't supposed to happen this way. He was the adventure seeker—the daredevil. If something bad had to happen, it should have been to him. Not his brother. None of this made any sense.

A flurry of motion drew Apollo from his thoughts. The wedding guests took their seats. Not wanting to stand out any more than he already did with his casual attire, Apollo took a seat in the back. The classical music started. Two pretty women started up the aisle.

And then Popi appeared at the end of the aisle, holding a bouquet of teal blossoms. She looked radiant. Her smile lit up her whole face. All he could do in that minute was stare at the most beautiful woman he'd ever seen in his life. It was the same sort of stunned reaction he'd experienced at her place, when he'd found her in the very short, very revealing pink robe. He couldn't decide which look he preferred on her. Both looks had their alluring qualities.

It was in that moment her gaze lifted, meeting his. The breath caught in his chest. Her big brown eyes were mesmerizing. He felt as though he were being drawn into her chocolate-brown depths. His heart beat faster, as time felt as though it had been suspended.

She was looking right at him as she stepped forward. His mouth grew dry. He should turn away, but he couldn't. She was amazing in every way.

And then she passed by him and kept going to where the priest and groom waited. Apollo didn't take an easy breath until the bride moved to the end of the aisle.

The wedding proceeded slowly and they had finally come to the blessing of the rings. The wedding bands were exchanged three times. Apollo rolled his shoulders. He willed the wedding to hurry up and end, but they were just now taking three sips of wine as a symbol of sharing for the rest of their marriage. He'd forgotten about three being such a significant number in Greek culture.

When they made it to the traditional readings, he resisted the urge to squirm in his seat. He'd done far too much sitting on planes in order to get to this little, out-of-the-way island as fast as he could. And his injuries were not taking all the sitting in one position well.

When the ceremony finally ended and the guests were directed to the garden area next to the café where the reception was being held, Apollo fell in step with everyone else. He was surprised when he only received a few odd glances at his choice of casual attire. How was he supposed to know when he'd ventured to Infinity Island that his trip would include a wedding?

He kept trying to catch Popi alone, but she was forever talking with this person or that person. He just wanted a brief word with her. He hoped once she knew he wanted custody of the child that she'd withdraw her petition. And in the meantime, he'd pay for her medical expenses and anything else she needed. Could it be that simple?

Apollo didn't miss how Popi spoke to everyone she passed. There were a lot of hugs and smiles. Everyone was enjoying themselves. He was impressed with how this group of people could act like one big, happy, functional family, whereas his own blood relatives had never experienced anything close to this easiness with each other. Not that he ever needed a close-knit family. He did fine on his own.

Apollo's father had had two loves in his life while Apollo was growing up: the family business and his bottle of bourbon. Nile inherited their father's passion for the family business. Apollo never forgot Nile's obsession with all things Drakos. The thing Apollo never figured out was whether his brother's interest in the business was an effort to please their demanding father or if Nile just loved the business world to the exclusion of all else—until he'd met Andrina.

Everything had changed after Nile fell for Andrina. It was evident in his phone calls with his brother. Nile's voice had been full of happiness and he'd grown excited about the future, which was no longer centered on the business, but instead Nile was excited about the family he and Andrina were creating. However, Apollo didn't believe that happiness lasted.

And then he'd been proven right, again. The news of their deaths was like a one-two punch to the kidney. Emotionally it had knocked him out.

In a blink, his brother had been stolen away. Even now the pain of loss emanated outward from Apollo's chest. He didn't know how Popi was holding it all together—maybe it was due to the baby. She was being strong for it. He had to admire such strength and courage.

It was then that Popi approached him. And by her stiff posture, he was certain she was not happy about him crashing this wedding. Maybe this hadn't been such a great idea after all, but he was there now so he might as well stay and get this over with.

He was propped against a tall white column. He didn't move, as Popi was headed straight for him. "What are you doing here?" Her gaze narrowed. "You aren't part of the moving crew, are you?"

"Never said I was."

"But you let me believe you were."

"As I recall, you were in too much of a hurry to get the details."

Popi crossed her arms and glared at him. "Who are you?"

He cleared his throat. "I tried to tell you back at the bungalow—"

Just then there was the tinkle of a glass as people were called to take a seat for dinner. The bride motioned for Popi to join her at the head table.

Popi signaled that she was coming before she turned back to him. "I have to go."

Without waiting for him to respond, she turned her back to him and walked away. His gaze naturally followed the sway of her hips.

"This isn't over." The gentle breeze carried his words, but Popi was too far away to hear him.

He'd walked away from his brother, not intending for it to be forever, but that's exactly what had happened. He would never again speak to Nile, argue with him or take comfort in his brother's concern for his well-being. Without Nile, he utterly felt adrift in this great big world.

And then when he'd been informed about Nile's child—his last living link to his brother—Apollo knew in that moment that he had to set things right. Or as right as was possible. He owed Nile that much and so much more.

In the next breath, the attorney had informed him that Popi was seeking custody. If he didn't stop her, he would lose a tangible link to his brother—his only chance to do the right thing as far as his brother was concerned.

Apollo had vowed then and there to never walk away from the baby. It was all the family he had left. He would learn from his past and not make the same mistakes again—the stakes were too high.

Apollo was generally straightforward, but with a baby involved perhaps a gentler approach was in order. His father had been a very blunt man. Apollo knew how it felt to be on the receiving end of that bluntness. He wouldn't wish it on anyone.

Maybe a bit of charm and a few kind words would smooth the path to claiming his niece or nephew. He didn't know if it'd work, but it was worth a try. He didn't want to make this harder on Popi than it needed to be. But in the end, he intended for the baby to live with him at the Drakos estate.

CHAPTER FOUR

POPI BARELY ATE her dinner at the reception.

Her gaze kept moving over the crowd of well-wishers, searching for the strikingly handsome man. He seemed so familiar to her and yet she was certain they hadn't met before, but how could that be?

And what did he want with her? If he was a disgruntled client, he would want to speak with Lea, as she was the owner of the island and the wedding business. But Popi hadn't noticed a wedding ring on his finger.

Lea leaned over. "Is everything all right?"

Not wanting to alarm the bride on her big day, Popi said, "Yes, of course."

Lea's brows drew together. "Then why haven't you eaten?"

Popi glanced down. At one point, the food had looked appetizing, but now her stomach was a twisted-up ball of nerves. "I…um…was just distracted."

Lea arched a fine brow at her. "Distracted, huh? With that handsome guy I saw you chatting with?"

Popi's gaze searched the area, not finding any sign of him. She didn't know what to say to Lea. She didn't want the bride worrying about the mystery man.

"Popi?"

She turned back to the bride. "He's, um, with the movers. There was some kind of mix-up and he showed up a day early. I hope him crashing the wedding hasn't upset you."

A look of disappointment skittered across Lea's face. "So he wasn't here at your invitation?"

Popi gave a firm shake of her head.

"I'll have him escorted off the island—"

"No. Don't." There was something about his serious tone and the feeling she should know him that had her anxious to learn his story. "I've got it."

Lea looked hesitant. "You're sure?"

Popi nodded. The truth was she wasn't sure about anything—especially why this man was so eager to speak with her.

Lea let the subject drop. And with the mystery man now gone, Popi forced herself to eat a few bites of food. The evening moved along with the groom, Xander, dancing the traditional *zeibekiko*. The crowd clapped as Xander's arms rose over his head. He snapped his fingers as he moved in a tight circle. He stopped in front of Lea and dropped to his knees, still waving his arms over his head. The crowd loved it, most especially Lea. The smile on the bride's face lit up the whole room.

One dance led to another. The bride and groom were all smiles, as they had eyes only for each other. Popi considered this wedding a success. She took her first easy breath.

And the next thing she knew, she was being led around the dance floor by the best man, Roberto, who was also Xander's close friend and second-in-command. She'd met him more than once, and though Lea was anxious for them to hit it off, it wasn't going to happen. Popi couldn't put her finger on why. He was definitely handsome and successful, but neither one was into the other. They were becoming fast friends, but that's all it would ever be.

Partway through the song, there was a tap on Roberto's shoulders. Popi's gaze followed the finger up the arm and then her gaze settled upon the sexy stranger's face. Apparently it was time for their talk. She had to admit that she was anxious to learn his identity and what he had to tell her.

"Can I cut in?" The stranger wore a serious expression.

Roberto, looking caught off guard, stopped dancing. "Um…" His gaze moved to her and she nodded. "Thank you for the dance." Roberto turned back to the other man. "She's all yours."

The man took Popi in his quite capable arms, but there was no escaping their closeness with her protruding abdomen. No one had long enough arms to allow for much room between them—not even this man.

"What are you doing?" Her voice came out in a heated whisper.

"Dancing. With you." He led her around the dance floor.

"But I don't know your name. I don't even understand why you're at the wedding—"

"Shh… I'll answer all your questions after one dance. That seems like a fair bargain, doesn't it?" He smiled at her, but it didn't quite reach his eyes.

His words were smooth, but she got the impression there was more going on here than him trying to pick her up. Although, a man with his striking good looks being interested in dancing with a woman almost nine months pregnant was an offer she couldn't turn down.

She nodded her consent.

His muscled arm moved to her waist while he took her hand in his and held it to his chest. Her heart was racing madly. She assured herself it was the physical activity and nothing to do with the handsome man holding her in his arms.

His gaze met hers and held it. She wasn't able to read his thoughts, but that didn't keep her heart from continuing to race. Was it wrong to acknowledge that he was the sexiest man at the wedding? On the *island*?

As she stared into his blue eyes, she was caught off guard by a glimmer of pain lurking just beneath the surface. Normally when she looked into someone's eyes, there was a light there, but in this mysterious stranger's case, it was as if that light had been snuffed out. Someone had hurt him—hurt him deeply. Sympathy welled up in her. She was all too familiar with pain that balled up inside and made it difficult to eat, sometimes to inhale a full breath.

He glanced away, breaking the contact. So he wasn't into sharing either, not that it was any of her business. But she couldn't help but be intrigued by him. Again, she was struck by his familiarity, but she was certain they hadn't previously met. There was no way that she would forget someone as good-looking as him.

The song playing in the background was a classic: "Moondance." As the singer's deep voice wafted through the air, Popi's dance partner guided her around the crowded dance floor. White twinkle lights were strung overhead, casting a soft glow over the area.

But all Popi had eyes for was the handsome man holding her in his arms as though she belonged there. For just this moment, reality, with all its sorrow, rolled away.

When his gaze met hers once more, there was something different reflected in his blue eyes. Was it interest? In her? Her heart skipped a beat. How could he desire her in her current condition? Impossible. Wasn't it?

For this one dance, she allowed herself the luxury of pretending that he was her lover. What could it hurt? It'd been so very long since she'd felt anything but the heavy weight of guilt and the darkness of grief.

For this one dance beneath the starry sky, she'd allow herself to be happy.

It'd been a long time since he'd danced.

And he was surprised to find he enjoyed holding Popi close.

Realizing he was enjoying it too much, Apollo guided them off to a quiet corner of the dance floor. His intent was to have a serious conversation with her, but this close contact was detrimental to his thought process.

He drew in a deep breath, but it did nothing to cool his heated blood. There was something about this woman that got past his practiced defenses. And right now, talking was the last thing on his mind.

Blindly following his desires was how he'd gotten himself into a number of jams in the past, from angry fathers with shotguns to returning to camp, where a tribal leader and anxious bride awaited him. He was older now, more responsible. But that didn't make Popi any less enchanting.

Get it together. He mustered up an image of the legal documents—papers that would steal away his last link to his brother. Suddenly his heated blood cooled and his thoughts became more focused.

And then he turned his gaze back to Popi. Perhaps he'd made a miscalculation by lingering at this wedding. He should have waited to speak with her. But he'd already waited too long to take his rightful place in the Drakos family. Guilt and determination kept him from walking away.

If only Popi didn't look so captivating, he'd be able to sort his thoughts—to speak his mind. His gaze continued to take in her beauty. Her hair was pinned up with just a few wispy strands of hair around her neck—ringlets that teased and tempted him to reach out and wrap them around his finger. And her gown hugged her curves and dipped low enough to hint at her tempting cleavage.

His mouth grew dry and his hands grew damp. Testosterone challenged his common sense. She looked so fine—very different from his sister-in-law, whom he recalled being a lot less curvy and had portrayed a more serious demeanor. And his old self would have swept Popi off her feet by now. It was so difficult being responsible and doing what was proper when his entire body longed to do all those improper things with Popi.

He blamed this instant attraction on this island. His research had unearthed that Infinity Island was famous for its romances. Marriages started here were rumored to last forever. Was it possible that it did hold some sort of magical power? Instead of a love potion, perhaps the island cast a love spell over its inhabitants.

Because right now, he was losing the struggle. All he could think about was kissing Popi. It didn't matter that they barely knew each other or that she was very, very pregnant. It was the way the moonlight was reflected in her eyes.

And then there was the way she looked at him when she hadn't thought he was paying attention. She was just as drawn to him as he was to her. That was the final part of his undoing.

Popi tilted her chin upward until their gazes met. "What's the matter?"

"In this moment, nothing."

"Then why did you stop dancing? Are you ready to answer my questions?"

He smiled at her tenacity, but he wasn't ready to ruin this moment with the harshness of reality. It would happen soon enough. He drew her close again as the remaining verses of the song played. He heard the swift intake of her breath as her eyes widened. "The song isn't quite over."

Their bodies swayed together, but their feet didn't move.

He lowered his head to her ear. Softly he said, "Do you know how beautiful you are?"

And then without thinking of the consequences—the right and wrong—he turned his head. He caught her lips. Part of him expected her to pull away—another part of him willed her to meet him halfway.

And then her mouth moved beneath his. His heart slammed into his ribs. Her glossy lips moved with eagerness. His tongue sought entrance. Her mouth widened, causing a moan to swell in the back of his throat.

Was this really happening? Could this amazing woman really be this into him? In that moment, he couldn't think of anything he wanted more than her.

Being alone for so long—just him and nature—it got so lonely at times. Not that he'd ever admitted it to anyone. But with Popi in his arms, he had a glimpse of what life might be like if he were to let someone get close.

Her hand reached up and wrapped around his neck. In that moment, he lost his fingertip-hold on reality. Popi leaned into him. Her lips moved over his, taking the lead in this arousing dance. She was so hot that everywhere she touched him, he felt singed. And he didn't want her to stop.

He'd kept to himself for too long. He told himself that was why her kiss was sweeter than the passion fruit Moscato wine being passed around the wedding. He assured himself it was all an illusion that would soon pass. But the longer they kissed, the more he craved her.

Apollo let go of her hand to wrap his arm around her waist. Her baby bump kept him from being able to pull her as close as he would like. It was a reminder that this wasn't a fantasy. Popi was very much flesh and blood.

He should stop this. He should put some distance between them. He took a small step back—at least he thought it was a step—but Popi was still leaning into him as their lips moved hungrily over each other.

Her fingers spread out over his chest, scattering his thoughts of ending things. The V-neck of his shirt allowed her fingertips to touch his bare skin. It was as though just by her touch alone, she branded him as her own.

No woman, no kiss, had ever affected him so deeply.

It was like they'd been made for each other. She was the half that made him whole.

A drum roll echoed through the garden and pounded reality back into his head. He pulled back and looked at her. It took them each a moment to catch their breath. He hadn't come here to kiss Popi. His fingers moved over his mouth, still remembering the softness of her touch. He drew in an uneven breath.

Kissing her had been a mistake. He didn't know if he was going to be able to talk to her—to look at her—without recalling that earth-moving kiss. And he couldn't afford to be distracted. There was too much at stake.

He stepped away. "That shouldn't have happened."

Popi's gaze darkened. "The song has ended. Now I want answers. Who are you?"

"Do you really not recognize me?"

"No." She studied his face. "Why should I know you? Are you famous?"

"In a manner of speaking." He'd been fodder for the tabloids off and on his whole life. Billionaire heir spotted here…spotted there. "I'm Apollo Drakos."

Her mouth gaped. Her eyes reflected the rampant thoughts racing through her mind. It took her a moment to press her glossy lips together.

Popi's gaze narrowed. "Where have you been? We tried to reach you right after the accident, but no one knew what had happened to you."

"It doesn't matter—"

"Of course it matters." Her voice assumed an accusatory tone. "You should have been here."

His muscles tensed as yet another person heaped guilt on him. He deserved the condemnation and accusations, but there was nothing she could say that he hadn't already said to himself.

"I'm here now."

"Then you know about the accident and that we had the funeral—"

"I know all of it. My attorney filled me in."

Her gaze searched his. "Then what are you doing here on the island?"

"I'm here to claim the Drakos heir."

CHAPTER FIVE

NO. THAT CAN'T be true.

Popi's arms immediately wrapped around her midsection. She'd heard rumors about the man standing before her. Apollo was known to be reckless and selfish. No way was he going to steal away into the night with this baby. Not on her watch. But try as she might, the rush of words clogged up in her throat. The back of her eyes stung with tears of frustration and a flurry of hormones.

Popi's sister, Andrina, had said Apollo was a playboy—taking what he wanted and leaving a string of broken hearts across the globe. But Popi considered herself lucky. He'd stolen a kiss, not her heart.

Okay, maybe they'd shared much more than a fleeting kiss. But something had clicked between them when they'd been chest to heaving chest, lip to eager lip.

Maybe she'd let herself sympathize with the pain that had been reflected in his eyes. Maybe her own grief had her acting out of character. Whatever had her lip-dancing with him, it had nothing whatsoever to do with her heart.

She knew Mr. Globetrotter over there lived off his very large trust fund. He never put down roots anywhere. From all Popi had gathered, she had been certain he wouldn't want to complicate his carefree life with a baby.

And with her own parents getting older, they weren't up to the day-to-day care of a baby. That left her to raise her sister's child. And that's why she'd spoke with an attorney to get the adoption started.

"This surely can't come as a surprise," he said.

Her brows drew together in confusion. "You mean you

showing up on the island unwanted and uninvited? Or
did you mean you trying to charm me with your smooth
words and kiss—"

"I wasn't trying to charm you. We both got caught up
with the music and the dancing. It wasn't all one way."
His pointed gaze met hers. When she opened her mouth
to deny the accusation, he continued. "Don't bother. Remember I was on the other end of that kiss."

Wordlessly, she pressed her lips together. Perhaps it
was best to pretend that kiss hadn't happened—for both
of their sakes.

Though the music of the reception floated in the background, Popi was no longer in the mood to laugh and smile.
Yes, she would have to go back to the party and put on a
happy face, but not before she set a few things straight.

"You've wasted your time coming here," she said.
"When this baby is born, I'm not going to allow you to
walk away with it." Not a chance. She'd heard way too
many stories about this guy, who acts first and thinks later.
The baby wouldn't be safe with him.

He pressed his hands to this trim waist. "You can't stop
me. I'm its uncle."

"I'm the aunt."

They stood quietly, glaring back and forth. Each waited
for the other to back down. He'd be waiting a very long
time, because she was never going to back down. This
baby was too important.

From the stories she'd heard of Apollo, he had been
a wild child. And as an adult, he did and said what he
wanted without care to others. So why had he grown quiet?
Why not say what he really thought? That she wasn't de-
serving of raising his niece or nephew, because secretly
she had her own reservations. The guilt over her sister's
death continued to eat at her.

Popi shoved aside the troubling thoughts. "You have

some nerve coming here months after your brother and sister-in-law's deaths and throwing around demands. Where were you for the funeral?"

Apollo glanced down at the ground. She'd hit a nerve. Perhaps he wasn't as self-centered as her sister had let on. Perhaps there was a bit more to Apollo. But not enough to just turn the baby over to him. That wasn't going to happen, even if this man turned out to be a saint, which she knew he wasn't.

When her sister had first approached her about being a surrogate, Popi had outright rejected the idea. She'd thought she was too young to go through everything involved with pregnancy—not to mention the associated pain.

She'd told Andrina to find another way. Looking back, Popi felt so bad about giving her sister such a hard time. At the time, she hadn't known about her sister's repeated miscarriages that had devastated both Andrina and Nile. Her sister had held it all in, not wanting her family to know that she felt like a failure as a mother and wife. But when the news came out, not one of them thought any such thing.

When Andrina had finally let her guard down with Popi, something wonderful had happened. As Andrina had explained about the emotional roller coaster that she and Nile had been on, the sisters grew closer than they'd ever been before. Popi then saw the surrogacy in a new light—a chance to cement their relationship—to be more like blood siblings than two adopted orphans.

And this stranger wasn't going to walk in here after the fact and take away her last link to her sister. It just wasn't going to happen.

"Where have you been all of this time?" Popi hoped to drive home the fact that she had always been there. When her family needed her, she was there for them. Just like she'd be there when this baby needed her.

Apollo rubbed the back of his neck. And then in almost a mumble, he uttered a response, but it was too soft for Popi to pick it up over the sound of the music.

"What did you say?"

He lifted his head. In his eyes, she could see the torment reflected in them. For a moment, it stilled her breath. She didn't know what to do with this new information. It was so much easier to fight him when she thought he was a selfish jerk without any worry for anyone else.

"I was out of contact while hiking in the Himalayas."

That would explain the tan and the very defined muscles. And it would also explain his absence from the funeral. As much as she wanted to cling to his absence from that awful time, she could tell he was riddled with guilt over it. She knew a lot about being plagued with guilt.

But that didn't change the fact that she was better suited to be a parent. She had a job. A stable life. A home. And lots of caring people to help her raise this child. What was it they said? Oh, yes: it takes a village. And she was blessed enough to have a loving village.

What did he have?

Popi thought for a moment before speaking. She didn't want to escalate this situation. If she could reason with him, it would be best for everyone concerned—most especially the baby.

"I know you're concerned about the child." She noticed he didn't try to argue and so she continued. "I also know you lead a very active lifestyle, which isn't conducive to having an infant or a small child." When he started a rebuttal, she held up her hand, stopping him. "I also understand you might feel the pressure to do the right thing. But I want you to know that the right thing is to leave the baby with me to raise while you continue to explore the Amazon and hike the Himalayas or whatever."

His gaze narrowed in on her. "So that you can take control of the Drakos fortune?"

"What?" She knew her brother-in-law was rich—more than rich—but she never considered the money when she'd decided to adopt the baby. She never stopped to realize that the baby would be heir to a fortune. "No, that's not it."

Apollo's gaze said that he didn't believe her. "You will never get your hands on that money."

Her heart sunk. She thought Apollo had come here to claim the baby out of some sort of obligation or maybe even love for his brother. It never even occurred to her that this would be some sort of power move. A chance to control the family business that he'd been excluded from in favor of his older brother.

She shook her head in frustration. At that point, she could hear voices over the speaker system. It was time for the champagne toast, followed by the bridal-bouquet toss. Though Lea had been adamant about incorporating the Greek traditions in honor of her groom, she'd also introduced some American traditions and married them, as Lea liked to say.

"I have to go," Popi said. "In the future, your attorney can contact mine." And with that she walked away, not even waiting for him to speak.

Before Apollo's arrival, Popi had been determined to protect the child and keep it with her, and this conversation had only solidified her position. Apollo was going to walk away empty-handed.

That kiss.

Oh, that kiss.

Apollo inwardly groaned. It was the most arousing, addictive kiss of his life. And it had ended much, much too quickly. The fact that Popi had wanted him just as much had been a surprise.

As good as the kiss had been, it had been a mistake. And just when he'd promised himself that he was going to be responsible and do what was best for the family—for the baby. Because he owed it to his brother's memory.

And right about now, he was certain Nile would be frowning at him. He'd let his desires rule, but that was the last time. He didn't care how beautiful Popi was, as he could ignore her charms. He could be the responsible man his brother always believed he was capable of being.

That meant stepping up and becoming a father to his niece or nephew. The acknowledgment of that was immense.

But Apollo was done walking away.

He'd done that enough in his life.

This time he was staying. He would do what was right.

Being a father meant giving up his freedom. Nile would say that it was past time, and perhaps he was right after this latest accident. It had opened Apollo's eyes to what was important—family. He never got to tell his brother that—he never got to thank his brother for never giving up on him.

The only thing he could do now for his brother was to make sure his son or daughter was raised as a Drakos and received all the privileges that afforded them.

And that left Popi. Unlike her and her claim for sole custody, he would not exclude her from the child's life. He didn't know how exactly it would work, but he wouldn't exile Popi from the child she'd carried. There had to be a reasonable compromise. He just needed time to think.

It was late in the evening and Apollo was still on the island. In fact, he'd taken up residence on Popi's porch. He didn't like being dismissed. His father used to do it and it grated on Apollo's nerves.

He settled back in the chair and stared into the night. He recalled the determination written all over Popi's beautiful face when it came to raising the baby. But it wasn't going to stop him. He hadn't been there for his brother, but he was here now for his nephew or niece.

He'd already had the most highly recommended nanny put on retainer. She was just waiting for his word and she would move into his family's grand estate, just outside Athens. There was a very talented cook. And then there was Anna, the housekeeper. A smile tugged at his lips when he recalled Anna. She never put up with anyone's nonsense, including his. Everybody necessary to provide for his niece or nephew would be awaiting them. It would be just as it was when he was young.

Apollo stopped rocking the chair on Popi's porch. Was that what he wanted for the baby? A life like he had?

Crunch. Crunch.

The sound of footsteps on the crushed-seashell walk drew Apollo from his thoughts. It was dark out now. The reception had gone on for quite a while. And then there had been the toot of the ferryboat sweeping the guests off to the mainland.

The bright moonlight streaming down illuminated Popi's face. Apollo had to admit that if circumstances were different—way different—he would have been drawn to Popi. The fact that she was single and carrying someone else's baby didn't diminish the attraction.

The distinct intake of breath let him know that she'd spotted him, not that he'd been hiding.

Popi stomped up the couple of steps to the porch. She turned to him and pressed her hands to her hips. "What are you still doing here?"

He got to his feet. "I told you I wasn't leaving."

In the shadows, he wasn't able to see her clearly, but he got the distinct impression she was glaring at him. So be it. He wasn't here to make her happy—nor himself for that matter. He was here to make sure the right thing was done concerning the child. And that was for it be raised as a Drakos. He would teach them what they needed to know to take over the Drakos legacy, the way his brother would have done.

Toot-toot.

Another ferry was about to pull out with its load of happy but weary wedding guests. And that was just fine with him because he didn't want any other interruptions. He needed to get through to Popi that whatever she had planned for the baby wasn't going to happen.

She moved toward the door. "I'm tired. It's been a long day."

He moved in front of her. Having the entire evening alone, he'd formulated a plan. "I think you should move to Athens until the baby is born."

"Where I give birth is none of your concern. Now I'm going to bed. Good night, Mr. Drakos."

And without another word, she moved past him and entered the bungalow. The door slammed shut behind her.

When he'd arrived on the island, he hadn't known what to expect. It certainly hadn't been this very determined, very frustrating woman. But he could be just as stubborn.

He would not walk away from the baby—not like he walked away from his brother. He would be the man his brother wanted him to be. It was the least he could do.

CHAPTER SIX

HER BACK ACHED.

And it was getting worse the longer she lay there.

At least that's what Popi blamed her sleepless night on. She refused to admit that she couldn't stop thinking of Apollo. Each time she closed her eyes, she envisioned his blue gaze staring back at her. His eyes were spellbinding and totally unforgettable.

And then there was that toe-curling, spine-tingling kiss. Popi knew no matter how long she'd live, she would never forget that starry night in Apollo's arms.

She scrunched up her pillow and struggled to roll over, eager to find a more comfortable position. In the past week, there didn't seem to be any position that was comfortable for long. It wouldn't be too much longer until the baby arrived and she was able to get a good night's sleep.

In the meantime, with sleep being elusive, she played over the events of the evening. What was Apollo doing here? There was nothing she'd heard about him that said he wanted to raise a baby. He couldn't even take time away from goofing off in order to attend his own brother's funeral. What sort of person did that?

Her arms moved protectively around her baby bump. This little one needed someone to adopt him or her that saw them as more than a Drakos heir. She could do that. She was uniquely qualified to be a loving adoptive parent—just like her adoptive parents had done for her and Andrina. They'd taken them both in at the tender ages of three and four and shown them that not all promises were broken. And most importantly that real love was in fact unconditional.

Could Apollo offer that to this child? Or would he be too worried about the position this child would hold in the Drakos dynasty? No matter his intentions, she would not be parted from this child of her heart.

Her sister and brother-in-law hadn't had the opportunity to make a will. Now it would be up to a judge—a total stranger—to decide the fate of this baby. She hoped and prayed they'd come to the right decision.

Was she scared of becoming a mother? Definitely. Did she have a clue what she was doing? Not at all. Just the thought of this little baby growing into a teenager with an attitude made her palms grow damp. But with love and a heaping dose of patience, they'd get through the growing pains. Popi had faith that all the good times, from the first words to the first steps to the first day of school, would greatly outweigh the challenges. That's what her parents had told her when she asked them how they put up with her through the teen years.

She would do her very best. It's the least she owed her sister...

Guilt welled up in her.

It felt wrong to be stepping into her sister's role as mother. Maybe if their last conversation hadn't gone so terribly wrong, Andrina would still be here. If Popi had been more understanding, maybe it would have made the difference between life and death.

But no matter how many times she went over the scenarios in her head, it wouldn't bring back her sister. Andrina was gone. And Popi had to pick up the pieces and move forward. No matter how difficult it could be at times.

Popi kicked off the sheet that was twisted around her legs. Using her arms to prop herself up in bed, she swung her feet over the edge of the mattress. She sat there for a moment. She never thought getting out of bed would be so much work.

She struggled to her feet, pressing a hand to the small of her back. She felt like she'd swallowed a beach ball. The baby agreed with a stomp of a foot or punch of a hand on her bladder. Popi waddled off to the bathroom for about the fourteenth time that night.

After answering the call of nature, she didn't feel like lying in bed and staring into the dark. And standing made the discomfort in her back ease a bit. Without turning on the lights, she paced around the bungalow. She paused next to the window.

She glanced out at the moonlight-drenched sand beyond her small yard filled with lush foliage. She was so fortunate to live in paradise. But even this beautiful land couldn't keep nightmares from landing at her doorstep...

A movement in the corner of her eye caught her attention. That was when she noticed an unusual shadow on the porch. It could be an animal. But as she peered closer, she realized that it was a person. The breath caught in her throat. Who would be on her porch at this hour of the night?

Apollo?

Popi squinted harder into the night. Yep, it was him. She let out the pent-up breath. He was sitting in the older rocker on her porch. His head was tilted back and his arms were crossed over his chest as he slept. He'd repurposed an old crate that she'd turned into a plant stand and used it for a footrest.

It was then that she realized by his waiting for her to come home from the reception, where she'd stayed late to oversee the cleanup, that he'd missed the last ferry to the mainland. And since the island was shut down for the pending renovations, there was nowhere for him to stay but with her. She sighed.

She should just turn away and let him be. After all, it was his choice to stay here. Just then the baby gave a hard kick that nearly doubled her over.

Rubbing her now sore side, Popi whispered, "Okay, little one. I hear you. He is your flesh and blood. As much as I want to pretend he doesn't exist, I won't kick him out of your life. He's the only one who can tell you about your father and his side of the family."

As an orphan who never knew her blood relatives, Popi knew the importance of family roots. She wouldn't deprive her child of that link—no matter how aggravating the uncle may be.

Popi grabbed a throw from the back of her couch that she hadn't had time to pack and moved to the door. Ever so quietly, she let herself out on the porch. She expected him to wake up at any moment, but he didn't stir. His breath was deep and even.

She tiptoed toward him and ever so gently draped the blanket over him. As soon as she had it over him, his breathing halted. He shifted positions as though getting more comfortable. Popi froze, knowing if she moved he'd wake up for sure. But then as quickly as his deep breathing had halted, it resumed, and so did Popi's.

She quietly tiptoed back inside the house. Tomorrow was going to be a very interesting day. Very interesting indeed.

Apollo jerked.

His eyes fluttered open just as his feet hit the floor. His heart pounded in his chest as he gulped down one breath of air after the other.

He glanced around, not knowing where he was. In the distance was the view of the sea. Slowly it all started to come back to him. The island. The baby. And the surrogate.

He was safe. He was on solid ground. And everything

else had been a nightmare. Or more like a vivid memory. One that played over and over in his mind. It was one reason he'd considered giving up his nomad existence, but one tragedy had only led him to another much worse tragedy.

Apollo rubbed his thigh. The wound, though mostly healed, still bothered him at times, especially when he'd been on his feet a lot. And he was certain the dancing last night hadn't helped things. But he was a determined man. He had a lot to make up for and nothing was going to stop him.

It was only then that he noticed the blanket pooled around his waist. It took him a second to realize that Popi must have brought this out to him. So she knew he was still here and yet she hadn't woken him up to kick him off her property. Off the island. Interesting.

He would take that as a good sign—maybe she was starting to come to terms with the situation. With the sun barely above the horizon, he got to his feet and stretched. His stomach rumbled a complaint. He hadn't eaten since he was on the mainland yesterday.

The creak of the door announced Popi's presence. "You're still here?"

"Good morning," he said, hoping to get the day off to a good start.

He smiled at her as she stood there with no makeup on and her long hair pulled back in a loose ponytail. She looked so down-to-earth and approachable. He resisted the urge to move. As he continued to look at her, he noticed a glow about her. He'd heard it said that pregnant women get a glow about them, but he'd never known what that exactly meant, until now.

She didn't smile, but she didn't frown at him either. He'd take that as another good sign—something he could build on. Because the only way he was going to keep the unborn baby close was to keep Popi close.

"I started a pot of coffee. You might as well come inside. You can clean up and then have a cup."

She didn't have to invite him twice. He grabbed his backpack. After all these years, he didn't go anywhere without it. He followed her in the doorway. "Thank you."

After she handed him a towel, he grabbed a quick shower. The hot water beat on his sore neck, easing the painful kinks in his muscles. All too soon, he turned off the water. He didn't want to dally, as Popi seemed as though she might be in the mood to talk.

As he dried off and dressed in some fresh clothes, he hoped now that her shock over his sudden appearance on the island had subsided that she'd see him as something other than the enemy. He wanted to convince Popi to accompany him back to the Drakos estate, which was situated so much closer to a hospital.

Apollo entered the kitchen and inhaled the most delightful aroma. "The coffee smells wonderful."

"Help yourself. The cups are in the cabinet right above the coffeemaker."

He liked that she didn't stand on formalities and instead believed in a feel-at-home approach. He grabbed a cup and then glanced over his shoulder. "Can I get you a cup?"

She shook her head. "I can't have any. You know, being pregnant and all."

She'd made this pot of coffee just for him? It was just a simple act, but it got to him. It'd been quite a while since someone went out of their way for him. Usually when people figured out that he was "that Drakos," they wanted something from him—access to his brother, money to invest in some get-rich scheme and the list went on. But Popi didn't seem to want anything from him.

His gaze dipped to her baby bump. "I didn't know you couldn't drink coffee." And then he felt guilty. "I can dump it out."

Again, she shook her head. "Why should you go without? I'm the one that's pregnant. Pour yourself a cup and enjoy it for the both of us."

He arched a brow. She gestured for him to get on with it. And so he poured himself a cup. He'd learned a long time ago that milk was hard to come by out on the trail and sugar attracted all sorts of insects, so he'd learned to drink his coffee black.

The timer went off and Popi moved past him. She added eggs to the tomatoes simmering on the stove. As she continued to work in the kitchen, he moved to a stool at the small kitchen island, where he was out of her way.

"Whatever you're making, it smells good. Real good." His stomach rumbled in agreement.

"It's Peloponnesian scrambled eggs with fresh tomatoes and herbs. And it's almost done, if you'd like some."

"I'd love some."

Popi used a spatula to stir the contents of the pan. "My mother used to make them for me. But it's been a while. I don't get home to visit my parents as much as I'd like."

"Our housekeeper used to have these prepared for me on special mornings." He sent Popi a smile, hoping today would be a new start for them. "Looks like you're serving up a bit of nostalgia for both of us."

"I must admit that nothing I try makes the eggs as good as the ones from my childhood."

"I think sometimes our memories deceive us—makes the good things so much better than they truly were."

Popi lowered her gaze to the counter. "And the bad things?"

"I don't know." Because he tried to keep his bad memories locked up in the back of his mind. He didn't like to share them with anyone—including his late brother.

After adding some freshly chopped herbs and feta to the dish, she served it up. "Let's see how I did."

They ate quietly for a bit. He noticed that Popi was doing a good job at clearing her plate. He glanced down at his almost-full plate. The food was good but he was distracted by the change in Popi's mood. First the blanket and then being nice to him this morning. What was up with that?

He knew not to let his guard down because that's when people took advantage of you. It'd happened to him in the past—once by a vivacious blonde and another time by a fellow hiker that Apollo had come to think of as a close friend. Both turned out to be more interested in what he could do for them than being friends.

Is that what prompted Popi's change of mood toward him? Was she worried he'd take the heir to the Drakos fortune away from her? Because honestly, in the beginning, that had been his plan. He already had his team of attorneys working to quash her application for adoption. But now he wasn't sure that was the right approach. If they could handle this outside the courts, it'd be best for everyone.

Unable to take the curiosity any longer, Apollo asked, "Popi, why—"

Ring-ring. Ring-ring.

Popi held up a finger. "Hang on. I have to get this."

As she talked on the phone with more yeses and nos than anything else, he cleared the empty breakfast dishes. He stacked them in the sink as he would do if he were at home and there was a staff to finish cleaning up. But this wasn't his home. This was Popi's place. And this place didn't have a staff. There was just a very pregnant woman that for some reason was giving him a second chance.

Apollo picked up the first dish and started washing it. And the funny thing was he didn't mind. When he'd been off on his adventures, he'd learned to clean his own dishes, and in definitely more harsh terrain.

See, big brother, my travels weren't all a waste of time. I've learned to be a real human being and not just a spoiled brat.

The pain of loss engulfed him. It was so hard to believe that Nile was gone. He kept expecting him to walk through the door, slap him on the back and give him some verbal jab about his latest expedition. And then he'd tell Apollo all about his upcoming baby and how he was anxious to know him or her. Sadly, that was never to be—

"Sorry about that," Popi said, cutting through his painful and sorrowful thoughts. "That was the moving crew."

He placed the last of the dishes in the cupboard and turned to her. "That must be who you mistook me for yesterday."

She nodded. "Sorry about that." She got to her feet. "The ferry to the mainland will be here shortly. You can head down to the dock to wait for it." Popi started for the bedroom.

"Thank you for breakfast," he called out. "It was delicious and a nice reminder of the past."

Did she really think things were settled between them? Was that why she'd been so nice to him with the blanket and feeding him? Did she think he'd just quietly disappear?

He'd wait until she changed out of that flirty little pink robe and then they'd talk. He would tell her that there was no way he was giving away his own flesh and blood. And it doesn't matter how nice she is to him or how her smile lights up her eyes and causes a warm feeling within his chest. He was immune to her charms—if he wanted to be.

CHAPTER SEVEN

Toot-Toot.

The ferry was pulling into the dock. The work crew had arrived. It was time to get to work.

Popi tried to put socks on her feet, but her feet now seemed so far away. After a couple attempts, she tossed aside the socks. Flip-flops would have to suffice. Besides, with the swelling in her feet, she wasn't even sure she could get shoes on her feet.

She definitely didn't know about all of these discomforts when she'd signed on to be a surrogate. Not that it would have changed her mind. She would have done anything for her sister.

Like the time when they were young and her sister had strep throat. They were supposed to go with friends on a trip to the beach. They'd been waiting months to go and then Andrina had gotten sick. Popi could have gone without her big sister, but she knew how disappointed Andrina was about missing the trip. So Popi stayed home and they had a movie marathon instead. Their parents had promised them a trip to the beach when Andrina was better.

The memory brought a smile to her face, but it was fleeting, as the guilt over Andrina's death came back to her. Unlike when they were kids, Popi had let her sister down in the worst way. Popi never understood the true power of words until that moment.

And sometimes the lack of words was just as important.

The breakfast preparation had definitely paid off. There had been no arguing, and now Apollo was on his way to the dock and then on to the mainland. Oh, she had no doubt that their paths would cross again. And she also realized their attorneys would be hashing out the custody arrangement. But that didn't mean she had to deal with him one-on-one.

She pressed a hand to her lower back. With her stomach pushed so far to the front, it was really putting a strain on her back. And nothing she did would ease the pain. The only thing she could do was try to ignore it—like that was possible.

Popi changed into some work clothes, which was a challenge all its own. She was so far along now that barely any of her clothes fit comfortably.

When she at last slipped on some flip-flops, she headed for the door. Once she coordinated the transfer of everyone's belongings to the warehouses, she would be on her way to her parents' house. She was anxious to put her feet up and wait for this little one to make an appearance. In another couple of weeks, it'd be her due date.

Having her parents around would be a comfort. Her parents' home wasn't the place she'd originally envisioned waiting for the baby—that had been with her sister and her brother-in-law. It was amazing how fast life could change—with the flip of a coin. Her grieving parents were cheered with the prospect of becoming grandparents for the very first time.

Giving birth to this baby would be such bittersweet joy for all of them—

Someone cleared their throat.

Oh, no. Please say it isn't so.

Popi turned. There sat Apollo in the same chair that he'd slept in last night. That was it. That chair was going away. All it did was attract the riffraff.

"You better hurry," she said, trying to keep the agitation from her voice. "You don't want to miss the ferry…again."

Apollo got to his feet. "I'm not leaving. This—" he gestured between the two of them "—isn't finished."

"It is as far as I'm concerned. Our attorneys can handle it from here. Now I have work to do."

"Work?" A look of concern flickered over his face. "In your condition?"

"Yes, in my condition. I'm pregnant. Not dying."

"But still—"

"What did you think? That I'd lie around in bed all day and let the staff wait on me?" With dramatic flair, she pressed her fingertip to her chin. "Oh, wait. I don't have a staff. There's just me. And I do just fine on my own."

Without waiting for him to protest again, she turned and headed down the crushed-seashell walk. There was no way she was letting this man—this pushy guy—tell her what she could and couldn't do. It wasn't like she was planning to do any heavy lifting. She doubted she could bend over and right herself again without some help, much less bend down to pick up a piece of furniture. No, she already had a full load on board. She rubbed her belly, feeling a small bulge in the side, wondering if it was an elbow or a knee. Even the agitation of Apollo couldn't douse the smile the baby brought to her lips.

The crunch of seashells behind her let her know Apollo hadn't given up on his pursuit of her. Whatever. Let him waste his time. He could leave when the movers did—and that wouldn't be soon enough.

"Don't just walk away," Apollo called out. "I'm not letting this go."

She kept walking. "And I have work to do."

"Then I guess I'll help."

She sent him a warning glare. She had a lot to coordinate today. She didn't need him getting in the way—

A sudden pain wrapped around from her back to the

front. It knocked the air from her lungs. She stopped. She closed her eyes, for a moment blocking out the world—blocking out Apollo. But she could feel his presence lingering next to her.

"Popi, what's the matter?" Urgency and concern laced his words. "Is it the baby?"

She opened her eyes to find herself staring straight into his piercing blue gaze. Instead of it being disturbing or upsetting, she found herself comforted by his genuine concern.

And there was something more, but she couldn't quite name it. Or rather she didn't want to admit it, not even to herself. But her heart thump-thumped harder and faster. No man had a right to have such piercing blue eyes. It was as though they could see straight through her—see what she was hiding from the world.

But how could that be? She didn't even know him. And he certainly didn't know her. That's the way it must remain.

Because what she did know of him told her that he was the last person that she should count on. He was here today and gone the next. Never one to linger in any one place very long.

She shook her head. "The baby is fine. And so am I." Maybe it was a little white lie. She'd been pushing herself with the wedding and now the island renovation. After today, she promised herself that she'd rest until her due date. But for now, she had work to do. "I just need you to back off."

He held up his hands in surrender. "This is me backing off."

Without another word, she made her way past him, making sure their bodies didn't touch. There was just something about him—something that got to her. And she couldn't afford to let herself get distracted.

Something told her his definition of *backing off* and her definition of *backing off* were two different things. After all, this man came from great wealth, so he was used to getting what he wanted. But this time would be different.

A different approach was needed.

Pushing was not going to do it.

Apollo didn't know how he was going to get Popi to get off her feet and rest, but he was determined to do everything he could to make that happen as quickly as possible. And so he attempted not to say anything else to upset her.

He soon learned the plan was to clear the resident bungalows of their furnishings and the boxes so that tomorrow work crews could come in and give these older bungalows a makeover. Apollo wasn't sure exactly why this was being done for the whole island. All he was able to discern was that it had something to do with yesterday's wedding.

But he really didn't care about the island's makeover. All he cared about was Popi and the baby she was carrying. That acknowledgment struck him as he helped carry a couch out to the waiting trailer that would then haul everything to the warehouse.

This was the first time in Apollo's life where he had to put someone else's needs and well-being ahead of his own. He realized, at the age of thirty-two, that was a sad commentary on his life. But his father never needed or wanted anyone to fuss over him—Apollo wondered if his mother had been the exception. And his older brother, Nile, took care of Apollo, not the other way around.

As for his romantic relationships, well, after college they never got serious. He was never in one place long enough for any of that to take place—not that he would let it. "Once bitten and twice shy" was what they said. He said he was better off alone—that way he didn't fail to live up to other people's expectations and they didn't let him down.

As the work crew moved on down the lane to the next bungalow, Apollo turned, looking for Popi. She was nowhere in sight. Thinking that she'd gone on ahead, he returned to the bungalow to close the door.

He'd just pulled it closed when he heard, "Here, kitty, kitty. Come here, sweetie."

What in the world?

He moved to the side of the bungalow to find Popi down on her hands and knees. Her butt was sticking up at him. As she moved to look under a bush, her backside wiggled. For a moment, he was tongue-tied. He just watched—unable to take his eyes off her.

What was it about this woman that had him acting so out of character? Until now, he could take or leave female companionship. He kept to himself for the most part—communing with nature and its wonders. And the only time he cooked for others was when they shared a camp in the wilderness. When traveling together, it was common for everyone to take turns with the cooking.

But Popi was getting under his skin. And it was more than the baby she was carrying. And then there had been breakfast. Well, it had been nice—almost domestic. Not that he was thinking of settling into a life of domesticity or anything.

"Come on, kitty."

Popi's cajoling voice stirred him from his thoughts and released him from the trance she'd cast over him.

He stepped up next to her. "You shouldn't be down there. Let me help you up."

Popi leaned back on her heels with a little gray kitten clutched to her chest. "Look who I found?"

"You have a cat?" He wasn't a cat person. Dogs, yes. Cats, no. Definitely not.

Cats couldn't go for walks or hiking or camping. When he was a kid, his friend had a cat. It was needy, pampered and wouldn't listen to a thing it was told. Apollo didn't need that in his life.

Popi shook her head, indicating that the cat was not hers. "It must have been left behind when all of the pets were moved to the mainland to be cared for until their owners returned from their cruise."

Apollo breathed a little easier. There were already so many distractions, so he didn't need more. As soon as he was done making sure Popi didn't overdo it today, they were going to revisit their prior talk and he was going to convince her that the best place for her and the baby was his family's home—the baby's future home.

He glanced down, finding Popi still sitting on the ground. "Give me your hand."

She appeared to be so distracted by the kitten clutched to her voluptuous chest that she did what he said without giving him a hard time about being able to do it herself. That was a first. Maybe if he was very lucky, it would be the start of something new between them. He could only hope.

"I need to get this little guy home," she said.

"But you don't know where he lives."

"Not his home. My home."

Apollo wasn't following her. "But you're moving out. You're leaving the island—"

"Not today."

"Of course you are. You have to."

Popi glowered, silencing him. "I've had a change of plans, which includes me staying until tomorrow."

"I'm confused." He rubbed a hand over the back of his head. He could feel the beginning of a headache coming on. "Why would you stay when everything is done?"

"Because I have to meet with the contractor tomorrow. Go over some last-minute details and hand over the keys." She sighed. "Not that it's any of your business."

She had a point. None of this was his problem. But that baby she was carrying, that was his responsibility. And like it or not, his feet were grounded to this island for the foreseeable future.

"I'd feel better if you were on the mainland, close to the doctor."

Popi made a note on her digital tablet. "I just had a checkup. Earlier this week. All is fine."

He pressed his hands to his sides. Why did she have to be so difficult? "It'd be safer if you were on the mainland—close to the hospital."

"You aren't going to let up, are you?" When he shook his head, she added, "Fine. I'll make you a deal. If you stop pestering me, I'll leave right away if anything seems worrisome."

It wasn't the answer he wanted, but it was better than nothing.

He nodded but didn't say what he was thinking. That pregnancy was dangerous—that his very own delivery had killed his mother. He didn't want history to repeat itself. It was one of the reasons he'd written off having a family of his own. He knew how devastating it could be when that dream fell apart.

But life had thrown him a twist. He was going to have a family—his brother's family. He just hoped he could be half the man his brother had been. The baby deserved nothing less.

Right now, the best thing he could do was to keep Popi off her feet as much as possible. In the morning, he'd get her back to the mainland—even if it meant he had to hire a helicopter to get them there.

He glanced at her as she fussed over the kitten. He had to admit he was a bit jealous of the kitten getting on Popi's good side, while she considered Apollo the enemy. But he was right about her going to the mainland. It was safest.

But if she refused to listen to him, then perhaps he could get her to put up her feet and rest.

"Why don't you go back to the bungalow?" he suggested. When she sent him a suspicious look, he added, "You know, to take care of the kitten."

He'd also noticed that, as the day progressed, she'd been experiencing a lot of discomfort. He didn't know if that was normal at this point in her pregnancy. She consistently rubbed the small of her back. A time or two, she'd even let him give her a light massage, but the relief was always short-lived.

Popi's questioning gaze moved from him to the kitten and then back again. "I can't leave now. I have to make sure everything is put in the right spot in the warehouse and categorized accordingly. Can you imagine everyone returning to the island and not being able to find their belongings? Or worse, getting someone else's things?"

It seemed like with every moment that passed, he was getting sucked further into Popi's life. But she wasn't leaving him much choice. Someone had to make sure she took care of herself. And that obviously wasn't going to be her.

"You go back to the bungalow," he said. "I'll make sure the warehouse is taken care of."

She arched a brow. "Why would you do that?"

He stifled a sigh. Couldn't she just accept his help? Why did she have to question everything?

"Because you are tired. It's written all over your face." His gaze moved to the wiggling ball of fluff in her hands. "And because you aren't going to be able to hold on to the kitten much longer."

Just then she caught the kitten before it could climb the whole way up onto her shoulder. She settled it back in her arms. "Stay there," she said to the kitten as though it could understand her. Then her gaze lifted to meet his. "And why should I trust you? I don't even know you."

"Our siblings were married, so that makes us family. Right?"

She hesitated. "Not really."

"Close enough. And if my brother were here—" just saying the words caused a large pang of hurt "—he would…he would vouch for me. I may not have been like him, but he understood that I had to follow my own path in life. Even if that path led away from him and our home."

Popi was quiet for a moment as her gaze searched his. "You really cared about him, didn't you?"

"Of course." He frowned at her. Why would she doubt such a thing? "Is that what my brother said? That I didn't care about him?"

She shook her head. "Forget it."

"Not a chance. I want to know why you would say such a thing."

She shrugged. "It's just that you were never there for the birthdays, the holidays. You weren't even there for their wedding or…"

She didn't have to say it. His mind filled in the blank. He wasn't there for the funeral. But he was here now. However, the look in Popi's eyes said that it was too little, too late.

Her gaze searched his. "You weren't interested in being part of the family then, so why the sudden interest now?"

Her words were like jagged rocks, beating against his chest. He hadn't meant to miss out on all of that. After each adventure, he told himself that he'd go on just one more excursion. He'd told himself that soon he would slow down. Soon there wouldn't be just one more mountain to conquer or one more adventure to go on. He'd always thought that there would be a tomorrow for him and his brother.

He of all people should have known that tomorrow is not guaranteed. The only thing you can count on is the here and now. That had to be enough. All the wishing in the world couldn't make the hands of time roll back. He knew this for a fact because it's what he'd been doing ever since he got the news of his brother's death.

He noticed the expectant look in Popi's eyes. She wanted him to argue with her. Well, she was in for a surprise.

"You're right." His voice was filled with remorse. "I wasn't there for those events, but I should have been. I was too wrapped up in my own life to realize what I was missing. I regret all of the missed opportunities."

She studied him for a moment, as though trying to discern the truth. "Do you really mean that?"

It was a sad commentary on him and his life when his devotion to his brother had to be questioned. "Growing up, Nile and I were close. I was the annoying little brother, but Nile put up with me. He took time out for me. When I wanted to quit college, he said that one day I would need to be able to run Drakos Industries. I just never thought it would be like this."

Popi glanced away. "I'm sorry. I shouldn't have doubted your relationship with your brother."

"It's not your fault. I've given you every reason to think I didn't care about Nile. I'll never forgive myself for losing track of what is truly important." He meant it. He had so many regrets that it was chewing him up on the inside. He wasn't about to add to that list. "I'm going to the warehouse now to make sure everything is completed. When I get back to the bungalow, we need to talk about the baby."

She handed over her digital tablet with all the necessary information about the furniture and boxes. "We can talk, but it's not going to change my mind about raising my niece."

"Or nephew."

She nodded. Without another word, she turned and did that really cute waddle thing. Eventually he caught himself standing there, staring as her. He gave his head a shake and then turned in the opposite direction.

CHAPTER EIGHT

There were definitely some benefits to being second-in-charge of the island.

Popi didn't feel that way most of the time. Most of the time being second-in-charge meant she had to run her ideas past Lea. It meant that any extravagances had to be preapproved by Lea. And sometimes being second-in-charge meant being the second place for a client to file a complaint, even if the situation was out of Popi's control.

But today Popi's position meant she could let herself into the small grocery store that carried so much more than food. She picked up some essentials for the kitten, from food to a litter box, and then she left an itemized list at the register of everything she'd taken. She would settle up when the island opened back up for business in a couple of months.

So much was about to change in the next six or seven weeks. Nothing would be as it had been. And her sister would not be there for any of it. And Popi blamed herself. If it wasn't for her making a fuss, her sister wouldn't have been on that boat when it exploded.

Popi shoved aside the guilt and pain. She had other matters to attend to now. There was the kitten locked up in her bathroom. And there was the sexy Greek man who insisted on staying in her life until he got his way. They'd see about that.

She wasn't just going to hand over this baby because he was a Drakos. Everyone in Athens—in Greece—knew his last name. They knew it was synonymous with old money and great power.

That wouldn't stop Popi from fighting for what was best for this child. Apollo might be the child's blood relation, but she was the one carrying the baby—making it possible for it to be here. And she wouldn't stop fighting for this little bundle of joy.

Once back at the bungalow, Popi was relieved to find that Apollo hadn't returned. But she didn't have time to rest. She had a kitten to care for.

In the bathroom, she was amazed to find that one little kitten could wreak such havoc. The toilet paper was strewn across the floor. Her purple-and-teal bath loofah that had been sitting on the edge of the tub was now across the room, and there was a kitten attached to it. The little guy was lying on his side while holding the loofah with its front paws and kicking it with his back. Popi could only hope that he wore himself out after making such a mess.

A little while later, the bathroom was set right and there was litter in the litter box. The kitten took right to the box. Popi could only hope that litter training was truly that easy and that there weren't any future accidents.

"Is everything okay?"

The sound of Apollo's voice made her jump. She hadn't heard him return. She turned in the hallway, finding him standing right behind her—so close that she could reach out and touch him. The thought was tempting—very tempting—but she resisted the urge.

"I didn't hear you come in," she said.

"Sorry. I didn't mean to startle you." He sent her a guilty grin.

When he wasn't frowning at her, he was really quite handsome. She wondered if the baby would resemble him in some way. She hoped so.

"Relax. I'm okay. I was just focused on the kitten." She frowned.

"What's wrong? Is it the baby? Did you overdo it today? I told you to rest earlier today, but you wouldn't listen."

"It's okay. It's not the baby. In fact, I think he or she is sleeping right now."

"Then why did you have that look on your face?"

"I was just thinking that I can't keep calling the kitten 'kitten.' It needs a name."

"And then you know what will happen, don't you?"

She sent him a puzzled look, not sure what he was getting at. "What will happen?"

"A cat with a name is a cat with a home."

She had to admit that she liked the idea. "Unless it already has a home."

"Something tells me that it isn't going anywhere." He was looking behind her.

She turned to see what he was staring at. There was the kitten dragging the loofah up to her. The kitten sat next to her.

"Looks like you have a shadow," Apollo teased.

"Shadow?" She looked at the dark gray kitten with the white neck and belly. She knelt down to pet the little guy. "What do you think? Are you a shadow?"

The kitten looked up at her with its pretty blue eyes and let out a little baby meow. Popi's heart swelled with love for it. Unless the owner showed up, it looked like she had a baby kitten to raise too.

Then she envisioned the baby with a kitten to grow up with. Somehow that seemed right to her. Now that she had her heart set on this vision of her family, she had to hope the kitten hadn't run away from a loving home and gotten left behind when everyone was shipped off the island for the renovations. And most of all, she had to pray that Apollo came to his senses and realized that the baby was best left here with her. Because if it came down to a court case, she had no doubt that he had the money to hire the very best army of lawyers and they would beat any defense she could muster.

Popi eyed Apollo, wondering if he'd really be that ruthless. There was a glint of determination in his eyes. Maybe she would have to mount her defense in a very different way—a way that didn't include lawyers and judges. She would have to appeal to his mind and his heart.

What was she thinking?

Apollo noticed the looks Popi had been giving him off and on all day. She had something on her mind, and he was pretty certain he wasn't going to like it.

It wasn't like she was just suddenly going to change her mind and hand over the baby when it was born. She had her mind made up about him, and he didn't know if he could change it.

When he was out in the wilderness, he didn't have to feel like he wasn't living up to other people's expectations of him. And he didn't have to feel like he didn't stack up to his big brother—the brother who had the perfect life, the perfect wife and the perfect career as CEO of Drakos Industries.

When Apollo was off on one of his adventures, the world became a lot smaller. He could focus on the more basic parts of life, such as his next meal and where he would sleep that night. Maybe that made him selfish—he wasn't sure. But at the time he'd gone off on his first adventure, he just couldn't stand to listen to one more of his father's lectures about how he was a disappointment. That was something Apollo would never say to his nephew or niece.

But he was starting to get similar looks from Popi—looks that said he'd let down his family and she would never trust him with the baby. The looks made him uncomfortable. After all, Popi barely even knew him. But she had heard stories from his brother. He could only guess at what his brother had to say about him, most likely none of it any good. In the last year or two, he and his brother had clashed—a lot.

Yet Popi still hadn't kicked him out. And he didn't miss the part about the village being deserted and it just being the two of them on the island. Did that mean he'd jumped to the wrong conclusions? Was it possible she trusted him? Just a little?

If so, it was a starting point from which he could reason with her and avoid a long, drawn-out, nasty court case that would be fodder for the headlines. The whole thing would be a mess.

"You really didn't have to stay here." Popi's voice drew him from his thoughts. "I'm fine on my own. And I have a phone should an emergency come up." Then she frowned as though realizing she'd said too much. "Not that there will be an emergency or anything."

He wasn't going anywhere. "I just feel better being here."

She arched a brow. "Are you saying you care?"

He suddenly felt as though there wasn't a right answer to her question. Not wanting to complicate things any further, he knew it was time to change the subject. "What would you like for dinner?"

A small smile pulled at her lips, letting him know she'd caught on to his diversionary tactics. "I don't know what's in the cabinets." She rubbed her back as a frown settled over her pretty face. "But I'm not hungry—"

Thunk. Thunk.

They both turned to the front door as it swung back and forth. The sun had set by then, leaving them in the dark. There wasn't even any moonlight tonight.

"The wind is really kicking up," Popi said. "I've been

so busy with the wedding and packing that I haven't had time to check the weather in days."

She moved to the open front door. Another gust of wind rushed through the doorway. She pushed the door closed against the wind and secured it.

"Do you get bad weather here?" he asked.

"Once in a while. But not often."

Apollo started opening the kitchen cabinets. "It looks like we have pasta." He continued to name off the various food items. And then he turned to her. "What do you feel like?"

She rubbed the small of her back. "Um…nothing."

He moved to her. "Is your back still bothering you?"

She nodded. "I guess I overdid it today."

"You should be resting." He noticed the lines deepening between her brows.

She shook her head. "It'll pass. It always does."

Apollo expelled a long sigh. "I told you not to lift anything today."

"I didn't." When he arched a disbelieving brow at her, she amended her response. "Okay. But that box wasn't heavy at all. It had paper products in it."

"Maybe you were just on your feet too long." He glanced around the room for a place for her to sit, but they'd emptied most of this bungalow, as well as all the other bungalows on the island.

He scanned the now empty living room. He'd tried to convince her to keep some of the furniture, but Popi had been insistent that she could manage for one night with bare bones. He wondered if she was now regretting that decision.

He walked to the master bedroom to retrieve an inflatable mattress from the closet. He returned to the living room with it, some pillows and a blanket. He put them all down in the middle of the floor.

Popi was pacing back and forth. Her hand was still pressed to the small of her back. "What are you doing?"

"You need to rest and take some strain off your back."

"I'm fine."

"Don't take this the wrong way, but you don't look fine."

"Well, aren't you just full of compliments." She sent him a teasing smile.

"I try." At least she hadn't lost her sense of humor. They were going to need it to get through this night.

It took a bit to pump up the full-size mattress. Once he detached the pump, he fixed the mattress up with pillows and blankets. But what he hadn't counted on was trying to get a nine-month pregnant woman down to the floor. It took some maneuvering and cooperation, but at last Popi was off her feet.

She moved this way and that way, trying to get comfortable. And yet she continued to frown. She rolled onto her side and he placed a pillow behind her back.

"How's that?" he asked.

"It's good." But the look on her face said that it was anything but good.

He knelt down beside her. "We need to get you to the mainland."

He didn't like taking chances where her pregnancy was concerned. He knew what could happen. His family had already sustained so many losses. He didn't think he could bear another.

She smiled at him, but it didn't quite reach her eyes. "I'm good, really. You were right. I overdid it today. I should have listened to you."

Had she just admitted that he was right about something? He smiled. "You're sure?"

She nodded. "See. The pain is already lessening."

He studied her for a moment, trying to figure out if she was telling him the truth. There was no way they were staying on this island if she was going into labor. Not a chance. She needed to be in the hospital with a full, knowledgeable staff and equipment for any emergency. But in the end, even that hadn't been enough to save his mother.

Why exactly couldn't he have stayed gone for just a little longer? Just until the baby was born—when the beautiful surrogate mother and little one were safe and sound. He wasn't any good at this stuff. This waiting and wondering was taking its toll. But he didn't want Popi to see how worried he was.

"Maybe I should call your doctor." He straightened and reached for his phone. "Just to be sure."

"Don't." Her eyes pleaded with him. "I already ran to the doctor when I thought I was in premature labor last week. They assured me it was just Braxton-Hicks contractions."

"What's that?" He didn't like the sound of it.

"It's the body's way of preparing for the birth of the baby."

His gut was knotted up. "And you're sure that's what this is?"

She nodded. "We're good."

He still wasn't convinced that all was well. But what did he know about pregnant women? He could only trust that what Popi was saying was the truth.

His gaze searched hers. "You'll tell me if anything changes?"

"I will."

He released a pent-up breath. He needed something to do besides pace. "I suppose I should find us something to eat."

Just then Shadow emerged from whatever hiding spot he'd been cowering in since the winds started beating on the bungalow. The kitten let out a tiny cry, as though letting them know that he was hungry too.

"And I'll get you a bowl of kitten food." Apollo couldn't resist running his fingers over Shadow's downy-soft fur.

"And water. He keeps knocking his water bowl over." Popi added just as the kitten climbed up on the mattress to be next to her.

Luckily Apollo had put down a couple of blankets to cover the mattress. Hopefully it'd protect it from the kitten's needlelike nails.

CHAPTER NINE

COULD HE TRUST HER?

Apollo studied Popi while she fussed over the kitten. She was so stubborn and one determined lady. He worried she'd let these Braxton-Whatevers go too far. But she seemed all right for the moment.

Maybe she was right. Maybe there was nothing to worry about…for now. Besides, it wouldn't take long to get to the mainland by boat or helicopter.

One more pain and he didn't care what she said, he was calling for help. She was better safe than sorry.

In the meantime, he turned to the kitchen. Since Popi's newly remodeled kitchen wasn't being renovated, she hadn't felt the need to pack it up. That made it convenient for him. He set to work.

He needed to prepare a meal that was simple—something that was in his wheelhouse—yet it needed to be something with a bit of substance. He settled for *fakés soúpa*. Popi had everything on hand, from the lentils to the onion and garlic. He warmed up a pot while he diced up the vegetables. It was a very easy recipe—

"What are you making?" Popi asked.

"Fakés soúpa." He added the chopped onion and minced garlic to the pot. "I hope that's all right."

"It's fine with me. So, tell me. Where did you learn to cook?"

"Here and there. It's a necessary skill when you're out on your own."

"And the soup? Was that something you made when you were hiking around the world?"

He glanced at her, finding genuine interest reflected in her eyes. "No. This is something I learned when I was a kid. When I would get in trouble with my father—which was most every day—Anna, our housekeeper, would either send me outside or if it was raining, she'd have me help in the kitchen."

"You and your father weren't close?"

He shook his head. "My father and I had a very strained relationship."

"I'm sorry to hear that."

"It's ancient history. But while I was in the kitchen, the cook told me that idle hands were the devil's workshop and so he put me to work. I actually didn't mind cooking. As it was, the cook and the housekeeper were the only ones besides my brother to have any one-on-one time with me."

"That sounds very lonely."

He shrugged. "I learned how to entertain myself and how to go it alone in life."

"And that's why you spend so much time off in some far-off jungle or climbing some mountain? It's all you've ever known."

She was right. But how had she done that? How had she read him so easily? He'd made it a point to close himself off to others. He'd built a wall around himself so no one would ever get close enough to hurt him again. And in such a short period of time, Popi had already scaled his wall and had a glimpse inside.

He cleared his throat. "I assure you the baby will never go through something like that. I'll make sure to give him—"

"Or her."

"Or her all the attention they need."

"You're still assuming the baby will be living with you."

It was time that she accepted reality. He placed the lid on the pot and let the soup simmer. He moved to the edge of the kitchen, where he could face her. He noticed how the kitten had curled up to Popi's chest and fallen asleep. She kept running a finger over its back. And when Apollo listened really hard, he could hear the kitten's purr. It sounded like the soft idling of a small engine.

"I'm waiting." Popi's voice drew him from his meandering thoughts.

His gaze met hers. "You have to realize that baby you're carrying, it's special. It's not your baby any more than it's mine. And it has a special place in life as the Drakos heir."

Popi's brows drew together. "Isn't that you?"

He shook his head. "My father wrote me out of the family business. He said I didn't have what it took to keep the company running. But Nile did. He was my father's favorite."

"But your father couldn't just cut you out of your inheritance—out of what is rightly yours."

"My father was powerful. No one told him what to do. He made up his own rules and expected everyone to follow them. He removed me from having anything to do with the company. While I was included in the will, it was my brother who inherited the controlling shares of the company."

"But with him gone, who's running it now?"

"At the moment, the board of trustees have stepped in to make sure there are no disruptions."

"And after that?"

"Well, since the baby is too young, there will be a conservator appointed."

"And that will be you?"

He shook his head and backed up. "It's not going to be me."

"Can't you do the job?"

"I could, if I wanted to. I might finally get some use out

of that expensive education that my brother convinced me to get. But I'm not going to do it."

"You're just going to turn your back on your legacy."

"That's where you're wrong. It's not my legacy. It never was." The memory of his father's harsh words came rushing back to him. *Worthless. Stupid. Mistake.* Each hurtful word was like a nail in his heart. How could those words still have such power to hurt him after all these years?

"Apollo—"

"No, I'm done talking about my past." His words came out more harshly than he'd intended. "We need to talk about the future. The baby needs to grow up in its home in Athens."

Popi glared at him. "You mean the same place where you were so obviously unhappy."

He sighed. She did have a point. "It will be different now. My father is no longer there."

"But will you be there? What about all of your adventures?"

That was something for him to consider. After being on the go for the past ten or so years, he couldn't imagine waking up in the same place day after day. Maybe when the baby got a bit older, he could take him…or her…on an adventure.

The outing would need to be more docile than he was used to taking. There would definitely be no thrill seeking, but something to get them out and about. He could teach the child about the world and how to care for it.

"I will deal with it."

Popi sent him an *I don't believe you* look. "Until you get bored."

"I won't get bored." Would he? He hoped not. But raising his nephew or niece would be such a different sort of lifestyle than he'd become accustomed to.

Before he'd only had himself to worry about. Now he'd

have a tiny human counting on him for everything. The enormity of that responsibility did not elude him.

Popi sat up straighter. "You say that now, but things will change. Babies aren't always that easy to manage."

And just as she was talking him out of his plan, he recalled what his brother had done for him. "I understand that, but I also remember what my brother had sacrificed after our father died. He stepped up and became my legal guardian. He didn't have to do it. No one made him. But he said that family stuck together in good times and bad."

"I...I didn't know. Your brother never spoke about those times."

Apollo rubbed the back of his neck as the memories started to flood back to him. "It wasn't an easy time back then. There was a power grab for control of the company. They said my brother was too young and inexperienced to run such a large entity. And then the attorneys wanted me to go off to live with strangers. It was a horrible time. And I didn't make life any easier for my brother. I was full of anger. My brother was the undeserving recipient of a lot of hostility."

"It couldn't have been easy for either of you. You were both so young, and to lose both of your parents..."

"Even though everything was against us, my brother didn't give up. He fought tooth and nail to keep us together and to hold on to our father's legacy."

Outside, the winds continued to rage, beating upon the bungalow with force. Inside, Apollo's feelings were just as fierce. His emotions swung between remorse, love and guilt.

He didn't know why he was opening up to Popi like this. He'd never divulged any of this to another person. The only other person that knew of the struggles was his brother and he was no longer here to make Apollo feel connected to his family. That tie was gone and would soon be replaced by his brother's offspring.

"Your brother was an amazing man," Popi said, drawing Apollo from his thoughts.

"He definitely was." Those were words he was certain no one had ever spoken of him. You have to earn that sort of respect.

And before, that hadn't bothered him, but now he wanted his nephew or niece to be able to look up to him. Not because he wanted the praise, but rather because he wanted to be that kind of person—the solid, dependable person that his brother had been for him. But was that even possible?

"And he loved you."

Apollo cleared the emotional knot in the back of his throat. "He tolerated me."

Popi shook her head. "It was much more than that. He stuck by you. No matter what. Even at his wedding, when someone would start to say something about you not attending, he would shut them down. He would tell them that you would be there if you could."

Apollo's head hung low as the weight on his heart grew more intense. "I should have been there." His voice was soft. "I wanted to be there."

A moment of silence passed.

"Why weren't you?" There was no tone of accusation to her question, but more a matter of wanting to understand.

Though they'd never met before now, they had shared a family. His brother, her sister. Popi had been there from the beginning of his brother's romance, through to the wedding and beyond…to offering to carry their baby. And Apollo had missed all of it. He'd chosen to isolate himself—to protect himself. Instead his plan had backfired. He'd hurt everyone, including himself.

"I had been in the Amazon rainforest. I had all my travel

plans for the wedding, but then I was stung and came down with a bad case of dengue fever. I had some complications and it prevented me from traveling." But he should have pushed himself—he should have made it.

"I didn't know. Your brother didn't go into details."

"I'm sure that's because he was angry with me. And he had every right to be. When I needed him, he was always there. When he needed me, I failed him."

"But it wasn't your fault. It's not like you went out and sought out the illness. I'm sure you brother was disappointed but he understood."

"Really? Because I'm not sure I would be so understanding."

Just then the sky filled with light as a bolt of lightning shot through the inky night. Seconds passed and then thunder shook the bungalow, as well as them.

"I didn't know it was going to storm this bad," Popi said.

Apollo couldn't help but wonder if she was running out of words to comfort him and had decided it was best to change the subject. Before they let go of the past, he had one more thing to share with her.

His gaze met hers. "I've changed since the wedding. I've done a lot of growing up. I've witnessed a lot. I've had someone die in my arms. A good man. I've learned that we aren't guaranteed tomorrow and to make the most of today. I've learned to treasure those who care about you because there are many more that won't." When he saw the confusion in her eyes, he said, "What I'm trying to say is that I think I'm a better person now. I think—no, I know—that I can do this. Be a parent."

Another crack of thunder rattled the bungalow, making the glass of the windows rattle.

"I think we should check the forecast," Popi said.

He'd wanted her to acknowledge what he'd just said but then realized that she would probably disagree with him. After all, how could she not? He had missed his own brother's funeral. Who does that?

But he did have his reasons...

Popi struggled to stand up.

"Stay there," he said, seeing the lines of pain etched upon her face. "Your back—it isn't getting better, is it?"

She shook her head. "I think it's getting worse." She settled down on the mattress once again. "Why do these practice contractions have to happen now? Couldn't they have just waited a day or two?"

He couldn't tell if she was talking to him or herself. Regardless, he didn't think she was expecting a response. And so he remained silent.

"Could you hand me my laptop? I want to check the weather." She told him where he could locate it in her bedroom.

Once he returned to the sparse living room, he said, "I don't think you're going to need this. I have a strong feeling we're in for some rain tonight."

Just then the first drop of rain pinged off the window. And so the stormy night began. Apollo had this feeling deep in his gut that they were in trouble. And it wasn't like him to worry needlessly. After all, he was used to camping in jungles with wild animals, on top of mountains in the unforgiving snow and even lost in the desert during a sandstorm.

But there was one thing he'd learned from all of his experiences and that was to listen to his gut. He had some kind of crazy sense of imminent peril. But that's all it was—a feeling. It didn't come with any warnings of what to avoid or how to prepare. He just knew to be on guard.

While Popi used her computer, he moved to the front door. With the wind still blowing, he decided against opening the door. Instead he moved to the window. Even with the covered porch to protect the window from the now-pounding rain, he couldn't see more than a foot past the window. It was the blackest night he could remember.

He turned back to Popi. Her face was scrunched up in pain as her hand pressed to her rounded abdomen. The feeling of doom came over him again.

He rushed to her side. "Is there anything I can do?"

She shook her head as she let go of the laptop and leaned back against the pillows. "I don't understand it. The pain is getting worse. Usually it subsides by now."

And then he had the worst thought possible. He internally struggled with whether he should put voice to his thoughts. Saying it out loud and putting it into the universe was like tempting fate. But something told him that their fate had already been written.

CHAPTER TEN

APOLLO'S PULSE RACED.

He knew what was happening. Popi was going into labor.

In the next breath, he calmed himself with the knowledge that it was too early for labor. She'd told him earlier that day that she still had a couple of weeks until her due date. Everything was going to be all right. But he had to be sure.

"Could you be in labor?" he asked.

"Um. No. It'll stop."

That wasn't good enough. "We had a deal. I'm calling for the ferry."

"They won't come out this late. And certainly not to pick up the two of us."

"Then, a helicopter."

She shook her head. "It costs more money than I have."

"Don't worry about the money. We have to make sure you're okay."

Popi sighed. "There."

"What?"

"The pain, it subsided. Everything is going to be okay."

He didn't say it, but he didn't think they were in the clear. He thought this was just the calm before a stormy night. And he prayed he hadn't made the biggest mistake of their lives by letting her insist they remain on the island.

"You better check on the soup," she said, sending him a small smile. "I hear the lid rattling."

"How can you hear anything over the noise outside?"

As he moved to the kitchen to tend to the soup and adjust the temperature, he realized that he needed a plan. If the worst happened, he needed to get Popi to the hospital. Because she may be fine now, but she wasn't a few moments ago. And he was worried that it was going to happen again.

Flashes of his childhood raced through his mind. *It's your fault she died.* His father's drunken rants hadn't taunted him in many years. But these were extraordinary circumstances—a position he'd never wanted to find himself in. Ever. *If it wasn't for you, she'd still be here.*

"You're awfully quiet. Is everything okay?" Popi asked.

Apollo turned to find her getting to her feet. He rushed to her side to lend her a hand. "What are you doing? You're supposed to be resting."

"I feel better now. The pain in my back has lessened. And I don't have any cramping. It's time to get the table set for dinner."

He stared at her. What had just happened? She'd been miserable and now she wanted to set the table for dinner? Was she really feeling that okay?

Not paying him the least bit of attention, she headed for the cabinets and retrieved two bowls. She moved without hesitation. And the little lines on her face had smoothed out. Maybe he'd just let his imagination get the best of him. After all, what guy wouldn't worry about being alone on an island with a pregnant woman—a very pregnant woman?

Lightning lit up the sky at the same time the power in the bungalow went out. Before either of them could speak, the lights flickered back on as a resounding clap of thunder shook everything. The storm was on top of them. And from the sounds of it outside, the island was definitely taking a hit.

He saw the worried look on Popi's face. "It's okay. It's just a little thunder."

She turned to the window. "It's not the thunder that worries me."

It was the lightning. It worried him too, as it was especially bad. But Popi didn't need anything else to worry about. "Don't worry. It should pass over in no time."

"Not soon enough."

He silently agreed.

The truth was that he couldn't wait until tomorrow. The contractor would arrive and they would leave the island. Soon they'd be part of civilization again—close to doctors, nurses and a state-of-the-art hospital. And maybe then he would be able to breathe easy. He didn't care how good she looked now—he still had that uneasy feeling in the pit of his stomach.

While he filled their bowls with steaming-hot soup, Popi paced the floor. Her hand pressed to the small of her back as though it were permanently attached there.

"Are you okay?" he asked.

"Um, sure. Fine." But those little lines returned to her face.

She wasn't fine—

The trickle of water caught both of their attention. They both glanced down to find a small puddle around Popi's feet. Either she just peed herself or they were in some *serious* trouble.

The breath stuck in his lungs as his gaze rose to meet her worried look. This was not good. Not good at all. He was freaking out on the inside but doing everything he could not to let it show. Like that was possible.

After all, he was a guy. He was used to traveling in the deepest, darkest jungles. He'd scaled rock walls. He'd lived through an avalanche. He been attacked by a bear and had the scars to prove it.

But this baby stuff. It scared him silly.

"My water broke." Popi's voice wasn't much above a whisper. And the look in her round eyes was one of fear.

The two of them couldn't freak out at the same time. That much was for sure. And then he saw her eyes shimmer and a tear splash onto her cheek. Okay. She got the first turn at freaking out.

He told himself to pretend he was on one of his missions. Popi was just another adventurer. And his niece or nephew wasn't about to born. He also slammed the door on his past and stories of his birth. He just had to deal with the here and now.

He strode toward her. "You need to sit back down."

"Not like this. Not in these wet clothes."

In the next few minutes, Apollo did things that he'd never done before. And he did them in an almost out-of-body experience. He got Popi fresh clothes and, to both of their embarrassment, helped her change. Sometimes you just have to do what you have to do. And then he cleaned up the mess on the floor.

He'd never considered himself a squeamish person before, but then again, he'd never dealt with childbirth. And what little he'd been exposed to let him know it wasn't for the faint of heart. And it certainly wasn't for someone that didn't know what in the world he was doing.

Inside he was yelling: *Why did you do this? Why did you stay on this island when you could be near the hospital? Why would you take a chance with your life and the baby's?*

He strained, not letting his rolling emotions show on his face. It wouldn't help the situation. But it was tough to hold it all in when he knew what this early delivery could mean if they didn't get to the mainland soon.

"Go ahead and say it." Popi's voice drew him from his thoughts.

"Say what?"

"What you were thinking."

Had he let something slip? He didn't think so. "I'm not thinking anything."

"You're thinking this is all my fault." Her voice wavered. "You're thinking I made a mistake staying here. That I should have known better."

He avoided looking at her. He knew he should disagree with her. He should reassure her that none of this was her fault, but right now he couldn't.

He didn't think she'd used her best judgement by staying on the island. He thought she should have been close to the hospital throughout this whole pregnancy. Or maybe she shouldn't have gotten pregnant at all. Pregnancy was dangerous. It could take away those that loved you the most.

"Go ahead. Say it." Popi's voice rose with emotion.

"I don't have anything to say." Nothing that would help the situation.

"I just went to the doctor a few days ago." She blinked away unshed tears. "She said that everything was okay. She said that the baby was doing well. I thought—I thought wrong." Her shoulders hunched and her head hung low.

"That's good," he said, struggling to find something positive to say. "You know, that the doctor said everything is good with the baby."

Popi went on as though he hadn't even said anything. "I should have known the backache meant something. I should have known I was going into labor. If I can't figure out this stuff, how am I going to be a good mother?"

He couldn't just stand by and let her beat up on herself. Maybe he didn't agree with all of her choices, but he wasn't in her shoes. This island is her home. She would feel safe and secure here. That was a feeling he'd never experienced. His father's mansion had always been like a war zone when Apollo was growing up. And the worst part was he never knew when a verbal bomb would be lobbed in his direction. He banished thoughts of his past. He had to stay focused on the present.

The soup on the table was long forgotten. Apollo was running on autopilot. And his goal was to get them off this storm-ravaged island ASAP.

He reached for his phone. He started to dial for help but then noticed there were no bars. He had zero reception.

"Where's your phone?" he asked.

Popi grabbed it from the side of her bed and handed it to him. "What's wrong?"

He checked her phone too. "There's no cell signal."

"The storm must have taken out the tower."

The storm wasn't letting up. In fact, he'd swear it was getting worse, not better. But he wasn't about to tell Popi that. All she needed to do now was focus on that baby.

"There has to be another way to contact the mainland." He was certain of it. Okay. Maybe certain wasn't the right word. But he was desperate. It seemed reasonable that an island which hosted so many guests would have a backup plan.

"I don't know." Popi's eyes were open wide and her face was pale. "I...I can't think. The baby. It's coming."

A contraction stopped her from speaking. She began panting. He wondered if that was normal or not.

"Can I do anything?"

Right now, all he wanted to do was turn and walk out that door. He didn't care if it was storming or not. It had to be better than watching Popi's beautiful face contort in pain. And he didn't even want to think about what lay ahead.

First, he had to do whatever he could to make her comfortable. He ran to the bedroom and grabbed any lingering throw pillows and blankets from the moving boxes. He propped all of the pillows against the wall and helped her settle back against it.

"What are we going to do?" Popi looked at him like he should have all the answers.

Meanwhile he was a wreck on the inside. He was just making stuff up as he went along and prayed that he was right. All the while reminding himself not to have a meltdown.

"We're going to get you off this island and to the mainland, where there will be help. Don't worry." Yeah, because he was worrying enough for the both of them. "This is all going to be okay. You and the baby will be fine."

The worry reflected in her eyes made the knot in his gut cinch tighter. He didn't believe what he was saying. He didn't believe this was going to be all right. There was no way he could do this alone. He had to get help and fast.

"Who is on this island besides us?"

"I...I don't know." She stared down at her protruding abdomen.

"Popi." When she didn't look at him, he placed a finger beneath her chin and lifted her head until her gaze met his. "Popi, think. Who is on the island?"

"Um, just some goat herders. Everyone else is off on a Mediterranean cruise for the next couple of weeks."

Apollo highly doubted goat herders would be any better at delivering a baby than him. So that idea was nixed. But he wasn't giving up. Their cell phones might not work, but there had to be another way to contact the mainland.

"Popi, what is the island's backup communication? You know, when the cell tower isn't working. How else can you reach help?"

Popi worried her lip as another contraction seized her focus. He took her hand in his, hoping to lend her whatever comfort he could offer. She squeezed his hand as her face scrunched up. The seconds seemed to last for minutes before the pain subsided. He couldn't even imagine what it must be like for Popi. If it were up to men to have the babies in this world, he'd been willing to bet there wouldn't be a population problem.

Once Popi relaxed, Apollo tried again. "Popi, think. How can I reach the mainland?"

"Um…" There was a moment of silence. "There are satellite phones on the boats."

That would work. He just had to make it through the storm that was raging outside. "Great. You did awesome." He leaned over and kissed her forehead. "Don't worry. I'm going to get you out of here."

"Wait. What are you saying?" She clutched his hand tightly. "You aren't going to leave me here. Are you?"

"I have to." He really did hate leaving her alone. "But it won't be long. I promise."

"Please don't go."

Just then the kitten came bounding out of the bedroom. Without the thunder, the kitten must have decided it was safe to come out.

"Look," Apollo said, "Shadow is here. He'll keep you company."

Apollo grabbed a couple of small objects from the countertop, a paper flower from the wedding and a foam ball. "Do you mind if I let the kitten play with these?"

Popi shook her head.

It didn't take much to gain the kitten's attention. When it rolled over on its back, Apollo noticed the small smile pulling at Popi's lips. Thank goodness.

"Now, take care of Shadow while I'm gone."

"Take care how?" The worry returned to her eyes.

"Just play with him. And in no time, I'll be back." He lifted her hand to his lips and kissed it. "I promise. And I never break my promises."

And with that he headed for the door, having no idea what awaited him outside. But something told him it wouldn't be nearly as scary as what awaited him inside.

CHAPTER ELEVEN

PAIN UNLIKE ANY other gripped her.

Popi breathed through the contraction like she'd learned to do at her prenatal class. All the while, frantic thoughts raced through her mind. One worrisome thought proceeded the next.

Her sweaty palms rubbed over the blanket. Nothing about this delivery was right. It was too soon. She wasn't ready. Not even close. There was so much to do.

This wasn't how any of this was supposed to be. Her sister was supposed to be here by her side. This was supposed to be a joyous occasion. Not frightening and tinged with sadness.

The pain rose like a wave increasing with each heartbeat. And then it crested. It felt like it would go on forever. And then it rolled away, subsiding into nothing. At last Popi could breathe easily again.

She leaned back against the pillows and savored this pain-free moment. Maybe if she relaxed and didn't move, the contractions would stop. And then she remembered that her water had broken. There was no way out of this one. Birth was imminent.

But if it would slow down, that would be awesome. She needed off this island and quickly. Why did she insist on staying? Why?

She had to get it together for the baby. And for Apollo. He made a point of acting tough for her, but she could see in his eyes that he was afraid of this premature birth. He wasn't the only one.

This was her fault. She shouldn't have been lifting

things yesterday. At the time, they hadn't been that heavy. She hadn't thought she was doing anything wrong. She'd just wanted to get the work over with so she could go home and rest.

She should have listened to Apollo when he'd told her to stop doing things. She should have gone to the mainland with everyone else. She should have been more prepared.

The regrets and—

Pain started again in her midsection, putting a halt to her rambling thoughts. The shortness between the contractions didn't escape her attention. She grabbed her phone so she could start timing them.

As the pain increased, she used the skills she'd learned from the midwife on the island and the prenatal class. She desperately tried to recall everything they'd told her. She just never thought she would be having the baby here.

She knew at nine minutes apart, she would still have some time before the baby. They needed all the time they could get to get off this island and to the hospital on the mainland.

She'd truly thought she would have more time before going into labor. This was her first baby and everyone had assured her that first babies were notoriously late. This baby apparently didn't want to be like everyone else, as it was coming a couple of weeks early—eager to put its stamp upon this world. And there was nothing and no one to stop it.

Now that the panic over the impending arrival of the baby was subsiding, she knew that she couldn't just lie here. The storm wasn't letting up—

Thunk!

Something heavy had hit the roof before rolling away. Popi glanced upward. She was relieved that there was no hole in the roof. The winds howled as greenery smacked the side of the bungalow. The storm wasn't letting up. In fact, it was getting worse.

With the tiny kitten cowering in her arms, she said, "Don't worry, Shadow. We'll be okay."

She had to get to the storm shutters on the windows and close them. The problem with that was they were on the outside of the bungalow. And she didn't relish the idea of heading out into the storm. But with Apollo already off trying to reach the mainland, that only left her.

She placed the kitten in a pile of blankets. "Stay there. I'll be back."

And so she struggled to her feet and headed for the door. It was pitch-black out. Definitely not a good sign. And the thought of Apollo being out there, alone, worried her.

He just had to be safe. She prayed he would return to her unharmed. She didn't know how she'd get through this without him.

He may have made mistakes in the past. And he may not have been there for his family when he should have been, but he wasn't the same man her sister had told her about.

The old Apollo—she could imagine him heading for the door at the first sign of trouble. He wouldn't have stayed with her, cooked for her and risked his life trying to get her help.

Maybe he wasn't exactly doing all of this for her, but he was doing it for the baby. At last he was learning that being part of a family meant being there for the good and the not-so-good.

Nile would be proud of his brother. She was proud of Apollo. She just wished he'd hurry back. With each passing minute, her worry escalated.

The fierce wind and rain stung his face.

The night was pitch-black.

Apollo squinted, trying to see where he was going. He

stumbled over a tree root but somehow managed to stay upright. With the power outage, there were no lights to mark the path.

Apollo refused to be stopped. Walking against the fierce winds made each step a challenge. But in his mind's eye, he saw Popi's face contorted in pain and he remembered his father's mutterings that if they had gone to the hospital sooner, his mother might have lived. Apollo didn't know if that was true or not, but he also knew getting help as soon as possible was most definitely in everyone's best interest.

Thankfully he'd been down to the marina a number of times that day, hauling the overflow items that wouldn't fit in the island's warehouse. The extras were shipped to the mainland to be stored at another location. At the time, he hadn't been thrilled about taking trip after trip to the dock, but now he was grateful that he was able to draw on those memories to navigate his way in the dark.

It wasn't until he made it down to the marina that there was some light. He didn't know how. The rest of the island was cast in darkness. But down here, light reflected off the dock and the boats. There must be some sort of backup generator. Whatever it was, he was extremely grateful.

Because the storm had stirred the sea into a frenzy. The normally serene water now moved toward the island in swells, with white caps that crashed upon the shore. The anchored boats moved to and fro, straining against their moorings. It was a miracle they hadn't broken free.

The rain was now coming in sheets. He was soaked to the bone. And he was cold, but he brushed off his discomfort. This was the most important thing he'd done in his life. If he didn't get help, Popi and the baby might die.

That thought sent an additional flood of adrenaline rushing through his body. Once on the dock, he was left with the decision of how to get on a swiftly moving boat. And on top of it was the fact that the deck was wet. So even if he made the jump, who was to say that his feet wouldn't slip off the edge. His body tensed. It would not end well if he were caught between the boat and dock.

Once he decided upon a boat, he studied it. In. Out. In. Out.

At least the boat appeared to be moving at a predictable speed. Before he could talk himself out of this, he jumped. Grabbing a rail and holding on for his life. For a moment, he didn't move, as he struggled to gain his footing.

And then he moved cautiously from the stern of the small yacht toward the bow. It was easy enough for him to find the control room. He wiped the rain from his face before swiping his dripping wet hair back, out of the way.

Once he turned the lights on, he went to work. With all of the adventures he'd experienced over the years, boating hadn't been one of them. He'd just never gotten to it. When it came to his excursions, he'd always favored the kind where he was physically challenged. When he thought of boating, he thought of lazy days on the deck, enjoying the sunshine. Obviously there was more to boating than he'd first assumed.

A strong current struck the boat. Apollo lost his balance. His shoulder hit the corner of a cabinet. That was going to hurt in the morning.

All he knew now was that he had to radio for help because there was no way he could deliver a baby. He didn't know the first thing about childbirth.

Another wave struck the boat, sending him stumbling to the floor. He didn't have much time before this yacht broke free of the dock. And there wasn't anything he wouldn't do to make sure Popi and the baby were safe.

CHAPTER TWELVE

THE BUNGALOW WAS SECURED.

But Apollo hadn't returned.

With every passing minute, Popi's concern for him mounted. She should have insisted he stay here. It wasn't fit for man or beast out there. But it wasn't like he would listen to her. It hadn't taken her very long to deduce that he was a stubborn man.

The door flung open. Apollo stepped inside. Wind rushed into the room, sending the kitten scurrying away. With effort, Apollo closed the door, shutting out the storm. He kicked off his wet shoes.

He was drenched with rivulets of rain racing down his face. She tossed him a towel that she'd used earlier to wipe off after venturing outside. He swiped it over his face before running it over his hair.

Holding the towel to his chest, his gaze turned to her. "How are you?"

She pressed a hand to her rounded abdomen. "Still pregnant."

"And the contractions? Did they stop?"

She shook her head. "They're coming at seven minutes apart."

"What does that mean?"

She shrugged. "I think there's still time to get to the hospital if this storm would let up." Now it was time for her to ask a question. "Were you able to reach anyone?"

He nodded but his gaze didn't quite meet hers. "I did—"

"You did? That's great!" But the look on his face said otherwise. "When will they be here?"

"They won't be."

"What? But why?"

"The storm is a lot worse than we thought. They can't get to us via sea or air until this storm is over."

"Oh." Another contraction stole her voice away.

Apollo rushed to her side. He grunted in pain as he knelt down next to her, but she couldn't ask him about it—not yet. He took her hand in his. His hand was dry but his skin was cold to the touch. The wave of pain rose...rose...and crested. And then it was slow to ebb away.

When the pain fully passed, she sighed. "I can't believe the pain is going to get worse. This feels plenty bad right now."

"Don't think about it. You're doing great."

"I sure don't feel like it."

He gave her hand a quick squeeze before he released it. As he went to straighten, she noticed his cargo shorts had risen up slightly on his muscular thighs. That was when she noticed a long scar starting near his knee and snaking up under his clothes. It was still pink, as though the scar were recent.

Once fully upright, he said, "I'll be right back. I need to get out of these clothes." He turned toward the bedroom but then paused and turned back. "Do you need anything first?"

She shook her head. "I'm good. Thanks."

The truth was she had a lot of questions for him. She wanted to know when this storm was going to move on. She wanted to know if he got any other information from the mainland. And she wanted to know about the scar on his leg. Did it have something to do with why he'd missed his own brother's funeral?

Seconds ticked away as Popi flipped through her pregnancy book, gleaning any information that would help them. She wondered if there was any way to delay this delivery until help reached them. She didn't recall read-ing anything like that, but maybe she missed it. Originally she'd been planning to stay with her sister in the city. And when that plan had fallen through, she'd made the backup plan to stay with her parents. At this point, they didn't even know that she was in labor, and she had no way of telling them.

Apollo entered the room again. His gaze moved to the kitchen island. "You didn't want to eat?"

She shook her head. "I didn't think it was a good idea under the circumstances."

He nodded in understanding.

"You can go ahead and eat," she said. "In fact, I insist."

"That's okay."

But she knew it wasn't. He had to be starving, espe-cially with his hike to the marina. "Please eat. You don't know how long we're going to be here."

His hesitant gaze moved between her and the food.

"Go ahead," she said.

His worried gaze turned back to her. "Shouldn't you eat something too?"

She shook her head. "I'm good."

He moved to the counter. "You know I feel really guilty about eating when you aren't."

That touched her. "Tell you what, after this baby is born, I'm going to be starved. You can feed me then." She thought it would make him feel better, but instead the worry re-flected in his eyes was now written all over his face.

"You bet." His voice lacked enthusiasm. "Anything you want."

Another contraction stole her voice. She sucked in her breath, holding it. She leaned forward and squeezed her eyes closed as the pain increased. She willed the pain to go away, but it seemed like the pain grew in strength and length as her labor progressed. Would she be able to hold out until help reached them?

The next thing she knew, there were hands on her back. She opened her eyes in surprise to find Apollo kneeling next to her. His big hands and long fingers gently kneaded her back.

"Breath in," he reminded her. His voice was deep and soothing.

She did as he said.

"And breath out." All the while, his hands moved over her aching back. "Now again." He breathed with her as though they were in this together.

After a while, the pain slowly ebbed away. She leaned back on the mound of pillows. "How did you know how to do that?"

"I did a little research while I waited for you to return from the wedding. I had a lot of time to kill and knew nothing about pregnancy. I wanted some idea of what to expect."

She looked at Apollo with a new kind of appreciation. There was definitely more to this man that anyone ever gave him credit for. She wondered what else there was to him. Because the more time she spent with him, the more curious she became.

"So, tell me about yourself," she said.

He shook his head. "There's not much to say."

"Really? I'd think there would be quite a lot to tell."

"I'm sure it's nothing you'd be interested in."

Why was he so insistent on putting her off? He was an adventurer. He'd been to more places on earth than she could ever imagine going. She would have thought he would be full of stories—of conquests. She would imagine him at pubs, entertaining the men and women with his brave and daring feats.

And needing something to concentrate on besides the

inevitable next wave of pain and whether help would reach them before this baby decided to make its appearance, she had to get him talking. Besides, if they were to co-parent, she wanted to know exactly what sort of man she was getting involved with—in a purely platonic sort of way. Though the thought of something more between them was certainly very tempting—even if it was completely out of the question.

She patted a spot on the mattress next to her. "Come sit beside me."

"I don't think that's a good idea."

"Why not? It's not like there are a lot of other seats around here, with the furniture already moved to the warehouse."

His hesitant gaze moved from her to the spot next to her. Still, he made no motion to move. "Maybe I should—"

"Entertain me." When he sent her a puzzled look, she said, "I'm serious. Come talk to me so I don't sit here and think about how soon the next contraction will hit me."

Still, he didn't move.

"Please." She pleaded with her eyes. "After all, I'm doing all of the hard work here."

That seemed to have done it. The next thing she knew, the mattress dipped as he lowered himself next to her. It wasn't until then that she realized just how small the mattress was. Apollo's thigh brushed up against hers, sending her heart aflutter. Which was totally insane, considering she was getting ready to give birth. But she was beginning to think there wasn't anything that could keep her from noticing Apollo and his sexiness.

She swallowed hard. "So, um, tell me about one of your adventures."

"Is that really what you want to talk about?"

She nodded, not trusting her voice.

"I've visited the Amazon rainforest. I was there for a few months."

"Months?" When he nodded in confirmation, she asked, "You mean out in the jungle, with all of those insects and snakes?" Her nose curled up at the thought of pitching a tent and having some creepy-crawly come curl up with her.

Apollo let out a soft rumble of laughter.

Her gaze met his, and it was then that she realized just how close he was. He was so close that it would be nothing for her to lean over and press her lips to his. Her gaze momentarily dipped to his mouth. She remembered just how skilled he was at kissing. And as tempting as the thought was, now was certainly not the time. There wasn't a chance he could find her attractive as he ran a cloth across her forehead. He'd probably never find her attractive again. She smothered a sigh.

"Popi?" His voice startled her from her rousing thoughts.

And it came just as another contraction ruined this perfectly nice moment. She turned away and ground her back teeth together. The breath hitched in her throat as she braced for the pain to reach its peak.

Apollo took her hand in his. His thumb stroked gently over the back of her hand. "Remember to breathe through the pain." His voice was gentle. "That's it. In. And out. In. And out."

And then he did the breathing with her. It touched her heart that he was trying so hard to be there for her. Neither one of them were sure exactly what they were doing. And as this pain was worse than the last, she knew the chance of the storm letting up and allowing help to reach them before this baby made its grand entrance was slipping away with each passing contraction.

"You're doing great." Apollo continued to hold her hand.

As the pain neared its strongest point, she squeezed his hand. Tight. Very tight. He didn't say anything. Nor did he try to pull away. And though in the beginning she hadn't wanted him here for any of this, she now found comfort in his quiet strength and took solace in his encouraging words.

But she wasn't sure either of them was up for all of this. If this was how bad the pain was now, how much worse was it to get when the baby was finally born? The thought sent an arrow of fear through her.

She couldn't do this. She never should have agreed to have this baby for her sister. Sure, women had babies all the time, but they were different than her—they were braver and stronger.

As the pain ebbed away, she said, "I don't know if I can do this."

Apollo placed a finger beneath her chin and turned her head until their gazes met. "You can do this. You are doing amazing so far. I've never seen anyone as brave as you."

She didn't believe him. "You're wrong." Panic clawed at her. "I can't do this."

"I swear you are the bravest."

"But you've done all kinds of brave things, from hiking and camping in the jungle to mountain climbing. I'm just having a baby."

"Having a baby is one of the bravest things a person can do. And climbing a mountain doesn't even compare." His voice faded away, as though he were lost in his thoughts.

She was supposed to have another couple of weeks before all of this. Even her doctor hadn't said anything about her going into preterm labor. If she was going to be a parent, she had to do better—be more prepared.

"Popi, I'm in awe of you."

He was? Had she heard him correctly? He was in awe of her?

She turned to him and found warmth reflected in his eyes. "You really mean that, don't you?"

"I do. This little baby is going to have the most amazing mother."

What did that mean? Was he telling her that he was going to relinquish his quest to have custody of the baby?

She never got to ask the question, as another more powerful contraction swept her breath away. She held on tight to Apollo's hand as she rode the painful wave.

CHAPTER THIRTEEN

WHAT EXACTLY HAD he gotten himself into?

Time passed slowly. Very slowly.

Apollo sat by helplessly as Popi writhed in pain. It was more horrible than even he had ever imagined, not that he thought about childbirth much. In fact, he'd spent his whole life avoiding the subject. But he hadn't been able to avoid the guilt that shrouded his youth over him surviving while his mother had not.

But that wasn't going to happen with Popi. She would make it. The medevac would be here shortly. He was positive of it. Because there was no way he was delivering that baby.

As more time passed, Popi's contractions were a mere two minutes apart. The winds and rain continued to pummel the bungalow. His hopes of a quick rescue were slipping away.

It was going to be up to him to make sure Popi held the baby in her arms at the end of all of this. That seemed like a very daunting task.

"Talk to me." Popi's voice drew him out of his thoughts.

"What do you want me to talk about?"

She pulled her hand from his and ran her finger along the uneven scar trailing down his thigh, where his shorts had ridden up. "Tell me about that."

"You don't want to hear about it."

"I do. Please tell me. Give me something to concentrate on besides the contractions."

With all she was going through to bring a healthy baby

into this world, he had no right to withhold her one request. But where did he begin?

He cleared his throat. "I was on an extended trip in the Himalayas when it happened."

"What were you doing there?"

He shrugged. "Would you believe me if I told you that I threw a dart at a map and that's where it landed?"

She looked at him with disbelief reflected in her eyes. "Are you serious?"

"Pretty much. The dart method has taken me to some of the most interesting places on this earth. Some places I'd rather have not visited. This was one of those places."

"You mean because you got hurt?"

Just then her hand sought out his, and he knew what was coming—another contraction. He couldn't believe the contractions just kept coming one right after the other. It was well into the middle of the night by now. And lines of exhaustion were written on Popi's face.

"Keep talking," she said before groaning in pain.

And so he did as she asked. "I spoke to Nile before I went on the trip. I wanted him to know that I'd be completely out of touch for a couple of months. Nile told me about the baby and wanted me to be available in case there was any news about the baby. In fact, he demanded I forgo the trip and pick up the slack at the office so he could spend more time at home." Apollo paused and wiped the sweat from her brow, never once letting go of her hand. "I didn't know it at the time, but it would be the last thing that he ever asked of me. So we ended up arguing." Apollo expelled a sigh. "If I had known—if I'd had any clue that was to be my last conversation with him, it would have ended so differently."

"I'm sure Nile knew how much you cared about him."

"Really? Because the last thing I told him was to butt

out of my life. He wasn't my father and he couldn't boss me around."

Apollo could tell Popi's pain was lessening, as her grip on his hand loosened. He didn't think that his hand would ever be the same after this night. If he made it through without any broken bones, he would count himself as lucky. But right now, that would be a small sacrifice compared to what Popi was going through.

"You couldn't have known it would be your last conversation. None of us knew what was going to happen."

"But my brother didn't ask much of me. For years, he just let me be to chase one adventure after another, like some overgrown kid. And the one time he needed me, I'm too busy for him."

"He wanted you to be happy. He knew you'd had an unhappy childhood."

"It's something I never want this baby to go through." His gaze met hers. "I want us to figure out a way for the child to be happy."

"We will." She gave his hand a quick squeeze. "But what happened on the hike?"

"There was an earthquake. The ground beneath my feet literally disappeared. And that is the last thing I remember."

"That's horrible." Her gaze moved back to his leg.

"They say I fell, tumbled, rolled—you get the idea—about two hundred to three hundred meters. I ended up buried in rocks. Luckily I wasn't alone on the hike. Others were more fortunate than me. They called for help and dug me out."

The color drained from Popi's face.

He knew this wasn't the story to tell her—especially now. If only she hadn't insisted. "I was unconscious when they found me. I'm told I had a broken leg, fractured ribs and a collapsed lung."

Popi gasped. "You're lucky to be alive."

He nodded. "For a while, I wondered why I'd been spared while others hadn't. Now I guess I have my answer." His gaze moved to her baby bump. "But it shouldn't be me here. It should be my brother. What kind of mixed-up fate is this?"

The pressure on his hand tightened. Another contraction was building. While Popi panted her way through it, he kept talking.

"While I was in the hospital, I'd slipped into a coma. Apparently the hard head I've been accused of having isn't much of a challenge to rocks."

Another contraction commenced. He wasn't sure Popi could hear him at this point, but he kept talking just like she'd asked. "I was in a coma when they died. It's why I didn't make it to the funeral. I remember dreaming of Niles. You know, while I was in a coma. I don't remember anything else, just seeing him and talking to him. He was as real to me as you are."

He recalled how Nile had said that he was proud of Apollo. They'd walked and talked like…like brothers.

"Do you think it was your brother saying goodbye?"

Apollo didn't say anything at first as he pondered the question. He wasn't sure what he believed about the hereafter. Did he think the dead could speak? No. He certainly didn't believe in ghosts.

As though Popi were privy to his internal debate, she said, "You know you were in a coma at the same time as… as the accident."

He knew what she'd meant to say—he was in a coma at the same time that his brother had died. Was it possible that it was truly Nile speaking to him in his dreams? Would Nile really have said that he loved and forgave Apollo? He wanted to believe it, but he knew it had just been wishful thinking on his part.

Not wanting to think about it any longer, Apollo steered the conversation away from the ghost of his brother. "I never thanked you for making all of the funeral arrangements. You don't know how bad I felt when I woke up in the hospital and found out that I had lived while my brother had died."

"That must have been horrible." Popi leaned her head against his shoulder. "I'm sorry."

Not being there for his brother and cutting Nile most of the way out of his life—they were the regrets that weighed upon his heart. He wasn't sure he would ever forgive himself for living while his brother died without ever getting to meet his little son or daughter.

Though Apollo did find comfort in Popi's words, he didn't feel he deserved them. "You have nothing to be sorry about. You lost just as much as I did that day."

Popi didn't say anything. He felt her body grow rigid. And then her grip on his hand tightened once more. The baby was almost here.

His gaze moved to the window. It was still dark out. But as he listened, he noticed that the turbulence of the storm had dissipated. But would help be able to reach them before the baby arrived?

"I need to push," Popi said between pants.

His blood ran cold with the thought of being responsible for the lives of Popi and the baby. His mother hadn't survived childbirth, and she'd been in the hospital, with people who knew what they were doing. He didn't have a clue besides what he'd read, and that hadn't been much.

Please let them be okay. Please.

CHAPTER FOURTEEN

"WAAH... WAAH... WAAH..."

Popi used her last bit of energy to smile.

They'd done it. Together they'd brought a new life into the world. And it was amazing. It was miraculous. And she'd never known such happiness.

"It's a boy." Apollo placed the baby, wrapped in a soft towel, on her chest.

Popi glanced up at her hero and noticed how pale he looked. In fact, he looked as though he were about to pass out.

"You should sit down." She attempted to move over, but her body protested the thought of moving so soon.

"Maybe I will." Apollo sunk down on the floor. He didn't seem to care that there was no mattress beneath him. He drew his knees up and rested his arms on them. He glanced over at her. "You were amazing."

"We were amazing." She turned to the baby in her arms, who'd calmed down now. "But you are the star of the day."

Apollo leaned in close. His finger stroked the baby's cheek. "You are a miracle, little guy."

"I just wish…"

She didn't have to say it, because he'd felt the same way. "I wish the same thing. His parents would be so proud of him."

A tear rushed down Popi's cheek. "They definitely would."

Whup. Whup. Whup.

The sound of an approaching helicopter gave Apollo his

second wind. In a heartbeat, he was on his feet. He rushed to the door and swung it wide open.

He stepped out onto the porch. The early morning sun was shining brightly as a gentle breeze circulated through the bungalow.

"How is it out there?" she asked.

"Blue skies and a calm sea."

"What about the island?"

"It's nothing for you to worry about."

Which is exactly what it did—worry her. If it was so bad that he wouldn't even tell her the damage, it must be really bad. Thank goodness they had a crew showing up today. It would appear they had more work ahead of them than they'd originally been planning on. She just hoped they were up for the challenge. Because she wasn't. She had other priorities now.

She turned her attention to the cutest little boy in her arms. He had blue eyes that seemed to take in everything around him. And a head full of dark hair. He was definitely going to be a heartbreaker when he grew up—just like his uncle.

Just then Shadow decided to make an appearance after hiding for most of the night. He crept forward, stretching his neck out and sniffing the new baby. Popi smiled. Something told her that these two were going to be good friends.

As for her and Apollo, she didn't know how things were going to work out now that they were about to leave the island. But their time on the island had most definitely changed things between them. The Apollo that she thought she'd known was much different than the actual caring, giving man that was now crouching next to her to fuss over the baby.

But even though she'd come to know this caring and gentle side of him, she knew that he still had an adven-

turous side. Would that mean he would leave the baby
with her?

There were still so many unanswered questions. But
as the paramedics made their way inside the bungalow,
she knew any answers would have to wait until much
later.

CHAPTER FIFTEEN

HOME FROM THE HOSPITAL.

Home. The word felt so strange.

Apollo opened one of the ominous oversize black doors with bronze fixtures. The Drakos estate had staff to open doors and such, but he'd been fending for himself for so long that he was no longer used to being fussed over. He knew that would change by moving back into this gigantic mausoleum of memories.

He hadn't alerted any of the staff of his exact arrival. He'd wanted his return to be low-key. He wasn't sure how he would feel first walking in here. While Popi had been in the hospital, he'd stayed in a hotel close by, not wanting to be far from her or the baby should they need him. And perhaps a tiny part of him had been relieved to have a legitimate reason to put off his return.

He glanced around the grand foyer with its gleaming marble floors. He recalled as a boy running into the room in his socks and sliding across the floor. His gaze moved to the grand staircase, where his father used to stand at the top with a glass of bourbon in one hand, while with the other hand he'd point an accusing finger at Apollo for one offense or another.

He recalled one specific instance when his father had stood at the top of the steps and glared down at Apollo like he was master of the universe. Apollo would get blamed for misdeeds he'd done and sometimes for misdeeds that were not his. And as he grew older, his attitude toward his father became more hostile.

There was a specific day when his father had blamed

him for something that was clearly not his fault and called him worthless, and Apollo had shouted that he hated his father. His outburst had been rewarded with his father raising his hand and launching his still-full glass of bourbon down the steps at Apollo. The vivid memory caused Apollo to flinch.

Popi's hand touched his shoulder. "Are you okay?"

He glanced down at the marble floor, where he'd been standing that day. If he hadn't moved, the glass would have hit him. He choked down the lump in the back of his throat. But when he spoke, his voice had a hoarseness. "I'm fine."

Looking back now, he wondered if that was the day his father wrote him out of the family business, or had that already been a forgone conclusion from the tragic day when he was born? Not that it mattered to him. He could take or leave the business world.

He'd learned a lot about the world and himself when he'd been off on his adventures. He was no longer the kid filled with rage over his crappy childhood, where he'd never known his mother, and his father had said one abusive comment after the next.

He shoved the dark memories to the back of his mind. Things would be different for the baby. Apollo would make sure their precious little boy never had to run from hateful words or flying glasses. The only time he would run from Apollo was when he was threatening to tickle his nephew.

Apollo turned to Popi, who was holding the sleeping baby in her arms. "Let's get you and the little guy situated."

"Thank you for letting us stay here while my parents are recovering from the flu."

"Not a problem." In truth, it had all worked out the way he'd wanted. He just didn't realize after all these years that this place would still get to him.

Just then Anna, the housekeeper, entered the foyer. Her face lit up with a big smile that made her warm eyes twinkle with genuine happiness. "Mister Drakos, you're home. It's been too long."

"Hello, Anna."

It was then that she broke with protocol and gave him a hug. It wasn't the first time, nor would it be the last, that she bent the rules that had governed the Drakos estate for as long as Apollo could remember. Maybe that's what the place needed—a break with the routine of the past.

He hugged her back. She was the closest thing that he'd ever had for a mother. And it was only now that he realized how relieved he was that she was still here for him to come home to. Between Popi, the baby and Anna, he would do his best to make peace with living here amongst the ghosts.

Anna pulled back and turned to Popi. "And who do we have here?"

She knew because Apollo had called ahead to make sure the house was spiffed up and a room had been set up for Popi and the baby. But he knew that Anna was fishing for an introduction.

"Popi, I'd like you to meet Anna. She is the housekeeper, but in truth she's the one that keeps this house functioning. Without her, the place would fall apart."

Anna's cheeks took on a pink hue, but she didn't say anything.

"It's so nice to meet you." Popi smiled.

"If you need anything at all," Anna said, "just let me know." And then she stepped closer. "May I see him?"

Popi pulled the blanket away from the baby's face to give Anna a good look at him. "Would you like to hold him?"

Anna's eyes widened and her face filled with excitement. "I would."

Apollo watched as the two women interacted with ease. He breathed a little easier. This would definitely help with his ultimate plan—getting Popi to agree to stay here with him and the baby.

One day passed into the next in what felt like a five-star hotel.

Every need was met but this place lacked that relaxing, comforting feel of home.

The Drakos estate certainly wasn't where Popi had planned to end up after leaving the hospital, but with the island undergoing renovations and her parents stricken by the flu, Apollo's offer had seemed like the only logical offer.

They'd agreed to use the name their siblings had chosen for the baby, Sebastian. As it was quite a mouthful, they'd nicknamed the baby Seb. It suited him.

The mansion, on the other hand, took a lot to get used to it. The place was enormous. It was possible for them to both be home and not even run into each other. The home was older but it had been updated over the years with all the modern amenities without losing its classic charms.

Popi felt like she was living in a museum. Everything in this enormous foyer was some priceless work of art. This place was definitely more museum than home. No wonder her sister and brother-in-law had never considered living here, preferring a smaller house near the sea. And it in some way explained why Apollo never came home. This place, though stunning with its marble floors and soaring columns, was cold. It was the complete opposite of her own cozy, colorful and warm childhood home. And nothing like her bungalow on Infinity Island. In fact, her entire place could fit within the walls of the foyer alone.

Was the lack of hominess within the mansion the reason Apollo had made himself scarce since they'd brought the baby home a week ago? Or was he avoiding her? Did he regret extending an invitation to her while her parents were dealing with a string of illnesses?

Well, she was done being ignored. If Apollo wouldn't come to her, she would go to him. And that meant a trip to the gardens. It appeared to be his passion and, in all fairness, the gardens were more weeds than flowers or foliage. If someone didn't tend to them immediately, the weeds would win.

With the baby fed, changed and down for a nap, Popi left the nanny Apollo had insisted on hiring in charge and went to seek out her host. She made her way down the sweeping steps off the grand patio at the back of the home. She could see how this area had been stunning at one time, but time and the elements had done a number on just about everything.

Popi followed the stone path until she heard the sounds of work being done. To her surprise, Apollo wasn't out here alone. At least he'd had sense to call in a work crew, because an enormous garden like this would take him years to restore on his own.

After being pointed in the right direction, Popi came across Apollo adding dirt around the base of what she surmised to be a small fruit tree. And then as her gaze took in his shirtless appearance, her mouth grew dry. He looked good—too good.

His skin was deeply tanned. His corded muscles flexed as he moved a shovel of dirt from the wheelbarrow. No man had a right to look that good. She should just tiptoe backward and slip away. Because without his shirt on, she had a hard time stringing two thoughts together, much less trying to speak.

Apollo glanced up as though he sensed her presence. "Is something wrong? Is it the baby?"

"Uh…" *Come on, Popi. You can do better than that.*

She swallowed hard. "The baby is fine." She forced a smile to her face as her insides shivered with nervous energy. "I promise."

It was sad that upon seeing her that he would jump to the conclusion that something was amiss. Was it such a leap for him to consider another reason for her being out here to see him?

She was right to have come here. If they were going to do this co-parenting thing, with the child splitting time between her on the island and Apollo here at the estate, they needed to be friends—not just two people who coexisted during a brutal storm. Even though he'd opened up to her that special night, he'd since shut down again. She hoped to bridge the gap once more.

Apollo's brows drew together. "Then why are you out here?"

Again, it was sad that he had to ask that question instead of just enjoying her company. She worried her bottom lip and glanced away. And then she wondered if coming here to the garden—to his private area—his sanctuary—had been a mistake.

"I came out here because… Well, I thought we, um…" Being near him was making her unusually nervous.

"How are you at gardening?" He turned back to the tree and finished packing the dirt.

"I, uh, don't have any experience. We always lived in the city, so the only plants we had were in pots in the windows. I must admit I never bothered with them. That was my mother's territory."

"It's never too late to learn." He gave her outfit a quick once-over. "But I'm sure you don't want to get your nice outfit all dirty."

She glanced down at her blue capris and white knit top. She did like this outfit. It fit her well and yet it was also comfortable. But she had a choice to make: stain her favorite outfit while making inroads with Apollo or walk away, leaving the awkward distance between them.

Without hesitation, Popi moved next to him and dropped down to her knees. "Where do we start?"

For the first time since Seb was born, Apollo smiled at her. "This sapling is done."

"Oh." A frown pulled at her lips. She must have mis-understood him.

"Don't worry. I have plenty more waiting to be planted." He got to his feet, pulled off his gloves and then held his hand out to her.

She placed her hand in his, and immediately a jolt of awareness raced up her arm and set her heart aflutter. Her gaze met his. The cool indifference that he'd shown her since they'd returned home with baby Seb was gone. In its place was warmth and, dare she say it, a twinkle of interest.

He led her to another secluded spot, where he'd already removed a patch of weeds and was ready to plant a lemon tree. Out here in the garden, he was chatty. So long as she supplied questions about anything pertaining to the gar-den, he gave her lengthy, informative answers.

Was it possible it was the house that put him in a sul-len mood and not her? He did say he and his father had a turbulent past. Perhaps there were too many bad memo-ries tied up in the house.

As they worked together, adding the water around the roots, followed by the loose dirt, Popi asked, "Why did you return here?" When he sent her a puzzled look, she added, "You know—instead of selling the estate and get-ting a place, um…" She knew she had to be careful how she phrased this, as she didn't want to undo the progress they'd made so far. "Someplace smaller for just you…and Seb."

Relief filtered over his face as though he were expecting some other question. He shrugged and returned to adding the dirt back around the tree. "It's the Drakos estate. And I'm a Drakos. And this is Seb's home."

Where he had been giving her lengthy answers, she noticed that he'd reverted back to his short answers. She also noticed how he said this was the baby's home—not his. There was more he wasn't saying, but he didn't need to. He was drawn to this place because it was part of his heritage, but it was also mired in bad memories. She wondered if there was any way to untangle the two.

"Stop." Apollo's voice drew her from her musings.

"Stop what?" She glanced down at her hands, but she hadn't been doing anything.

"Not the gardening." He shook his head. "Stop trying to figure out ways to fix me. Some things and some people can't be fixed."

She didn't believe that. But she knew arguing with him would be pointless—

"Miss Costas?"

Popi glanced over her shoulder to find one of the young maids heading toward her. Popi got to her feet and brushed off the gloves that Apollo had loaned her. Apollo moved beside Popi with a concerned look on his face.

The young woman stopped in front of her. "You wanted to know when the baby woke up. He's up now and in a fine mood." The young girl looked at Apollo and blushed. "I should get back to the house."

Popi held back a laugh until the young woman was out of sight.

Apollo studied her. "What's so amusing?"

"Someone has a crush on you."

His gaze moved from her to the young maid and then back to Popi. He shook his head. "No."

"Yes. Didn't you see her blush?"

He noticeably swallowed. "I should probably replace her."

Popi shook her head. "Don't do that. I'm sure she needs the job. Besides, if you replace all of the females that have a crush on you, then you'd have a very small staff."

Apollo's mouth opened but nothing came out. He pressed his lips together. Was that a tinge of color in his cheeks?

"As long as you don't encourage her, you shouldn't have a problem with her."

Apollo's brow arched. "Who else should I be cautious around?"

Popi shrugged. She didn't want him to become even more withdrawn. This was the only maid to make her infatuation blatantly obvious.

"What about you?" he asked.

"What about me?" Suddenly she felt quite uncomfortable. Surely he wasn't asking what she thought.

His blue eyes studied her. "Do you have a secret crush on me too?"

"Uh…" The breath got caught in the back of her throat. And suddenly the sun was quite uncomfortably hot. "I should go check on the baby."

She turned and walked as fast as she could without breaking into a run. She should have answered him, but she hated lying. And there was no way she was admitting to him that she too had a crush on him, because it was nothing more than a rush of hormones.

After giving birth, her body was all over the place. Plus Apollo had helped her through the scariest, yet most profound moment of her life—giving birth to Seb. For that she would always be grateful to him.

Right now Apollo was just having some fun at her expense. Nothing more. His deep laughter followed her up the path. It wasn't like he was truly interested in her answer. Right?

CHAPTER SIXTEEN

THINGS WERE CHANGING...

For the better, she liked to think.

Popi refilled her coffee cup and moved to the terrace. Now that she knew about Apollo's passion for gardening and his willingness to teach her, she regularly joined him when Seb didn't need her.

But she found that their conversation centered on agriculture. And she simply didn't have the same passion for flowers and trees that Apollo did. She'd been hoping they would connect on a deeper level. Because if he couldn't connect with her, would he be able to do it with Seb?

She leaned back in the cushioned chair and sipped her morning coffee. The baby had already been up, eaten and played before going back down for a morning nap. That had been Popi's cue to grab some coffee before heading to the garden.

It was at Apollo's insistence a nanny had been hired. She was an older woman with years of experience and stellar references that were all verified. In the end, Popi realized that having another person devoted to the care and nurturing of Seb could only ever be a good thing. And it in no way detracted from her interactions with the baby.

"I thought I might find you here." Apollo's voice interrupted her thoughts.

She turned to find him approaching the empty chair next to hers. "I was beginning to wonder if you'd slept in."

"Not a chance. I've been getting up with the sun for so many years that I don't know if I could sleep late even if I needed to." He sat down. "I take it the baby had you up early."

She nodded. "I suppose he takes after his uncle."

A smile pulled at Apollo's lips. "Do you really think he's like me?"

"I think he looks a lot like you."

His smile broadened. "But I think you've totally won him over. Every time I pick him up, he cries. When you hold him, he's all smiles."

So, he'd noticed that too. She hadn't said anything about it, as she didn't want to make him feel bad. Seb was just as much Apollo's nephew as he was hers. They'd been dancing around the subject of a split-custody arrangement since they'd been discharged from the hospital.

She couldn't stay here forever. The repairs to Infinity Island were almost complete. They had to get the legal issues taken care of so that they could both move on. Because even though they'd become friends, there was nothing more to this arrangement than mutual respect for each other and their devotion to the baby.

"Apollo, we need to talk—"

"I agree. I've been giving this a lot of thought. And I think I've come to a solution."

"A solution?" Was he talking about the same thing as her?

He nodded. "We both love Seb. And he is the Drakos heir. That little boy will one day come into great wealth and wield unimaginable power."

She had an uneasy feeling in the pit of her stomach. When he started talking about the baby being the heir, she knew she was in trouble. Apollo was seeing Seb not as a sweet baby in need of love and nurturing but rather of the power that the baby will hold one day and the guardian that must handle the business affairs for the baby until its of age.

Apollo continued, even though she'd missed part of what he'd said. "It's for this reason that the baby should remain here—at the Drakos estate."

"I thought we'd agreed on split custody."

"I said I'd think about it. And I did. It'll will be less confusing for him to stay here at the estate. He'll have an entire staff to watch after him."

Popi set aside her coffee, no longer having the stomach for it. She sat up straight. "I didn't know that you still looked at Seb that way."

"What way? You mean as the heir?"

She nodded. "He's just a little baby." She waved her hand around. "None of this means anything to him."

Apollo's eyes became shuttered, blocking her out. "This place means everything. I may have walked away from here because I didn't feel as though I belonged here, but I never doubted the importance of the estate. My brother was always the chosen one. He was the one my father appointed to step into his shoes. And that role will now fall to my nephew."

That was a lot to put on a small, helpless baby. "But what about you?"

"I will help the army of trustees selected to run the business until Seb is old enough to take over."

"And then what? You're just going to turn your back on your family's business again?"

"Sure. Why not? It was not my calling like it was my brother's. Nile was the one obsessed with all things Drakos. He would want his son to be raised here."

"And what about you and your future children? Won't they want a place in the family business?"

He gave a firm shake of his head. "I'm not having children. I'm not going through that again."

"Through what?"

He glanced away. "Nothing."

"It was definitely something." She didn't understand why he would resolutely write off the possibility of children. He surely didn't think he would be climbing mountains and hiking the Amazon the rest of his life, did he? "Apollo, talk to me."

He looked at her with emotions reflected in his eyes. But she couldn't discern if it was anger at her for pushing the subject.

He cleared his throat. "I won't be responsible for another person dying."

"What?" Was he referring to his brother? If so, she didn't see how he could feel responsible. He wasn't even in the country at the time. Or was it someone else? "Who?"

A few seconds passed before he said, "My mother."

He killed his mother? No. That couldn't be right.

She was most definitely missing something.

Her gaze searched his face for answers but found none. "I don't understand."

He stared out at the vast landscaped yard with its elaborate water fountain and gorgeous flower garden. "My mother died after giving birth to me. And my father blamed me for her death until his own dying breath."

Suddenly she understood him so much better. This was why he was always on a new adventure. Who would want to stick around to be blamed for something that was in no way his fault?

Popi reached out, placing her hand on his arm. "Surely you understand that it wasn't your fault."

"I understand that I was an accident. Once my father got my brother, he wasn't interested in having more children, but he was willing to indulge my mother. But when it all went so horribly wrong, I was blamed. I was just a child but I knew my father hated me."

"He didn't hate you." She just couldn't believe that was true. Could a parent really hate their child? She couldn't accept such a horrible reality for him. "Your father was grieving his wife."

Apollo turned a haunted look at her. "For years?" He shook his head. "I don't think so."

"I'm sorry you lived through that."

"I had my brother. He did his best to shield me. He stood up to my father when I wasn't old enough to do it myself."

"I had no idea you and your brother were that close."

"We used to be. In fact, we used to play hide-and-seek out in the gardens. I was good at hiding. My brother, not so much. We used to have all sorts of adventures out there."

"And this place, it reminds you of those times?" She couldn't help but ask. She'd noticed he spent a great amount of time either running errands or working in the gardens. If he kept working outside, she was pretty certain the entire grounds, and that was a massive amount of property, would end up being one enormous exotic garden.

He rubbed the back of his neck. "I guess. My brother inherited the controlling shares of the family business, while I inherited a much smaller share and this estate."

"I understand now why you think Seb should be raised here, but what about my sister's wishes?" Andrina wasn't here to speak for her herself and without a will, Popi had to do it. Because they might not have been blood relatives, but they were as close as two sisters could be. "She would want her son to know me…to have a mother figure…someone who understands that families come in all shapes and sizes. His family will be different than most of his friends', but his life will be filled with love that he can always count on."

Apollo nodded in agreement. "You are right. So, you think it is best for him to split time between here and Infinity Island?"

She smiled, knowing she'd finally gotten through to him. And then she nodded.

"Or you could stay here."

"Here?" The smile slipped from her face. Was he serious? "With you?"

"That's the general idea, but I can see you don't like the idea."

"It's just that my career…my home…it's back on the island." She loved Seb, but she loved her job too. She didn't want to have to pick one over the other. And living here with Apollo, knowing the chemistry between them—it was a recipe for disaster.

"Keep my offer in mind. This mansion is more than big enough for both of us." He paused as though waiting for her to respond, but she didn't know what to say. She'd been caught off guard. And so he continued. "Speaking of the mansion, I keep forgetting to tell you that I've started a household account in your name."

"My name?"

He nodded. "It's so you can set up the nursery any way you want. Feel free to paint, buy new drapes or whatever you want. If there isn't enough, let me know."

He was now Seb's financial guardian. Plus from what she'd gleaned about him on the internet, Apollo came with his own great wealth. Still, it felt weird to take money from him. She was used to standing on her own feet and paying her own way. She'd been doing that ever since she finished college. And she liked her independence.

But then she realized the money, though under her control, wasn't for her. It was for the baby. And the nursery really could use an overhaul. The white paint was now yellowing. There were some cracks. And the windows stuck when she tried to open them to let in some fresh air. They definitely needed to be replaced.

"Thank you. The nursery could use some sprucing up. I'll try not to spend much."

Apollo smiled at her, making her stomach flip. "You

don't have to worry about the money. Do what needs to be done. I'll cover it."

She was used to living on a budget. Things in Apollo's world—and now Seb's—were a lot different. "I better get started with the plans. I want to make sure I have time to finish the room."

Soon she'd be returning to Infinity Island. She hoped they were able to repair all of the damage from the storm and make it as though it had never happened.

The truth was that she wasn't homesick for the island like she'd thought she'd be. In truth, she liked it here at Apollo's home. And it had nothing to do with living in a mansion that was straight out of the movies. Or the fact that Apollo had insisted on employing a household staff the size of a small army—

"I must be going." He abruptly got to his feet. The smile had faded from his face. "I have a new shipment of plants arriving today."

"Are you creating your own exotic jungle?" She meant it to tease him, but it did nothing to soften the frown now pulling at his lips.

"Perhaps." And with that he walked away.

She could tell it was killing him to stay here. And that saddened her. When they'd been on Infinity Island, he'd been happier, but now it was like a dark cloud was following him. It wasn't good for him and it certainly wasn't good for Seb to see Apollo so unhappy.

And if Apollo was unhappy living at the estate, it meant when the baby was with her, Apollo would be off on another dangerous adventure. She told herself she was upset on behalf of the baby that would miss him, but she wasn't that good of a liar. She would miss him too. And she worried that his body wasn't healed enough and he would re-injure himself.

While she pondered how or even if it was possible to

fix this problem, she drank the last of her coffee and got to her feet. She had a room to make over. It was a task she welcomed. It would keep her from thinking about the sexy man with the eye-catching tattoo that wrapped around his sculpted bicep, and his deep, sexy voice that made her insides melt.

What had he been thinking?

Two weeks later, the nursery was nearly finished. Popi was astonished at the amount of money Apollo had set aside to redo the room. Even with a rush order for new windows, doors, fixtures and paint, it had barely made a dent in the amount. She'd been about to return the remainder of the funds, but then she had a thought.

What if she was to give the rest of the home a makeover?

At first she'd dismissed the idea. As this wasn't her home, it wasn't up to her to redecorate. But something told her Apollo never would. It wasn't his thing. He spent almost every waking hour outdoors.

But she could see how uncomfortable he was when he was inside. He'd frown at a portrait and then turn away. He'd avoid the study altogether. There were many rooms which he didn't visit or would only step into for just a moment or two.

As the idea took root, she just couldn't dismiss it. If she could help Apollo get past his bad memories and not have them constantly pop up in his mind, she felt compelled to do it. What else could she do until Infinity Island was back up and running? She wasn't used to having idle time.

Organizing and creating visions was her job. Sure, she normally did it in the form of a wedding, but she was certain she could take those skills and create a home that didn't make Apollo feel like running back to the Amazon as soon as he walked in the door. Or keep him outside digging up more and more of the grounds to create the biggest and most impressive garden in the region. People were starting to say that the gardens were going to rival the mansion in size and elaborateness. And Popi had to agree. The gardens were breathtaking.

So, that evening at dinner, Popi brought up the subject of repainting and updating some of the other rooms with the extra money. Apollo gave her the go-ahead with his blessing.

And so she started in a wing that Apollo didn't visit. One room led to another room, putting portraits and decorative pieces in storage and replacing them with pieces more in line with Apollo's tastes, from animal prints to foliage paintings. The paint on the wall was warmer, and accent walls with vibrant colors were done.

A few weeks later, she'd completed a cosmetic makeover of the east wing of the mansion, but she wasn't ready to show Apollo what she'd accomplished—not yet. She wanted to work on the study first.

When the house phone rung, Popi rushed for it. But when she picked it up, Apollo spoke before she could. Popi remained quiet. She was expecting a call from the home-interiors store about some specialty wallpaper that she'd chosen to create a very special accent wall in Apollo's study. She waited to see if this was in fact the store calling.

"Apollo, is that you?"

There was a slight pause.

"Matias?"

"It's me, buddy. I hadn't heard from you in a while—"

Popi was disappointed that the call wasn't about the order, as they couldn't progress with the study until she was certain the store could get enough of a particular wallpaper. Hopefully they would call soon. If she could get Apollo to relax in his home, maybe he wouldn't be so eager to head out on his next adventure.

Popi moved to hang up the phone when something caught her attention. The man, Matias, said, "...you joining me on my next safari. And I'm just about to head out."

"A safari. I've always wanted to do that but never had the chance."

"Well, this is your chance."

"So it is."

That's all Popi needed to hear. Her hand moved quickly to slam down the phone in frustration, but she stopped herself just before placing the phone on the receiver. Instead she hung up gently, all the while mulling over what she'd learned.

So nothing they'd shared meant anything to him. He was just putting in time until what? The baby was comfortable with the household staff? Or was he going to ask her to watch Seb every time he got the urge for an adventure?

The blood warmed in her veins. Sure, she'd love having the extra time with Seb, but the baby wasn't a possession to be passed around at will. Eventually Seb would start asking questions. She was about to go momma bear on Apollo. He needed to be a devoted parent to Seb, not just a guardian of the child's vast inheritance. If that was too much for Apollo to handle, then she would raise Seb on her own.

And then there was the thing between them. The way he looked at her when he didn't think she was paying attention and the way he flirted with her, it had to mean something, right? Or was she building up this relationship in her mind when in fact it was nothing to him? Something to pass the time? Or was it something more sinister? Was he trying to win her over so that she wouldn't fight him for the baby?

She immediately dismissed the idea. Apollo may not see a future for them, but he wasn't devious. He was kind. And he was thoughtful. She'd never believe that he had an ulterior motive.

Did that make her foolish? She hoped not. But she needed to stop concentrating so much on making this stone-cold mansion into a warm, inviting home and worry more about getting back to Infinity Island.

She rushed downstairs to confront him, but as she searched room after room, she realized that she'd missed him. Seb shouldn't be left with a nanny. He needed to live with her on Infinity Island, where there was an entire village of extended family and friends. She dialed the number of her attorney—the one who had handled things after her sister and brother-in-law's deaths.

Popi probably should have waited to phone until she'd calmed down. Maybe then she wouldn't have had to pay the attorney's steep fees to listen to her vent about Apollo, their messy situation and her concerns about him leaving the country.

She didn't want Apollo to leave. She thought that they were growing closer. But had she only seen what she wanted? Was Apollo the same carefree, free spirit he'd always been?

CHAPTER SEVENTEEN

HE NEEDED OUT of the house.

The only problem was, he hadn't wanted to walk out the door.

Apollo's car sped down the road. He never thought he would want to stay at the mansion. But it wasn't the same place as when he was growing up. It was different now—now that Popi and Seb were there. The sound of laughter was now common around the house. And each morning all the drapes were pulled back, flooding the mansion with bright, rejuvenating sunshine.

At first he'd started working on the neglected gardens as a way of getting out of the house, but now he had to force himself to go work on the project. He'd much rather stay inside and follow Popi around. But he knew that was a fool's errand.

Popi was planning to leave the estate—leave him—just as soon as Infinity Island's updates were completed. The closer the time for her departure came, the more he realized he didn't want her to leave.

He'd even considered giving her a reason to stay—with him. The only reason he'd resisted the urge was knowing he couldn't give her what she wanted. Long-term relationships didn't work out for him. Every one that he'd had ended in disaster. And he wouldn't subject Seb to a broken home.

Apollo slowed the car as he neared the *bistrot* where he was to meet up with Matias. He found a parking spot on the busy street and slipped his black Greek supercar into the spot.

As he walked into the darkened *bistrot*, he realized he should have turned Matias down on the phone. His life had changed and his wings had been clipped.

An image of Seb filled his mind. He knew that giving up his old nomadic ways was for the best. He loved Seb with all his heart. But sometimes he let himself imagine what his next adventure might entail—until his thoughts turned to holding Seb in his arms. Then Apollo knew he was right where he belonged—embarking on the most important adventure of his life.

Matias waved from across the room.

Apollo made his way to him, ordering a dark ale on his way. He took a seat across the table from a friend he'd made while trekking through Nepal. He'd met so many interesting people along his travels. In an effort to keep people from flocking to him because of his family's fortune, he typically used his mother's maiden name. Some would exchange information, along with a promise to keep in contact, but it was rare he would hear from anyone again. Matias was different.

They had kept in contact over the past eight years. Like him, Matias's family was influential in Madrid. It made it easy for them to open up to each other because neither wanted anything from the other. And along the way, they found they had a lot in common, like avoiding commitments, not living up to family expectations and enjoying the thrill of an adventure.

"Hey, man." Matias got to his feet. They clutched hands, pulled each other close and, with their free hands, clapped each other on the back. They quickly pulled apart. "It's good to see you, man. I mean it's really good to see you."

"Thanks. I'm surprised to see you in Athens."

"I'm just passing through. After I heard about your accident, I wanted to see that you're truly in one piece."

They both sat down and a waitress brought their drinks.

Apollo took a sip of the dark brew. "Yeah. That was a bad one. Doctors weren't sure if I was going to make it or not."

"I would have been there for you if I had known about it."

Apollo shook off the idea. "There was nothing you could do. Nothing anyone could do. It just took time."

"And so you've decided to spend some time at home?"

With reluctance, he told Matias about his brother's death and the new baby. He skimmed over the subject of Popi. He wasn't sure how to describe his relationship with her. Was that right? Did they have a relationship?

His mind slipped back to the steamy kisses they'd shared. And they'd have shared so much more if not for her pregnancy. But did that equate to a relationship?

Then again, they were sharing a home. And they were sharing a baby, not to mention the time they spent gardening together and the meals they shared. The more these facts piled up, the harder it got for him to stick his head in the sand and refuse to accept what was right in front of him.

He was involved in a romantic relationship with Popi. And he was committed to being a full-time father to Seb.

His heart stilled for a moment as the significance of this acknowledgment settled in his mind. But where did it go from here? Where did he want it to go? Would Popi stay at the estate with him if he asked her?

"Hey." Matias waved his hand in front of Apollo, gaining his attention. "Where'd you go?"

"What?" He had no idea what Matias had been saying. That wasn't like him. But this was a situation that he'd never been in before. "Sorry. I guess I just have a lot on my mind."

"It sounds like it. So, what's her name?"

Apollo frowned. "Why do you just assume it's a woman?"

"Because I know you. And there's a look on your face—"

"What look?"

Matias smiled and shook his head. "Never mind."

"I do mind. What look?"

"Like you're a lovesick pup—"

"I'm not!" The denial came so quick and so vehemently that even he didn't believe it.

Matias's eyes widened as he held up his hands. "Hey, you asked." He glanced down at the table. "So, back to the reason for my visit. How soon are you ready to set off on a new excursion? I've got guides set up for a walking safari. We'll get up close and personal with the wildlife."

It was something that Apollo had never done. And it was something that he'd always wanted to do. But he'd never found it challenging enough. Until now, he'd always wanted to push himself to the edge. But with this last adventure, he'd gotten too close to the edge and it had cost him.

The safari was exactly what he needed while his body continued to heal. But that would mean leaving Seb. That was something he couldn't do. It was up to him to look after the little guy. And more than that—he'd miss Seb something awful.

He shook his head. "I can't, man."

"You mean because of your injuries?"

"No. I mean I'm still not one hundred percent, but I have the baby now. I have to put him first. I owe that much to my brother."

But that wasn't exactly the truth. His desire to stay here in Athens wasn't born out of duty but rather out of desire. He wanted to stay home—to be there with Seb—and Popi. To share his life with them.

Matias stared at him. "Is that the only reason holding you here?"

"What else would there be?" Popi's beautiful face filled his mind, but he quickly dismissed it.

"I don't know, but you have that look on your face again."

Finally deciding that he needed some advice about his situation with Popi, he opened up to his friend. He told Matias about the first time he met Popi and that undeniable immediate attraction. He went on to mention that Popi's life was on Infinity Island and how she planned to return to her life there as soon as possible—with the baby. And how he would once again be alone.

"You'd be able to get back to your adventures," Matias offered.

Apollo lowered his gaze and stared blindly into his drink. "I don't know if it was almost dying on this last excursion or what, but I'm not anxious to get back out there. At least not yet."

"Is it that? Or have you finally found a reason to stay at home?"

"You mean Popi?" When Matias nodded, Apollo said, "But this arrangement is about to end and then she'll be gone." Just like everyone else in his life.

"Unless you give her a reason to stay."

Apollo looked up at his friend, finding that he was perfectly serious. But what could he offer Popi to stay here? Her career and friends were on the island. When she spoke of the island and the weddings she'd planned, it was obvious how much she missed it.

But her family was here in Athens. A flicker of hope sparked within him. If he were able to give her another reason, maybe he could change her mind. But how?

He searched his mind to come up with some reason that would rival her desire to return to Infinity Island. There had to be an answer. It wasn't like money would be an obstacle. But he also knew throwing money at Popi wouldn't be the answer. She was so stubbornly independent.

"Can I offer you a bit of advice?" When Apollo nodded, Matias said, "Be careful. I know things seem really good now. But move cautiously. I just got burned by a woman who was only interested in my bank account. She put on such a good show that I didn't see it. I was just about to propose to her when I learned the truth."

"Is this the reason you missed the last trip?"

It was Matias's turn to avoid Apollo's gaze as he nodded.

"It's just as well. As you can tell, it didn't go well." Apollo rubbed his surgically repaired thigh, which still had a dull ache to it.

"Just be careful is all I'm saying. Make sure if you move forward with her that she's interested in you and not what you can offer her."

Apollo didn't believe it was the case with Popi. He was certain she had a heart of gold. He pushed his friend's advice to the back of his mind.

"This place is more impressive than I ever could have imagined."

Two days later, Popi's mother stood in the nursery, holding Seb while gazing out the window at the estate grounds. The nursery had an excellent view of the extravagant gardens that Apollo was creating. Popi joined her mother at the window. She gazed down, catching a glimpse of Apollo as he worked in the bright sunshine without a shirt on.

He was too far away to make out the detailed lines of his well-defined muscles. But the memory of him working shirtless was vividly imprinted upon her mind. She'd been tempted more than once to reach out and smooth the flecks of dirt from his tanned skin, but each time she'd resisted the urge, unsure of his reaction.

Sure, they'd kissed, but she still didn't understand where that left them—except for wanting more. And since she'd had the baby, he'd been so reserved around her—even if she saw the desire reflected in his eyes. It wasn't like he was going to stay here in Athens. He was a nomad, always on to the next adventure.

"Looks like you find it impressive too." Her mother's voice drew Popi out of her thoughts.

"Mmm… What?"

Her mother sent her a knowing smile.

"What?" Popi asked.

"I'm thinking you're enjoying the view a little too much."

Heat rushed to Popi's chest and headed north to her cheeks. "I…I don't know what you mean."

Her mother arched a brow. "Popi, don't play coy with me. I saw you looking at Apollo. Is there more to this playing house than caring for Seb?"

"Of course not." Did her response sound like a lie? Because it sure felt like one.

Disbelief reflected in her mother's eyes. "Just make sure that whatever you do with Apollo, it's for the right reason."

That was it? No lecture? No telling her that he was absolutely the wrong person for her? Popi struggled to keep her mouth from gaping open.

"What?" Her mother placed the sleeping baby in the crib before turning back to her daughter.

"It's just that I expected you to tell me not to get involved with him…to stay away from a man who never slept in the same place more than a few nights."

"Is that what you expected me to say? Or is that what you've been saying to yourself?"

Popi shrugged, not wanting to answer. "I don't know

what to make of him. He's so much different than the picture Andrina painted of him."

"That happens a lot. People are never quite what other people say of them. Usually there's so much more if you look beneath the surface."

Popi moved to a basket of fresh baby clothes and began placing them in the new chest of drawers. "It was so much easier when I was certain he was an irresponsible playboy, out to have a good time instead of taking responsibility for himself and his family. But now…"

"Now you've found out there might be reasons for his globetrotting."

Popi stopped and turned to her mother. "How did you know?"

"Your sister. She didn't know the whole story, but from what she was able to glean, Apollo had a harsh childhood, with an alcoholic father."

"She knew there was more to him?"

Her mother sighed. "She didn't know for sure, but she hoped when the time came that he would step up and be there for the family. And perhaps have a family of his own."

This was all so unexpected. Her sister had never said anything like this to her. In fact, Andrina had warned her, should she ever meet Apollo, to be on her guard. Maybe Popi had misinterpreted that warning. Maybe her sister had known just how dashing her brother-in-law was and she worried that Popi would fall for him and he would end up breaking her heart. Was that going to happen?

Had she already lost her heart to him? Was that why she was still here even though she'd received word that all the renovations had been completed on her bungalow?

She looked at her mother, who was wise in the ways of the heart. "But how am I to know what he wants?"

"The question you have to answer first is what do you want?"

"I…I don't know."

"Listen to your heart—it will guide you."

"If only it was that easy." But every time she listened to her heart, her mind intervened with all of the reasons that pursuing anything with Apollo wouldn't work.

"Don't push yourself. You've been through a lot, and so has he. But I have to say that your sister would be so proud of you."

Popi's heart stuttered. How could she be so caught up with Apollo? It wasn't right.

If it wasn't for her sister's death, she wouldn't be here. And Andrina wouldn't have died if it hadn't been for her. Which meant that she didn't deserve Apollo. She didn't deserve to have the perfect family that her sister had been robbed of.

"No, she wouldn't." Popi couldn't meet her mother's gaze. "Andrina should be here, not me."

"That's nonsense. I know that it's hard without your sister. I miss her every day. But one life is not more important than the other. I love you both, equally."

Her mother's unconditional love is what had gotten her through so much in life, including her sister's death. But there was something her mother didn't know—that she was the one who'd insisted that her sister be on that boat. She just didn't know how to admit to something so horrible.

"Mum, there's something you don't know—"

Knock-knock.

Apollo stuck his head in the doorway. "I heard we had company."

Introductions were made, and as though the baby sensed Apollo was in the room, Seb fussed, wanting to be picked

up. Apollo readily lifted the baby into his arms as though
Seb had always belonged there.

She noticed how Apollo had changed into clean clothes.
Still, he had the worst timing. But then again, maybe it
was for the best. Her mother would just end up trying to
make Popi feel better for what had happened to her sister.
Her mother wouldn't throw around blame—that wasn't
her way. And Popi didn't deserve her mother's sympathy
and understanding.

And most of all, she didn't deserve Apollo…no matter
how much she wished it was otherwise. Because this was
the life her sister should have been living—an adoring
man, a beautiful home and a smiling, happy baby.

Popi thought she was coming to terms with losing her
sister and learning to live with the loss, but every time she
held Seb and that little boy stared up at her with those big
brown eyes—so much like Andrina's—the guilt washed
over her.

She was the reason Andrina was on that boat. Popi's
ultimatum was the only reason her sister had reluctantly
gone out on the water. And that was why Popi couldn't
let herself enjoy a family that was hers out of default. It
wasn't right. Andrina should be here, watching her beautiful baby boy grow.

CHAPTER EIGHTEEN

HE COULDN'T SLEEP.

It wasn't from worry. And it wasn't from unpleasant memories.

In fact, it was quite the opposite.

For the first time in his life, Apollo was content and happy right here at home. He never thought that could happen. In fact, he had been quite certain that returning to the Drakos estate would be like a life sentence of misery.

And all this happiness was due to Popi.

His friend's warning about Popi echoed in his mind. He quickly dismissed it. Matias didn't know Popi. If he did, he'd realize she would never intentionally hurt anyone. After all, she even rescued helpless kittens.

She was like a ray of sunshine on a cloudy day. She could make something as mundane as breakfast be like a grand meal with her comical stories of Seb, her radiant smiles and her genuine interest in him. No one before her had ever taken such an interest in his life—not even his brother.

And he didn't want to miss a moment of the sunshine Popi had brought to his life.

Because he knew in the end that this wasn't going to last. This peaceful serenity that had taken over his life would end as soon as Popi walked out the door. And then what? He'd long to escape once again on one of his adventures?

But there was Seb to think of. He couldn't just leave him—not even with the best nanny or Anna, the housekeeper. No, Seb was his responsibility—his and Popi's.

Because what he was quickly learning was that the baby needed both of them.

And then a thought began to percolate in his sleep-deprived mind. But it was so far out there that he was certain it was all fantasy without any substance. Because there was no way Popi would want a future with him. Would she?

"*Waah... Waah... Waah... Waah...*"

There was no time to answer the question. He obviously wasn't the only one not sleeping. Apollo sprang out of bed and headed for the nursery that was situated between his and Popi's bedrooms. He hoped to get there before Seb woke Popi too. There was no point in them both being awake.

Not taking the time to dress, Apollo rushed out of the bedroom in nothing more than his blue-and-white boxers. After all, the whole mansion was asleep. No one would see him. And Seb needed him.

Apollo rushed into the nursery. He immediately turned off the baby monitor so as not to wake Popi. She needed her rest. He'd noticed her at dinner and she had been quieter than normal. She'd even yawned through the main course. Maybe he'd been spending too much time in the garden and leaving her to deal with the baby more than he should. He made a mental note to be on hand more instead of losing track of time in the gardens.

"Hey, little man. It's okay." Apollo spoke softly as he picked up the baby. He cradled Seb against his bare shoulder. "What's the matter?"

Seb's crying softened but it didn't stop.

"Did you have a bad dream?" As he lightly bounced the baby in an effort to comfort him, he noticed that Seb's diaper was wet. A problem that he could solve. The nurse had instructed him on how to do this in the hospital. Be-

tween Popi and the nanny, he didn't have time to put the lesson to use until now.

"I see the problem. You need a diaper change. No problem. We've got this."

Until this point, he never thought he'd want a baby—another human counting on him for everything was daunting. But Seb was teaching him that he was capable of being there for someone—did that include Popi?

The baby's cry had woken her.

Popi hadn't moved at first. One book she'd read about parenting said not to rush to the baby at their first cry. Sometimes the baby would self-soothe and go back to sleep. Waiting didn't come natural to her. Her natural tendency was to rush to the nursery and comfort Seb. But she wanted to be a good parent—the best possible—even if it wasn't always easy.

But the sound of Apollo's voice over the monitor surprised her. Usually that man slept like a log and didn't hear a thing. It didn't bother her. She'd opted to take the baby monitor so she could keep a close eye on Seb. She didn't want a nanny soothing the baby at night. Seb needed his mom holding him and letting him know that all would be right in the world again.

Popi sat up in bed, waiting to see if her assistance was needed, but then the baby monitor went totally silent. Apollo must have turned it off.

She knew he deserved some one-on-one time with the baby. It was good for both him and Seb. Since they'd re turned from the hospital, Seb had grown a strong bon with Apollo. In the beginning, Seb would cry when Apo picked him up, but now the baby would fuss for Apo to hold him. At least that's the way it seemed to her. she couldn't help worrying that Apollo would need h

She'd never worried this much in her life. She wa

stantly thinking of ways to keep Seb safe or happy. She wondered if this was how it felt to truly be a mother. At times it could be exhausting. But the when Seb smiled, he made all of it worthwhile. He was a bundle of love.

Popi couldn't go back to sleep. She had to know what was going on, so she slipped out of bed and put on her robe. She tiptoed into the hallway, not wanting to startle Apollo or the baby. She paused at the doorway to the nursery. Apollo was inside with his bare back to her, as he had Seb on the changing table.

"I've got this, little guy. We'll have you all dried up in no time."

Popi enjoyed watching her two guys together. She quickly realized her mistake. Apollo wasn't her guy, even if they were living together and had shared a life-changing moment on the island—not to mention the toe-curling kiss beneath the stars.

With the soiled diaper off and the baby cleaned up, Apollo said, "Hang on, I just have to get a fresh diaper."

With one hand on the baby, he bent over to grab a fresh diaper off the lower shelf. Popi was about to say something when Apollo straightened and the baby peed—all over Apollo.

Popi couldn't help it—she burst out laughing.

Apollo turned a frown in her direction. "You saw that, huh?"

"Uh-huh." She stepped farther into the room and wiped the tears of laughter from her eyes. "I should have warned you to always have a fresh diaper ready so that doesn't happen. I can finish so you can go clean up."

He shook his head. "I'll finish changing him."

Apollo dried off, cleaned up the little guy again and then put a fresh diaper on him before handing Seb off to her. Holding the baby in her arms felt so right—so

natural. So did sharing this moment with Apollo. They seemed like—dare she think it—a real family.

And the sight of Apollo standing there in nothing more than his briefs—*wow*, it had grown warm in the room. She resisted the urge to fan herself as she took in the view of his muscular chest and his six-pack abs. There were a few scars on him that she longed to run her fingers over and ask him about their origin, but she resisted the urge. Those scars only added to his sexy factor. They definitely didn't detract.

"We've got a lot to learn, little man." Apollo's voice drew her from her thoughts. "But we'll work on it."

When Apollo stepped forward to kiss the baby on the head, his lips came so close to hers. Was it her imagination or did he pause ever so slightly as though considering kissing her too?

Their gazes connected. The breath caught in her throat. She willed him to kiss her again.

If not for the baby in the crook of her arm, she would have looped her hands around Apollo's neck and pulled him down to her level. And then she would—

Apollo's head turned away. He kissed the baby goodnight and headed for the shower. Popi was left standing there with her heart racing madly and the realization that she wanted this relationship to be more than two people sharing a space. She wanted the one thing she didn't deserve—this family.

CHAPTER NINETEEN

SHE WAS SOMETHING SPECIAL.

Very special.

And it wasn't just some pumped-up compliment to cover for all Popi had done by not only giving birth to his nephew but also her willingness to come here and make a home for the baby. Apollo really meant it. Popi was special. With every day that passed, he realized just how much Popi was changing his life, in big and little ways.

Most of all, he found that staying here in Athens was nothing like he'd originally envisioned. He found himself anxious to get up in the morning to seek out Popi and to hold Seb. He found that gardening was something he really enjoyed. He'd learned a lot about vegetation while he was off on his adventures from both the tour guides and the locals. And now he was able to put that knowledge to use.

He had a very special evening in mind for Popi. It was his way of thanking her for giving him a new outlook on life. And he'd worked on this plan all day, including a trip to the barber. His longish hair was now cut short. Everything had to be perfect for her.

As afternoon faded to evening, he rushed through the shower, shaved not once but twice and dressed in some dark jeans and a white collared shirt with the sleeves rolled up. He stopped in front of the mirror, which was something he seldom did, but tonight was different. Tonight he had to look decent—no, he had to look good. Really good. Popi deserved nothing less. He swept his fingers through his hair and then he was out the door.

He located Popi in the nursery. She placed the baby

in the crib for a nap. Seb had a set routine. A nap before his evening feeding and then he'd stay awake for the late show and go down for the night, not waking up again until morning.

"I was looking for you," Apollo said.

Popi put a finger to her lips. "Shh…"

Apollo mouthed *sorry*.

She nodded in understanding, but didn't speak until they'd quietly backed out of the room. With great care, she eased the nursery door closed.

She turned to him. "What did you need?"

"You." He'd already made sure the nanny would keep an eye on Seb for the rest of the evening.

"Me." Her beautiful eyes widened. "For what?"

"It's a surprise."

"I…I don't know if I'm up for it."

"Sure you are. Come on. I promise you'll like it." At least he hoped she would.

He didn't give her time to talk herself out of joining him. He took her hand in his, liking the way her skin felt next to his. He laced his fingers with hers as though it was something they'd been doing for years. And then he started for the grand staircase.

At the top of the stairs, Popi stopped. "Wait. I don't even know where we're going. Is it dressy?"

"Not unless you want it to be."

It was then that she noticeably took in his attire. Her gaze skimmed down over one of his dressier shirts and down to his newest pair of jeans. When her gaze finally met his, there was a hint of pink in her cheeks. The color only enhanced her beauty.

"See anything you like?" He couldn't help himself from teasing her.

"You…you've changed. Your hair is all cut off. You even shaved. And you're dressed up. You look incredibly handsome. Did you do all of this for me?" When he nodded, her cheeks turned a deeper hue of pink. "Then I have to change. I can't go anywhere like this. I have baby drool on my shirt."

"I promise no one will notice."

She frowned at him. "I'll notice."

She pulled her hand from his, turned and then headed back down the hallway.

Apollo sighed. He didn't have the patience to wait around for her. Actually it was more than that. He was afraid the baby would wake up and then Popi would refuse to leave Seb until he was asleep again.

But Apollo knew his anxiety ran deeper than that. He was afraid he would come up with an excuse not to follow through with his plan. It felt like he was standing at the edge of a two-hundred-foot cliff and getting ready to step off with nothing but water to catch him.

Even though his gut was twisted up with nervous tension, he couldn't walk away. He had to see if this thing growing between them was real or not. Because today marked six weeks since Seb's birth, and Popi had just been to the doctor's and gotten the all clear. Apollo no longer had to hold her at arm's length or worry about things getting out of control between them. Tonight was a new beginning for them.

While Popi changed clothes, Apollo rushed to the kitchen just to check on things. Nothing could go wrong with this evening. He owed Popi a memorable night.

To his relief, the food was all on track. Now he just hoped Popi didn't change her mind. However, when he returned to the foyer, he found Popi standing there in a sleeveless black-and-white high-low dress. With her hair pinned up, she looked like a runway model. She took his breath away.

"I hope this is all right," she said. "I picked it up when I was in the city."

"It's better than all right. You look stunning."

His compliment brought a smile to her kissable lips, and his heart thumped against his ribs. It was all he could do to hold himself back and not take her in his arms right then and there. But he assured himself there would be plenty of time for that later.

He stepped up to her and pulled a black silk handkerchief from his pocket. "Turn around."

The smile fell from her face. A worried look reflected in her eyes. "What's that for?"

"It wouldn't be a surprise if you saw it." When his words did nothing to ease the stress lines etching around her eyes, he said, "Trust me. You will like this."

Her gaze moved from the blindfold to him. "Couldn't I just close my eyes?"

He smiled and shook his head. "You'll peek."

"No, I won't."

"Liar." He sent her a teasing smile.

Her mouth gaped in mock outrage.

"Don't give me that look," he said. "We've been living together for a while and I know that you're terrible with surprises."

"I am not."

"Really?" He arched a challenging brow. "Then how come you told me that I couldn't see the nursery before you'd finished with it, but then you showed me the paint and then the crib and then—"

"Okay. Okay. So I get excited sometimes and it's hard to keep it to myself."

"Uh-huh. Hence the blindfold." He gestured for her to turn around.

She hesitated.

"You don't want to miss the surprise, do you?"

Without a word, she turned around and let him affix the blindfold. He was careful not to draw the loose curls of her hair into the knot. And then he tucked her hand securely in the crook of his arm. Joined together, he led her outside to the garden.

"Where are we going?" Popi asked.

"You'll see soon."

They continued walking. He was careful to keep her from walking into the statues in the garden or from running into any garden walls or vegetation.

"This isn't the way to the car."

"No, it's not."

"So we're walking to the destination?" When he didn't respond, she said, "Apollo, at least give me a hint."

He stopped walking. He glanced around, making sure that everything was how he'd envisioned. To his great relief, it was.

"Apollo? What is it? Would you say something?" She tugged on his arm.

A smile lifted his lips. "Is someone impatient?"

"Yes."

She sniffed the air. "Mmm... It smells so sweet."

He'd made sure to include some aromatic flowers in every part of the garden. He'd wanted it to be a more-than-visual experience.

"Okay. Stand still." He moved behind her and removed the blindfold.

Popi gasped.

She stepped forward, checking out the table for two in the garden path. The table was set with white linen and candles. She glanced back at him. "You did all of this for me?"

He nodded. "Do you like it?"

"I love it." Her gaze lifted to the glass lanterns with candles dangling from tree branches.

Those had been a bit more of a challenge than he'd been planning, as he'd had to move the dinner spot to an older section of the garden, where the trees were mature enough to handle the weight of the lanterns. In the background, a romantic ballad was carried by the gentle breeze.

"This is much more than a little something."

He held his hand out to her. "Would you care to dance?"

Without a word, she slipped her hand in his and he drew her close. His arm wrapped around her slender waist, while his other hand wrapped around hers. Their bodies swayed together as the sun sank below the horizon and the lanterns cast streaks of light across the garden.

She lifted her head so that her gaze met his. It was then that he realized how close they were. If he were to lean just a little bit forward, he could kiss her. The temptation lured him. But he wondered how Popi would react. Would she welcome the advance? Or would she push him away?

The look in her eyes wasn't telling him anything. Had he always been this bad at reading women? Or was it his worry about messing things up with Popi that had him second-guessing his every move with her?

"Why did you do this?" she asked. "It's so special— so amazing."

"Because I wanted to make you smile." And it did make her smile.

Before he could say more and explain how much she'd come to mean to him, their dinner arrived. A parade of three servers carried covered trays and placed them on the small table.

Apollo held his arm out to her. "Shall we?"

Popi once more placed her hand in the crook of his arm and let him escort her to the table, where he pulled out her chair. As they enjoyed the meal, the lanterns cast a warm glow around them. It was as if they were in their own secret world.

He glanced down to find her moving the food around her plate. "Don't you like the food?"

Her gaze lifted. "It's delicious."

"Then why are you barely eating?"

"I'm sorry." She took a bite.

The magic of the evening was slipping away and he desperately wanted to get it back. There was something weighing on Popi's mind, but how did he get her to open up to him? Was it something he'd done? Was this cozy dinner a bad idea?

This was the sweetest gesture anyone had ever done for her.

And she didn't deserve it.

If only he knew the truth.

Popi couldn't get the conversation with her mother out of her mind. Everyone seemed to think she was someone great, but the truth was she was not—not even close. She felt like a total imposter.

"I think they're playing our song." Apollo got to his feet and held his hand out to her.

She didn't want to dance. She didn't feel like she belonged here in this scene right out of a fairy tale. Yet she couldn't turn Apollo down. He'd obviously worked so very hard on this evening. And he'd done an amazing job. He thought of everything, down to the finest detail.

And it would be so easy to be swept away into the romantic evening. But how could she do that when she knew how she'd gotten here? She was living her sister's life and being showered in baby smiles and giggles, when it was her sister who should be experiencing the joy of raising Seb.

The guilt weighed on her as she once again let Apollo guide her into his very strong, very capable arms. She lifted her gaze to thank him for such a wonderful evening, but when her gaze strayed across his mouth, she hesitated. Maybe it was the soft, lilting music in the background that had her thinking about lifting up on her tiptoes and pressing her lips to his. Or maybe it was the way his thumb stroked the small of her back.

As though he could read her thoughts, he lowered his head and caught her lips with his own. Her heart jumped to her throat. This is what she wanted—what she'd longed for all through dinner. She wanted to lean into him and let herself get swept away. His kiss was gentle and coaxing. And it'd be so easy to forget everything except the way it felt to be in his arms…but she couldn't.

It took all of her determination and a good amount of guilt to pull away from him. Though her heart and body yearned for the warmth of his touch and the heat of his kiss, she knew she couldn't do this. She didn't deserve this precious moment—a moment she'd gained at her sister's grave expense.

Apollo gazed at her with confusion reflected in his eyes. "What's wrong? If I moved too fast…if I went too far—"

"No. It's not you. It's me." She realized the line was such a cliché, but that's because it was very accurate, especially in this instance. She lowered her gaze to the ground. "If only you knew what I've done."

Apollo stepped toward her and reached for her hand. "I can't imagine anything you've done that can be that bad."

"It's worse than bad." She pulled her hand away, refusing herself the comfort of his touch.

He cleared his throat. "Maybe you should tell me about it. Maybe we can figure out how to make it better."

She wished. Boy, did she wish. "It's not possible."

He led her over to a bench in the shadows and sat down. She didn't want to sit next to him because she knew if she did that the whole nightmare would come spilling out. But she'd had it bottled up for so long now. She should have told her mother, but what good would that have done? Her mother didn't deserve to be burdened with the truth—her truth. It wouldn't change anything. It wouldn't bring her sister back.

But Apollo was different. He was looking at her as though he wanted more from this relationship than a casual flirtation. And she wanted something more too—something like a real family, a family that her sister and brother-in-law should have had.

And she just couldn't let things go on like this.

"Talk to me, Popi." Apollo's voice was soft and comforting.

"You wouldn't be so nice to me if you knew the truth."

"Let me be the judge of that." When the staff approached to clear their dinner dishes, he sent them away. There was no one around now but him, her and the looming truth. His gaze searched hers. "I promise. Nothing you could say will be bad enough to put that look of worry on your face."

"You haven't heard my story yet."

"Then tell me."

She searched for what to say—how to begin. "I…I don't know how."

"Sure you do." He took her hand in his. His thumb lightly rubbed over her skin. "Start at the beginning."

Ever since the baby had been born, she'd been so busy, and at night so tired that she'd been able to push aside the haunting memories. But now that the baby was on a normal schedule and she was feeling better than ever, the guilt had been eating at her.

"It started at the beginning of spring." Her voice was unsteady as she attempted to keep her emotions in check. "My parents' fiftieth anniversary was approaching. You do know that my sister and I were adopted?" When he nodded, she continued. "My parents were childhood sweethearts and had married as soon as it was legal. But when they went to have kids, they found that they couldn't have them biologically. Which was lucky for my sister and me. But by the time my sister and I came along, our parents were older, not that it ever slowed them down."

Apollo remained silent, but she was certain that when he said start at the beginning, he hadn't meant to go this far back. But he'd realize shortly that it was all relevant. Or at least it had seemed so at the time.

"Anyway, with their golden anniversary quickly approaching, I wanted to do something super special for them—something they couldn't do for themselves."

"I'm sure anything you'd have done for them would have been appreciated."

"I know. But I wanted—no, I needed—this event to go above and beyond the norm. I wanted to show them just how much they meant to me and my sister. But Andrina was distracted with planning for the baby. I tried splitting up all of tasks that needed to be done for the party, but my sister kept forgetting to do this or that."

"Was this something unusual for her?"

Popi shrugged. "Not really. My sister wasn't much of a planner. She liked to do things spur of the moment. Day planners were foreign objects to her."

"And so she left all of the party preparations up to you?"

"Yes. But I was busy with the island weddings, plus I had morning sickness."

"You'd think your sister would be bending over backward to help you—what with you having her baby and all."

"She was in the beginning. I think as the thought of a baby became the reality of having a baby, she got jealous." Popi had never thought of it before, but looking back now as the pregnancy had progressed, Andrina had slipped into the shadows of her life. "It must have been so hard for her to face that I could have a baby when she couldn't."

"She's lucky to have a sister like you. Not everybody would step up and have a baby for their sibling. You are special."

Popi shook her head as though driving away his compliments. "Trust me. I'm not great."

"So, what happened? Did you two have a fight?"

"Yes. But it gets worse."

He tightened his hand around hers. "Go ahead. I promise nothing you say is going to drive me away."

"That's because you haven't heard it yet."

He placed a finger beneath her chin and lifted her chin until their gazes me. "We'll work through this together. Just like on the island, we can do anything together."

She wanted to believe him. She truly did. But she knew this was going to be a game changer. And not in a good way, like the baby.

She drew in an unsteady breath as she turned her head to stare straight ahead into the black night. She just couldn't bear to witness the disappointment, the hurt and the anger that would surely cross his handsome face.

She drew in a calming breath. "I had a lot going on that day. I'd been dealing with a rather difficult client who had gone full-blown bridezilla on me. Not that there's any excuse for what I did." She sighed deeply in resignation that nothing would undo the past, no matter how much she wished that it were so. "And by the time I spoke with my sister that evening, I was exhausted and had little patience."

"I'm sure your sister understood. Everyone has had those days."

Popi shook her head. "Not like this. We were arguing over our parents' party—again. I felt like I was doing all the work. Calling the caterers. Setting up appointments with bands. Ordering invitations. You know. And my sister was just sitting back, letting me. She said that was because I was a party planner and I could do it better than her. When she said that, I lost it. I was tired of being taken for granted by her. Every time she needed something or when she didn't feel like doing something, she dumped it on her little sister. She'd been doing it all of our lives."

"I guess that's how Nile must have felt about me too. I was always ditching events to go off on a new adventure."

"But you had a legitimate excuse."

Apollo shrugged. "But was that reason enough to leave my brother to deal with everything from the family business to dealing with my very difficult father?"

"Your brother loved you."

"How do you know?"

"Because he never said a bad word about you and he wouldn't let anyone else speak ill of you."

Apollo's eyes widened. "Really?"

She nodded. "When he spoke of you, it was always positive."

"Even though I didn't deserve it." Apollo blinked away the moisture in his eyes. "Thanks for telling me. It means a lot."

"He'd tell you himself how much you meant to him…if he was still here. If that day had never happened."

"So, you and your sister were arguing. I still don't see how that has anything to do with the accident."

"Because I threatened my sister. I told her if she didn't go check out the private island for my parents to have their second honeymoon after the party that she would no longer be my sister. I had drawn a line in the sand— at the time, I was perfectly serious. And she knew it." Tears stung the back of Popi's eyes and she blinked repeatedly. "Why did I do it? Why did I have to give her that ultimatum?"

"Surely she knew you would forgive her. Is that what

has you all upset? That you argued with her before she died?"

"No. It's that I forced her on the boat ride that killed her and your brother. Don't you see—if I hadn't made that threat, they wouldn't have been on that boat when it had a malfunction and blew up? It's all my fault."

Apollo got to his feet and knelt down in front of her. He reached up and swiped away a tear that streaked down her cheek. "It's no more your fault than it is mine."

She lifted her head. "How could it possibly be your fault? You weren't even here when it happened."

"Exactly. Maybe if I'd have been around, it would have changed the course of events. Maybe they wouldn't have been so distracted and would have researched the island sooner. Maybe your sister was so busy trying to keep up with my overworked brother and that was the reason she let so much work fall on your shoulders. Maybe in the end, the blame is mine."

"No. Don't say that. It isn't true. It's not your fault."

"Neither is it yours. I believe that when someone's time on earth is up, it doesn't matter where they are. It was the end of their time and there's nothing you or I could have done to change it. We both have to learn to accept it. The only thing we can do for them is to raise that little boy to the best of our ability and tell Seb about his biological parents. That's what they'd want us to do."

Popi blinked repeatedly. "Is that what you truly believe?"

"It is. And you deserve as much happiness as you can find in this world."

Without thinking, she asked, "With you?"

"I was hoping you'd want that." He reached up, his hand drawing her face to his. And then he kissed her. It was a kiss full of promise of all sorts of delights yet to come.

All too soon, he pulled back.

"Why did you stop?" she asked.

"I thought we'd have dessert up at the house."

"Dessert?"

A wicked smile lit up his face. "Dessert in bed. What do you think?"

"It doesn't get any better than that. Lead the way."

CHAPTER TWENTY

HE HADN'T SLEPT much the night before.

It was the best sleepless night of his life.

As the sun glowed brightly in the morning sky, Apollo was filled with energy and a sense of purpose. He'd slipped out of bed quietly to let Popi sleep. He'd fed Seb his breakfast, taken him for a stroll in the gardens and now Seb was back down for a midmorning nap.

Apollo sat down in the sunroom to drink some coffee and peruse the morning news. He'd been rolling around the idea of stepping up and running the family business for Seb. Now it was time to put his thoughts into action.

He had a degree in business that was about to get a workout as he eased back into the family business. He never thought he would be comfortable here at the estate, where he had so many bad memories, but Popi was helping him to make new memories—happy memories. And he never thought he'd be a businessman, but the thought of providing for his family appealed to him.

"What can I get you?" Anna, the housekeeper, asked.

He leaned back in his chair. "I'm thinking Popi should be up soon. How about lots of fresh fruit, eggs, pastries, the works."

Anna smiled brightly. "Am I to take it that she approved of your surprise?"

"Yes, she did." He'd always liked Anna. She'd always done her best by him. "Thanks for the suggestion."

"I'm just glad I could help. I'll go have the kitchen start your meal." She started to leave and then backed up. "Would you like me to wake Miss Popi?"

He continued to smile. "No need. I'll do it."

Just as Anna exited the room, his cell phone rang. He honestly wasn't in the mood for business today. Tomorrow was to be his first day in the office. But still, he checked the caller ID. When he found it was the number for a local merchant, he was about to send the call to his voice mail, but they didn't make a habit of calling him and curiosity got the better of him.

"Mr. Drakos, this is Manolas Decorating. Your nanny— or was it your decorator—was in here the other day, wanting to place a special order. We got the quote back from the manufacturer and it is quite costly. We wanted a verbal confirmation from you before we place the order."

"And this is for the nursery?"

"No, sir. I can't imagine that anyone would put this particular wallpaper in a child's room. Nor the flooring that was picked out. And there were some other items selected, as well."

"Just how much are we talking about?"

When the salesman spoke, Apollo sat straight up. That was more money than he'd allotted for the nursery. What was Popi thinking? And what was she planning to do with the supplies?

"No. Do not charge them to the account. There has been a mix-up." Apollo ended the call.

He sat there, staring blindly ahead. His friend's warning came back to him. Was it possible Popi was using him for the money? Would she use Seb to extort more money from the estate? Were these purchases just the beginning? Or was there truly some sort of misunderstanding?

"Sir, your mail." Anna placed a stack of envelopes on the table.

He didn't feel like sorting through it, but there was a large manila envelope that stuck out from all of the rest.

In the corner was the address of an attorney located right here in Athens. A family law attorney. Popi's attorney.

He knew what was inside before he even opened the envelope. But like watching a horrible accident about to happen, he kept moving, letting the scene play out. Because he had to know the truth about Popi.

He removed the papers and scanned the top sheet. It was the paperwork requesting Popi gain full and immediate custody of Seb. Apollo didn't have the stomach to read a list of reasons that he wasn't adequate to raise his nephew. He was about to toss aside the papers when he noticed at the bottom a request for support. This was something new. And the number was staggering.

The breath hitched in his throat. She wanted money.

He'd been so wrong about her.

And this time he wanted to be right—more than he'd ever wanted anything. He wanted Popi to be different than the other people that had let him down.

His hopes were dashed. He didn't know why he let people in, because in the end they hurt him every time. And he'd so wanted to believe in Popi—in what they'd shared. But now he was beginning to see what was important to her.

And it wasn't him.

Popi couldn't believe she'd slept so late.

But then again there hadn't been much sleeping going on during the night.

As soon as she entered the sunroom, she noticed that Apollo's mood had changed. The morning after was the awkward part. Maybe if she just acted like nothing had happened—like that was possible—things would eventually smooth out.

"Good morning." She flashed him a bright smile, even though her insides shivered with nerves.

"Morning." His gaze didn't meet hers.

She took a seat next to him and poured herself a cup of coffee. Now that she was no longer pregnant and the baby wasn't breastfeeding, she was free to drink all the caffeine she desired—and this morning, she desired the entire pot. Every muscle in her body was sore, but in a good way—a very good way.

"You should have woken me to take care of Seb."

"No need."

She arched a brow. "You took care of him?"

A dark line formed across his brow. "Yes."

"Sorry. I just know how fussy he can get in the morning. And you've never handled him right when he wakes up. Did everything go okay?"

"Yes."

"That's good. I'll set my alarm for tomorrow." Her attempt at making conversation was failing miserably.

He turned his attention to his phone and appeared to be scrolling through emails. So much for pretending that last night didn't happen. She might as well face the big pink elephant in the middle of the room.

She took a sip of coffee before setting aside the cup. "About last night—"

"I don't want to talk about it."

When he looked at her, it was with skepticism and something else—was it anger? Or pain? But in a blink, his emotions were hidden behind a wall. She felt cutoff and adrift.

He regrets our night together.

When she'd confessed to her part in the death of her sister and his brother, Apollo had said all of the right things. In that moment, he'd convinced her that what had happened was fate. She should have known that once he thought over her confession about what had happened to his brother that he would blame her just like she blamed herself.

They'd let themselves get caught up in the moment—wanting to believe their attraction could overcome the obstacles. At least that's how it had been for her. Maybe for him it had been something much less—something more physical. Either way, it was over.

And there was the email that she'd received from Lea, confirming that the renovations to Infinity Island were almost complete. Popi's bungalow had been completed first and it was ready for her and Seb to return. She'd been planning to delay her return, just until she knew where things were going with Apollo. But now she knew and there was no reason to put off their departure. It was time to introduce Seb to his new home.

"I received an email this morning. The work on the island is wrapping up. It's time I leave."

Apollo's head lifted and his guarded gaze met hers. "It's probably for the best. Last night, it shouldn't have happened."

His words broke her heart. The breath stilled in her lungs as the pain of loss and rejection seeped into her bones. It was with effort that she sucked in some much-needed oxygen.

Just keep it together. Just a little longer.

"I…I slept too late to catch today's ferry. I still have all of my stuff to pack and the baby's—"

"He stays here." Apollo's blue eyes were ice-cold.

"I can't just leave him." Her voice wobbled.

This can't be happening. Everything is falling apart. All because I couldn't resist him last night.

Apollo placed both hands flat on the table and leaned toward her. "You're free to leave, but that little boy upstairs is my flesh and blood. Not yours. He stays."

His sharp words stabbed her heart. Was that what he'd boiled everything down to? Blood relations? Tears pricked the back of her eyes. She blinked. "But...he'll wonder what happened to me."

"I'm not heartless. I won't cut you completely out of his life." Apollo looked at her accusingly, like she'd do the same to him. "You can visit him here at the estate."

"And that's it?" She struggled to keep from shouting, but with every word her voice rose. "I'm not the baby's biological aunt, so I'm not important—"

His gaze didn't meet hers. "I didn't say you weren't important."

"Just not as important as a Drakos." Anger, pain and resentment balled up within her. She felt like she was on the verge of losing absolutely everything that truly mattered to her. She couldn't just give up that precious baby boy. Not without a fight.

"What's wrong with being a Drakos?" Apollo's gaze lifted to meet hers. There was a challenge reflected in his icy-blue eyes. "My brother was a Drakos and he was a great man. The best man I've ever known."

Apollo was right on that point. Nile was a wonderful brother, from what she could tell, and an adoring husband. He would have made an amazing father if he'd had the chance. But there was something Apollo didn't seem to understand.

"It takes more than a name or blood ties to make a family." Her voice cracked with emotion. "It takes love—lots of it—and it takes time, one-on-one quality time. Without those you're nothing more than relatives—not a family."

Apollo stepped closer. His eyes flared with emotion. "I will always be that little boy's family. Don't you ever doubt it."

Popi had witnessed Apollo pull himself together over the past couple of months. She had no doubt that if he put his mind to it, he would make a great father. With the passion he'd shown just now, she believed he would always be there for Seb. And no matter how upset Apollo was with her at the moment, he wouldn't keep her from having access to Seb.

In the end, she didn't want Seb constantly dragged back and forth between Infinity Island and the Drakos estate. Deep down she knew it was best for Seb to be settled in one place.

She attempted to tell Apollo that she would be back for regular visits with Seb, but when she opened her mouth, a lump of emotions blocked the words. Her heart was so full of love for her sister and for that little bundle upstairs that she'd been carrying around inside her for months. But she was also consumed with guilt for being the reason her sister and brother-in-law were on the boat. Maybe this was her penance.

Apollo got to his feet. "I'm needed at the office. I'll probably be in the city until late, so don't hold dinner for me. And my attorney will be in touch about visitation rights."

Without waiting for her to say a word and without a goodbye, he was gone. And Popi was left sitting alone, wondering what in the world had just happened in the last twenty-four hours. How could everything have gone from being so good—so happy—to this utterly desolate feeling?

CHAPTER TWENTY-ONE

SHOWERED AND DRESSED in a new suit, Apollo stepped in front of the floor-length mirror in his bedroom.

He didn't want to go to the office, especially a day early. But he couldn't just skulk around the house with Popi right here. He knew that sooner or later he would be drawn to her. He would want her to explain away the money and the custody papers. Like that could be done.

Why did he let himself think Popi was going to be different? Why did he think with her in his life that he could have a happy future? Happiness wasn't in the cards for him.

He moved to the table by the French doors, where fresh coffee had been left for him. He picked up the mug, knowing he would need some caffeine in order to get through the day. He took a drink, but it lacked its usual good taste.

The only thing he could do—his mission in life—was to look after his nephew. And he was going to throw all of his resources into blocking Popi's attempt at gaining custody. Seb was a Drakos. He should grow up here in the family home.

And as upset as he was with Popi, he was mostly upset with himself. The thought of going after her—of ripping the baby out of her arms—sickened him. He set aside his coffee, no longer having the stomach for it.

Knock-knock.

"Come in."

Anna entered the bedroom, clucking her tongue and shaking her head just like she used to do when he would get in a row with Nile. He wanted to ignore her. He wanted to just sit here in his own puddle of self-pity. After all, he was the one who always came up with the short stick where relationships were concerned. Why didn't Anna sympathize with him instead of acting like he'd done something wrong?

"What is it?" His tone was short and curt.

She arched a brow at him and he suddenly regretted aiming his frustration at her. "I can't believe you are sending her away."

"I'm not sending anyone anywhere. Popi is leaving because she wants to. She can't get out the door fast enough."

"Uh-huh. You just keep telling yourself that."

Apollo got to his feet. "What is that supposed to mean?"

Anna crossed her arms as her determined gaze met his. "What else was she supposed to do with you being so closed off and short with her? This place was starting to feel like a home again. You were at last starting to be happy, just like I'd always wanted for you. What happened?"

Apollo turned away from Anna's probing eyes and moved to the window overlooking the garden—a garden he'd planted with Popi. "She wasn't the woman I thought she was."

"What sort of woman would that be?"

"One that cared." His voice was nothing more than a whisper.

"I think there's something you need to see."

"Not now. I just want to be left alone."

"It's important. Come with me and then if you want, I'll see that no one disturbs you the rest of the day."

He knew better than to argue with Anna. The woman was a force to be reckoned with, and it was easier and quicker to placate her than to argue the point.

He followed her to the other side of the house—the side that he made a point of avoiding. He didn't want to go there. He didn't know why Anna would take him here. She knew this part of the house had once been his father's sanctuary. For Apollo, it had been where he took his punishment for whatever his father felt like accusing him of that day.

He stopped. "Anna, I can't."

She turned to him. Determination gleamed in her eyes. "You must."

"Why? What's so important?"

"Something that just might change how you see the future." Without waiting for him to respond, she turned and kept walking.

Though every part of him wanted to turn and walk in the opposite direction, he found himself following Anna. What could possibly be so important?

As they walked, he noticed the hallway had been painted. Instead of that dingy dark gray color that had adorned these halls all his childhood, they were now a much cheerier off-white. And the portrait of ancient wars was replaced with portraits of landscape scenes. Where had they come from? Was this something that Popi had splurged on?

They turned a corner and stopped in front of a set of double doors. Anna turned to him. "I wasn't supposed to show you this. It was meant to be a surprise but under the circumstances, I thought you should see what Popi has been up to while the baby naps."

Anna pushed open the doors and then stepped aside. Why would Anna let Popi mess around in this room? Anna knew the bad memories he had in here. But when he stepped inside the room, the big oak desk where his father would sit and drink his bourbon was gone. In its place was a modern glass desk. Everything in the room was light and bright—something his father would have hated. And greenery was everywhere. The bookcases that had lined the wall behind his father's desk were gone. The wall was blank as though it wasn't finished.

Knock-knock.

He turned to find two delivery men with a big roll in their arms, plus some other supplies.

The men paused at the doorway. "We're from Manolas Decorating with a delivery."

Apollo was confused. "But I refused payment."

The man looked at the paper in his hand. "It says that it was paid in full. A Miss Costas paid."

And it had to be with her own funds.

While the man placed the supplies off to the side of the room, Apollo tried to make sense of everything. The money Popi had spent had been for him. She was trying to wipe away the sadness of the past and paint him a new future full of light and hope.

If he was wrong about her and the money, what else had he been wrong about?

The memory of the custody papers sitting on the table haunted him. How could that be a misunderstanding? Popi had to know what she was doing.

But another part of him wanted to believe there was an explanation he hadn't thought of. He couldn't leave things like this. He needed answers before it was too late.

He retrieved the custody papers and headed for Popi's room. He rapped his fingers on the door, hoping she was there. Surely she wouldn't have slipped away to a hotel or anything. To his relief, the door opened.

Popi's normally bright and sparkly eyes were dulled and red. Had she been crying? Because her plans were about to go awry? Or was it something more?

He held up the papers. "Was this your idea?"

"Was what my idea?" Confusion reflected in her eyes.

"To sue me for custody of Seb and to ask for large support payments?"

"What?" She paused as though making sense of what he was saying. "Can I see those?"

"You don't know what they say?"

She frowned at him. "Obviously I don't or I wouldn't ask to see them."

Hope started to swell in his chest, but he tamped it down. It was too soon and he still had questions. "Then why else would your attorney send me these papers?"

Popi sighed and turned to walk farther into her room. "Because I accidentally overheard you on the phone. You were making plans to leave on a safari—another one of your dangerous adventures. And...and I wanted to make sure the baby is with me when you're out of town."

"I'm not going anywhere. I'm not sure what you heard, but my life is here with Seb." He stopped himself from saying that his life was with her too, because he still had unanswered questions. "I have no intention of leaving Seb. And I told my friend exactly that."

"Oh, I didn't know."

He had one more important question. "And the really large support payments?"

"I don't know anything about those. I called my attorney and I was a bit worked up at the time. I told her to do what was best. I thought she would send the papers to me first—not you."

His gaze searched her eyes, finding nothing but honesty reflected in them. He knew that his next move would determine the ultimate fate of their relationship.

"I have to go."

He turned and exited the room. His mind was already churning through this new information and what it meant.

He didn't have time to bask in the hope that filled him. Instead he needed to act. His questions had been satisfactorily answered, but he couldn't just apologize and expect

Popi to give up her life on Infinity Island. He had to give her a reason to stay here—with him.

Goodbyes were so hard.

Popi's dream of raising Seb alongside Apollo had been dashed. That acknowledgment slashed through her heart. How had she read everything with Apollo so wrong?

As she stood in the dimly lit nursery, Popi blinked repeatedly, stemming the river of tears threatening to spill onto her cheeks. If she gave into her emotions now, she didn't think she'd be able to stop crying.

It was time for her to head back to the island…back to her job…back to the welcoming embrace of the island's close-knit community. Seb would be loved and cared for here. Apollo would see that this precious baby had a hands-on, adoring father. Of that she had absolutely no doubts.

Raised as a Drakos, Seb would have every opportunity to live a fantastic life. And once a formal visitation agreement was drawn up, she'd see Seb every single chance she was allowed. She'd be around so much that he'd get tired of seeing her, but she would never get enough of Seb's smiles and laughter.

She held Seb in her arms until he fell asleep. Tears clouded her vision. She whispered, "You will be safe here. Your uncle will see to it. You will be loved by Apollo and Anna and the rest of the staff that think you hung the stars." When Shadow meowed from his spot atop the chest of drawers, Popi smiled through her tears. "And Shadow will love…" Her voice cracked. "He'll love you too."

She blinked repeatedly as unshed tears clouded her vision. If she didn't leave now, she was afraid that she wouldn't have the strength to do the right thing—leave Seb here. This was his home—his destiny. She'd watched Apollo over the past weeks and he was up to being a good father.

"I love you, little guy." She placed the sleeping baby in the crib. "Your mum and dad are watching over you. Always. And I'll be back just as soon as I can." She swiped the tears from her cheeks.

And then she slipped an envelope from her purse and placed it against the lamp on the chest of drawers. With all her things packed and the baby down for the night, there was nothing left to do but leave.

With every step she took toward the door, it felt like her heart was being ripped from her chest. Without allowing herself to glance back, she exited the mansion and walked down the long driveway, to where a taxi was waiting to take her to a hotel for the night. Tomorrow she would catch the ferry back to Infinity Island—where she belonged.

CHAPTER TWENTY-TWO

WOULD THIS WORK?

The next morning, after a few hours of restless sleep, Apollo had his plan in motion. It was the only thing he could think of to change Popi's mind about leaving—about leaving him for being such a jerk.

Apollo had to admit, for a man used to making decisive decisions in the spur of the moment with potentially deadly consequences, he was totally unsure about this one. Would it be enough to convince her to stay?

The one thing he did know was that she had changed things for him. Little things and big things. And if he didn't do everything he could to keep her from walking out that door for good, he would lose his chance at happiness. He was certain of that.

He'd heard it said by the elders that there was one true love in the world for each person. Popi was that person for him. And he had to show her that a future with him was worth pursuing. But would she believe him?

It was time to find out. He went to her room and knocked on the door. There was no answer. After he knocked again and called out her name, he opened the door. Her bed was made up as though it hadn't been slept in. He checked the bathroom, finding no sign of her things. The closet was empty. The dresser was empty.

She was gone.

But why? It was way too early to catch the ferry.

And then his thoughts turned to Seb. Had they both slipped away without even so much as a goodbye? His chest tightened. That couldn't be. Popi wouldn't do that, would she?

Apollo rushed down the hallway to the nursery. He barreled through the doorway and came to a halt when he saw Seb in the crib, kicking his feet and smiling up at his mobile.

Apollo rushed over and picked up the baby. "Thank goodness you're still here. That means Popi must still be here. I have to find her."

It was then that his gaze strayed across the white envelope on the dresser with his name on it. He knew that writing. It was Popi's. His heart sunk down to his loafers.

He called for the nanny. Once the baby was tended to, he took the envelope and walked back to his room. He didn't want to be disturbed when he read what Popi had to say to him.

Apollo,
I'm sorry for disrupting your life in so many ways. I'm sorry for so many things these days. The one thing I'm not sorry for is having Seb and getting a chance to see you with him. You are going to be such a great father. Seb will thrive under your care.
    I'm going back to where I belong—back to Infinity Island. In the morning, I will contact my attorney and have the custody case withdrawn. Seb belongs with you.
Take care of yourself,
Popi

Things couldn't end this way. He had to find her. He had to prove to her that they were better together than apart.

Life would be better once she returned to Infinity Island. That's what Popi had told herself all night—a very long night. Memories of Apollo kept coming one after the other. She missed the sound of his voice, the twinkle in his eyes when he smiled at her and most of all she missed the utter bliss of feeling his arms around her.

But once she made it back to the island, she would be busy. There would be so much to do to get the wedding business back up and operating. There would be receptions to plan. People to talk to. And lots to keep her mind from straying to the two men who meant the world to her.

Leaving was for the best. And she couldn't take a baby away from his doting uncle and the home that belonged to him. They would get along fine without her—she couldn't bear to think it would be otherwise.

And maybe someday soon, Apollo would find love—

She halted her thoughts there. The thought of him with someone else was just too painful to contemplate. The best she could do at the moment was to hope he found happiness.

The long, low blow of the ferry whistle let her know it was time to move to the dock. And yet she didn't move. She didn't want to move.

The truth was she'd been happy in Athens with Apollo and Seb. Happier than she'd ever been in her life. Her mind began to replay snippets of memories, from their walks in the garden to their shared meals to their candlelit dinner, where they danced beneath the stars. That had been such a perfect night. Too perfect.

The truth was she had no right to be so happy. How was she supposed to have the perfect family and the perfect life when her sister had been robbed of her happiness? Life was not fair. Not at all.

Popi didn't know how long that she'd sat there when someone bumped her suitcase and jarred her back to reality. She needed to get on that ferry before it pulled out without her. And then she'd have to spend another night alone in a hotel room, with nothing but her memories and regrets to keep her company.

She got up from the bench and lifted the handle on her suitcase. She started to roll it toward the busy dock when she thought she heard her name being called out. She glanced around but didn't see anyone she recognized. It was probably her imagination, combined with her abysmal night's sleep.

"Popi! Wait!"

That time she was certain of what she'd heard. It was Apollo's voice. She stopped and turned, but there were so many people behind her. And they were none too happy that she had stopped and held them up.

She should keep going. There was nothing left for them to say to each other. But then she thought of Seb. Maybe there was something wrong. She worried her bottom lip for a moment and then got out of line.

Apollo approached her. "We need to talk."

"Is it Seb?"

"Don't worry. He's fine."

"Then I have to go." She couldn't bear to drag this out any further. The pain of loss was still so deeply etched in her heart. "Please leave me alone."

"Not until we talk." His tone brooked no compromise.

She turned to him, pleading with her eyes. "You don't know how hard leaving was for me. I just can't drag this out."

"Not even for Seb's sake?"

Worry for herself ceased. "Is Seb all right?"

"Yes. I didn't mean to imply otherwise. But he misses you. He wants you to come back. Let's talk."

She gave a determined shake of her head. "There's nothing left to say. It's time I go home." She turned to walk to the end of the long line of people heading for the dock. Some people were day laborers. Others were heading out on boats bound for various destinations. And some were like her and going home—at last.

"Popi," he reached for her arm. "Please don't walk away. Not until you've heard what I have to say."

She didn't know what he could say that would make a difference. Surely he'd read her note that she wasn't going to fight him for custody of Seb. Even if she wanted to, she didn't have the resources to challenge his deep pockets. But she still planned to have regular access to her nephew. She hadn't written that in the note. She'd been too worked up at the time to think to include it. Maybe now was the time to make it clear that she wasn't totally backing out of Seb's life. She wanted a binding agreement written by their attorneys.

She turned back to him. "I'm listening."

"Not here." He glanced around at the crowd of people. "How about over there?" He pointed to a vacant bench off to the side of the marina.

She followed him to the bench and sat down. She turned to him, knowing she had to say this quickly before she lost her nerve. "Before you say anything, I want you to know that I'm not abandoning Seb. I still plan to be a part of his life and visit him as much as possible. I think that's what my sister would have wanted under the circumstances. I can tell him about his mother. Things that no one else would know."

Apollo stared into her eyes. "I would never keep you from Seb."

"Thank you." Her heart was breaking as they were talking. All she wanted was for this conversation to be over. It was too painful to be this close and yet this far away from him. "I should go."

"Not yet."

The truth was she didn't understand why he was here.

She'd given him everything he'd wanted—a life with Seb. There was nothing left for her to give.

A couple blasts of the ferry whistle let her know the boat was about to pull out. But not without her. She had to get back to Infinity Island.

She jumped to her feet. "I've got to go."

She rushed toward the dock. She sensed Apollo behind her. Why was he being so insistent? Was he afraid he couldn't handle the baby on his own? That was just nerves. Seb loved him. And so did she...

The thought sent a wave of fresh pain coursing through her body. Her feet moved faster. Apollo was right behind her. How was she supposed to get over him when he wouldn't go away?

Apollo was speaking but with the crush of people and the sounds of the dock, she couldn't make out his words— she didn't want to make them out. She wanted to forget that she ever knew him—though she knew that would be utterly impossible.

When she finally made it through the congestion and reached the end of the dock, the walkway had been drawn up. The ferry was just beginning to pull out.

"Wait!" This couldn't be happening. "Please. I need on the boat."

"Sorry," yelled a young sailor. "You'll have to catch the ferry tomorrow."

"But please. It's important."

"Can't stop the ferry now."

Popi was so anxious to get away from Apollo that, for a moment, she considered swimming for the boat. But she knew that would cause pandemonium, and the water wasn't exactly inviting right next to the dock. It was murky, unlike the clear blue water on the island.

With a resigned sigh, she leveled her shoulders and

turned. She knew Apollo would be standing there. What was it going to take to make him go away?

Her gaze met his and her heart thump-thumped like it did every time he stared deep into her eyes. "Say whatever it is you have to say and then be on your way."

"I'd rather show you."

"Show me what?"

"Come with me."

She hesitated. "I...I don't think that's a good idea."

"How about we make a deal?"

"What sort of deal?"

"You come with me and if you don't like what I have to show you, I will chopper you out to the island today. You won't have to spend another night on the mainland."

That deal was too good to pass up. But what did he have to show her that was so important?

CHAPTER TWENTY-THREE

THIS HAS TO WORK.

Apollo wanted this more than he'd wanted anything in his life.

And he was more nervous than he had been while crossing the Amazon with its many dangers.

"What are we doing back here?" Popi asked.

"You'll see." He drove past the front of the house, toward the back.

"Apollo, what's going on?" Popi stared out the window at the big white tent he'd erected the night before. "If this is some sort of party—"

"It's not. I promise."

He got out of the car and came to her side. He opened the door and offered her a hand out but she didn't accept it. She got out on her own.

"But I don't understand." She walked to the edge of the drive. "The gardens look like they are set up for a wedding." She turned to him. The color faded from her face. "Are you trying to tell me you're getting married?"

"I'm not. At least not right now. I put this together for you."

She pressed a hand to her chest. "For me? But I'm not getting married."

"Come see. And then I'll explain."

He held out his arm to her. She hesitated at first, but then slipped her hand into the crook of his arm. He led her down the aisle. And in that moment, he knew without any shadow of a doubt that he was doing the right thing. They belonged together. But how did he convince Popi of that?

At the end of the aisle, he turned to her. "I did this for you. I wanted to show you that Infinity Island isn't the only place for beautiful weddings."

Confusion reflected in her eyes.

He cleared his throat. "I'm not saying this very well. What I mean is that you could—if you wanted, that is—run a wedding business right here at the estate."

"But why?"

He gazed deep into her beautiful brown eyes, willing her to truly hear what he was saying. "Because I want you to stay. I've made such a mess of things. I wasn't expecting to fall in love with you—"

"You love me?"

He smiled and nodded. "I think I have since we danced at your friend's wedding. But I didn't know it at the time. And then after we made love, I panicked and I let my doubts and insecurities overrule what I knew about you."

"Which is?"

"That you are beautiful both inside and out. That you would do anything for the people you love—even sacrificing your happiness."

"I can't believe you're saying all of this...even after the part I played in the deaths of our siblings."

He stepped closer to her and brushed the back of his fingers gently down over her cheek. She couldn't resist leaning into him and drawing on his strength.

His gaze met hers. "You have to stop blaming yourself. You didn't do anything wrong. Sometimes bad things happen and there's no one to blame."

"Really?" Hope gleamed in her eyes.

"Really. Quit being so hard on yourself. It isn't what your sister would want."

Popi paused as though considering his words. He was right. This not what Andrina would want. "My sister could procrastinate with the best of them, but she was never vindictive."

"See. The only one who has to forgive you…is you."

Popi nodded in understanding. "I'll work on it."

He was winning her over—he was certain of it. "So, what do you say? Would you like to stay here with me— with Seb? And start your own wedding business?" And then he realized he'd forgotten something. "And that tent off to the side, it's going to become a conservatory with glass walls and ceiling so you can dance beneath the stars. And you may use it for your weddings. Use whatever you desire."

"You'd do all of that?"

He nodded. "And more, if you'll say yes. I've traveled the world searching for something—something I never found. Until now. I've found my home right here with you and Seb." He pulled a ring from his pocket and dropped down on one knee. "I love you, Popi, with all of my heart. Will you be my partner on the biggest and grandest adventure of my life?"

Tears splashed onto her cheeks. "I will. I love you."

EPILOGUE

Five months later...
The Drakos Estate, Athens, Greece

THIS WAS GOING to be the wedding of the season.

Every newspaper, television network and paparazzo was in attendance.

But the guest list was quite selective—only family and friends.

And so the media was left outside the gates. But that didn't stop them from hiring helicopters to whirl above the big white tent in the lawn of the Drakos estate. But with a few well-placed calls, Apollo was able to get the helicopters removed, letting the peaceful chirp of the birds and the rustle of the wind be the only backdrop to this occasion.

In just a few hours, Popi was going to become Mrs. Apollo Drakos. And then the adoption of Seb would become official. Popi moved to the crib and lifted her future son into her arms.

Popi held Seb so that she could look him in his eyes. "Very soon Apollo and I will be your legal parents. But don't worry, we'll make sure you know all about your very special birth parents. They loved you so much. We all do."

"What's going on in here?" Apollo's voice came from the doorway.

Popi turned to him. "You aren't supposed to see the bride before the wedding. It's bad luck."

He stepped farther into the room and didn't stop until he was next to her. He planted a quick kiss on her lips and then one on the baby's forehead. "We don't need luck. We have love on our side."

Aww… This was one of the reasons that she'd fallen in love with him. Once he'd trusted her enough to let down his guard, she'd found an optimistic side to him. And Apollo truly believed what he said. And she believed in him. They didn't need luck, because their love was strong enough to see them through anything.

The smile slipped from his face. "I just have one question for you."

"What's that?"

"Are you sure about starting your own wedding business here? I will understand if you want to return to Infinity Island." He gazed deeply into his eyes. "My home is wherever you are." At that point, the baby let out a cooing sound. Their gazes moved to Seb. "And you too, little guy."

"And my home is here." With her free hand, Popi reached out to Apollo. Her fingers traced down over the stubble trailing down his jaw. "My heart belongs to you. And I can't wait to start my own business. I've already been working on a new website and deciding what colors I'll use for my brand."

"You have?" When she nodded, he said, "I can't believe you've had time with all our wedding plans, the baby and finishing the remodel. I'm so proud of all you accomplished in such a short amount of time. You are amazing."

She smiled. When he talked to her that way, she felt as though she could accomplish anything. It meant so much that he believed in her.

Before she could put her thoughts into words, there was a knock at the door. Lea stepped into the room with the newest addition to their group. Baby Lily was in her arms, sound asleep.

Lea smiled. "Hey, you two aren't supposed to be together before the wedding."

Popi nodded toward her soon-to-be-husband. "Someone says that we don't have to worry about luck."

"Really?" There was disbelief in her voice. "I wouldn't want to tempt fate." She narrowed her gaze on Apollo. "That means you need to go." When he didn't make any move to go, she added, "Now."

Popi turned to Apollo. "I think she's serious. You better go."

He sighed. "But the wedding isn't for hours."

"You'll be fine." Lea smiled once more. "I've never seen a more perfect couple."

"She's right," Popi said. "It's only three more hours—"

"And three minutes," Apollo added.

"In three hours…and three minutes, I'll be all yours. And you can have me all evening."

"Mmm… I like the sound of that." He leaned in close and pressed his lips to hers.

"Hey! Hey! Hey!" Lea said. "You have to wait for that until after the vows."

Apollo groaned as he pulled away. "It won't come soon enough." And then he looked at Seb. "I will see you soon, little guy. Hopefully you haven't outgrown your tux."

"We just got the outfit for him last week," Popi said.

"He's a Drakos. He's growing quickly."

"Don't rush him. I'm enjoying having a baby."

"Me too." His gaze sought hers out. "Maybe we should discuss having another one."

"Really?"

"Mmm-hmm." His gaze reflected his sincerity.

Lea moved between them and, with her free arm, gave Apollo a shove toward the door. "It's definitely time you go. Out. Out."

When Apollo closed the door behind him, Lea turned to her. "Wow. That guy is really crazy about you."

"It goes both ways."

"I'm really going to miss you on the island. But I totally understand why you want to stay here. You have a devoted guy. And this mansion and the grounds are amazing."

"Apollo created the garden where we're getting married. Together, we're turning this into our home with our memories."

"Then we better start getting you ready. We have a blissful memory to make."

"Yes, we do."

This was just the beginning of the greatest love story. Popi smiled. She never knew life could be this good. And it was all due to Apollo. She loved him with all her heart.

"Popi, come on." Lea placed Lily in the crib. "You have to put down Seb. We have to get you ready for your groom. It's almost time for you to say 'I do.'"

Popi's feet barely touched the ground.

There really were happily-ever-afters...

* * * * *

THE COWBOY'S
SECRET FAMILY

JUDY DUARTE

To "Honey" Colwell,
my fur grandchild and the inspiration for
Sweetie Pie, the rescued stray dog in
The Cowboy's Secret Family. No matter how many
times Honey gets sprayed by Eau de Stink,
she's determined to catch the rascally skunk
that prowls the neighbourhood at night.
Maybe next time, Honey.

And to Jeff and Sarah Colwell.
Thank you for the opportunity to spend a
special summer with Emalee and Katie, my
two granddaughters, and a barnyard menagerie
consisting of one overly protective shepherd mix,
six free-range chickens, two 4-H lambs and a
couple of horses. Love you, guys!

Chapter One

The new Dodge Ram pickup bounced along the graveled drive that led to the Double G Ranch, where Matt Grimes intended to hole up until he recovered from his injury and could return to the rodeo circuit.

The afternoon sun's glare was damn near blinding, so he reached for the visor, only to miss spotting another pothole, this one bigger than the last. Pain shot through his bum knee, and he swore under his breath. He'd have to convince Uncle George that it was finally time to pave the blasted road or they'd need an all-terrain vehicle to get to the house.

Matt hadn't been home since the Christmas before last, so he probably should have called to let his uncle know he was coming, but he'd decided to surprise him.

He swerved to avoid another hole, a quick move that

jarred his knee again, and he gritted his teeth in pain. The last bull he'd ridden, Grave Digger, had thrown him to the ground, stepping on him in the process. He hadn't suffered a fracture, only tissue damage. But it hurt like hell, and the doctor seemed to think it would take a while for him to heal.

But come hell or high water, Matt was determined to compete in the Rocking Chair Rodeo, which would benefit two of his favorite charities—a local home for retired cowboys, as well as one for abused and neglected kids. On top of that, Esteban Enterprises had used Matt's name to promote the rodeo, and all the ads and posters sported his photo and practically claimed *Local Boy Makes Good.* Hopefully, he'd heal quickly so he could live up to the hype.

When he pulled up to the small ranch house and parked, he remained behind the wheel for a while, rubbing the ache in his knee and stunned as he scanned the yard and noticed how different things were. Damn. His uncle had been busy. No wonder he hadn't gotten around to fixing the road yet.

A lamb stood under a canopy covering part of a small pen near the barn. A new chicken coop had been built, too, with several hens clucking and pecking at the ground. A black-and-white Shetland pony was corralled near the house and an unfamiliar car was parked in the drive.

What in the hell was going on? Had Uncle George hired someone new? He had ranch hands who worked the cattle, but he'd never put a lot of effort into the yard.

Matt climbed out of the truck, wincing when he

put weight on his right leg. As he reached for his cane, a mixed-breed dog wearing a red Western kerchief around its neck rushed at him, barking as if it had super-canine strength and planned to take on a pack of wolves.

Before Matt had to fend off the shepherd-mix with his cane, Uncle George stepped out onto the porch from inside the house, squinting at the glare caused by the sunlight hitting a metal wind chime—a fancy addition that hadn't been there before.

George lifted his hand to shade his eyes and called off the stupid mutt. It obeyed the old man's gruff tone, but it still eyed Matt as if it wasn't yet convinced he wasn't a burglar who'd come to rob the ranch at gunpoint.

"What's going on?" Matt asked, his voice edged with irritation.

The screen door screeched open again, and out walked a little girl in pigtails wearing a white blouse with a green 4-H kerchief tied around her neck, blue jeans and sneakers. The dog took a look at her, wagged its tail and then began barking at Matt all over again.

The girl hurried to the mutt, dropped to her knees and hugged the dog's neck. "Shush, Sweetie Pie. It's okay."

"Well, look what the cat dragged in," Uncle George finally said. "My long-lost nephew. What'd you do? Lose your cell phone?"

"I've been busy." While that was true, Matt still should have called. Maybe then he'd know who that little girl was. Had his uncle taken on a babysitting gig to supplement his Social Security? And what was with the menagerie—ponies, chickens, dogs and who knew what else?

A soft breeze kicked up, causing the wind chime to tinkle, while Matt tried to make sense of it all. Before he could prod his uncle for an explanation, the girl turned to the house and called out, "Mommy! Hurry up. We're going to be late to the 4-H meeting."

Matt leaned on his cane, confused. Dazed. He shot a glance at his uncle. The white-haired man still favored jeans and flannel shirts, like the red one he wore today. His clothes fit him much better. The tall, lanky man had filled out since the last time Matt had been home.

Apparently, "Mommy" was a good cook.

As Matt took a step toward his uncle, his bad knee nearly gave out, causing him to wince and wobble. He used his cane for balance and swore under his breath.

"You'd better sit down before you fall down," George said. "What'd you do to yourself?"

"Crossed paths with the wrong bull." Matt hobbled up the steps to the wraparound porch, which was adorned with pots of red geraniums and colorful pansies. He had no idea how long "Mommy" had been here, but long enough to make her mark.

"One day a bull is gonna break your neck instead of your leg," Uncle George said. "I hope you learned your lesson this time and are finally giving up the rodeo. You're getting too old for that crazy kid stuff."

"It's barely a scratch. I'll be ready to ride again—or even have another run-in with Grave Digger—in a few weeks." Matt glanced at the colorful heart-shaped welcome mat at the door. "Is my room available?"

His uncle gestured to one of the rockers on the porch. "Your room is always ready for you. I keep thinking you'll finally come to your senses and move home where you belong."

Matt limped to a chair. He didn't really *belong* anywhere, a lesson he'd learned early on. He took a seat, rested his cane against the small wicker table and set his rocker in motion. His uncle sat in the chair next to his.

For a moment, he savored the familiar earthy scent of the only place that came close to being the home he could actually call his own. But now he wasn't so sure about that. Apparently, a lot had changed in the past year and a half.

Matt lowered his voice and asked, "So what's going on?"

His uncle shrugged a single shoulder, then placed an arthritic index finger to his lips and shushed him. "Hold your questions for a while."

Matt nodded as if that made perfect sense, but nothing about this situation did, and his curiosity grew to the point that it was downright troublesome.

He studied the child. She was a cute little thing. He guessed her to be about six or seven.

She cocked her head to the side, one brown pigtail dangling over her shoulder, and eyed Matt carefully. "Who are *you*?"

He could ask her the same thing, but he supposed

he'd have wait until after she and her mother left to have the bulk of his questions answered.

"I'm Matt," he said.

"Oh." She nodded, her pigtails swishing up and down. "You're the cowboy who used to live here. That's what I thought. I'm Emily. Me and my mom are staying here. We'll probably go home someday, but I hope we don't. I like having a big yard."

So Emily and "Mommy" lived in a town. Or in a city.

The screen door squeaked open once again and a twenty-something brunette stepped onto the porch. She shielded her eyes from the sun's glare off the metal chimes with her hand, blocking her face, but recognition slammed into Matt like a bull out of the shoot.

Miranda Contreras.

His old teenage crush. The girl who'd strung him along before breaking his heart beyond repair. And here she was again, all grown up, prettier than ever and rocking Matt's world again, just as she'd done the day she arrived at Wexler High, a pretty sophomore with a bubbly laugh.

She stepped out of the sunlight's glare, and when her eyes met his, she flinched. Her lips parted and she placed a hand on her chest as if she hadn't expected to see him ever again. *"Matt?"*

"Miranda." His body tensed, and he kept his tone cool. But inside his gut coiled into a knot.

She swept a glossy strand of dark hair behind her ear. A nervous gesture?

"It's been a long time," she said.

"Yep." Too long, it seemed. But maybe not long enough.

Matt's gaze swept across the yard, from the pony in the corral, to the chickens in the coop, to the lamb in the pen and then to the little brown-haired girl hugging the dog.

Was Miranda responsible for all of...*this*?

She had to be.

But why in the hell, after all these years, had she come back to the Double G? And how long did she intend to stay?

Uncle George had made it clear that he ought to hold his questions until after they left, but the curiosity was eating him alive.

"I see a pony in the corral," Matt said to the child. "Did you bring it with you when you came to the Double G?"

"No, she's brand-new. I mean, she's not a baby. She's just a little horse. And she's already grown up. Uncle George gave her to me because I'm going to be a cowgirl when I grow up."

Uncle George? Back in the day, Miranda had claimed his father's uncle as her own. And now she'd encouraged her daughter do the same thing. It hadn't bothered Matt a bit when they were younger, because if things had worked out between them, that relationship might have become official. But that's not the way their teenage romance had played out.

For that reason, having Miranda here knocked his blood pressure out of whack, especially since he had the feeling she'd moved in permanently. Her daughter might think they were going back home one of these days, wherever that home was. But flowers on the porch, a pony in the corral and a dog guarding the yard suggested otherwise.

"Guess what?" Emily asked, as she placed her small hands on her denim-clad hips. "I can saddle my pony all by myself."

"Good for you." As angry as Matt might be with her mother, he couldn't fault the cute little girl with a splash of freckles across her nose. He wondered whether she favored Miranda or maybe her father, whoever he might be. It had been years since he and Miranda had split. When had she had Emily? How old was she?

Before he could ask the little girl her age, Miranda stepped off the porch, her purse slung over her shoulder. "We'll have to play catch up later, Matt. If Emily and I don't leave now, we'll be late."

Good. Uncle George had some explaining to do.

Miranda turned to the old man and blessed him with a smile. "I have a pot roast in the oven."

"Is it big enough to feed a drifter?" George asked.

She hesitated, then smiled. "Yes, of course." She turned her gaze to Matt. "There's plenty." Then she held her hand out for Emily. "Come on, honey."

Matt watched them walk toward her car. Miranda wore a loose-fitting summer dress—a soft yellow with a floral print. She looked as fresh as spring, although she'd obviously grown up—and changed. She had womanly curves now. And, if anything, she was even prettier than before.

Once she started the car and headed down the drive, Matt turned to his uncle. "Okay. What gives?"

"Miranda and Emily needed a place to stay for a while, and I had plenty of room. They've been good company."

The subtext was clear. Matt hadn't been around much. He shook off a twinge of guilt, promising himself he'd have to do better from now on. Then he leaned back and set his rocker in motion again. "So what's her story?"

"She needed time to sort through some things, and we both figured this was the perfect place for her to do it."

"What'd she need to think about?"

"Back in February, she broke her engagement. I 'spect she's got a few things to sort through."

Two months ago? Damn. Each answer George provided only stirred up more questions. "What made her back out?"

"You know me. I don't like to pry."

Matt blew out a sigh. "Does Miranda's father know she's here?"

"Nope. And she doesn't want him to know."

Matt stiffened, and the rocker stalled. "Are you kidding? No one's come looking for her yet?"

"Not here. She told him she was staying with a friend, and her dad must have assumed it was someone she'd met in college. He's called her cell phone a few times, but he doesn't have any idea where she is."

"That's not good." Matt blew out a ragged sigh.

"You remember what happened the last time he found her here."

"I sure as hell haven't forgotten." George's rocker picked up speed, creaking against the wooden floor. "He got so angry and red in the face that I damn near thought he was either going to have a stroke or I'd have to shoot him full of buckshot."

Matt hadn't forgotten that day, either. Or the words Carlos Contreras had said to Miranda. *I can't believe you've been sneaking around with a good-for-nothing-wannabe cowboy who won't amount to a hill of beans.*

Matt had spent the past eight years riding his heart out—what was left of it, anyway. He'd shown the rodeo world that he was more than good enough for anyone, even Carlos Contreras's daughter. But he doubted his skill and a collection of silver buckles had done a damn thing to change the old man's opinion of him. Not that it mattered. That teen fling had ended a long time ago, validated by a phone that never rang.

"So what's the deal with Emily?"

George stopped rocking, leaned to the side and grinned. "She's a real sweetheart. Spunky, too. And she loves animals. You've met Sweetie Pie, the stray she talked me into keeping."

"Yeah, I met the dog. But that name doesn't suit a mutt who nearly chewed off my leg when I got out of my truck and started walking toward the door."

His uncle chuckled and folded his arms across his chest. "Animals love her, too. She really has a way with them, including the chickens. I can't tell those hens apart, but she can. Heck, she's named each one."

"That wasn't what I meant." Matt leaned toward his uncle and lowered his tone. "How *old* is she?"

"Seven or eight, I reckon."

A feeling of uneasiness began to niggle at Matt. Something about the timeline felt…wrong.

"Who's her father?" Matt asked, watching for the hint of a smile or a twinkle in his uncle's tired blue eyes, which seemed to be a lot livelier these days. But George had a talent for donning a good poker face when he wanted to.

"You'll have to ask Miranda," George said, the rocking chair creaking against the porch's wooden flooring.

"Didn't *you* ask?"

Uncle George shrugged and said, "You know me…"

"Right. You don't like to pry." Normally, Matt didn't, either, but that didn't mean he wouldn't do it as soon as he had the chance to get Miranda alone.

By the time Miranda drove within a mile of the Wexler Grange Hall, where the 4-H sheep group was gathering this afternoon, her nerves were still on edge and her mind scrambling to control her jumbled emotions.

When she'd come outside to tell Emily it was time to leave, she'd just about dropped to the ground when she'd spotted Matt at the Double G. Sure, she'd known that he could show up any day, but the rodeo circuit was in full swing, and George had told her that he rarely came home these days. So he was the last thing she'd expected to see this afternoon.

Hardly a day went by that she didn't think of her teenage love. The way she left. The guilt she felt. The secret she kept... She glanced in the rearview mirror at the eight-year-old secret that was sitting in the back-seat right now.

But it wasn't just the negative feelings that struck her. She often thought of the good things, too.

Wherever she went, indoors or out, the memories dogged her. Riding horses out by the swimming hole. Fishing for trout with a makeshift pole. Having a pic-nic on the trail. Eating a bowl of ice cream with two spoons. And sharing sweet stolen kisses—here, there and everywhere.

So when she first spotted Matt, she'd assumed her mind was playing tricks on her again, just as it al-ways did whenever she saw a shadow in the barn or heard George talking to someone only to find out it was his horse. After staying with George for the past two months, she'd begun to think Matt wouldn't come home while she and Emily were here. A champion bull rider like him would never do that while the rodeo sea-son was in full swing.

But she'd been wrong. The minute she realized the handsome cowboy wasn't an illusion—that she was actually looking at Matt in the flesh, that she was gaz-ing into those expressive green eyes—her heart took a flying leap, only to belly flop into her stomach, threat-ening to stir up the morning sickness that had stopped plaguing her six weeks ago.

Somehow, she'd managed to rally and find her voice. She just hoped it had sounded polite and unaffected.

"Mommmmy!" Emily called from the backseat, her

voice raised, her tone irritated. "I called your name *three* times. Aren't you *listening* to me?"

Obviously not. She'd been too busy daydreaming about the past... "I'm sorry, honey. I didn't mean to ignore you. What did you say?"

Emily blew out a dramatic sigh. "Can Janie come over after the meeting with us? And if her mom says it's okay, can she spend the night?"

Miranda glanced in the rearview mirror. Emily's eyes—the shape of them, not the color—were so much like Matt's that her heart squeezed. "No, honey. This isn't a good time to have a friend over."

"But it's Saturday, and we don't have school tomorrow. Why *can't* she?"

"Because we have a full house at the ranch already." And this evening, things would be awkward at best. But she wasn't about to reveal the real reason to her daughter. "Besides, Matt hasn't been home in a long time, and he's probably just passing through. So until I find out when he's leaving, I don't want to schedule a play date."

Surely, he'd be gone in the morning. Monday at the latest. But he was using a cane, so obviously he'd been injured. Had he come home to recuperate? If so, how long would that take?

Miranda broke eye contact with her daughter and studied the road ahead, watching for the entrance of the Wexler Grange Hall. But she couldn't keep her mind off Matt. He'd certainly grown up since she'd last seen him. His lanky nineteen-year-old body had filled out. His muscles were bulkier, his shoulders broader. He'd been sitting in a rocking chair on the porch, so it was hard to know for sure, but she suspected he'd grown a bit taller, too.

He wore his sandy-blond hair longer than she remembered—or maybe he just needed a haircut. Either way, she liked it.

An inch-long scar over his brow and a five o'clock shadow gave him a rugged edge, which, for some strange reason, added to the perfection of his face.

If he'd smiled or flashed his dimples, suggesting that he was glad to see her, her heart would have soared. Instead, he hadn't seemed the least bit happy that they'd crossed paths. Of course, she really couldn't blame him. She'd left him without saying goodbye, let alone offering an explanation.

She suspected he was long over her by now. She'd followed his rodeo success and heard rumors of the parade of buckle bunnies that followed him from city to city, hoping for a date—or whatever. From what she'd heard, Matt was even more footloose and reckless now than he used to be.

As she turned the car into the parking lot, a thought slammed into her like a deployed air bag, a possibility she hadn't considered.

What if his injury was permanent? What if he'd made a career change? What if he planned to stay on the Double G indefinitely? There was no way they could all live in the same house. And then there was the baby to think of...

Her first impulse was to go back to the ranch as soon as the 4-H meeting was over, pack their things and leave as quickly as possible. But she couldn't do that. Dodging uncomfortable situations had become a habit, one she was determined to break. Besides, a move like that was likely to crush her daughter.

Before shutting off the ignition, she took one last look in the rearview mirror and watched Emily wave at her friend Janie. The two girls planned to show their lambs at the county fair in a couple of weeks, and Miranda had never seen her daughter happier.

For Emily's sake, Miranda would deal with her feelings, as jumbled as they were. Besides, how hard could that be? She could handle the discomfort and awkwardness for a day or two.

But if Matt's stay stretched much longer, she'd be toast.

Chapter Two

Now that the dinner hour had arrived, and they'd gathered around the kitchen table, Matt and Miranda sat in silence. Once friends and lovers, now strangers at best.

She studied her plate, her glossy brown hair draping both sides of her face and making it difficult to read her expression. Matt bet she felt nearly as uneasy about their unexpected reunion as he did.

The past stretched between them like a frayed rubber band ready to snap. But he'd be damned if he'd be the first to speak.

"Emily," Uncle George said, "how'd your 4-H meeting go?"

"It was good. Miss Sadie, our leader, gave us the schedule for the county fair." The girl looked at Uncle

George with hopeful eyes. "You're going to come watch me, too. Right?"

"Honey," he said, "I wouldn't miss it for the world."

Matt swept his fork across his empty plate, stirring the leftover gravy. The fair was a couple of weeks away, so Miranda clearly planned to stick around for a while, and that left a bad taste in his mouth in spite of the fact that the damned meal she'd fixed tonight was delicious. He might have asked for seconds, but he wanted an excuse to leave the table.

Hell, as it was, he'd thought about going somewhere else to recover. At least until after the fair ended.

"Miranda," Uncle George said, patting his belly, "this pot roast is the best I've ever had."

She glanced up from her plate, which had held her interest for the past ten minutes, even though she hadn't taken more than a couple of bites. "Thank you. I'm glad you liked it." Then she returned her focus on her food.

Matt had planned to order plenty of meals for him and his uncle at Caroline's Diner since George's favorite kitchen appliance was a can opener. Now, he supposed, he wouldn't have to. That is, if he could deal with having Miranda around, stirring up the memories, both good and bad.

He supposed he ought to compliment her cooking and thank her, too. He might feel like shutting her out of his mind, like she'd done to him, but he hadn't forgotten his manners.

Before he could open his mouth, his uncle added, "I really lucked out when you came to visit, Miranda.

I'm eating better than ever, my check register finally balances and the ranch books are finally in order."

Matt dropped his fork on the plate. The thought of Miranda looking over the Double G's finances struck a ragged nerve—and for more reasons than one. George Grimes might be rough around the edges, but he had a soft heart, which sometimes got him into trouble when he put too much trust in the wrong person.

"You've got a good eye for detail, Miranda. You spotted things in the books that my accountant missed." George chuckled and crossed his arms. "I liked being able to point them out to him, too. I told him I had my very own CPA living right down the hall."

"I'm glad I could help," Miranda said, her voice almost too soft for Matt to hear.

Apparently, she'd become an accountant. That wasn't surprising. She'd been a good student when she'd been in high school, which was one reason her father had made such big plans for her.

So why was she here, when she could be helping her wealthy old man run one of the biggest berry farm operations in Texas?

Uncle George mentioned that she'd broken her engagement recently. Why? And who was the guy she'd planned to marry? Did he work for or with her father?

George said he hadn't quizzed her, which seemed doubtful since he'd always had a soft spot for her. He also had a way of getting people to open up and tell him things without the need to ask.

Either way, something wasn't right.

Matt glanced across the table at Emily, who was

stirring her carrots with a fork, trying to make it look like she'd actually eaten her veggies.

She was a cute kid, petite and dark-haired like her mother. He still wondered about her dad. And Matt was determined to learn more. Uncle George wasn't the only one in the family who was adept at ferreting out information indirectly.

"Emily," Matt said, first making eye contact with the girl before shifting his focus to her mother. "I think it's cool that you're in the 4-H. When I was in school, I knew a couple of kids who were in the 4-H, but they were older than you. Isn't there an age requirement?"

Miranda stiffened.

"I'm old enough," Emily said. "People sometimes think that I'm younger than I am because I'm small for my age, just like my mom. When I joined, the lady who signed me up wanted to put me in Cloverbuds, but that's for kids who are five to seven."

"So you just made it, huh?" Matt smiled at the child, then turned to her mother, whose lovely tanned complexion had paled.

"My birthday's on August third," Emily said, a grin dimpling her cheeks, her eyes bright. "I'm going to be nine."

It didn't take a CPA to do the math. Miranda left town nine years ago last October, which meant she must have been pregnant at the time. And if so, that meant… Matt's hand fisted and his eyes widened. *Emily was his.*

Matt knew. And he clearly wasn't happy about the secret Miranda had kept from him.

What little dinner she'd eaten tonight churned in her stomach, swirling and rising as if it had nowhere to go but out. Thankfully, she was able to hold it down. She placed her hand on her stomach, only to feel her growing baby bump. But this was one bout of nausea she couldn't blame on pregnancy. Her morning sickness had passed more than a month ago.

The frown on Matt's face and the crease in his brow suggested it was taking every bit of his self-control not to...

Not to *what*? Throw something across the room like Gavin once did when he'd come across a mess Emily had left in his family room?

This time, it was Miranda who'd made a complete mess of things. But Matt wasn't like the man she'd nearly married, the marital bullet she'd dodged.

At least he hadn't been like that in the past.

"Guess what." Emily speared a potato, but rather than lifting her fork, she smiled and directed her words at Matt. "Uncle George said I could have my birthday party here."

"He did, huh?" Matt's demeanor, so stiff and strained moments ago, seemed to soften ever so slightly. His expression did, too, although it was unreadable. "Is your dad coming?"

Miranda's lips parted. She wanted to respond for the child, but the words wouldn't form. The time had come to tell Emily about Matt and vice versa, but Miranda wasn't sure what to say in front of an audience. Especially this one.

"No, he can't. Because my dad died when I was a baby."

Matt shot a fiery look at Miranda. He didn't say a word, but he didn't have to. She saw the anger, the pain, the accusation in his eyes.

She wanted to defend herself, to tell him that Emily hadn't gotten that idea from her. She must have come to that conclusion on her own. Instead, she watched as Matt got to his feet, wincing as he reached first for his cane with one hand, then stacked his glass and silverware on his empty plate with the other.

As he started for the sink, Miranda pushed her chair away from the table and stood. "Don't worry about clearing the table or doing the dishes."

He glanced over his shoulder, his glare enough to weld her to the floor, the silent accusation enough to suck the air out of the room.

"I'll explain later," she said, her voice soft, wounded.

"Don't bother." He rinsed his plate and placed it in the sink. Then he left the kitchen, his cane tapping out his anger, disappointment and who knew what else in some kind of weird Morse code.

This was *so* not the way she'd intended to tell him,

She stole a peek at George, his craggy brow furrowed, his tired blue eyes fixed on Emily. She knew that the sweet but crotchety old man had put two and two together the minute he spotted Miranda and Emily standing on his front porch. He hadn't asked any questions or judged her. He'd merely stepped aside and welcomed her, his so-called niece, and her daughter into his cluttered but cozy home. Then he'd done his best to make them feel comfortable and told them they could stay as long as they wanted.

God bless that man to the moon and back.

"Emily." Miranda sucked in a deep fortifying breath, held it for a beat, then slowly and quietly let it out. "What makes you think your daddy died?"

Emily bit down on her bottom lip and scrunched her brow as if struggling with the answer. Finally, she lowered her voice and sheepishly said, "*Abuelito* told me."

Miranda winced. Her father had overstepped once again, although he hadn't done so in years. Not since Emily was a baby and Miranda had finally put him in his place. Or so she'd thought.

"Honey," Miranda said, "if you had questions about your father, you should have asked me."

"I would have, but *Abuelito* said you didn't like to talk about my father because it made you sad. So it was better if we forgot about him." Emily glanced down at her half-eaten meal, her long pigtails dangling toward her plate, and bit down on her bottom lip again. After a couple of beats, she looked up, eyes glistening with unshed tears. "I'm sorry for hurting your feelings."

Miranda's feelings were a mess, but that wasn't Emily's fault. "No, honey. You didn't hurt me. I'm just sad that you were afraid to talk to me about your father. I'd wondered why you didn't ask, and now I know. And no matter what anyone might say, you can always come to me with your questions."

"About my dad?"

"About anyone and anything." Miranda glanced

across the table at Uncle George. "Would you mind if I let you and Emily wash the dishes alone tonight?"

"Of course not." He blessed her with an affectionate smile, then turned to Emily and winked. "I know where your mama hid the chocolate chip cookies. And there's a brand new carton of vanilla ice cream in the freezer."

Miranda didn't usually let Emily eat sweets this close to bedtime, but she would gladly make an exception tonight. If the two dishwashers wolfed down a dozen cookies and a gallon of ice cream, she wouldn't complain.

After rinsing her plate in the sink, Miranda left the kitchen and headed down the hall until she reached Matt's bedroom. She held her breath, then knocked lightly on the door.

As footsteps, punctuated by the heart-wrenching tap of his cane, grew louder, her heart flipped and flopped in her chest like a trout on a hook, frantic to return to a safe, familiar environment. But she remained rooted to the floor, determined to face him, and waited for him to let her in.

When the door swung open, Matt stood before her, broad-shouldered, bare-chested and more muscular than she'd imagined. Her gaze drifted down his taut abs to his jeans, the top button undone. As much as she wanted to continue to take him in, to relish the manly changes that had taken place, she zeroed in on his eyes, once as clear and blue as the Texas sky, now a stormy winter gray.

He'd worn a similar expression the day her father

arrived at the Double G, raising hell and setting the breakup of their teenage romance in motion.

"I, uh…" She cleared her throat. "I need to talk to you. Can I come in?"

His only response was to step aside, cane in hand, and limp to his bed, where he took a seat on the edge of the mattress, leaving her to shut the door behind her.

Miranda scanned the room. The same rodeo posters and a schedule, long since outdated, still adorned the off-white walls. The maple chest of drawers and matching nightstand hadn't been moved. Even the familiar blue-plaid bedspread covered the double bed.

Too bad the angry cowboy glaring at her wasn't the same guy she used to know.

If only he were. She could have faced the *old* Matt in all honesty, without choosing her words, without holding back. She would have been able to fall into the comfort of his arms and tell him she was sorry for the delay in contacting him, for the hurt she'd unintentionally caused him—for the hurt she'd caused them both.

She leaned against the closed door. "I'm sorry. I should have told you about Emily sooner."

He rolled his eyes. "A *lot* sooner."

Right. "But I didn't tell her you'd died. Apparently, that was my father's doing."

Matt rolled his eyes. "I'm not surprised. Your dad never thought I was good enough for his little berry princess."

Talk about direct hits. She remained standing, clasped fists hanging at her side. "Just so you know, I didn't find out I was pregnant until after we broke up."

Matt crossed his arms and frowned. "You should have called me as soon as you knew."

"Yes, you're right. But if you remember, my dad limited my cell and telephone usage."

Matt chuffed at what sounded, even to her, like a lame excuse. "Your father didn't let you date, either. But you found a way around it."

True. She'd lied to her father, telling him time and again she was going to the library to meet with her study group. Her dishonesty hadn't sat well with her then—or now. But that was the only time she'd willfully deceived him. She had too much respect for him, for all he'd been through, all he'd accomplished in life. As a young boy, he'd gone to work with his father in the strawberry fields, learning the ins and outs of farming. When he grew up, he and his father purchased their own berry farm, then expanded it into an impressive operation with fields all over the state.

Matt slowly shook his head. "Your old man must have really blown a fuse when he found out you were going to have a baby, especially mine."

He certainly had. But going into detail about the early days of her pregnancy wasn't going to do anyone any good right now, so she cut to the chase. "He was smitten with Emily the very first minute he saw her and held her in his arms. And, for what it's worth, he's been a good grandfather to her."

Matt clicked his tongue. "Don't you think that lying to her about me ought to throw him out of the running for Grandfather of the Year?"

"If she'd asked me, I would have been honest. I

had no idea my father would tell her something like that. There was no reason for it. And it was way out of line."

"Sounds like you finally learned to stand up to him."

"I guess you could say that. But whenever I roll over, it's out of respect, not fear." She tucked a strand of hair behind her ear. "My dad was strict and expected a lot out of me, but he's a loving father and grandfather. I hope, one day, you'll be able to see that."

"Not gonna happen."

She supposed it wouldn't. Not for a long time, anyway.

"Does your old man know where you are?" Matt's harsh tone and narrowed gaze shot right to the heart of her. And so did his question.

She sucked in a deep breath, hoping the oxygen would clear her head and cleanse her soul, then slowly let it out. "Not exactly, but he knows we're safe. And that I'm staying with a friend."

Matt arched a brow.

"Okay," she admitted. "That could be considered a lie of omission. But believe it or not, I've always meant well and wanted the best for everyone involved."

So why had she begun to feel like the villainess in this mess?

While tempted to make her way to the edge of Matt's bed and sit beside him, she realized she'd have to earn the intimacy of his friendship. So she stood her ground and crossed her own arms. "I don't blame you for being angry at my dad—and not just because he told Emily you were dead. When we were kids, you saw a bad side of him."

"I don't care about your old man or the past. What's done is done."

"Okay, but I'd like to make things right."

Matt's gaze softened slightly, but not enough for her to make any assumptions or to move toward him.

"Is that why you came to the Double G?" he asked.

Not really. And not at first. But the compulsion to finally make things right was why she was standing in his room now. "Yes, that's pretty much why I'm here."

He nodded, then glanced at the cane that rested within reach on the edge of the mattress where he sat.

She placed her hand on her womb, caressing the small baby bump that she wouldn't be able to hide much longer with blousy tops and dresses. In fact, she'd suspected George already knew she was pregnant, since he was pretty observant. Not that he'd say anything.

When Matt looked up, she let her hand drop to her side and offered him a shy smile. "Like I said, I'm sorry. I should have told you that you were a father."

"You've got that right."

"I've made mistakes, but Emily isn't one of them. She's a great kid. So for now, let's focus on her."

"All right." Matt uncrossed his arms and raked a hand through his hair. "But just for the record, I would've done anything in my power to take care of you and Emily."

"I know." And that's why she'd walked away from him. Matt would have stood up to her father, challenged his threat, only to be knocked to his knees—and worse.

No, leaving town and cutting all ties with Matt was the only thing she could've done to protect him.

As she stood in the room where their daughter was conceived, as she studied the only man she'd ever loved, the memories crept up on her, the old feelings, too.

When she'd been sixteen, there'd been something about the fun-loving nineteen-year-old cowboy that had drawn her attention. And whatever it was continued to tug at her now. But she shook it off. Too many years had passed, too many tears had been shed.

Besides, an unwed, single mother who was expecting another man's baby wouldn't stand a chance with a champion bull rider who had his choice of pretty cowgirls. And she'd best not forget that.

"Aw, hell," Matt said, as he ran a hand through his hair again and blew out a weary sigh. "Maybe you did Emily a favor by leaving when you did. Who knows what kind of father I would have made back then. Or even now."

At that, Miranda longed to cross the room and take his hands in hers. The Matt she used to know would have been a great dad. And something told her the new Matt would be, too.

But he was a rodeo star now, with all the good and bad that came with it. So if he wanted to be a part of Emily's life, what kind of role model would he be?

But that was beside the point. He deserved a chance to know his daughter.

"Matt," she said, "I think you're going to be an awesome father, if you want to be. Either way, I'm going to talk to Emily and tell her that her *abuelito* was mistaken, that her father is very much alive."

"So you're going to tell her that I'm her father?"

"Yes." She eyed him carefully. "Unless you'd rather I didn't."

He didn't respond right away. Was the decision that hard for him to make?

When he glanced up, his gaze seemed to zero in on hers. But this time, it wasn't in anger. "I'd like to be there when you tell her. If that's okay."

She blew out a breath she hadn't realized she'd been holding. "Of course. I think that would be best."

For the first time since Matt arrived home, his expression grew familiar. Not completely, but enough to remind her of the old Matt and to stir up old feelings. But she'd better keep her wits about her—and her emotions in check.

"When should we tell her?" he asked.

"Whenever you're ready."

He nodded pensively. "Tomorrow, I guess."

"Okay then." She managed a smile. "I'll see you at breakfast."

Then she turned and let herself out of his room. The hard part was over.

Or was it?

It was one thing to think they'd be able to co-parent their daughter. But what about a child that wasn't his? The future and the possible so-called family dynamics were worrisome at best.

And what about those sexy buckle bunnies who thought Max was God's gift to womanhood?

No way could Miranda ever compete with them, especially as her pregnancy advanced, as new stretch marks developed…

She swore under her breath. Now that she'd opened up a Pandora's box of emotion—real or imagined—she had no idea how much her heart or her ego could bear.

Chapter Three

Last night, after talking to Matt, Miranda had turned in early, emotionally exhausted. But she'd barely slept a wink. Memories—both the good and the bad, happy and sad—plagued her, making it impossible for her to unwind.

When she finally dozed off, her dreams refused to let her rest.

Sirens and flashing lights.

The snap of handcuffs.

A gavel banging down. Again and again.

A cell door clanging shut.

Knees hitting the courtroom floor. A sobbing voice screaming, No!

Miranda shot up, her heart racing, her brow damp from perspiration. She'd had that nightmare before, but it hadn't been so real.

Once her pulse slowed to normal and her eyes adjusted to the predawn darkness, she threw off the covers, got out of bed and padded to the bathroom, where she washed her face, brushed her hair and dressed for the day. She chose the maternity jeans and a blousy pink T-shirt she'd purchased in town last week, after her last obstetrical appointment.

Most pregnant women liked showing off their baby bumps, but Miranda wasn't one of them. Not now. Not yet.

It wasn't that she didn't want the baby—a little boy she planned to name after her father, which might soften the blow when she told him she was expecting. It's just that she hadn't wanted the news to leak out. If Gavin learned that she was having his son, he might want shared custody.

As she headed for the kitchen, she relished the aroma of fresh-brewed coffee and ham sizzling in a pan.

George stood in front of the stove, while Emily—her hair pulled into an off-centered ponytail and adorned with a red ribbon—sat on the counter next to him and chattered away about what she and Sweetie Pie planned to do today.

"Good morning," Miranda said. "You two are awake earlier than usual."

"Emily usually gets up first," George said, "but I figured I'd better get busy this morning and fix a hearty breakfast. Matt's looking a little puny."

He'd looked pretty darn healthy last night when he'd answered the bedroom door bare-chested.

George adjusted the flame under the blackened,

cast-iron skillet, then turned to Miranda with a smile. "I found my mother's old recipe box last night. I won't have much use for it, but I thought you might like to... look it over. She was one heck of a cook."

"I'd love to see her recipes. And if there's a special meal or dish you'd like me to make, I'd be happy to give it a try."

George laughed. "I'd hoped you'd say that." Then he nodded toward the teapot. "The whistle isn't blowing yet, but the water should be ready. How 'bout I pour you a cup?"

"Thanks. That would be nice." Miranda made her way to the pantry and retrieved a box of herbal tea bags. She'd no more than turned around when Matt entered the kitchen, fresh from the shower and looking more handsome than ever.

He gave her a distracted nod, then using his cane, limped to the coffee maker and filled a cup to the brim.

Miranda placed a hand on her baby bump, which seemed to have doubled in size overnight. She supposed that was to be expected, now that she was approaching her fifth month. She hadn't given the maternal habit much thought before, but she'd better be careful not to draw any undue attention to her condition. So she quickly removed her hand and stole a glance at Matt, who was watching her over the rim of his coffee mug, his brow furrowed.

Her cheeks warmed, and her heart thumped. Did he suspect...?

Not that it mattered. He'd find out soon enough.

She took the cup of hot water George had poured

for her and carried it to the scarred antique table and took a seat.

While her tea steeped, neither she nor Matt said a word. But she imagined him saying, *Apparently, you have a habit of running away from your baby daddies.*

Just the thought of him having a reaction like that struck a hard blow, a low one. But then again, she couldn't blame him for being angry, resentful. Judgmental.

And he didn't even have to say anything to her. As it was, she felt guilty enough, which was why she wasn't looking forward to facing her father and announcing she was, once again, unmarried and pregnant.

Nor was she ready to admit to Matt that she was having another man's baby.

As Matt took his first sip of coffee, he studied Miranda, who looked a little pale, if not green around the gills. But so what? She deserved to feel guilty. She'd kept his daughter away from him for years.

Carlos Contreras, the Texas berry king, had made it perfectly clear that, at least in his opinion, Matt wasn't good enough for his precious daughter. And apparently, Princess Miranda felt the same way.

Miranda's deceit and the unfairness of it all rose up like an index finger and poked at his chest, jabbing at an old wound that, apparently, hadn't healed. It hurt like hell to know he'd been shut out of a family once again.

Last night, after Miranda came to his bedroom and admitted that Emily was his, a secret she'd kept for nine years, Matt hadn't been able to sleep a wink. He'd even popped a couple of the pain pills the doctor had prescribed and he rarely used. But even that hadn't helped. Not when the real pain had very little to do with his knee.

He kept rehashing old conversations he'd put to rest years ago, like the last one he and Miranda had had.

Let's take a break for a little while, Miranda had said. *I'll call you when Daddy's cooled down and had a chance to think things over.*

But that call never came.

Matt leaned his left hip against the cupboard under the kitchen counter, taking the weight off his left knee. He lifted his mug, but didn't take a drink. Instead, he gazed at Miranda. She'd grown prettier with each passing year. Even in a pair of loose-fitting blue jeans and a baggy T-shirt, she was a knockout.

Her waist, once flat and perfect, had a paunch now. He'd noticed it before and had assumed it was to be expected after having a baby. That is, until she'd caught him watching her a few moments ago. An uneasy expression crossed her face, and the hand that had been resting on her rounded stomach dropped to her side.

Was she pregnant?

She might be, but he'd never ask.

All he knew was what Uncle George had told him yesterday. She'd recently ended a relationship and needed time to think.

She sure looked pensive this morning, as she stirred a teaspoon in her cup long after any sugar had dissolved.

What was she thinking about? Whether she should reconcile with her ex?

Or had she deserted another expectant father, leaving him completely unaware of her pregnancy? That is, if Matt's suspicion was right.

He glanced at his uncle, who was cracking eggs into the skillet he'd used to fry ham. Did he know more about Miranda's condition, her situation, than he'd let on?

He had to, since he'd clearly taken her under his wing, going so far as to provide housing and food for her and Emily, not to mention hosting a menagerie.

Then again, his uncle had always liked Miranda. *That lil' gal has a sweet way about her, Matt. She's smart and funny, too. If I'd had a daughter, I'd want her to be just like her.*

And Miranda had felt the same way about Uncle George, too. Or so she'd said.

Matt turned his focus to Emily, who kept glancing out the kitchen window, then at the clock on the microwave.

She was a cute kid. He couldn't say that she looked like him, other than maybe the shape of her eyes—but not the color. Still, he didn't doubt that he was her father. The only doubt he actually had was whether he could be the kind of dad she deserved.

The dog padded through the kitchen and into the service porch. It whined a couple of times and scratched at the back door. Since no one else seemed to notice, Matt reached for his cane and headed to the service porch to let it out.

"No!" Emily jumped down from her perch on the counter, where she'd been watching George fry eggs, and ran to the door, grabbing the dog by the collar before it could go outside to pee.

What the hell?

"Sweetie Pie can't go outside until the sun comes up," Emily said, her voice coming out in short frantic huffs. "Or else she'll chase that skunk again. And she always gets sprayed and stinky."

"Always?" Matt asked. "How many times has she gotten sprayed?"

"Four." Emily knelt before the dog, cupped her furry face and made kissy sounds. "Wait a little bit longer, Sweetie Pie. I'll open the door as soon as it gets light and after that ornery ol' skunk goes to sleep."

A grin tugged at Matt's lip, and he slowly shook his head. "You'd think that getting a snout full of *Eau de Stink* more than twice would have convinced her to try chasing another critter."

Emily looked up at him, her sweet smile reaching into his chest and touching something soft and tender.

"You got that right," George called out from the kitchen. "Good ol' Lulu Belle was a smart dog, but Sweetie Pie is a slow learner."

Back in the day, Matt had been one, too. You'd think that, after his widowed dad had remarried and chosen his stepbrother over him, Matt would have known better than to harbor thoughts of family, hearth and home. But then he'd met Miranda, and she'd stomped on his wounded heart, leaving him feeling abandoned yet again.

Fortunately, Matt didn't need to get sprayed a third time before learning his lesson.

While refilling his cup, he studied his daughter. What would she say when she learned that Matt was her father?

And when would they tell her?

He stole a glance at Miranda, who hadn't said much of anything, even when she wasn't sipping from her fancy china teacup that used to belong to George's mother. He had no idea what she planned to do with her life. Her decisions were none of his business.

That is, unless they affected Emily. And if he didn't agree with the choices Miranda made—*or any her father made*, Matt wasn't about to sit on the sidelines and let them dictate his daughter's life. And if they thought they could shut him out, like they'd done so far, there'd be hell to pay.

By the time breakfast was on the table, the sun had risen and Sweetie Pie had gone outside to take care of her doggy business and to go in search of her black-and-white-striped nemesis.

None of the adults spoke while they ate their fill of ham and scrambled eggs, but Emily chattered away. And Matt hung on her every word.

As she chomped on a piece of ham, her eyes brightened. "Guess what? You know Suzy Reinquist, the new girl who brought an arrowhead to school for show-and-tell? She has six toes on each foot."

"Emily," Matilda said, "please don't talk with your mouth full."

The child swallowed, chased it down with a sip of orange juice and continued her story. "I didn't believe

Suzy when she told us, 'cause that would make twelve toes, and everyone knows you only have ten. But then she took off her shoes and socks so we could count them. And sure enough…"

Even if Emily weren't his daughter, Matt would have enjoyed listening to her. She had a unique way of seeing the world. And he liked hearing about her interests and friends.

Emily took another swig of juice. "I can't wait for spring break to get over. I love school. I like Mrs. Crowley, too. But she wasn't at school on Friday. We had a substitute. I forget her name, but she's kind of old and has a little bald spot on the back of her head. I didn't notice it until she turned around to write our math assignment on the board."

Before the girl could share another story, Uncle George pushed his chair away from the table. "You'll have to excuse me. The ranch hands will be arriving soon, and I need to get to work."

"Me, too." Emily downed the rest of her OJ, then got to her feet. "The chickens laid three eggs yesterday. I wonder how many I'll find today."

"Honey, wait a minute." Miranda glanced at Matt, then back at their daughter. "I have something I need to talk to you about."

"Am I in trouble again?" Emily placed her hands on her hips and frowned.

"No, you're not in trouble," Miranda said.

"Then can we wait until I check on Dumpling? The other chickens kept pecking at her yesterday."

Miranda rested her forearms on the table and leaned

forward. "No, honey. I've already waited too long to tell you."

Emily plopped back into her seat. "What is it?"

Miranda glanced at Matt, then focused on their daughter. "Your *abuelito* was wrong when he told you that your father died."

Emily cocked her head and furrowed her brow. "You mean my father *isn't* dead?"

"No. In fact, he didn't even know about you until recently."

Emily crossed her arms, leaned back in her seat and frowned. "Does *Abuelito* know that?"

Miranda nodded.

Emily's eyes widened. "You mean he *lied* to me?"

"Yes." Miranda drew in a deep breath, then slowly let it out. "I'm afraid he did."

Emily remained silent for a beat, then she rolled her eyes. "That *really* makes me mad. He told me to always tell the truth, no matter how hard it is. But then *he* didn't."

"I'm sorry," Miranda said. "That was wrong of him."

To say the least. Matt continued to watch the conversation unfold, his interest in his daughter growing. The kid had spunk. He liked that.

"I'm going to let your grandfather know how I feel, how we both feel about him lying to you the next time I see him."

That didn't seem to appease the child. But hell, why should it?

"Just so you know," Miranda added, "I'd planned

to tell you about your father when you asked me about him. But I shouldn't have waited."

"So where *is* my dad? And how come he didn't know about me? If he did, maybe he would have come to see me or called or…something." Emily shook her head, her ponytail swishing from side to side. "Does he even know when my birthday is?"

"It's August the third," Matt said. "And I'm going to try my best to be with you on that day from now on."

Emily's lips parted, and when she turned to him, her eyes widened in disbelief. "*You?* You're my dad?"

Damn. Did the kid not approve of him, either? Grave Digger had done a real number on Matt's body when he stomped on him, casting a shadow on all he'd accomplished, all the buckles he'd won. But Miranda's rejection, her father's disapproval and now Emily's reaction crushed him in a way that blasted bull hadn't.

"Yes," Matt said. "I'm your dad."

Emily eyed him carefully, taking in the news that had thrown him for a loop when he'd first heard it last night.

He held his breath as he awaited her response. For some reason, her assessment of him concerned him more than that of any high school principal, police officer or courtroom judge.

The crease in the girl's brow deepened, then she looked down at her empty plate, studying the smears of ham drippings as if they were tea leaves.

When she finally looked up, her expression eased into one of cautious curiosity. "Why didn't you know about me? Didn't you ever want a little girl?"

He could throw her mother and grandfather under the

bus, but that might make things even worse. "I'm here now. And I'm glad I finally got to meet my daughter."

She seemed to chew on that for a beat, then asked, "Does that mean you're coming to my birthday party?"

"You bet I will. I'll even bring a present. What would you like?"

She shrugged. "I don't need anything."

"Not even a bicycle?"

At that, she smiled. "I have a pony, remember?"

"Right. And you're going to be a cowgirl when you grow up."

"Yep. But I might be a veterinarian. That's a doctor for animals." She glanced at her mother. "Can I go now?"

That was it? She'd moved on to gathering eggs rather than locking in a birthday present? Hell, he was tempted to bring her nine of them, one for each birthday he'd missed.

When Miranda nodded, Emily turned to Matt and smiled. "You wanna go with me to get the eggs?"

A farm chore had never sounded so appealing. "I'd like that." In fact, he liked it a lot.

She got up from her chair, then walked out to the service porch. Matt glanced at Miranda, assuming she'd want to join them, but she shook her head and waved him off, allowing him some privacy when meeting his daughter for the first time.

He appreciated that, even though his anger and resentment hadn't diminished too much. Maybe, in time, he'd find it easier to forgive her than he'd thought.

As he followed Emily outside, she turned and

blessed him with a dimpled smile. "Want me to show you my pony and my lamb before we get the eggs?"

"Absolutely."

As they walked toward the corral, she pointed to his cane. "Why are you limping?"

"I tried to ride an ornery bull, but he didn't like it. So he threw me off and stepped on me."

She stopped in her tracks and turned to face him. "That wasn't very smart. You do know that bulls are dangerous, right?"

"Yeah. I know."

"You're lucky he didn't poke you with his horns and stomp you to death. And then I wouldn't have got to meet you at all." She lifted her index finger and wagged it at him, a gesture that touched his heart. "So don't do it again, okay? I just found you and don't want you to get hurt or die."

He couldn't help chuckling at her admonition. As much as he'd have liked to respect her wishes, he couldn't give up the rodeo. If he wasn't a champion bull rider, who was he? But she'd given him something to think about.

When they reached the corral, where the black-and-white Shetland pony munched on alfalfa that George must have fed him this morning, Emily pointed to the little gelding. "That's Oreo. Do you know why we call him that?"

"Let me guess." A grin stretched across Matt's face. "Because he eats cookies?"

She laughed. "No, silly. Because he looks like one. An Oreo cookie. Get it?"

"Aw. Yes. That's very clever. Did you name him?"

"No, the people who owned him before Uncle George bought him for me called him that. But I got to name Bob and the chickens."

"Is Bob the lamb?"

"Yep."

"Maybe you should have called him Baaaab?"

"You're funny!" Her smile darn near turned him inside out.

He'd always liked to make his friends laugh—and he did so often. But the pleasure he'd taken at seeing their happy adult faces paled in comparison to hearing the lilt of Emily's sweet laugh and seeing the bright-eyed smile that dimpled her cheeks.

"Come on," she said. "I want you to meet him. And you can watch me feed him."

"Uncle George doesn't do that for you?"

"Oh, no! I take care of Bob all by myself. I feed him and give him water and bathe him and everything. I'm going to show him at the fair. He's very cool, and he likes going for walks. He's my best friend. But don't tell Sweetie Pie."

A grin tugged at Matt's lips, although he tried to hide it. Implying that Emily might not be pulling her weight when it came to the ranch chores seemed to have horrified her, which filled him with a bit of pride. He would have felt the same way, when he'd first moved onto the Double G as a young teen.

After feeding Bob, Emily reached into her back pocket, whipped out a pink Western bandana and tied it to the lamb's neck. Then she led Matt to the chicken coop and pointed out each one. "That's Dumpling. And the brown and black one is Nuggets. Pot Pie is behind the coop and the one drinking water is Casserole."

"They're all named after chicken dishes, huh? Does that mean you're going to eat them?"

"No!" Her once happy expression morphed into one that was just as horrified as the last. "They're my friends. Besides, they give us eggs."

The little girl—*his* little girl—was a hoot. Smart as a whip, spunky and pretty to boot. And in spite of feeling awkward around her earlier, she'd managed to put him at ease.

Not that he expected to take to fatherhood the way he'd taken to riding a horse or roping cattle, but taking on a paternal role didn't seem nearly as scary as it had when he first learned he had a child.

Emily unlatched the door to the coop and went inside to check for eggs, but came back empty-handed.

"Looks like the girls aren't doing their jobs."

Emily shrugged. "Sometimes they don't lay them until later. That's why I check for eggs all the time."

After shutting the wired door and hooking the latch, she brushed her hands on her denim-clad thighs. When she looked up, her eyes sparkled. "You know what? I'm really going to like having a daddy."

Something deep in his heart warmed at the comment, the acceptance.

"I'm glad to hear that," he said. "I'm going to like having a daughter." Surprisingly, those words rang true.

He couldn't ask for more in a child, other than wishing he'd known about her when she'd been a baby. But there wasn't anything he could do about that now.

They did have today, and each one after this. Yet while he could envision himself bonding with Emily, he wasn't so sure how he felt about her mother.

Emily stopped and gazed up at him. "You don't believe in hitting kids, do you?"

He hadn't seen that question coming. "No, I don't."

"Good. That's why I don't like Gavin."

Matt's gut twisted into a knot, his senses on high alert, and he braced himself for her answer. "Who's Gavin?"

"The guy my mom was going to marry. I'm glad she didn't. Gavin wouldn't be a good daddy."

Matt stiffened. "Why do you say that?"

"Because he's a yeller. And a hitter."

The knot in his gut was nothing compared to the clench of his fists. "Did he hit you or your mom?"

"Only me. And he made my nose bleed."

A chill ran through Matt's veins. How dare that man hit a child. Especially *this* child.

"I really wanted to be a flower girl," Emily added. "And I really liked the dress I was going to wear. But not if we married Gavin."

"Is that why your mom left him?"

Emily nodded. "Yep. Because he hit me for crying when I had an earache."

Matt's gut clenched. What kind of monster had Miranda planned to marry?

"*Abuelito*, my grandfather, was mad, too," Emily added.

"At Gavin?"

"No. At my mom. Because he had to pay a whole lot of money for the wedding, even though no one went to it."

That figured. A snide comment formed on the tip of Matt's tongue, but he clamped his mouth shut until the urge to blurt it out passed.

"So where did your mom meet Gavin?" he asked.

"At *Abuelito's* Christmas party."

Matt glanced over his shoulder at the house, wondering if Miranda had come out to the porch to see how he and Emily were doing. He supposed he should be grateful that she'd allowed them to have this precious time alone. But he no longer wanted time with his daughter. He now wanted to get the straight scoop from Miranda.

No doubt she had made the right decision to leave. Had she pressed charges? She certainly should have. Questions began to pop up in his mind, one after another.

Why had it taken her so long to see through Gavin?

And how had she gotten involved with a guy like that in the first place?

As soon as Emily was out of earshot, Matt intended to learn the answer to all his questions. And in this case, he wouldn't be the least bit reluctant to pry.

Chapter Four

Miranda wanted nothing more than to go outside with Matt and Emily, to listen to their conversation and to watch their facial expressions, but she'd been reluctant to ask if she could join them. She'd kept Emily to herself for so long that it only seemed fair to let Matt have some time with their daughter without her hovering nearby.

But that didn't mean she'd go so far as to hole up in the home office, balancing the checkbook and paying the monthly bills. Instead, she brought her work to the kitchen and sat close to the back door, where she expected them to reenter the house after Emily showed Matt around the ranch and introduced him to her barnyard *friends*.

And while she had plenty to keep her busy, she

found it difficult to focus on anything other than the tour going on outside, on the possible conversations unfolding between Emily and her father.

Finally, the back door creaked open, and her heart dropped with a thud. For a moment, she froze like a possum in the headlights of an oncoming big rig.

As approaching footsteps sounded, her pulse throbbed harder and more intense with each tap of a cane. She turned away from the laptop screen, as if she'd been completely taken aback by Matt's and her daughter's entrance, and her eyes widened as if to say, *Oh. It's you.*

"We're back!" Emily's dimpled grin, the bounce in her step and the swish of her ponytail suggested the tour had gone well. On the other hand, Matt's expression was a little too solemn for a man who'd enjoyed his time outdoors with their daughter.

"Mom," Emily said, "can I ride Oreo? I wanna show my dad how I can saddle and bridle her all by myself."

Miranda arched a brow at Matt. "Are you okay with that?"

"Sure." He made his way toward the kitchen table, his very presence sucking the air from the room.

He might have just agreed to go back out to the corral with Emily, but Miranda wasn't convinced that he was actually *okay* with it. But then again, maybe his knee was bothering him. And if so, he'd probably appreciate having some time to sit down for a while and take the weight off his bad leg.

"All right," Miranda told their eager daughter. "You can ride your pony, but not until you clean your room."

"Aw, man." Emily let out a dramatic pout that lasted all of two beats, then she turned to Matt. "Will you wait? It won't take me very long."

"I'll be here."

As the child dashed off, Matt took a seat across from her and leaned his cane against the wall.

"How did it go?" she asked.

"It went great." He stretched out his bad leg, leaned back in his chair and zeroed in on her with a piercing gaze. "That is, until Emily told me that guy you were going to marry hit her and bloodied her nose."

Wow. Nothing like cutting right to the chase. But Miranda couldn't blame him. She'd been furious, shaken to the core, when she'd learned what Gavin had done. Not only had she been angry with him, she'd blamed herself for not seeing the signs sooner.

"I was appalled, too," she said. "That's why I left him."

Silence stretched between them, slowly sucking the air from the room, until Matt said, "Dammit, Miranda. What'd you ever see in a guy who'd do something like that?"

"I've asked myself that a hundred times. But he was sweet at first. We met at the company Christmas party a year before last."

"So he was a charmer, huh? Swept you off your feet?"

"In a way." In truth, the only one who'd ever swept her off her feet had been Matt, when he'd been in his senior year and she'd transferred to his high school as a sophomore. The first time she'd spotted him, looked into those bright blue eyes and saw that sweet but cocky grin, she'd been moonstruck.

But there was no point in reminding him how they'd once felt about each other. Matt had clearly moved on, and so had she.

"It might surprise you," she said, "to know that Gavin was wearing a Santa Claus suit that night and passing out candy canes."

Matt rolled his eyes. "Ho, ho, ho."

She understood his anger, his frustration, his concern, but before she could respond, Emily returned to the kitchen, wearing a bright-eyed smile, as well as the new boots and child-size black cowboy hat George had surprised her with last week. But Miranda knew her daughter's tricks when it came to having a higher priority than a tidy room.

"You know," Miranda said, "I'm going to look in the closet and under the bed. So you might want to double check and make sure you did a good job picking up."

Emily folded her arms across her chest and shifted her weight to one foot. "Can't I do that *after* I ride Oreo?"

"I'm afraid not. And when you're finished, please bring your hamper to the service porch so I can wash your clothes."

Emily let out an exasperated sigh, then turned to Matt. "I'll be back. It'll just be a few more minutes."

"I'm not going anywhere," he said.

After Emily skipped out of the kitchen, Matt zeroed in on Miranda again, the intensity of his gaze threatening to undo her. "I hate bullies. Always have, always will. And if that guy was standing here right now, I'd be tempted to take a couple of swings at him for hitting a child."

She'd watched him stand up for the underdog on quite a few occasions, one of which had landed him in detention. He'd been a real hero back then. Still was, she suspected.

Matt slowly shook his head. "I don't understand, Miranda. There had to have been signs that he had a mean streak."

"Not at first. But I have to admit a few red flags popped up during the last six weeks we were together."

"Like what?"

She felt compelled to tell him it wasn't any of his business, but then again, she wanted to assure him that she'd never willingly put her child in jeopardy. "Gavin began drinking more in the evenings and blamed it on stress at work. He'd always liked his scotch, but it became a nightly habit. And whenever he'd had too much, which seemed to be most nights, he'd snap at whoever he was talking to—a client on the telephone, me… Emily. It was then that I realized he had a temper, although I'd never realized he'd become physically violent."

For the first time since Matt arrived on the Double G, his expression softened, and he began to remind her of the old Matt, the one who'd been her best friend.

"Then why didn't you break up with him six weeks sooner?"

The *real* reason? She hated to admit it, but she hadn't wanted to disappoint Gavin's mother or her fa-

ther. They'd both been over the moon about the marriage. Her dad considered it a business merger of sorts
He'd tried for years to convince Gavin's father to invest
in a farming venture in Mexico, and their partnership
was finally coming together. Then there was Gavin's
mom, who considered her only child's wedding to be a
huge social event, one she'd been dreaming of since the
day he was born. And since the woman was recovering from a recent mastectomy, Miranda hadn't wanted
to disappoint her or create any additional stress on her
health. But none of that mattered the day she learned
Gavin had not only hit Emily, but that it hadn't been
the first time.

"I wish I had canceled the wedding sooner," she
said. "And for more reasons than one."

Matt remained silent, his eyes holding judgment.

Miranda took in a deep, fortifying breath, then
slowly let it out. "There were only about seventy-five
people on the original invitation list, which was about
all my dad's backyard could hold. But before I could
blink, that number quadrupled, and we needed a bigger venue. So my dad put down a huge non-refundable
deposit so we could hold it at a country club." And not
just any club, but the nicest and most exclusive in San
Antonio.

Matt leaned forward and rested his forearms—
stronger, bulkier than she remembered—on the table.
"Sounds like things got way out of hand."

"To say the least." Gavin's mother had gotten so
involved in planning the ceremony and reception that
she'd hardly talked or thought about anything else. On

the upside, it had taken her mind off her health issues and pulled her out of the resulting depression that followed her surgery.

Miranda didn't dare mention the flowers they'd ordered from Europe or the designer gown that had been altered. And who knew what they'd done with the white doves Gavin's mother had insisted would be a nice touch.

"I'll admit that I should have put my foot down a lot sooner," Miranda said, "but the closer it got to Valentine's Day, the worse I felt about calling it off."

"I'm glad you finally did."

Was he? She tried to read into his words, his expression, then she shook it off. Her curiosity was sure to lead her down a path she had no business taking. Not after all this time.

She glanced down at the table, where her clasped hands rested, then she risked a glance at Matt. His gaze locked on hers, and she spotted something other than anger in his eyes. Sympathy? Concern?

For a moment, he was the old Matt who'd swept her off her feet in high school. And while they'd never be lovers again, maybe, just maybe they could be friends.

"Did Gavin ever hit *you*?" he asked, as if nothing had changed, as if he still had her back. "Did he threaten you in any way?"

"No. He raised his voice a couple of times. But he never got physical with me."

"But given time," Matt said, "he probably would have. And he definitely would have hurt Emily again. Did you press charges against him?"

"I seriously thought about it, but my dad talked me out of it."

The crease in Matt's brow deepened, and any sign of sympathy faded from his eyes. "Are you *kidding*? Why in the hell would he talk you out of it? And worse, why would you let him?"

"When I told my dad why I'd broken our engagement, he completely understood. And he was angry at Gavin, too. But Gavin's father is one of the investors in a joint farming venture, a big one, and my dad didn't want to complicate matters. I would have argued with him, but I'd already broken our engagement, and since I'd left town, I knew Emily was safe."

Matt flinched, and his eye twitched. She wasn't sure what he was thinking—or feeling—but she reached out and placed her hand on his forearm, a bold move she hadn't planned, one she wasn't sure how to take back.

"Don't worry, Matt. When I left Gavin, it was for good. And if he ever came around and tried to talk to me, I wouldn't hesitate to file a restraining order or press charges."

Concern swept across Matt's brow once more, and she was tempted to stroke his arm rather than hold her hand in place. But she didn't.

"Do you *expect* him to come after you?" he asked.

"Maybe." She wouldn't put it past him. He'd called several times after she left, and when his apologies and pleas became demands, she blocked his number. "But he'd have to find me first. And no one knows I'm here."

The muscles in his forearm flexed, and she removed her hand, breaking the physical connection she had no right to make. She fingered the scarred surface of the antique kitchen table instead.

"No one?" His head tilted slightly.

She slowly shook her head. "Not even my dad. All I told him was that I needed to spend some time away from San Antonio and the office, but I didn't tell him where I was staying."

Matt rolled his eyes and let out a humph. "He'd burst an artery if he knew you were here."

"Probably. At first. But he'd get over it." Eventually, anyway.

"So what are you waiting for?"

"I don't want to tell him until I have a solid plan for the future." A future that now included Gavin's baby, something else her father didn't know. Yet. "But my plans are coming together."

"So what's your next move?"

"Finding a job and a place to live. I can't stay on the Double G forever, and I don't want to go back to my condo in San Antonio." Only trouble was, she couldn't put any of that into motion until after the baby was born.

She'd also have to level with her father and tell him where she was staying. She'd then have to tell him she was pregnant and that he was going to be a grandfather again, which would both set him off and please him. But she'd had enough confessions for one day. She'd call him tomorrow.

"So..." She took another deep breath and slowly let it out. "How did things go when you went outside with Emily? How are you feeling about...?"

"Instant fatherhood?" He shrugged. "That's left to be seen. But Emily is a great kid. You've done a good job with her."

"Thanks."

His gaze locked on hers, stirring old memories, old feelings. "I wish I'd known her sooner."

"Believe it or not, so do I."

He studied her for a couple of beats, as if judging her sincerity. But she meant those words from the bottom of her heart. If she could go back in time and make other decisions, handle things differently than she had, she would. But other than telling Matt about Emily sooner, she would still make the same choices she'd made before. And for the same reasons.

"All done!" Emily called out, as she skipped into the kitchen.

Miranda's hand slipped from the tabletop to her baby bump. She usually found comfort in caressing her little one, but it didn't seem to help today. Instead, it only served to remind her that life went on.

And that there were no do-overs.

When Matt first entered the kitchen after his tour of Emily's barnyard menagerie, he'd been angry and resentful, along with a few other emotions he couldn't put his finger on, all of them equally negative. But after confronting Miranda, after gazing into her pretty brown eyes and feeling her gentle touch, he'd begun to sympathize. In fact, he'd begun to soften so much toward her that he was thankful for an interruption, even if it was the pitter-patter of little cowboy boots.

Matt turned away from Miranda, breaking whatever fragile tie they'd just had, and focused on their daughter. With her olive complexion, dark brown hair and hazel eyes, Emily looked a lot like her mother.

Lucky kid. Miranda had been a beautiful teenager, and she was even more so now. The years had been damn good to her. Or maybe he'd just forgotten how attractive she was.

Emily took after him, too, he supposed—the shape of her nose, the dimples in her cheeks. Not to mention the occasional mischievous spark that lit her eyes.

"I've got my room all cleaned up now," Emily said, as she entered the kitchen carrying a laundry basket. "Even the closet. And there's nothing under the bed anymore. So now can me and Matt—I mean, my dad—go outside?"

"Yes, you can. But please take that basket to the service porch and leave it next to the washer." Miranda blessed the girl with a dazzling smile, a heart-strumming display Matt hadn't seen in a long time, one he'd never expected to see again. A smile that threatened to turn him inside out like it once had.

He reached for his cane and got to his feet. "All right then. Looks like it's time to cowgirl up."

"Yes! *Finally.* Let's go." Emily led the way to the service porch, where she deposited the laundry basket. On the way out the back door, she glanced over her shoulder and smiled. "I like the way you rodeo talk, because I want to be a barrel racer when I get a little older and my mom lets me get a bigger horse."

"If it's okay with your mom, I'd be happy to work

with you while I'm here." Matt stole one last glance at Miranda, who nodded her approval.

Apparently, she had faith in him, which was a relief. But it wasn't his horsemanship that worried him. He could do that in his sleep. On the other hand, he hadn't planned to be a father. And a relationship like that was going to take a bit more work.

His gaze dropped to Miranda's lap, where one hand rested and the other caressed her rounded stomach. At first, he'd noticed what he'd thought was a paunch, the lingering evidence of childbirth. But then he'd realized the bulge didn't appear to be soft or flabby.

He'd wondered if she was pregnant, but there wasn't any doubt about it now. That was definitely a baby bump.

Did Gavin know? Was that the real reason she was hiding out at the Double G? Was she afraid for the baby?

If so, she'd be safe here. Especially while Matt was around. Bum knee or not, that bully wouldn't stand a chance.

Then again, Uncle George had never had a problem pulling his shotgun off the rack over the fireplace and chasing off an uninvited guest. He'd give that jerk a run for his money, too.

"Are you coming?" Emily called out from the open back door. "I'm letting in flies, and Uncle George is going to get mad. And he's already in a bad mood because he can't find the keys to his truck."

"I'd never want to set off Uncle George." Matt followed his daughter outside.

Okay, cowboy. Now it's time to Daddy up.

* * *

Miranda watched Matt and Emily leave the house until they shut the back door behind them. Should she join them this time? If Emily was going to ride Oreo, Matt's attention would be focused on her. So it's not like Miranda would be intruding on their conversation.

She'd give them a few minutes alone, then go out and check on them. She'd no more than made that decision when Uncle George entered the kitchen, grumbling as he passed her and made his way to the service porch, where he searched the key rack near the door, only to come up empty-handed.

"Looking for something?" she asked.

"I can't find the blasted keys to my truck. I could have sworn I left them hanging right here. Dammit." He slapped his gnarly hands on his hips and then brightened. "Oh, for Pete's sake." He reached into his pocket. "Here they are."

Miranda bit back a chuckle. "Where are you going?"

"I've gotta run a couple of errands in town."

"If you're going anywhere near the post office, we're going to need another roll of stamps. I'd like to mail out the monthly bills tomorrow."

"You got it."

"Will you be home for lunch?" she asked. Not that she planned on making anything other than sandwiches.

"Yeah, I'll be back. But don't bother fixing anything to eat. I'll pick up a couple pizzas. Better yet, I'll get something from that new restaurant near the Night Owl

Motel. I ordered the hot wings last time I was there, and that was the best cluckin' chicken I ever ate."

This time, Miranda let the laughter flow. Uncle George wasn't just a hoot, he was special. One of a kind. How could a man be sweet and gruff, soft and tough, all at the same time?

"If you don't mind," she said, "I think I'll watch Emily ride Oreo for a while, then I'll finish the office work."

"Suit yourself. You're the one balancing the books. I'm just glad I don't have to do it anymore—or worry that someone is robbing me blind."

"And I'm glad you let me and Emily stay here for the time being."

George grimaced, then stroked his left arm from shoulder to elbow and back again.

"What's the matter?" she asked. "Is your arm bothering you?"

"I slept on it wrong. It's nothin' that a couple of ibuprofen won't take care of." He nodded toward the door. "It's burnin' daylight. I gotta go."

"If you give me a minute," she said, "I can drive you."

"Oh, hell's bells. I might be old, but I'm not an invalid. And if you don't stop fussin' over me, the only place you're going to drive me is crazy." He punctuated his snarky tone with a wink, then he opened the back door and let himself out.

After stopping in the service porch, reaching into Emily's laundry basket and placing a load of colors into the washer, Miranda went outside, too, where she found Matt leaning against the corral, his cane propped up next to him, as he watched Emily saddle her pony.

She took a minute to study the cowboy from a distance, the way his hat tilted just right. The way he cocked his head. The way the sun lit the blond streaks in his light brown hair. Broad shoulders, narrow hips. If he'd just turn a bit to the right, she'd catch sight of his profile, of his handsome face…

That's enough of that, she told herself as she shook off her star-crossed attraction and headed toward him. When she reached his side, she lifted her hand to her forehead to shield the morning sun from her eyes.

"How's she doing?" she asked.

"She's a chip off the old block."

Miranda's heart swelled. She'd noticed so many of Matt's mannerisms in Emily, and she was glad he'd spotted them, too. "You're right. She really does take after you."

Matt turned toward her, providing that glimpse of his gorgeous face, and tossed her a playful grin. "The *old block* I was referring to is Uncle George. Emily's a feisty little thing when she doesn't want help. But other than that, she's doing just fine."

After tightening the cinch, Emily turned to Matt, slapped her hands on her denim-clad hips and grinned. "See? I did it by myself."

"I'm *impressed.*"

So was Miranda, but not so much at her daughter's skill when it came to riding the pony, but at the way Matt and Emily seemed to have hit it off so quickly.

"Do you want me to give you a boost into the saddle?" Matt asked.

"Nope." Emily stood as tall as her little girl stature would allow, brushed her hands together, then reached for the pony's reins. "I can do that by myself, too. Just watch me."

An easy grin tugged at Matt's lips, and Miranda let out a soft sigh of relief. She knew better than to think that he'd forgiven her for keeping their daughter a secret from him for so long, but at least he didn't seem nearly as angry as he'd been.

"See how stubborn and insistent she can be," Matt said. "Maybe you should have named her Georgina, after our headstrong, favorite uncle."

"She's a little bullheaded. I'll give you that." But then again, so was her father.

Memories of that handsome young cowboy and days gone by popped up like spring flowers. First love, new life. Stolen kisses while frosting homemade cupcakes. Holding hands while watching TV and munching on popcorn.

What Miranda wouldn't give to roll back the clock and return to that simpler time.

"So," Matt said, drawing her back to the present. "When is your baby due?"

Miranda's heart darn near stopped, and she could hardly take a breath, let alone form a single word. Instead, she continued to lean on the corral for support and turned to him in stunned silence.

"I'm sorry," he said. "That's none of my business."

No, she supposed it wasn't. But that was another secret she couldn't keep from him any longer. "I'm due on September second."

He merely nodded.

"It's a boy," she added.

He glanced at Emily, who galloped her pony inside the corral. "Does she know she's going to have a little brother?"

"I'm sure she'll be thrilled, but I haven't told anyone yet." She expected Matt to address her confession, to offer an opinion, a judgment. Something. But his gaze remained on the child.

About the time she thought he'd dropped the subject completely, he asked, "So your father doesn't know?"

"No, but I plan to call him tomorrow. I'll tell him then."

At that, Matt's focus finally shifted, and he turned to face her, his elbow resting on the corral. His weight shifted to one hip, allowing him to take the burden off his bad knee. "Are you *afraid* to tell him?"

"No, I'm not." She'd been more afraid to tell her dad that she was going to have Matt's baby. Just as she'd expected, when he found out, he'd been more than a little upset. But he'd gotten over his initial anger when he realized he would be a grandfather. And once he'd seen Emily and held her in his arms, he'd made a complete about-face. So Miranda had no reason to expect a different reaction from him this time.

"So what are you waiting for?" Matt's gaze drilled into her, but not in an accusatory or judgmental way. He seemed more curious than anything. And wanting answers.

But she couldn't blame him for that. Her current situation could inspire a new reality TV show: *The Pregnant Runaway Bride*.

"Just to be clear," she said, "I regret ever getting involved with Gavin, but I'm actually happy about having another baby. It's not this little boy's fault that his unexpected arrival has complicated my life. My dad's, too."

"How so?"

"Besides the obvious?" She tucked a strand of hair behind her ear. "I play an active role in the family business."

"It doesn't look like you're doing a very good job of that now."

"You're right. My dad had to hire an accountant from a temp agency to cover for me. From what he told me, things are getting done at the office, but the temporary setup is getting old, and he'd like me to come back."

"He's always had big plans for you," Matt said. "Like graduating from high school as a valedictorian and attending an Ivy League college."

"True." Not to mention getting an accounting degree and eventually running the business he and his father started from the ground up.

"How long do you plan to stay with George on the Double G?" he asked.

"If your uncle doesn't mind, I'd like to stay until after the baby is born. But eventually, I need to find a place of my own, something with some property. Not a ranch, but I'll need room for all of Emily's barnyard friends."

"That's for sure," Matt said, a smile tilting his lips.

Miranda relished his upbeat mood for a couple of beats, wishing it was here to stay, then glanced into the corral, where her daughter—*their* daughter—and Oreo loped in a figure-eight pattern.

The kid was a natural. Was horsemanship genetic? In this case, it certainly seemed to be.

Over the years, Miranda had tried her best to forget her first—and *only*—love and move on, but she'd never been able to. How could she? Every time she looked at their daughter, she was reminded of the cowboy who'd stolen her heart when she was in high school.

And now, seeing the two of them together for the first time was surreal. And heartwarming.

Without a conscious thought, she risked another glance at Matt, and something stirred deep in her soul, something warm and…tender. Special.

Or was it more than that?

Not that Miranda was interested in rekindling an old flame. She knew better than to waste her thoughts on something crazy like that.

Matt might be willing to step up and be a father to Emily. But she couldn't expect him to want to take on a baby who wasn't his.

Chapter Five

As a rumbling engine sounded outside, Miranda glanced out the office window and spotted George returning to the ranch in his old pickup.

As planned, she'd spent the rest of the morning paying the monthly bills and balancing the ledger, a task she'd just completed. So she gathered up the checks George needed to sign and placed them in a stack.

She'd no more than started down the hall, headed to the kitchen to greet him, when George called out, "Chicken's on the table."

Since Emily was probably still outside, Miranda would have to find her and tell her to wash up for lunch. As she entered the kitchen, she expected to see George laying food out on the table, but all she found were several heat-resistant boxes containing the meals he'd brought home.

She suspected he must have gone to tell Matt and Emily it was time to eat, so she proceeded to pull out napkins and paper plates from the pantry.

Her cell phone rang before she could take a step. She glanced at the lighted display. Spotting her father's name, she let out a little sigh, then swiped her finger across the screen of her iPhone and answered. "Hey, Papa. What's up?"

"Everything, it seems. From the moment I woke up, if something could go wrong, it did. I started out the day with a routine dental exam only to end up having a root canal. Then Diego Martinez called. That new farming venture in Mexico is going south, and I need to fly to Los Mochis later this afternoon to straighten things out."

"That's too bad. I'm sorry, but I guess some days are like that."

He sucked in a deep breath and blew out a heavy sigh. "I know you wanted to distance yourself from Gavin. And I don't blame you. But when are you coming home, *mija*? I could sure use someone in my corner right now."

Miranda chewed her bottom lip. She'd planned to tell her father everything tomorrow, after she'd gotten her thoughts in order. Then again, she had him on the phone now.

Just get it over with and put it behind you.

She opened her mouth to speak, but a response shriveled up in her throat like a dried sponge, and her tongue couldn't seem to find any words. The poor guy was having a bad day already, and her news would send him over the edge.

Boy, she could sure use a drink of water. Not to mention a believable excuse. So she crossed the room, cell phone pressed to her ear, and headed for the fridge. "I'm sorry I'm not there for you, Papa, but I'm not quite ready to come back yet."

If truth be told, she wasn't sure she wanted to return at all, other than to pack up her belongings and call a moving van.

"But it's been three months, *mija*. I know you're staying with a friend, but aren't you afraid you'll wear out your welcome?"

She cringed at the reminder of the excuse she'd given him when she'd first told him she needed time away. She was staying with a friend, but she'd led him to believe it was someone she'd met in college.

For a woman who'd always prided herself on being honest, she'd certainly pushed the limits on more than one occasion.

"Besides," Papa said, "the office isn't the same without you."

"I miss you, too." She removed a cold bottle of water from the refrigerator.

As she closed the door and turned away, she noticed a torn wadded-up piece of paper on the floor next to the metal trash can. She picked it up, realizing it had once been a small white bag with a red pharmacy logo, its contents—most likely medication—hastily removed. It hadn't been there this morning. Had Uncle George gone into town to pick up a prescription? That was a little unusual, since she'd never seen him take anything.

"So how're you doing?" her father asked. "And how's Emily? I sure miss my girls."

"We're both having a good time. And Emily couldn't be happier. She loves playing outdoors, especially with my friend's dog, pony and other barnyard critters. I wouldn't be surprised if she decided to become a veterinarian."

"That's great. It won't hurt for her to start thinking about college. But you know I'm not a fan of home-schooling, so I hope that's only going to be temporary, while you're away. I think she'd do better in a regular classroom."

"I agree." That's why Miranda had enrolled her in Brighton Valley Elementary, which was currently on spring break.

"When will you two be home? I don't have anyone to spoil with glazed doughnuts on Sunday mornings."

"I'll bring Emily to see you in a week or two." And she would. That would give her time to tell him about the baby and for him to get used to the idea. But that visit would be brief. She wasn't going to stay in San Antonio any longer than she had to.

"By the way," she asked, "is that accountant from the temp agency still working out?"

"He's okay. He tries hard. But he's not you, *mija*."

Just then the backdoor creaked open. Emily entered the house first, followed by George.

"What kind of chicken did you bring us?" Emily asked.

Miranda's heart slammed into her chest.

"Listen," she said, "I have to hang up, Papa. I'll give you a call in a couple of days."

Then she disconnected the line before he overheard a name or recognized a voice that would unravel her secret before she had a chance to reveal it at a better time.

And in a much better way.

By the time four o'clock rolled around, Matt had built up a powerful thirst, so he went to the kitchen, where he found everyone had gathered. Emily and Miranda were working on a jigsaw puzzle at the table, while George was standing in front of the freezer, filling a glass with ice cubes. Even Sweetie Pie was seated on her haunches, tail thumping the floor, yet eyeing Matt as if she still wasn't convinced he could be trusted.

"We finished off that chicken at lunch," George said. "So how about chili beans for dinner? I've got a couple of cans in the pantry. There should be a box or two of that cornbread mix. But if not, I'm pretty sure we have saltines."

Matt had survived his teen years eating simple fare that didn't require much effort on the cook's part, but canned chili had never sounded very good to him. Besides, he didn't come to the Double G expecting someone to wait on him or to take care of all his needs. "It's my turn, so I'll get dinner tonight."

"All right." George took the jug of sweet tea from the fridge and filled his glass.

"I don't mind cooking," Miranda said. "I can make a run to the grocery store."

"You can do that tomorrow," Matt said, as he fixed himself a glass of tea. After taking a big swig, he made his way over to the table to check out the puzzle, a colorful scene with a fairy tale theme.

Emily looked up and gifted him with a dimpled grin. "Want to help us, Matt?"

He returned her smile. "No, I'll just watch. You two seem to be fine without me."

George took a sip of tea, then asked, "What do you have in mind for dinner, Matt? If you want to grill, there's plenty of meat in the freezer, so it'll need to be thawed. Or you'll have to go to the market. And, come to think of it, we're getting low on propane."

"Let's make this easy. I'll drive into Brighton Valley and order something from Caroline's Diner to go."

"That's a great idea. Simple, tasty and filling." George reached into his back pocket. "And while you're there, check out the desserts. I've got a hankerin' for something sweet, especially if Caroline made it fresh today."

When George withdrew the beat-up leather wallet that had molded to fit his backside, Matt raised the flat of his hand. "Put your money away. I've got it covered."

"All right-y," George said. "Then I won't fight you."

Matt felt a tug on his shirtsleeve and looked down at Emily.

"Can I go with you?" she asked, her soft brown eyes hopeful.

Matt didn't mind taking her, but he glanced at

Miranda, seeking her approval. "You'll have to ask your mom."

Miranda, who'd just removed a puzzle piece that had been placed in the wrong spot, looked up and caught his eye. She didn't respond right away, so he figured she was uneasy about him taking Emily on his own. But why wouldn't she be worried about that? Matt didn't know squat about kids, especially little girls.

After a beat, she asked, "Are you sure you don't mind taking her with you?"

"No," he said, "not at all. You can even go with us. Unless you've got better things to do."

She nodded toward the puzzle, then turned to him and laughed. "Are you kidding? This is the only project I have going on right now, but it can wait until we get back. Give me a minute, and I'll meet you outside."

Matt had learned that, most of the time, when a woman asked for a minute, she took much longer than that, but Miranda surprised him by actually making it quick.

As he opened the truck's rear passenger door to let Emily into the backseat, Miranda came outside wearing a pretty pale green dress and a pair of boots. She'd brushed out her dark brown hair and let the curls tumble over her shoulders. And she'd freshened her lipstick. As she headed toward his pickup with a spring in her step and a breezy smile, she looked more like a woman who belonged on a ranch than a CPA who spent her days working in an office.

He hated to admit it, but he still found her stunningly attractive—with or without the baby bump.

"I haven't been to Caroline's Diner in years," she said, as she climbed into his pickup, filling the cab with a hint of her perfume—something soft and alluring that reminded him of spring flowers. "Has it changed much?"

"Not that I know of," Matt said. "Unless Caroline did some remodeling since I was there the winter before last."

"Does Margie still work there?"

Matt chuckled. "I'm sure she does—unless she landed a job as the gossip columnist at the *Brighton Valley Gazette*. And even then, she'd probably hang out at the diner to pick up the latest news."

"I remember her being a bit nosy and talkative," Miranda said. "But she was very sweet."

"You have her pegged just right. Some people never change." Matt glanced across the seat at his former high school sweetheart. And of course, some did.

Two days ago, he never would have thought he'd see Miranda again, let alone learn that she'd given birth to his daughter. And now look. Here they were, riding together to Caroline's Diner, kicking up dust along the long driveway to the county road and stirring old memories he'd thought that he'd forgotten.

After parking along Brighton Valley's quaint tree-lined Main Street, they climbed out of Matt's pickup and headed to the diner. In spite of the addition of a fancy steak house and the Italian restaurant that opened a couple of years ago, Caroline's was still popular with the locals.

The last time Miranda and Matt had come to Caroline's for a burger and fries, they'd sat in a corner booth, hidden from view, and she'd prayed her father or one of his friends or associates wouldn't spot her. Little had she known that he'd hired a PI to find her, a man who'd followed them inside, then told her father what she'd been up to.

The bell over the diner's door jingled, announcing their entry, but other than two old men seated at the lunch counter, the place was surprisingly empty. Miranda scanned the interior of the familiar eatery, with its pale yellow walls and white café-style curtains on the front windows.

"Look!" Emily pointed to the refrigerator display case that sat next to the old-fashioned register. "Are we going to have dessert tonight? I love chocolate cake."

"You bet," Matt said. "I like chocolate, too. I'll also pick up a lemon meringue pie. That's Uncle George's favorite."

Emily turned away from the desserts long enough to notice the chalkboard where Caroline posted her daily specials.

As usual, she'd written it in yellow chalk: *What the Sheriff Ate—Pork Chops, Mashed Potatoes and Gravy, Buttered Green Beans, Biscuits and Peach Cobbler.*

"What's that mean?" Emily asked, pointing to the board.

"Caroline's husband used to be the sheriff," Miranda explained. "He's retired now, but everyone still refers to him with that title."

"And so he ate pork chops for lunch?" Emily

scrunched her brow. "Why do people need to know that?"

Margie, who was still in the kitchen, must have heard the bell at the door jingle-jangle because she called out, "Y'all don't need to wait to be seated. Take any table you like."

"It's going to take a while for them to get our dinner orders ready," Matt said. "And there's hardly anyone here now, anyway. Let's go ahead and sit down."

When he pointed to a table near the window, Miranda placed her hand on Emily's shoulder, then steered her to the spot he'd selected. She would've preferred that they sit in the corner booth, even though it might provoke memories neither of them ought to poke at. A few of her dad's friends still lived in town, although he probably hadn't kept in touch with them after moving to San Antonio. He ran in a different social circle these days.

Besides, she had every intention of being the one to tell him where she was staying. And she'd do that soon. Very soon.

"This place is funny," Emily said, as she took a seat. "They have bells on their doors, and they tell each other what they eat."

"You're right," Matt said, as he leaned his cane against the wall, then pulled out his chair.

They'd no more than taken their seats when Margie stopped by the table with two adult menus and one for a child, as well as a plastic cup filled with crayons. The instant she recognized Matt, she offered him a bright-eyed grin and winked. "Well, if it isn't our local bull riding champ! Welcome home, cowboy. We're all looking forward to seeing you compete in the Rocking Chair Rodeo."

Matt didn't respond.

When Margie glanced at Miranda, her jaw dropped. "Well, now. Isn't this a nice surprise. I haven't seen you in years."

"It's been a while," Miranda said. "How are you?"

"I'm doing just fine. Thanks for asking." Margie zeroed in on Emily, who was busy checking out the puzzles on her menu and removing a red crayon from the little cup.

"And who is this sweet little thing?" Margie asked.

Emily looked up from her work long enough to offer the waitress a smile, then went back to a word search.

"This is Emily," Miranda said, "my daughter."

"*Our* daughter," Matt corrected.

Margie gasped, and Miranda wanted to slip under the table, although she wasn't sure why. Shouldn't she be glad that Matt had claimed Emily as his child?

"Well, now." Margie studied Emily for a beat, then her eyes twinkled. "Isn't that nice?"

Isn't it? Miranda's life story was about to be blasted on the front page of the *Brighton Valley Gazette*. Thank goodness, she didn't need to use the bathroom—yet. The last thing she needed was for Margie to see her baby bump and jump to conclusions. She shot a glance at Matt, but he didn't seem to be concerned.

"I had no idea you two got married," Margie said. "The last I heard, your daddy didn't approve of Matt."

He probably still didn't, although Miranda knew,

with time, her father would come around. He always did. It's just that he was prone to having knee-jerk reactions at first.

"Miranda and I didn't get married," Matt said, as he placed his hand on Emily's shoulder, a move that appeared awkward until the child looked up at him and smiled. "But we couldn't be happier to share this little girl."

"I can sure see why," Margie said. "She's a real cutie."

"Not only that," Matt added, "she's smart, too. And she has a big heart."

The door swung open, and the bell jingled, announcing that a new customer had just entered. Margie turned toward the front of the diner, offered the entrant a bright-eyed grin and waved. "Come on in, Doc. Take a seat anywhere." Then she returned her attention to Matt. "While you look over the menu, I'll get y'all started with some water."

"Actually," Matt said, "we're going to order four meals to go. And while we're trying to decide what we want to take home, we'll have three slices of that chocolate cake."

"You've got it," Margie said, as she headed for the refrigerator display case at the front of the diner.

"Hey, Rick." Matt waved over the dark-haired man Margie had referred to as Doc. In a flannel shirt, jeans and boots, he didn't look like a doctor. Then again, Matt and his high school buddies all had nicknames, but she'd never met this guy.

"Well, I'll be darned," Rick said, extending a hand

for Matt to shake. "I heard you had a hard ride. How are you doing?"

Matt nodded toward his cane. "All right, I guess. But I'm not getting better as quickly as I'd hoped."

"It takes time to mend, but I'm sure you'll be back to fighting weight in no time."

Matt turned to Miranda, introduced her as an old friend and Emily as his daughter. "This is Doctor Rick Martinez. About five or six years ago, when Doctor Grimes retired, Rick bought his practice."

Miranda had met Dr. Grimes once, when he came out to the Double G to treat Bandit, Matt's prized gelding. He and George were cousins, if she remembered correctly.

"So now Rick is the town veterinarian," Matt added. "And he's a darn good one at that."

Emily set down her crayon and gave the man her full attention. "I'm going to be a veterinarian when I grow up."

"That's awesome," Rick said. "You must be an animal lover like me."

She nodded proudly. "I have a dog, a pony, a lamb and chickens."

"You don't actually *have* those animals," Miranda corrected. "They belong to Uncle George."

Emily clicked her tongue. "Sweetie Pie is mine because I found her, and he said I could have her. And when we move to a new house with a big yard, I get to take them all with us. So they're practically mine already."

Miranda could hardly argue that. And no matter

where she decided to live, she'd never end up back at her condo in San Antonio. They allowed pets, but the landlord would never agree to chickens, a lamb or a pony.

As Emily chattered away, Miranda glanced at Matt, who was smiling as he watched the conversation unfold between Dr. Martinez and their daughter. If Emily decided not to major in veterinary medicine, she should consider a career as an investigative reporter. She certainly appeared to have an aptitude for it.

"Do you operate on animals, too?" Emily asked.

"Whenever I have to. I have a small surgical suite in my clinic, but if my patient is a large animal, like a horse, I refer patients to the equine hospital in Wexler."

Emily scrunched her brow and bit down on her bottom lip, then looked up at Dr. Martinez. "Do you ever operate on chickens?"

A smile tugged at the vet's lips. "Not usually. Why do you ask?"

"Because I have a chicken named Nugget, and she has a crooked toe. I don't know how it happened, but it's been like that ever since we got her. And I think we should fix it for her."

Dr. Martinez stroked his chin, as if giving the medical dilemma some thought. "Can Nugget walk?"

"Yes."

"Does she limp or act like it hurts?"

"No."

"Then I wouldn't recommend surgery. She's adapted just fine."

Miranda liked the doctor already. He seemed to have

an amazing bedside—or rather diner-side—manner, and he was great with kids. Rather than tell Emily that an injured chicken was more likely to end up in a roasting pan than an operating table, he took her questions seriously.

"The other chickens peck at her sometimes," Emily added, "and I think it's because of her toe."

"Chickens have what we call a pecking order. They rank each other, and those on the low end get pecked more often. So whatever their reason for pecking on Nugget, I don't think it has anything to do with her toe."

Emily seemed to think about that for a while.

When the bell attached to the diner door jingled again, Dr. Martinez glanced over his shoulder and waved. "I'll be right with you, boys."

"Is that Lucas?" Matt asked.

"Yep. He's in high school now. I'm meeting him and one of his classmates here to discuss colleges that offer degrees in veterinary medicine."

"Already?" Matt furrowed his brow. "I can't believe Lucas is already thinking about college."

"He's sixteen," Rick said. "And the twins are four."

"They were practically newborns when I saw them last." Matt laughed. "Time flies, huh?"

"You've got that right." Rick nodded toward the teens who were studying the desserts in the refrigerated display case. "I'd better go before they eat up all the good stuff."

"Give Mallory my best," Matt said.

"I'll do that. And if we don't get together before

the rodeo, we'll see you there. I've already purchased our tickets."

As the vet turned away from the table, Matt said, "Hey, Rick. One of these days, I'd like to bring Emily to your clinic for a tour. I'm sure she'd like to see your pet rescue, too."

"Absolutely. You can bring her by anytime. Just give me a call to make sure I'm there and not visiting one of the ranches."

"You got it."

Rick had barely taken two steps when Miranda caught Matt's attention and mouthed, "Thank you."

Matt shrugged a single shoulder, as if he hadn't done anything worthy of her appreciation.

As his gaze fixed on their daughter, a slow smile curved his lips and dimpled his cheeks.

Miranda's heart fluttered to life and beat in a way it hadn't in years. And for a moment, she feared she was falling in love with Matt all over again.

Slow down, she told herself. *And be careful.*

If she let down her guard, she might fall hard. And if that happened, she didn't see things ending any better than they had nine years ago.

Chapter Six

Two days later, Matt sat on the edge of his bed and rubbed his aching knee. He had to admit it felt better, but he was a far cry from being at one hundred percent. And if he wasn't completely healed, that meant he couldn't compete in the Rocking Chair Rodeo, an event where everyone in town expected to see him.

Even if he could pull off climbing on the back of a bull, one more hard fall and bad landing could create a more lasting and permanent injury. And then where would he be?

He got to his feet and limped to the closet, holding the cane rather than using it. Then he slid open the door and placed the cane inside. Maybe, if he wasn't using it anymore, he'd convince himself that he'd be fully recovered soon.

As he stood in the center of the small but comfortable room that had once been his great-grandmother's, he scanned the interior, which hadn't changed in years.

After Matt's dad asked George to let Matt move in and live out his teen years on the Double G, George had purchased the blue-plaid bedspread that covered the bed, replacing the pink-and-beige quilt that his mother had made before she died.

The maple chest of drawers and matching nightstand, probably considered antiques, had once belonged to her, too. But other than that, there wasn't much to remind Matt of the woman he'd never met.

He'd added his own touches to the room—rodeo posters that still adorned the walls, several framed photos that dotted the chest of drawers. He crossed the room and picked up one of him and his buddies; they were wearing their football uniforms—dirt-smudged faces, happy grins and drenched in ice water after winning the division title.

Matt studied the picture of himself, along with Clay "Bullet" Masters and Adam "Poncho" Santiago, and couldn't help but smile. They'd been fun-loving, mischief-prone teenagers back then, and as a result, they were often in trouble at school.

The worst and probably last time any of them crossed a line was when a harmless prank went awry and injured a janitor. Charges were filed, and if Adam's foster dad, a respected police officer, hadn't gone to bat for them, they might have spent some time in juvenile hall. That was the first time Matt had someone defend him, and he'd never forgotten it.

Behind several other pictures, he spotted a photo of him and Miranda, standing next to Bandit, the horse he'd had to put down three months after Miranda left town. That second devastating loss had only made the first one worse.

Matt had been so hurt by Miranda's rejection that he'd been tempted to throw that photo in the trash or burn it or tear it to pieces, just like she'd done to him. But it was the only picture he had of Bandit, so he'd stuck it upside down in the lower dresser drawer instead.

So who'd gone through his things and put that picture back on display? Not that they'd placed it front and center. Still, Matt certainly hadn't done it.

It might've been his uncle, he supposed, but George had always respected Matt's privacy in the past. It didn't seem likely that he'd rummage through his drawers. He supposed it might have been the cleaning woman George hired to come in every couple weeks.

A knock sounded at his door—a loud rap, not one of the soft tentative knocks he'd come to expect from Miranda.

"Come in." He turned away from the photographs and watched George enter the room.

"I've got one of the new hands fixing the pump in the north forty," George said. "He's still a little wet behind the ears, so I need to go out there and supervise. Since you're taking Emily to tour the veterinary clinic today, I wondered if you'd pick up something for me while you're in town and save me a trip."

"Sure. What is it?"

"A prescription at the drugstore. No big deal if you can't. I'll find time to get it later this afternoon."

George rarely visited the doctor. "What's it for?"

"An antibiotic for an infected toenail. Like I said, it's no big deal."

"I'll get it after Emily's tour."

"By the way," George said, "she's waiting outside for you, next to your truck."

"Already? If we go now, we'll show up about twenty minutes early."

George chuckled. "She was so excited, she hardly touched her lunch. I'd say she's eager to get on the road."

"Yeah, I know." He'd figured that out when she darn near talked Rick's ear off at Caroline's Diner. "She's going to like visiting the clinic."

A slow smile slid across George's face. "You're going to be a good father."

"I don't know about that." Matt shrugged a single shoulder. "But I'm going to try. You can't expect more than that from a guy who's never been close to his own dad."

"It won't be hard. Just try to be the kind of man you wished your father would've been."

A man like George, he supposed. And maybe one like Adam's foster dad. Neither of them had had kids of their own, but they'd both stepped up and provided damn good role models for a couple of angry and rebellious teenagers.

"Speaking of fathers," George said, "have you talked to yours lately?"

"Not since I had that run-in with Grave Digger. He called me, but not because he was concerned about my injury. He asked if I could get a couple of VIP tickets for him and my *brother* to attend the Rocking Chair Rodeo." Matt rolled his eyes. "I told him I couldn't."

"Sounds like you're still holding a grudge."

"Shouldn't I?"

George seemed to chew on that for a while, then said, "Family is important. And for the record, I'm glad you're part of mine."

Matt was pretty much George's only relative—other than Matt's dad, who rarely visited him, even on holidays. But hell, why would he do that when he'd chosen his second wife's family over the one he'd had?

"I don't think you call two people a family," Matt said.

"You know what they say about quality over quantity."

"I suppose you're right, but since I got shut out of the only real one I had, I don't have the foggiest idea how to create one, let alone be a part of one."

"You'll figure it out."

He'd have to. Things might have been different if his mom hadn't died when he was too young to remember her, if he hadn't spent so much time with babysitters or in day care. And it would've been a hell of a lot different if his old man hadn't fallen heart over brains for a woman with a kid of her own. But that's how it had all come down, and he'd dealt with it the best way he'd known how.

Matt studied the old man who'd become the only

father he really cared about, the man he'd come to love. "Did you put that picture of me and Miranda on my dresser?"

"You noticed, huh?" George grinned.

"Being snoopy or nosy isn't like you."

George arched a gray brow. "You mad about that?"

"Why shouldn't I be? You went through my drawers."

"I did your laundry the day after you left to follow the damned ol' rodeo. And I figured you weren't quite ready to throw it away, or you would have."

Matt let out a humph and slowly shook his head.

George nodded toward the bedroom doorway. "Like I said, Emily's waiting for you. And I suspect her mother would like to go, too, even if she didn't mention it."

Matt hadn't planned to include Miranda unless she asked. And even then he was reluctant to take her with him.

He might have built a heavy-duty wall around his heart—just ask some of the women who'd thought they'd be able get a commitment out of him.

But that wall had been a lot easier to maintain when Miranda was long gone—and out of sight.

Miranda hadn't asked Matt if she could go with him to the veterinary clinic, even though she really wanted to. Emily was going to enjoy the special tour, and Miranda would have loved to be a part of it. But she didn't want Matt to think that she and Emily were a package deal. And worse, she didn't want him to suspect that she had any romantic notions about starting up where they'd left off. She knew better than that. So she'd returned to the office to do the payroll, even though it was a day early.

She'd barely gotten started when a soft knock against the doorjamb sounded. She looked up from her work and spotted Matt in the open doorway, wearing a sheepish grin.

"I can see that you're pretty busy," he said, "but did you want to go to the clinic with us?"

She tamped down her enthusiasm and said, "Sure. If you don't mind. It sounds like fun. And my office work can wait."

And now here they were, entering a veterinary clinic with their delighted daughter, pretending to be a family, when they were anything but.

While Matt sat in the waiting room, Miranda studied his profile, the blond hair, neatly cut and styled, collar length, but not as wild as he'd worn it nine years ago. His eyes, as blue as the summer sky, were framed with thick dark lashes a woman would die for—pretty lashes their daughter had inherited.

He seemed so different from the guy she'd once loved, yet at the same time, there was a bit of the old Matt in him. And he hadn't shaken that cowboy swagger. If anything, he'd honed it, and she found it sexier than ever.

No wonder women flocked around him, eager to have a chance to spend some time, if not the night, with the champion bull rider.

Miranda rested her hand on her baby bump, which served as a nice reminder for her to keep those old memories at bay, and scanned the waiting room, with its pale green walls and built-in fish tank. She expected Emily to be immediately drawn to the colorful tropical fish. Instead, the girl zeroed in on a gray-haired man seated on one of the brown vinyl chairs and holding a cat carrier, a gray tabby resting inside.

"Can I see your kitty?" she asked him.

"Of course," he said. "Do you like cats?"

"Yes. I like *all* animals." Emily stooped to peer into the carrier. "What's her name?"

"It's a boy. His name is Archie."

"How come he's in a cage? Does he bite?"

"Oh, no. Archie's very friendly. But sometimes, there's a dog or two in the waiting room. And so I bring him in his carrier, where he's safe. He's much happier this way."

"Oh." Emily eased closer to the animal.

Miranda glanced at Matt, saw a grin curling his lips. He seemed to be as proud of their daughter as she was. And as intrigued by her friendly manner.

As if sensing Miranda's assessment, Matt turned to her and smiled. The glimmer in his eyes was that of a proud daddy, but then it shifted, morphing into the kind he used to shine on her. As their gazes locked, her senses reeled and her heart darn near stopped. Old memories popped up, taking her back to the days when things had been different between them. When she and Matt had envisioned a future together.

"Why is Archie here?" Emily asked the cat's owner. "Is he sick?"

"He was, but he's feeling better now. We came in

for a checkup, and we're just waiting to pick up his medicine."

The door to the back office opened, and a woman walked out holding the leash of a German shepherd wearing a plastic cone around its neck.

Emily's interest piqued, and she approached the dog's owner. "What happened to your dog? Why is it wearing that thing?"

The woman, her graying hair pulled up into a top-knot, smiled. "It looks a little silly, doesn't it? But Dr. Rick put this on Sophie to keep her from licking or chewing her stitches."

Before Emily could question the dog owner further, a blonde wearing blue scrubs came to the reception window. "Dennis, here's Archie's prescription. You'll see that Dr. Rick lowered the dose this time."

The older man got to his feet, and with the cat carrier firmly in hand, approached the opening. "Thanks, Kara."

When the door squeaked open again, Rick entered the waiting room and greeted Miranda and Matt. Then he turned to Emily. "Are you ready to check out my clinic and see where I work?"

"Yes!"

"Then let's go." Rick stepped away from the door-way, allowing the child inside, then motioned to Miranda and Matt. "Come on, Mom and Dad."

As the two awkward parents fell into step behind the veterinarian and their daughter, Miranda was tempted to reach for Matt's hand, to pretend they were the family Rick assumed they were.

But she knew better than to rock the boat.

* * *

As they entered the clinic, Matt glanced at Miranda, who mouthed, *Thank you*, as if he'd done her a favor.

He nodded to acknowledge her words, but he hadn't done anything extraordinary. He'd just coordinated a tour for their daughter. Or was she thanking him for including her?

If truth be told, he'd been reluctant to bring her along—and for a slew of reasons. But he couldn't think of a single one of them right now.

"These are the exam rooms," Rick said, pointing out three of them as he led the way through the clinic. Next, he showed them a pharmacy area and a small laboratory, where he let Emily look through a microscope at a blood smear.

Matt glanced at Miranda. Maternal pride glistened in her eyes.

Yeah, he decided. She had been thanking him for including her this afternoon. And in spite of dragging his feet about it earlier, he was glad that he had.

Rick led them to a glass window that provided a view of the operating suite. "If any animals need surgery, this is where it takes place."

They then headed to the boarding area, where several furry patients were recovering or waiting for their owners to pick them up.

"Oh!" Emily said, as she pointed to a cage that housed a mother cat and six nursing kittens. "What's wrong with them?"

"That's Mama Kitty. At least, that's what we're calling her. Kara, my vet tech, found her wandering around in her neighborhood and assumed she was a pregnant stray. The babies were born yesterday. She has a leg wound, which I'm treating. Once it heals, I'll take her to our animal rescue center out back."

"Then what?" Emily asked. "Will they live there forever?"

"No, only until we can find them good homes."

"I have a good home for them." Emily turned to her mother, eyes pleading. "Can we take them back to the ranch and keep them?"

"*All* of them?" Miranda laughed. "I'm afraid not. You've already pushed your limits with poor Uncle George. He's taken in enough strays as it is. And we don't want to wear out our welcome until we find a place of our own."

Did she plan to move to Brighton Valley? Matt wondered. If so, it would put some distance between her and her father, which would be good for her and for Emily. Good for him, too, he supposed. It would make it easier for him to see Emily.

And to see Miranda.

He stole another glimpse at the woman who'd rocked his teenage world. He'd been nineteen and a senior back then. And he'd had his choice of girls. But it was the new girl in school, a pretty dark-haired sophomore, who'd first caught his eye and soon stolen his heart.

Falling for Miranda had really complicated his life back then—in both good ways and bad.

She cast a look his way, caught him gazing at her and blessed him with a pretty smile that could turn a man inside and out. But he shook it off the best he could.

As they continued through the clinic, Rick pointed out his office, with its solid oak desk adorned with antique brass and a Mac computer on top. Then he led them to the back door and took them outside, where a six-foot high chain-link fence encircled a small white house.

"This is the animal rescue yard," Rick said. "I used to live in that house before Mallory and I got married."

Upon their approach, several dogs ran to the fence, barking and wagging their tails.

"You rescue dogs?" Emily asked.

"And cats, rabbits, a goat and, right now, we have a potbellied pig."

The front door of the house swung open, and a balding older man walked out. He squinted, then lifted his hand to block the sun from his eyes and grinned. "Oh. Hi, Doc. I wondered why Scout and Beauty were barking up a storm."

Rick introduced them to the tall, slender man as Roy Dobbins, Kara's grandfather.

"Roy's retired," Rick explained, "so this setup works out well for all of us."

After seeing the dog runs out back, as well as the Kitty Hotel, Matt thanked Rick for showing them around.

"No problem. It was my pleasure."

As they returned to the truck, their shoes crunching on the graveled parking lot, Emily sidled up to him and slipped her hand into his. "That was so awesome. Thank you for bringing me here."

"You're welcome. I was glad to do it. I had a feeling you'd like to see a real veterinary clinic."

She gave his hand a squeeze, then looked up at him with an adoring gaze that shot right through his heart. "You're the best daddy ever."

Matt could have walked on air, had his bum leg not held him back, and he shot a glance at Miranda. Her pretty brown eyes glistened as if she were holding back tears. Happy ones, it would seem, and they touched him in an unexpected way.

For a moment, nothing else in the world seemed to matter. Not her abandonment and his heartbreak. Not an eight-year-old secret she never should've kept. Not even the fact that she was having another man's baby.

Damn. If he wasn't careful, if he let down his guard, she just might complicate his life all over again.

Chapter Seven

As Matt backed out of the clinic parking lot, Miranda settled into the passenger seat feeling a lot more comfortable and at ease than she had when they'd started out.

"Thank you," she said.

Matt shot a glance across the seat. "No problem. I knew Emily would enjoy it. And that she'd learn a lot."

"I did!" Emily said. "That was the best field trip ever."

Miranda waited a beat, then explained what she'd actually been thanking him for. "You didn't have to include me, but I'm glad you did."

"Yeah, well…" He shrugged. "You're welcome."

As he shifted the truck into Drive, Miranda added, "Rick is a great guy, and he clearly loves his work."

"That's true." Matt turned to the left, instead of turning right onto the road, which would have taken them home. "I hope you don't mind, but Uncle George asked me to pick up a prescription for him at the pharmacy."

"Another one?" Miranda asked. "That's odd."

"Why do you find that so unusual?"

"I suppose it's not, but George always told me that he rarely goes to the doctor. Besides, a few days ago, I found a discarded white pharmacy bag. So I'm pretty sure this is a second prescription. Unless it was yours."

"It wasn't mine."

Miranda furrowed her brow. "I hope he's not sick."

"No," Matt said. "He has an ingrown toenail that's infected."

Men like George didn't often take care of themselves. Or seek medical attention. So if his toe bothered him enough to see the doctor, it might be more serious than he'd let on.

She thought about voicing her concern, but decided to confront George instead.

Minutes later, Matt pulled down Brighton Valley's tree-shaded main drag and parked in a space near the pharmacy, which was located a couple doors down from Caroline's Diner.

"It won't take me very long," Matt said. "You guys can wait in the truck if you want to. But if you come inside with me, I'll buy you an ice-cream cone."

"*I'll* come in with you," Emily said. "I *love* ice cream."

So did Miranda. She hadn't visited the old-style

pharmacy since she'd been a teenager. In fact, she and a girlfriend had been eating French fries and drinking cherry colas when Matt first approached her and asked to sit beside them at the counter. Both girls had plans to meet a couple of their classmates for a study group at the library, and it was almost time for them to go. But when Miranda looked into those gorgeous blue eyes, when she saw that dimpled grin, she'd opted to stay behind.

"Do they still have that soda fountain along the side wall?" she asked Matt.

"They sure do. The tourists and the locals would throw a fit if they didn't. But I don't think they offer food or fountain drinks anymore. Both the cook and the woman who used to work behind the counter retired, and the owner hasn't been able to find a replacement."

"That's too bad."

"They still serve ice cream, though. And it's just as good as you remember."

After getting out of the pickup, they entered the charming old pharmacy that had maintained its 1950s style while offering all the latest products and medications. Miranda took a deep whiff, relishing the familiar scent of sweet vanilla laced with something clean and medicinal.

Matt nodded toward the counter that ran along the wall. "Why don't you two have a seat while I pick up George's prescription?"

Miranda steered Emily toward one of the red vinyl upholstered swivel seats that sat in front of the long white counter. "You're going to love this, honey. This was one of my favorite things to do when I used to live in Brighton Valley with your grandfather."

"It's too bad you had to move away from here," Emily said. "Brighton Valley is a fun place to live. I like it a lot better than San Antonio."

So did Miranda. There was a lot to like about the small town, and it hadn't been her idea to leave. She stole a peek at Matt who stood in line, waiting to speak to the pharmacist. She couldn't help admiring the way the sexy cowboy leaned into the counter, the way he'd tilted his hat.

As much as she'd have liked to put Matt at the top of her list of reasons to stick around in town permanently—or at least indefinitely—she knew better than to let him sway her decision. In four short months, she'd be a single mother of two. And he'd still be a handsome rodeo star with his choice of women; a fun-loving man who was always ready to throw back a beer or to circle the dance floor, two-stepping the night away.

But if he wanted a relationship with Emily, which seemed to be apparent, it might be best if she did move back to Brighton Valley—or at least to the general vicinity.

But what would her father say when she told him she wanted to work from home, that she would rarely come to the office in San Antonio?

There's no way he'd agree. She'd heard his speech enough times to recite it verbatim. Mija, *my dad came to the United States as a young man with only the clothes on his back and a gunnysack carrying his few belongs. He had guts and grit and* ganas—*desire. He wasn't educated, so he worked in the berry fields. But he was bright. He learned the ins and outs of farming, literally from the ground up. And by the time I graduated from high school, he'd saved enough to send me, his only son, to college.*

Miranda remembered her grandfather, an older man with sun-ravaged skin, stooped shoulders and a warm smile. A man her papa loved and respected.

As a tribute to my papa, I excelled and received an agriculture degree with a business minor. And then I went home, where my father and I worked and saved so we could purchase enough fertile acreage to plant berries. Together, we built our business for you, mija. *And one day, it'll all be yours.*

Miranda blew out a soft sigh. How could she dash a dream that had carried the Contreras family through two generations?

Before she could ponder the answer, Matt returned to the counter. "The pharmacist is sending the stock clerk over to serve us."

"This place used to be a big tourist draw back in the day," Miranda said. "I remember when they served food here. They had these really cool plastic menus that offered hot dogs, burgers and fries."

"They still have them, although they don't use them anymore." Matt slipped around to the back of the counter and found where a couple of old menus had been stored. He handed one to Emily, then took a seat next to her, placing the child between them. Whether she was a wall or a connection was left to be seen.

Miranda scanned the nostalgic setting. "I imagine it would still be a big draw."

"You're right." Matt looked over Emily's head, which was bent so she could study the menu, his gaze on Miranda. "But Ron Jorgenson, the original owner, passed away a few years back, leaving it to his wife Hazel. His death was unexpected, and Hazel took it hard. The manager has been running things, so I have a feeling Hazel has lost interest."

"For a guy who's been away a lot and on the rodeo circuit, you seem to know a lot about what's going on in Brighton Valley."

"I stay in contact with Bullet and Poncho, who keep me updated. My info comes from a cop and a Life Flight pilot, so it's pretty solid."

"Hmm." She tossed him a playful smile. "So in some ways, you're able to keep your ear out for local gossip—like Margie at the diner."

"Whoa!" He lifted his index finger and moved it back and forth, like a windshield wiper. Yet, a glimmer in his eye told her he'd taken her teasing for what it was. "I wouldn't go that far. I like being in the know, but I'm discreet. My buddies know that I can be trusted not to spread gossip."

"Hey, y'all," a teenage boy said, as he approached the counter. "My name's Danny. What can I get you?"

"We'd like ice-cream cones, unless you still have banana splits." Matt nodded his head at Miranda and winked.

Talk about nostalgia and memories... She and Matt had shared a banana split at this very counter that first day, and he'd taught her how to tie a cherry stem in her mouth—without using her hands.

"We don't have any bananas, whipped cream or cherries," Danny said, "but I have chocolate sauce."

What a shame. Miranda had been prepared to show Matt that she still remembered how to do that amazing trick.

"Sounds like we'd better stick with three cones," Matt said.

At that, Emily looked up and grinned. "What flavors do you have?"

"Chocolate, vanilla, strawberry and black cherry. We can give you different flavor combinations if you order a double or triple scoop."

After they placed their orders, Danny got to work making their cones.

"I was talking to the pharmacist," Matt said, "and he told me they've lost a lot of business to that big super pharmacy that opened up on the border between Brighton Valley and Wexler."

"That's too bad. This place has an amazing small town appeal. Their customers like having the personal attention they can't get at one of the big chain stores."

"I agree. I'd hate to see it go."

Miranda again scanned the setting, then placed an elbow on the counter and turned to Matt. "You know, it might turn out to be a moneymaker and a good investment if Hazel refurbished it."

"Maybe. But I'm not sure if she'd be interested in doing anything other than selling it outright."

Danny handed Emily a strawberry cone, the top scoop tilted slightly off center. "Here you go."

Emily thanked him, then began to lick the side.

As Danny returned to make the other two cones, Matt said, "From what I heard, the woman who used to manage the soda fountain retired."

"And the one before that got pregnant with triplets," Danny added. "For some reason, people who work at the counter keep leaving. My friends and I call it The Curse of the Drug Store Soda Jerks."

"What happened to them?" Emily asked, her lips parted, her eyes open wide.

"They didn't die or anything." Danny carried a single-dip black cherry cone and handed it to Miranda.

"I don't believe in curses," Matt said. "People don't always stick with a job that doesn't pay a lot. But I have to admit, it's kind of weird. About forty years ago, Uncle George dated a woman who worked here. And she not only quit her job, she broke up with him and left him high and dry."

"Why'd she leave?" Miranda asked.

"She ran off with a musician bound for Nashville, and it really messed up George. He's sworn off women ever since—at least, when it comes to romance."

"Poor George." So that's why the man had never married. Miranda nibbled at her cone, then turned to Matt, caught a glimpse of his profile, saw his eye twitch.

He didn't say it, but he didn't need to. Miranda had run off, too.

As Danny handed Matt a double-deck chocolate

cone, Emily got off her swivel seat. "Can I look around the store?"

"I suppose." Miranda could see why the child would be curious. "But don't touch anything."

"I won't."

As Emily stepped away, leaving the two adults at the counter, Miranda made a quarter-spin in her swivel seat and turned to Matt.

"I had a good reason for leaving," she said, her voice soft, hesitant.

He zeroed in on her for a couple of beats, then broke eye contact to study his chocolate cone. "It doesn't matter."

Actually, it did. To her, anyway. And while she felt compelled to insist that he listen, Emily chose that moment to approach a display of colorful refrigerator magnets that was only a few steps away and within earshot.

So it wasn't the time for Miranda to either defend herself or to apologize for breaking his heart.

The afternoon they'd spent at Rick's clinic had turned out even better than Matt hoped it would. And they topped off the day with a simple but filling dinner Miranda had fixed them.

While they munched on baked chicken, rice pilaf and a tossed salad, the adults remained quiet, but mostly because Emily chattered up a storm, rehashing the things she'd seen and learned on her tour and sharing her plans to open her own veterinary hospital and rescue center someday.

Needless to say, no one else had been able to get

a word in edgewise. And that was just as well. Matt hadn't known what to say anyway. Spending time as a family had been pretty surreal.

His mom had died when he was in kindergarten, and since his dad's job required him to travel, Matt had spent a lot of time with babysitters or else he'd been placed in day care for hours on end. Then, when his stepmother and her son had eventually come into his life, she rarely included Matt in those kinds of activities. And that often left Matt alone.

"It's my turn to clean up," George said, as he got up from the table.

Matt didn't argue. Instead, he poured a cup of decaf and slipped out the front door, where he took a seat in one of the rocking chairs.

He'd no more than taken a couple of sips when Miranda opened the screen door and stepped into the soft yellow glow of the porch light.

"There you are." She smiled sheepishly, then tucked a strand of hair behind her ear. "Is it okay if I join you for a few minutes?"

You'd think that he'd resent having an interruption to his solitude, but for some reason, it didn't seem to bother him a bit. "Sure, go ahead."

She took a seat in the rocker next to his. "It's nice outside this evening."

That's why he'd come out here. Well, there was that. But he'd also wanted some time to think. About life. About parenthood.

About *her*.

"I really appreciate how kind you've been to Emily," she said.

How could he not be? He was her father. "She's an amazing kid."

Matt would never turn away from Emily, like his old man and his stepmom had done when they'd both favored her bratty kid over Matt.

Much to his stepmom's aggravation, the house became a battlefield, with Matt getting into trouble for starting the fights even when he wasn't to blame.

His father traveled on business and was gone most of the time, which was nothing new. But each night, when his old man called home, his stepmom would complain about Matt picking on her son or giving her a hard time. You'd think the guy would have at least listened to Matt's side of the story, but he hadn't. And by the time Matt was fourteen, his dad had gotten tired of hearing about every little thing he'd done wrong and shipped him off to live with Uncle George.

But hey. Things had worked out. And in time, Matt had put it all behind him.

He stole a glance at Miranda, who peered up at the sky. He assumed she'd come out here to talk to him, so he waited for her to broach whatever she had on her mind. But she continued to sit in silence.

Apparently, like him, she'd only come outside to enjoy the peaceful sights and sounds of the ranch at night. So he leaned back in his seat and took a deep breath of night air, picking up the ever so soft scent of night-blooming jasmine, listening to the evening breeze rustling the leaves in the maple tree and watching the occasional cloud hide the waning moon as it moved across the starlit sky.

"I enjoyed getting to know Rick a little better," Miranda finally said. "He's a great guy."

"You'll like his wife, too. Mallory is a social worker at the Brighton Valley Medical Center."

Miranda set her rocker in motion, the chair runners creaking against the wood-slatted floor. She seemed especially pensive tonight. When she looked out into the distance and bit down on her bottom lip, he realized that she actually did have something on her mind, something she found difficult to say.

"What's bothering you?" he asked.

She took a deep breath and slowly let it out. "When I called everyone in for dinner this evening, your uncle came in a bit winded. Did you notice?"

Now that she'd mentioned it… "Yes, but he'd been outside and had probably hurried to the house. He always used to fuss when I came in late at mealtime."

"That's possible, I guess."

Her concern for Uncle George didn't surprise Matt. Back in the day, the polished college-bound teen and the gruff old rancher had grown surprisingly close. In fact, his uncle had really taken a shine to her. He'd claimed that was because she kept Matt out of trouble. But it was more than that. George had never married or had kids, and having Miranda around seemed to make them a family.

You be good to that little gal, George had once told him. *She's got a sweet disposition and a great sense of humor. But she's also got a good heart.*

And more than once, after Matt's recent arrival at the Double G, when he'd seen the two of them together, George's words had again rung in his ears: *If I'd had a daughter, I would have wanted her to be just like Miranda.*

And Miranda had felt the same way about him. *I love your uncle. He might have a rough exterior, but he's a real softy, too. Don't get me wrong, I'm close to my father, but sometimes George is a lot easier for me to talk to.*

Miranda stopped rocking and turned her head toward Matt. "I don't doubt that he has an infected toenail, but I haven't seen him limp or heard him complain."

"You think he lied to me when he claimed that prescription I picked up for him was an antibiotic?"

"I don't know. It's just that…" She let out a soft sigh. "I think he's having some health issues… Maybe his heart. Or possibly his lungs."

At that, Matt stiffened. "What makes you say that?"

"He's obviously seen a doctor recently. And he's had two different prescriptions. Would they both be for his toe?"

"Maybe."

"I also caught him stroking his left arm the other day. So when he seemed to have trouble catching his breath this evening…? It's probably nothing, but I'm a little concerned."

Matt hadn't noticed anything unusual, but it had been a long time since he'd been home, let alone spent any quality time with his uncle. Once he went back on the circuit, he'd have to make a point of coming around more often. That is, *if* he went back.

"You know," Matt said, "if he's actually having health issues, I don't think he'd ever admit it. Maybe I should talk to his doctor."

"You won't find out anything by talking to his doctor. The HIPAA regulations won't allow him or her to discuss your uncle's health with you."

"Then I'll just have to ask George and not settle for a *nothing's wrong* answer." Hopefully, if there was anything to be alarmed about, the feisty old codger would open up and level with him.

"Good." Miranda set the rocker in motion again, as if that was settled, but then she looked into the darkness again and began to nibble on her bottom lip.

"What else is bothering you?" he asked.

She didn't respond right away, either to admit or deny it. After a few creaks of the rocker, she stopped the motion completely and turned to him. "I've tried to tell you several times why I left town."

"And I've told you it doesn't matter." Her father had had a strong hold on her back then—and he probably still did. "You were a minor. You had to do what you were told."

Even though she'd returned to the ranch, which showed that she'd grown up and had more gumption, she still hadn't told her father where she was. Nor had she revealed her pregnancy.

"Do you remember that trouble you and your friends got into at the beginning of your senior year?" Miranda asked.

How could he forget? They'd tried to play a trick on the football team, but it backfired and the janitor was seriously injured.

"You were on probation," she added.

And he'd been damned lucky, too. If Poncho's foster dad hadn't gone to bat for them, they could have faced time in juvenile hall or in jail.

"And remember that day things blew up?" she asked.

"When your dad showed up at the ranch?" What a disastrous day that had been. They'd been making homemade ice cream with an old hand-cranking machine on the front porch when her father had arrived, along with a private investigator. Her old man had pitched a real fit.

Matt had tried to tell the berry king that he was in love with his daughter, that he'd never hurt her, but that only seemed to make things worse.

I don't know what kind of picture you've painted for Miranda, Carlos Contreras had said, *but I'm not about to let my daughter waste her life by hooking up with a footloose cowboy hell-bent on trouble. She's destined for bigger and better things.*

Matt had expected Miranda to object, to stand up to her father, to defend their relationship, but she'd buckled instead and had gone home with him.

It had been a crushing and demoralizing confrontation, and in the midst of his anger and resentment, Matt realized that, even if he didn't understand why, Miranda loved and respected her father. So, for that reason alone, he'd been determined to win the guy over, although he hadn't had a clue where to even start.

Matt chuffed. And how had that wild plan worked out?

"When we got home," Miranda said, "my dad accused me of..."

She didn't have to say it. Matt had a pretty good idea what Mr. Contreras had said.

Miranda cleared her throat, then continued with the story that he'd already pieced together on his own. "I swore up and down that we'd never slept together. He eventually believed me and mellowed out some. That's when I called you and suggested that we take a break from each other. And you agreed."

Matt hadn't had any choice other than to go along with the decision her father had made and forced onto her. So he didn't call her for a few days, thinking her father would chill and that he'd talk to her at school. But she never returned to Brighton Valley High. Nor had she called him again.

Later, he found out that she'd left town, and no one would tell him where she went, leaving Matt feeling abandoned yet again.

Miranda might think she'd had a good reason for leaving without a trace. And she probably thought he understood. In a way, he supposed he did, but it was too late to go back in time. Too much had happened. Too much had changed. Yet, one thing hadn't.

He stole a glance at her and saw the way she bit down on her lip, the crease in her pretty brow. He could have reached out to her, taken her hand, given it a forgiving squeeze. Because, in a way, he did forgive her. At least, his anger and resentment had eased. But she'd always be her father's princess, under his wing and under his thumb.

Matt was no longer a *footloose cowboy hell-bent on trouble*, but he doubted that made any difference. The berry king wouldn't find a broken-down bull rider any better suited for his princess.

So he fought the urge to say or do something stupid. Instead, he let Miranda continue with her confession and the apology he couldn't quite accept.

Miranda had no idea whether her words were having any effect on Matt or not, but it helped her to unload the guilt and the painful memories that had plagued her for the past nine years.

"In order to keep us apart," she continued, "my dad pulled me out of Brighton Valley High and sent me back to the private school I used to attend."

"His plan certainly worked. I never saw you after that."

"True. And things only got worse. When I got nauseous several mornings in a row, he realized I was pregnant and that I'd lied to him." Miranda closed her eyes, hoping to blink back the memory, but it didn't work.

Her father narrowed his eyes, scoffed at her and spat out the most hurtful words she'd ever heard. *Apparently, rotten apples don't fall too far from the tree.*

He hadn't actually called her a tramp, but she'd known what he'd meant. Her mother had left them both for another man, a wealthy and influential oil-man. The loss and rejection had hit her dad hard, and he'd never quite recovered from it.

On the other hand, Miranda had only been a baby at the time, so it hadn't really affected her. At least, not directly.

Still, the hateful accusation had cut her to the quick. She might have turned on him right then and there, raised her own ruckus and stood her ground. But what he'd said next nearly knocked her to her knees.

That damned kid is nineteen, and you're seven-teen—which means you're underage. Stay away from him, or I'll call the sheriff.

Miranda sucked in a lungful of the cool night air, then slowly let it out and pressed on. "He threatened to have you charged with statutory rape. And since you were already on probation, I was afraid you'd end up serving time in jail." She looked at Matt, awaiting his reaction, but he merely sat there, stone-faced. Had he even been listening?

She would have gone on, but when he furrowed his brow, considering what she'd told him and possibly pondering his response, the words stalled in her throat.

Finally, he said, "So that's why you left without looking back."

That wasn't true. She'd looked back nearly every day since. She just hadn't contacted him.

"I was willing to do anything to protect you," she added, "so I agreed to never see you again. That's why I stopped calling."

Matt's gaze zeroed in on her. "Okay. I got that. It

was over between us. But you should have told me about the baby."

"Yes, I should have, but I knew what you'd do. If I'd told you I was pregnant, you would have challenged my dad. And then he would have followed through on his threat. So I agreed to live with his aunt in Brownsville and have the baby there."

His silence chilled the night air, and she gripped the rocker's armrests until her fingers ached, waiting for his understanding, if not his forgiveness.

"I can understand why you did what you did," he said. "Back then, anyway. But you're an adult now, and you're still afraid to cross him."

In some ways, she supposed, Matt was right. But these days, when she complied, it was by choice. "I challenge him when I have to."

"Like *when*?"

"The first time was when he called me at my aunt's house and told me that he'd talked to an adoption agency. When I refused to even consider it, he threatened to disown me if I didn't give up the baby and go to college as planned. But I never would have done that, no matter what the consequences."

"That was only a threat. He wouldn't have disowned you. He loves you too much."

"I know." At least, she knew it now. But at the time, after he'd compared her to her mother, she hadn't been so sure.

"So," Matt said, "your dad apparently softened his stance when it came to adoption. You kept Emily, and you went to college."

"That's true, but I threw a fit of my own when he suggested I go to a four-year university and move into a dorm. He actually thought I'd leave Emily with him and let a nanny raise her. But I refused. I went to a local junior college part-time, and eventually, when she was old enough to attend preschool, I transferred to Rice University."

The stifling silence returned, and Miranda pondered the past and the various choices she'd made—both good and bad. She suspected Matt might be doing the same thing.

"I realize you must resent my father," she said, "and under the circumstances, I can't blame you for having hard feelings or even hating him. But he absolutely adores Emily and has apologized a hundred times over for even suggesting I give her up."

Matt chuffed. "You still should have called me—at least once. It's been nine freakin' years, Miranda."

"After she was born, I *did* call, and George told me you'd gone out on the rodeo circuit. He and I talked a bit, but I didn't tell him about Emily."

"You could have asked him to contact me."

She'd thought about it. But news like that should be given face-to-face. "He asked if I wanted to leave a message, but I told him I'd call back after the rodeo season ended."

"But you didn't."

No, not after she'd done an internet search and then scanned various social media sites. She'd learned that Matt was whooping it up with the other cowboys and countless rodeo groupies. But even if she hadn't gotten a glimpse of what his new life was like, she wouldn't have followed him from arena to arena with a newborn.

"I'm sorry, Matt. I should have contacted you. But with each day that passed, the harder it got. Still, I wasn't going to keep it a secret. I planned to tell you about her eventually."

And that time had finally arrived.

She glanced his way, but he continued to look out into the night at the darkened ranch. Had he even begun to understand why she'd stayed away? Would he accept her apology? And more importantly, would he truly forgive her?

"I guess that's all in the past now," he said, without looking at her. "So it doesn't really matter."

But his feelings *did* matter. Call it young love or just a teenage crush from which she'd never recovered, she still cared for Matt, a lot more than she cared to admit. And if he still had any feelings left for her, it would help them co-parent their daughter, assuming he wanted to be that involved in her life.

"So now what?" he asked, as if filing away her excuses, along with her apology.

"I'm not sure." She hadn't gotten that far yet. But maybe he had an answer, a suggestion.

She turned to him, only to find him looking at her. His gaze was intense, but she couldn't spot any lingering anger. He continued to study her in silence, setting off a tingle in her chest, jump-starting her heart once again and sparking a dream she'd once had. A hopeless dream she'd been dodging since the day he arrived at the ranch.

But their lives, their careers, had gone in completely different directions. And the last thing Matt would be interested in was a woman who was pregnant with another man's baby, a single mom who'd be opposed to frequenting cowboy bars and spending nights on the town.

"I hope we can put this behind us and move on," she said. "For Emily's sake."

"It'll take time, but we probably can."

She let out the breath she'd been holding. "Thanks, Matt."

He continued to eye her, assessing her. Judging her?

She might have looked away, if his expression hadn't softened to the point that it seemed almost...hopeful.

"Matt!" George called from inside the house. "Your cell phone is ringing."

He didn't respond right away. Not to his uncle, not to her. After a beat, he nodded toward the front door. "I'd better get that."

Then he broke eye contact, as well as the frail, tentative connection they'd briefly shared, setting her adrift on uncertainty as she tried to avoid a slew of bobbing memories and emotions.

She watched him rise from the rocker, using the armrests as a brace. He moved with pride and strength, yet at the same time, he seemed vulnerable, and her heart went out to him.

As he took a step, his knee buckled and he listed to the side. She jumped from her seat and reached out to steady him. Her attempt worked, and he straightened.

His gaze met hers again, locking her in place. He didn't thank her. Nor did he move.

She didn't move, either. She didn't even dare to breathe.

Her brain tried to make sense of the silent words he spoke, the memories his touch provoked, only to fail miserably. But for some crazy reason, her heart didn't have that same problem.

In spite of herself, she placed her hand on his jaw, felt the light bristles of his cheek. And against all common sense, she drew his mouth to hers.

Chapter Eight

The second Miranda's hand slipped behind Matt's neck, her fingers lit his skin on fire. And when her lips met his, he was toast. His knees went weak, and his heart began to pump as if there were no tomorrow. And right now, there didn't seem to be any yesterdays, either.

The kiss started soft and tentative, but within a beat, it damn near exploded with pent-up desire and pumped up a demanding erection.

Before he knew it, he'd morphed back into that same stupid kid who'd yet to be hurt, disappointed and abandoned. And that kid only knew one thing. He'd missed Miranda something fierce. And he'd missed *this*.

Her mouth opened, and his tongue slid inside, where it met hers in a heated rush, twisting, tasting. He remembered how good it had been between them, how good it still was.

It was also crazy. What in the hell was he thinking? Kissing Miranda had to be the dumbest thing he'd ever done. Yet, he couldn't seem to help himself from pulling her close and holding her tight.

Her baby bump pressed into him, but even that didn't slow him down. Nor did it matter, as the years rolled away, taking the pain and anger with them and leaving him with this one magical moment in time.

Only the screen door creaking open brought him back to his senses, and he would've jumped a foot—if he hadn't had a bum knee—taking a startled Miranda with him.

"Whoopsy-daisy." George cleared his throat and chuckled. "You missed a call, so I thought I'd bring your phone out to you. But I guess I should've let the damn thing ring."

Matt didn't have the foggiest clue what to say, let alone how to explain this. Not to his uncle, and certainly not to himself.

He took the phone from George and thanked him, his voice thick with guilt and embarrassment and who knew what else.

George was still chuckling to himself as he returned to the house, allowing the screen door to slam behind him.

Matt wished he could do the same thing—slip away, disappear, forget what had just happened under the amber glow of the porch light. But it wasn't the light that had cast a spell on him tonight.

"I'm sorry," he said. But hell, why should he be contrite when she's the one who'd started it?

"Me, too." Her words came out soft and tender. Maybe even fragile.

"I…uh…" He lifted his cell phone to show her a plausible excuse for taking off without addressing what they'd just done, which would only open up a slew of emotion and pain he'd rather not wade through. "I've got a call to return."

"And I have a bedtime story to read." She smiled, then headed indoors, leaving him in one hell of a quandary.

He remained outside for a while, holding his phone, bewildered and kicking himself until his erection subsided.

Finally, he glanced at the lighted screen and saw that his buddy, Clay Masters, had called. If Clay wasn't married and the daddy to twins, which kept him and his wife both busy in the evenings, Matt might have suggested they meet at the Stagecoach Inn that very night for a beer. He could really use a friend right now. He needed someone to talk to.

Not about Miranda, though. His feelings were too convoluted to even think about putting them into words.

No, he was more concerned about his slow recovery—and what that might mean. And who better to open up to than a man who'd suffered an injury that had ended his military career?

Realizing they didn't need to go to the local cowboy

bar and throw back a couple of beers to have a conversation like that, Matt returned Clay's call.

"Hey," his buddy said, "what'd you do, lose your phone?"

"Nope. Just didn't hear it ring. What's up?"

"Not much. I hadn't heard from you in a while and thought I'd touch base. I finally have a little more time on my hands these days. And more energy since the babies are finally sleeping through the night."

Clay and his wife Erica were the proud parents of twins—a boy and a girl—which kept them busy.

"I'm glad you can finally get some sleep at night," Matt said. "That's got to be a relief."

"Yeah, life is finally settling down, In fact, Drew and Lainie are going to watch the twins for us on Saturday night so I can take Erica to a movie and dinner."

Drew Madison, the promotional guru Matt worked with at Esteban Enterprises, had married Erica's twin sister. The couple had recently adopted three little boys—brothers who'd been separated in foster care.

"Since Drew and Lainie have kids now and one on the way," Clay added, "we're going to babysit for each other once a week so we can have date nights."

"That's a great idea."

"The reason I called," Clay said, "is to check in on you. How are you doing?"

"Not as good as I'd hoped. I thought coming home to the Double G would make it easier for me to take it easy and to heal, but that's not working out as well as I'd hoped it would. To tell the truth, I'm a little worried about the slow recovery."

"I know what you mean. I eventually healed from my injury, but I had to make a career change. And that actually turned out okay. I'm a lot happier than I thought I'd be."

"Say," Matt said, "as a Life Flight pilot, you work with a lot of paramedics and probably run across medical professionals all the time. Can you ask around and get the name of a good orthopedic surgeon? I think I should get a second opinion."

"I don't need to. Call Brighton Valley Orthopedics and ask to see Jamal Hillman. One of the guys I work with was involved in a serious car accident and really did a number on his ankle. I thought for sure he'd be permanently disabled, and so did he. But he's coming along great. He's still moving slowly and seeing a physical therapist, but he raves about Dr. Hillman."

"I'll call and make an appointment tomorrow. Thanks."

"No problem, buddy. Keep me posted."

Matt almost mentioned Miranda, but that might lead to questions about how he felt about her, and he really didn't know. Even if he was foolish enough to think that something might eventually develop between the two of them, he certainly wasn't going to do a damned thing about it until he was back to fighting weight and on top of his game.

But keeping Miranda a secret meant he couldn't tell his buddy about Emily, either, which was too bad. The two men had something else in common these days, now that they were both family men.

So, for now, he let it all slide and ended the call on a happier note.

Matt would have plenty of time to tell Clay about all the changes going on in his life, starting with Miranda's arrival. But he had to make an appointment to see Dr. Hillman first. Then again, something told him he might need a miracle, rather than just a second opinion. If he wasn't a champion bull rider, then who was he?

He certainly wouldn't be a man her father would consider good enough for Miranda. And Matt had no intention of facing Carlos Contreras until he was all that and more.

Matt managed to avoid Miranda for the rest of the evening and the following morning. The last thing he wanted was for her to think that kiss meant anything, especially since he had no idea what to tell her.

So after having only coffee for breakfast, which he took outside to drink, he waited until nine o'clock and called Brighton Valley Orthopedics to make an appointment with Jamal Hillman, the surgeon Clay had recommended.

The sooner Matt saw the doctor and got a better idea of what lay in front of him, of what he could expect in the future, the better off he'd be.

Unfortunately, the first available appointment he could get was on Friday afternoon, and that was only because the receptionist was a big rodeo fan and had squeezed him in.

"Come early," she said. "And expect to wait."

That meant avoiding Miranda for another four days,

which wouldn't be easy. So he told George he had an out-of-town meeting with the Rocking Chair Rodeo promoters, then checked into the Night Owl Motel and tried to keep a low profile.

Talk about going to extremes.

By the time Friday rolled around, Matt was more than ready to get his life back on track. At the very least, he'd be happy just to get a good night's sleep in his own bed.

Now he was seated in the waiting room at Brighton Valley Orthopedics, holding a magazine he was too antsy to read and listening for his name to be called.

Minutes later, a matronly brunette wearing pale blue scrubs called out, "Matt Grimes?"

He set aside the *Field and Stream* and made his way to the open doorway that led to the back office.

Once he'd been asked to take a seat on an exam table, he waited another fourteen minutes until a tall young doctor wearing neatly styled dreadlocks entered the room introducing himself as Dr. Hillman and offering Matt a friendly smile and a firm professional handshake.

"Tell me about your injury," the doctor said.

Matt explained how it had happened and what the previous doctor had told him. Then he handed over the digital X-rays he'd been given.

Dr. Hillman studied them, then said, "The bone isn't fractured, although I see what could be a small crack in one of the inner bones."

That was news to Matt. Apparently, someone hadn't noticed that before.

The doctor turned away from the black-and-white image and probed Matt's knee. "It's still pretty swollen."

"The initial pain has eased up some, but at times, it still hurts like hell."

"I'd like to take another X-ray," the doctor said.

"To find out if it's healing?"

"Yes," Dr. Hillman said, "but I'd also like to see if there've been any new developments that have made things worse. I'm also going to order an MRI to see the extent of the tissue damage, and we may want to follow that up with an ultrasound."

Matt had always been leery of people in the medical field, but something told him that he was in good hands now.

"We can do it all in this office," Dr. Hillman added, "but we're a little behind today, so you'll have to wait until the tech is free."

"No problem. I don't have anything pressing to do. I just want this thing to heal. And the sooner the better."

An hour later, Matt had finished getting both the X-ray and the MRI, both of which he'd been told would be digital images. That, in itself, suggested Brighton Valley Orthopedics had a state-of-the-art operation.

Now he was back in the waiting room, thumbing through another magazine he couldn't quite get into. As much as he would've liked to complain about all the time this was taking, he realized he was partly to blame for the heavy schedule and kept his mouth shut.

Finally, a different woman wearing pink scrubs called him back to an exam room, and ten minutes later, Dr. Hillman came in, brought up the latest images they'd taken and pointed out his concerns.

"The crack appears to be mending," Dr. Hillman said, as he studied the new X-ray on the screen. "So that doesn't concern me. But you've got a torn patellar tendon, which is causing all the pain. You're going to need to take it easy, and once the swelling goes down, I'm going to order some physical therapy."

"I'll admit that I pushed myself too hard for a while, but now that I'm back home, I've made a point of taking it easy."

"Good." Dr. Hillman showed him the ultrasound scan. "I'm afraid both you and that bull have done a real number on that tendon. Bones usually heal faster than tissue. But the problem with this particular tear is that it could turn into patellar tendinitis if you're not careful, and that can have painful, crippling and lifelong consequences if not allowed to heal properly."

Matt braced himself for the answer to his biggest question. "But it will heal. Right? Completely?"

"With time." Dr. Hillman turned away from his computer screen to face Matt and crossed his arms. "I know how important it is for you to get back to competing, so let's take another look at your knee in three to four weeks."

That long? *After* the Rocking Chair Rodeo took place? Matt blew out a ragged sigh. "So, no riding until then?"

"I wouldn't recommend it—unless you're willing to risk a far more serious consequence that could keep you from any rodeo competition for the rest of your life, not to mention many day-to-day activities." The doctor placed his hand on Matt's shoulder and gave it a gentle squeeze. "Athletes tend to recover sooner than those who aren't as healthy and strong, but sometimes they don't take the time for their bodies to recover and push themselves too hard. And then all bets are off."

Again, Matt blew out a sigh.

"Hey," Dr. Hillman said, "no one gets this better than I do. I was a long distance runner in college, so I know what I'm talking about. You need to take off that mask and cape and give your body the time it needs."

"Okay. Got it."

"I'm also going to prescribe a brace that will help to stabilize your knee, as well as a pain medication."

"I…uh…already have some medication and a brace," Matt admitted. "I have a cane, too, but I…"

A wry grin slid across the doctor's face. "A real tough guy, huh? Well, the choice is yours, but I'd put it back on and wear it if I were you."

Matt nodded. "Okay. Thanks, Doc."

As soon as the doctor left the exam room, Matt limped to the front office, settled the bill and paid his deductible.

You'd think he'd have been happy to finally have his questions answered, especially by someone he'd come to trust, but those answers weren't the ones he'd hoped for.

Once he got back in the truck, he checked his cell and saw that Clay had called while his phone had been on silent. But Matt wouldn't return the call yet. He was still trying to wrap his mind around the news the doctor had given him, which would require an attitude adjustment. And that wasn't going to be easy for a guy who cherished his mask and cape.

In the meantime, he headed home. He couldn't stay away from the Double G forever.

Since it was nearing the dinner hour, he called the house to ask about the mealtime plans. If Miranda wasn't in the kitchen cooking and George had yet to open any cans of whatever simple fare he'd stored in the pantry, Matt would be happy to pick up something at one of the local restaurants or a drive-through and take it home.

The phone rang several times before George answered by saying, "I don't know who this is, but I hope you have a darn good reason for dragging me away from watching *Lonesome Dove.*"

Matt laughed. If anyone had been counting, his uncle had probably watched that Western miniseries on television twenty-three times or more.

"I don't want to keep you from your favorite evening entertainment," Matt said. "I just need to know if you guys want me to bring something home for dinner. Or does Miranda plan to cook tonight?"

"She probably won't be home in time to eat, so get whatever you'd like. I've been munching on tortilla chips and guacamole, so I'm not too hungry."

"Where is she?"

"Miranda? She and Emily have spent the last couple of days at the county fairgrounds with the other kids and their lambs."

No wonder it had been so easy for him to avoid her. "When's the auction?"

"Tomorrow. At one o'clock, I think. Are you going?"

"Of course." What kind of dad skipped out on an event that was important to his daughter? Actually, Matt knew exactly what kind of father would do that. And years ago, he'd sworn not to follow in those lousy footsteps.

"I wouldn't miss it for the world," he added.

"I'm a little surprised, though."

At that, Matt gripped the steering wheel a little tighter. "About what?"

"Emily agreeing to auction off her lamb. She loves Bob. And the animal loves her, too. She doesn't even need a halter or a lead. It follows her wherever she goes."

"You're probably right," Matt said. "I have a feeling it's going to be hard for her to let him go. Especially knowing he'll end up as lamb stew on someone's dinner table."

"Yeah. That's what I'm thinking. But when I mentioned the auction, she seemed excited and told me that some of the other kids got over a thousand dollars for their lambs last year."

Damn. With a business sense like that, Emily might have more Contreras blood than Matt had realized. He supposed that wasn't a bad thing to have, as long as she didn't let it go to her head.

And Matt would have to make sure that it didn't.

"About dinner," Matt said. "I'll pick up a couple of

cheeseburgers. You're not hungry now, but you might be later tonight."

"That sounds good to me. And while you're at it, pick up an order of fries and a chocolate milkshake for me, too."

So much for filling up on chips and guacamole. Matt let out a little chuckle and slowly shook his head. "You got it. But what about Miranda?"

"What about her?" His uncle's jovial tone suggested that the man who didn't like to pry was doing just that.

Curiosity was probably eating him up, especially after he caught Matt and Miranda kissing on Monday night. But even if Matt wanted to open up to his uncle, he still didn't have a clue what he ought to do about it—if anything. So he didn't bite and skirted the issue instead.

"Will Miranda be home later tonight?" he asked. "If so, I can get something for her and Emily, too."

"I'm not sure when she'll be in, but it might be a good idea to get something for them, just to be safe. And you probably know this, but I'll mention it anyway. She prefers chicken over beef."

Matt had noticed that.

"By the way," George said, "I have a question for you. And I want to know the truth."

The direct approach, huh? Matt rolled his eyes. He hadn't just been avoiding Miranda so he didn't have to talk about that blasted kiss, he'd been avoiding George, too. And for the same reason.

He braced himself for the inevitable and said, "Fire away."

"How'd your visit with the doctor go? What did he have to say?"

That wasn't the question Matt had expected to hear. "How'd you know I saw a doctor?"

"Clay called a few minutes ago. He tried to reach you on your cell, but you didn't answer. So he thought you might be home."

Matt hadn't planned to tell anyone that he'd been concerned about his recovery and that he was getting a second opinion. Other than Clay, of course. But it was too late to backpedal now.

"I'll be okay." Eventually. And *hopefully*. "It's just going to take a little more time." And sadly, way more than he'd expected.

"At least you'll be okay in the long run," George said.

"Yeah, but not in time to compete at the Rocking Chair Rodeo. And I hate letting everyone down."

"So what are you going to do?"

"It's still two weeks away, so I'll have to take it day by day."

And that's just the same plan he'd make for dealing with Miranda.

Miranda got home late from the fairgrounds, tired and ready to call it a day. But when she spotted Matt's truck parked near the barn, her breath caught and a surge of adrenaline revived her. She hadn't known when he'd return from his business trip, but she'd hoped he would be home in time for the auction. That is, if he wanted to attend. Emily would be disappointed if he didn't.

She glanced in the rearview mirror at her daughter, who'd fallen asleep on the drive home. Had Miranda not been pregnant, she might have tried to carry Emily inside and put her to bed. As it was, she opted to wake the sleepy child and guide her to the back door.

The house was dark, so she assumed that both George and Matt had turned in for the night, which was just as well. She wasn't up for a chat.

After putting Emily to bed, tucking her in and kissing her brow, Miranda returned to the kitchen for a cookie and a glass of milk, a bedtime snack she hoped would tide her over until breakfast.

When she opened the fridge, she spotted two boxed meals on the center shelf, which she suspected had come from Caroline's Diner. She assumed Matt had brought dinner home for them, which had been a nice gesture. But one she refused to read into. They'd shared an amazing kiss last Monday, but they'd never talked about it. And to be honest, she was afraid to think about it too long. Nor was she crazy enough to ask Matt how he felt about it.

So once she'd eaten an Oreo and downed her milk, she made her way to her bedroom and climbed into bed, too tired to think.

Morning rolled around before she knew it, and by the time she'd showered, dressed and headed to the kitchen, everyone else had beat her there. George stood at the stove flipping pancakes, while Emily was perched on the counter beside him, watching his every move.

But it was Matt who caught Miranda's eye and demanded her full attention.

He sat leisurely at the table, a mug of black coffee in his hand. He'd shaved, nicking his chin in the process, but that didn't mar him in the least. His hair, still damp from the shower, was stylishly mussed. When their gazes met, her heart took a tumble. Memories of that heated kiss she'd tried to forget came flooding back, threatening to carry her away.

Darn it. If Matt stuck around the Double G much longer, she'd have to find another place to live. And quickly. She wasn't going to hold up very well if she had to face him each morning.

"I hope you're hungry," George said, a raised spatula in hand. "It's going to be a long day for all of us, and a good one. So I whipped up some of my famous hotcakes. You had them once before, Miranda, and you said you liked them. And I got a bottle of that blueberry syrup, too."

Yes, of course.

Blueberry pancakes.

Breakfast.

She turned away from Matt, tamping down the thoughts she shouldn't have, the dreams she had no business resurrecting and blessed his uncle with an appreciative smile. "Yes, you make the best pancakes in the world. But I'd better only have one. I'm a little too excited to eat."

Actually, she was more nervous than excited. And not just about Matt and the kiss they'd shared.

She studied her bright-eyed daughter, who didn't

seem the least bit concerned about that auction, which seemed a little odd for an animal lover who'd bonded with Bob the day they'd brought him to the ranch.

"How 'bout you?" George asked Matt. "That coffee's gonna burn a hole in your gizzard if you don't put something else in your belly."

"You're not much of a cook," Matt said, "but your hotcakes are the best I've ever eaten. I doubt Caroline could make better. So yes, Uncle George. I'll take a short stack."

While Emily chattered away, Miranda put a cup of water in the microwave and set the timer for two minutes. After the beep sounded, she removed it and brewed a single serving of herbal tea.

"I can't wait to go to the fair," Emily said. "I bet me and Bob win a blue ribbon."

"What time are we supposed to get there?" Matt asked.

"I forget. I'll have to check." Emily jumped down from the counter and made her way to the fridge where they'd posted the flyer with a magnet.

Apparently, Matt planned to go with them, which was both personally unsettling and a maternal relief. But she shook off her uneasiness, glad to know his presence would make Emily happy. For that reason, she caught his eye and smiled gratefully.

Like usual, when she tried to silently show her appreciation, he answered with a half-shrug, as if it were no big deal. But this was a special day for their daughter, and his being there to cheer her on was huge.

"The fair opens at nine o'clock," Emily said. "And

after I check on Bob and make sure he's okay, we can walk around and look at stuff."

"That'll give us time to go on a few rides, too. I'm looking forward to riding the roller coaster with you." Matt winked at the little girl. "That is, if you're not afraid."

"Hey!" Emily slapped her hands on her hips. "I'm not scared to ride it. I saw it yesterday and it's super big. But it'll be fun." Emily turned to Miranda. "Will you go with us, Mom?"

And ignore the signs that warned pregnant women not to get on any wild rides?

"Not today." She placed her hand on her belly and caressed her growing baby bump. "I'll have more fun watching you."

Besides, now that Matt had reentered her life, she'd already boarded an emotional roller coaster that was taking her through more ups and downs than she liked.

Chapter Nine

Matt and Miranda, along with George and Emily, drove to the county fairgrounds right after breakfast. They parked in the main lot, which was filling fast, and headed to the barns to visit Bob.

Emily slipped into his pen, dropped to her knees and gave the lamb a hug. Then she kissed his wooly head. "You look so handsome with your new haircut, Bob. Everyone is going to see that you're the best lamb here."

George placed a curved hand to his mouth and mumbled something to Matt. Miranda strained to hear what he was saying, only to pick up a few words and phrases.

"I don't know 'bout this..."

"Bob? Should be Shish ka-Bob."

"You sure she knows...?"

Miranda caught enough to know what he meant. A similar thought had crossed her mind more than once. Emily didn't seem to mind that Bob was going on the auction block, which was surprising because she was so fond of him. But apparently she was okay with it because she'd already begun to list the things she wanted to buy with her money. And she'd even mentioned her plan to donate a hundred dollars to Rick's animal rescue operation.

After letting herself out of Bob's pen, Emily said, "We have to be back by twelve-thirty. But we can go on the rides until then."

"Then what are we waiting for?" Matt asked. "Let's check out that roller coaster and see if it's as big as you said it was."

They exited the barn, then walked through the exhibit hall and out to the actual fairgrounds. Excitement filled the air, along with the tantalizing smell of candied apples, peanuts and cotton candy.

It was still early in the day, but people were already in line to purchase deep-fried Twinkies and a variety of almost every other packaged pastry imaginable.

Matt stopped by the ticket booth and pulled out his wallet to purchase a package of tickets. He'd worn a knee brace today. Miranda first thought his leg must be bothering him, but then she realized he'd probably come prepared to do a lot of walking.

In the distance, children laughed and shrieked with glee, while a baby needing a nap or some cuddling began to fuss.

"There it is!" Emily pointed to the roller coaster. "See? I told you it was super big."

Matt reached for her hand. "Then let's go."

As the rodeo champ limped along with the excited child, Miranda couldn't help admiring him—and not just his awesome physical appearance. He wasn't letting a bad knee stop him from spending the day with his daughter and making sure she was having fun.

By the time Miranda and George caught up with them, Matt and Emily had settled into one of the cars, just as a ride attendant lowered the lap bar and locked it in place.

As their train of cars rolled off in a wheel-churning, metal-creaking rush, a thrill shot through Miranda, and she felt as if she were riding along with them, even though she remained on the sidelines with George.

By the time Matt and Emily reached the first peak on the track and began their descent, they raised their hands in the air. Matt, who must have taught Emily the fine art of roller coaster riding, laughed. And Emily squealed in both fear and delight.

Miranda placed her hand on her baby bump and reminded herself not to lose her head and let her emotions run away with her. No matter how she'd felt about Matt in the past, the young cowboy she'd once loved was long gone. And even if his lovemaking had been honed and was far better than she remembered, the kiss they'd shared the other night didn't mean a thing and would have to remain a sweet memory. She'd have to be content knowing that her happy daughter not only looked up to her father, but she adored him, too. And

Matt appeared to feel the same way about her. Only a fool would ask for any more than that.

When the roller coaster ride came to an end, Matt gave Emily a high five before climbing out of the car. As they approached Miranda and George, Matt's limp seemed a little more pronounced, but he wore a brighter smile.

Again, Miranda had to remind herself that she'd be foolish to dream of having any more than she already had—a happy child, a renewed friendship with the man she'd once loved, a man who was proving to be a good father.

But when Matt's gazed locked on hers, and her heart spun out of control, she feared that she was more foolish than she'd ever thought possible.

For nearly two hours, Emily led Matt from one carnival ride to another, while George and Miranda tagged along behind them, and the exuberant child didn't slow down until Matt insisted that it was time to take a break and get something to eat.

"That's a good idea." Miranda wanted to get off her feet, too. She should have worn different shoes because the new flats she'd chosen had rubbed her right heel raw. She'd have to look to be sure, but she suspected she'd find a blister.

"I'll tell ya what." George reached into his back pocket and pulled out his beat-up wallet. "If you'll take a seat at this table, I'll spring for lunch. Any one up for chili dogs? They can be a little messy, but they sure are good."

"I don't like chilies or cheese," Emily said. "I only want ketchup on mine."

Miranda and Matt both opted for regular hot dogs.

"All right-y," George said. "I'll have 'em pack up those dogs and all the fixin's, then I'll bring them back to you."

"Thanks. That'd be great." Matt took a seat, stretched out his bad leg and used his fingers to stroke his knee through the metal hinges on his brace.

"After we eat a good lunch, can we have cotton candy for dessert?" Emily asked.

Matt glanced at his cell phone. "We'd better wait to have dessert until after the auction. It's almost noon, and we'll need to head back to the barn pretty soon."

Forty-five minutes later, after they left Emily at the barn, they headed to the grandstand and took their seats, with Miranda in the middle.

"You've been a real trouper today," Miranda told Matt. "How are you holding up?"

"I'm okay." He glanced at her lap, where her hands had clasped around her belly, then looked up and caught her gaze. "How about you?"

Rather than respond to the quiet implication that pregnancy might be slowing her down, she skated over it by removing her right shoe and wiggling her toes. "Other than a blister on my heel, I'm holding up just fine." She nodded at his bad leg. "I'm more concerned about you. I hope you haven't set yourself back."

"You and me both. But I didn't have the heart to disappoint Emily when she was having so much fun."

"I know what you mean. Her enthusiasm can be a

little annoying sometimes, but I actually admire it."
Miranda admired Matt, too. He was turning out to be
a good father, one Emily could look up to. A man she
could be proud of.

Matt cocked his head slightly and eyed her face.

"What's the matter?" she asked.

He reached out and placed his index finger at the
side of her mouth, stroking her skin and sparking a
heated tingle that rushed down her throat and to her
chest.

Her breath caught. She would have asked what he
was doing, but she was so stunned by his touch that
she couldn't form a single word.

"You've got a little mustard there," he said. "But
I got it."

She opened her mouth to thank him for caring
enough to save her the embarrassment of walking
around the fairgrounds with the remnant of her lunch
on her face. But what if she stuttered and stammered?
What if he realized his touch still had a blood-stirring
effect on her?

She cleared her throat, shaking one single word free.
"Thanks."

Matt merely nodded, then pointed to the arena and
the parade of children and their lambs now entering.

George was the first to spot Emily and Bob. "Will
you look at that? She's doing great. She's leaving plenty
of room between Bob and the other lambs. And she's
making sure his legs are set and that his head is up
and alert."

"And she's keeping her eyes on the judge," Miranda added. "Just like she's supposed to."

"She's a born showman," Matt said.

Miranda pulled out her cell phone and began snapping pictures.

"Looks like you're having a proud mama moment," George said.

Miranda laughed. "You've got that right."

They craned their necks as they watched Emily show her lamb, going through the drills she'd practiced daily since Bob's arrival on the Double G.

After the judge handed Emily a red ribbon, she dropped to her knees in front of her lamb, cupped his face with her hands and pressed a kiss on his snout. Then she gave him a hug.

"Looks like she's having a proud mama moment, too," Matt said.

"Maybe so." George sat back in his seat and gripped the armrests. "But I don't have a good feeling about this."

"Neither do I," Miranda said. "But so far, she seems to be okay with it. I guess we'll have to wait and see how she does after the auction."

They didn't have to wait long. Ten minutes later, Bob was on the block. As the bids increased, Emily appeared delighted. And when he sold for nearly fifteen-hundred dollars, she lifted her hands to clap, then slapped them back at her sides as if remembering to curb her enthusiasm and to be a good sport.

"Her attitude blows me away," Matt said. "That girl definitely has ranching in her blood."

After the young handlers turned over their lambs to the ring steward, Emily scanned the grandstand until she spotted where her family sat. Then she hurried toward the fence.

Even though she lowered her voice, she couldn't hide her excitement. "Bob did it," she whispered. "He won a lot of money. Now I can buy another lamb. And I can give some money to Dr. Rick for his pet rescue, too."

Miranda looked at Matt, who shrugged as if he didn't know what to say.

When Emily started to turn back toward the ring, where the stewards were herding the lambs through a gate, she stopped in her tracks and glanced over her shoulder at Miranda, Matt and George. "Hey! Where are they taking Bob and those other lambs?"

"The man who just bought them is…" Miranda hated to remind her that they'd be taken to a slaughterhouse—eventually. "He's taking the lambs that he purchased."

"*What*?" Her eyes widened, and her jaw dropped. "He *bought* Bob?"

"Yes, in the auction."

"But Bob is *my* lamb. I want to take him *home*."

"I'm afraid you can't do that. I thought that you understood what was going to happen at the auction. Weren't you listening when they explained…?" Miranda paused, unable to complete the sentence, especially when it was now obvious the child hadn't paid attention.

"When you agreed to auction Bob, it meant you agreed to sell him. It meant that he'd…" Matt paused.

Miranda picked up where he left off, hoping to soften the blow. "That he'd have to go to someone else's ranch."

Emily's lip quivered, and tears welled in her eyes. "But I thought *auctioned* meant that they were going to give me money as a prize for taking such good care of him and for teaching him to obey and be good. What's that man going to do with him? Keep him? Put him in a pen with a bunch of other sheep he doesn't even know?"

Miranda didn't have the heart to reveal Bob's fate, and she looked at Matt, hoping he'd find the words once more.

But Matt only gazed at their daughter, who was now sobbing hard enough for her tears to fill a water trough. And if the sympathy Miranda read in his expression was a clue, it appeared that he might fall apart, too.

"I'll be right back," he said, as he got to his feet.

"Where are you going?" Miranda asked.

"To make a deal with the guy who bought her lamb. I might have to offer him more money than he spent, but I'm not going to turn my back on family. And apparently, Bob is now part of mine."

Miranda's heart soared, and her plan to keep Matt at an emotionally safe distance failed. Because she'd just fallen hopelessly in love with him all over again.

That evening, after driving everyone home and putting Emily's beloved pet back in his pen, Matt suggested they go to Mario's Pizzeria to celebrate Bob's return to the fold.

"That sounds good to me," Miranda said. "This has been the kind of day I'd love to celebrate."

Love? She cringed inwardly at the slip up. She hadn't meant to use the *L* word when talking to Matt, even though she'd meant dealing with her child's melt-down and walking all over the fairground until she ended up with a good-sized blister on one heel and a small one on the other.

George slowly shook his balding head. "You guys go on ahead without me. Those two chili-cheese dogs I wolfed down at the fair gave me indigestion."

"We can bring something home for you," Matt said. "You might feel better later and want to eat then."

"Don't bother." George tapped his fist against his upper chest a couple of times. "The last thing I want to eat tonight is something loaded down with pepperoni, sausage and spicy Italian tomato sauce."

"We could order a plain cheese pizza for you and ask them to hold the sauce," Miranda said.

George blew out a humph. "What kind of Texas rancher do you think I am? I wouldn't eat a tasteless, wimpy pizza like that on a bet." Then he topped off the snarky comment with a wink.

Miranda felt a little uneasy about leaving him home alone, although she wasn't sure why. Those two chili-cheese dogs had been covered with onions and topped with jalapeños. So it didn't surprise her that he was suffering indigestion now. Still…

"I realize you never have liked doctors," Miranda said, "but I also know you've seen one recently. Maybe you should give him or her a call and mention that indigestion. I also noticed that you've gotten a little out of breath lately."

George waved her off. "Me and the doc have it all under control. It's nothing a little pill or two won't fix. So you don't need to worry about me."

"All right," she said. "I'm glad you're taking care of yourself."

"I appreciate your concern," he said, "but I'll be right as rain after I take a couple of antacids."

He was probably right, so they left him home and went to the pizzeria without him.

Miranda had planned to check on him later that night, after they returned from Mario's, but by the time they'd entered the back door, the house was quiet and the lights had been dimmed. Clearly, he'd already turned in for the night.

But why wouldn't he? They'd all had a long, exciting day. Even Emily's shoulders had begun to droop, so Miranda told her it was time for bed.

"Aw, man." Emily rolled her eyes, but the effort lacked her usual dramatic flair. "Okay, but can I skip my bath tonight?"

"Absolutely not. And don't forget to brush your teeth."

Apparently, Emily couldn't come up with a reasonable argument because she turned on her heel and did as she was told.

"Matt," Miranda said, "if you're up for some decaf, I'll brew a small pot for you and then steep a cup of tea for me."

"Sounds good."

She would have suggested that they take their drinks out to the front porch, but she didn't want him to think she was trying to set up a repeat of Monday night. If they were to go outdoors, it would have to be his idea. And if that were the case, she'd jump at the chance, even though no good would come of it.

"I'd offer to help you in the kitchen," Matt said, "but my knee is killing me. I'd better plop my butt on the sofa and give it a rest."

She offered him a smile. "If I hadn't kicked off my shoes when we got home from the fair and traded them for a pair of flip-flops, I'd pass on the tea and plop down next to you."

Ten minutes later, Miranda placed a white coffee mug and her favorite teacup, both filled with their respective steaming hot brews, onto a wicker tray and carried it into the living room. After setting it on the coffee table, she took a seat on the sofa, next to the armrest, which put a wise and healthy space between them.

Rather than reach for his coffee, Matt stretched out his leg and removed the brace.

"How's your knee feeling?" she asked.

"A little achy today. But overall, it's about the same."

"No worse?" She nodded at the brace. "You weren't wearing that before."

"Actually, I was, but I took it off before I drove home to the Double G. Apparently—" he paused for a couple of beats "—I shouldn't have done that. I might have screwed it up for good. And if that's the case, I'll have to give up the rodeo, which I don't want to do."

He'd have to give up the fame, too, she supposed. But that really wasn't any of her business.

"You have no idea how much I appreciate all you did today," she said.

"It was no big deal."

"Oh, but it was. Emily couldn't be happier, and I... Well, I'm just glad the two of you are bonding."

"Me, too. But..."

She waited for him to continue, to explain, but it became a long wait. She lifted the delicate china tea-cup and saucer from the tray and sat back on the sofa.

"I'm not sure if you remember," Matt said, "but my dad and I didn't have a good relationship. We still don't. So when it comes to parenthood, I'm in uncharted territory."

"I do remember, and I'm sorry things never got any better between you. But just so you know, I think you were a perfect dad today."

Matt seemed to mull that over, then smiled. "You mean by offering to whip out my checkbook to save the day? What else could I do? You saw how heart-broken she was when she thought she'd lost her lamb. Besides, the fair adjusted the buyer's bill, and I didn't have to actually pay anything."

"I realize that, but you went to bat for Emily when you convinced the buyer to let us take Bob home. And you also trekked all over the fairgrounds with a bad knee. The way I see it, after today, you've already proven to Emily that you're the best daddy ever."

"Thanks. I appreciate that. But there'll probably be other days when things don't turn out so well."

"True. I've had days like that."

Matt lifted his mug, took a drink and said, "Rumor has it that Emily wants to get another lamb. A *girl one* so they can have a baby."

Miranda laughed and rolled her eyes. "The last thing she needs is another animal. And even if I would've let her buy a second lamb with the auction money—which I wouldn't have done—she can't afford it now. Besides, we can't stay at the Double G forever, and depending upon where we end up, she might not be able to take her animals with her. At least, not all of them."

"What are your plans?" he asked.

"I'm going to put my condo in San Antonio on the market and relocate, hopefully to a place with enough property for Emily's menagerie."

"Does that mean you'd consider relocating here?"

"That's what I'm thinking. Emily and I both like living in Brighton Valley, and she's making friends at school and in the 4-H Club. Hopefully, my dad will let me work remotely. Because if I do find a place and move here, I can't very well commute to San Antonio on a regular basis."

And if she couldn't work for Contreras Farms, she'd need to find another way to support herself and her growing family.

She glanced down at her lap, which seemed to be disappearing more and more each week. She'd also have to find a competent nanny.

When she looked up again, she caught Matt gazing at her.

"So you still haven't told your father?" he asked.

"I was going to, but then I got busy with all the county fair prep and 4-H activities, so I put it off for another week. But I can't wait much longer."

Matt didn't respond. He didn't even make a snide remark about her dad, which he'd been doing ever since he arrived at his uncle's ranch. So she took this as a good sign that they seemed to be working through the past.

"What about *your* dad?" she asked. "Have you talked to him?"

"About Emily? No, not yet. And I really don't want to. He'd probably ask to meet her, and I don't want him to disappoint her the way he disappointed me."

Miranda wouldn't want to see that happen, either. But maybe the man would turn out to be a better grandfather than a father.

"It sounds to me like you still keep in touch with him," she said.

"I guess you could say that. He calls me every few weeks, although I never have much to say to him. He wasn't much of a father, but then again, he didn't think I was much of a son."

She'd hoped that, over the past nine years, Matt and his father would've buried the hatchet, but apparently they hadn't. From what little the old Matt had told her in the past, his father had really hurt him. And it didn't look like the new Matt had gotten over it.

Matt took another drink of coffee, then he turned toward her. "Why have you waited so long to tell your dad about the baby? I'd think you'd want to get it over with."

She drew in a deep breath, held it for a beat, then let it out slowly. "If I had my way, I'd wait to tell my dad until the baby takes his first step."

Matt's brow furrowed as he pondered her response.

She probably should explain. "When he finds out, he'll pressure me to return to San Antonio, which I'll have to do anyway when I sell the condo and line up the movers. But once I'm back in the city, Gavin is bound to find out I'm pregnant. And I'd rather that didn't happen until it's not as easy for him to do the math and realize the baby is his."

Matt arched a brow. "I thought you said you weren't afraid of Gavin."

"I'm not afraid for myself. It's just that he might petition the court for visitation, and I know the baby wouldn't be safe with him. So I've been dragging my feet to protect both kids, since I don't want him showing up at my house—even for holidays."

Matt pondered her words for a beat, then said, "If Gavin had any suspicions, you could tell him the baby's mine."

Chapter Ten

You could tell him the baby's mine.

Damn. Hearing himself blurt out a suggestion like that surprised Matt as much as it had clearly taken Miranda aback. Then again, maybe not.

She continued to gape at him, her eyes wide and unblinking, as if he'd shown up at a rodeo wearing only his hat and boots. The fingers that held the delicate handle of that fancy pink teacup trembled until she lifted her free hand to steady it. But even supporting it with two hands didn't seem to help much.

Matt reached for the teacup before she dropped it to the floor, took it from her and placed it on the saucer that rested on the coffee table.

At that, Miranda blinked, and her stunned expression shifted into one that appeared more perplexed.

"Are you serious?" she asked.

He wasn't sure. He hadn't planned to offer her any advice, but for some stupid reason, the words had rolled off his tongue the second that wild solution had come to mind.

But what was he worried about? It wasn't as if he'd offered to pay her child support on an eighteen-year plan—and for a kid who wasn't his.

So he shrugged off his reservations and gave her the best explanation he had. "You're not the only one who doesn't want that guy showing up at your house."

A deep crease in the center of her brow suggested that she might be pondering his crazy idea and considering any other options she might have.

He doubted that she could come up with anything else that would keep Gavin out of her life.

Maybe she was worried about the possible repercussions they could face if they did lie about the baby's paternity. And there were sure to be some.

Her father's temper came to mind. The man had an image to protect, and he would have a conniption fit if he thought Matt had fathered another one of Miranda's kids, both of who were illegitimate.

Not that Matt got any pleasure from Miranda's current situation—neither this pregnancy nor the one he'd been responsible for. Besides, he would have married her in a heartbeat if she would have told him about Emily.

As he thought about her father's reaction to the news of Matt being the father of her second child, a smile began to form, and he almost chuckled.

Apparently, there was still a rebellious spirit inside of him, waiting on the sidelines, flexing its muscles and ready to jump into the fray, just to set off Miranda's old man.

"You know," Miranda said, "if you're actually serious, that idea just might work. How do you see this all playing out?"

Other than pissing off her dad? Matt really hadn't thought it through. So he asked, "What's the worst thing that could happen?"

"Well, at first, my father would probably want to punch your lights out."

From what Matt had heard, Carlos Contreras wasn't a man most people wanted to cross. But he'd been in his forties when Miranda was born, so he must be pushing seventy now. And since he'd quit working in the fields years ago, he'd probably gotten soft and would think twice about raising his fists.

"Things won't get physical," Matt said. "That is, unless your dad gets violent. But either way, I'm not afraid of him. So what else could happen?"

"I suppose Gavin could ask for a DNA test."

"He might. But then he'd probably rather not have to pay you any child support."

"You're probably right."

"And if he doesn't ask for proof of paternity, you wouldn't get the money."

"I don't need it."

She hadn't needed child support from Matt, either, which clamped a vise on his ego and tightened it. But he shook it off. There was no need to poke at the past.

"Just to make it clear," he said, "I'd walk away before risking a loud or physical altercation with your father. And I suspect Gavin won't ask for a DNA test. If he did, he'd have to deal with charges that he hit Emily. That might give him reason to reconsider."

She cocked her head slightly and studied him carefully, most likely trying to read into his offer and his take on all of it. But damn, when she looked at him like that, feelings rose up in his chest. Soft and tender ones that made him want to pull her into his arms and promise her the moon, tell her he'd do anything to make her happy and to keep her and the children safe.

"Listen," he said, tamping down the rising emotion that wouldn't do either one of them any good, "I just threw that idea out there to make sure you and the kids never have to deal with Gavin again."

"You want to protect the baby, too?" she asked, her voice soft, tender.

"Of course. It's not his fault that he has a crappy biological dad." Nor had it been Matt's fault that he'd been cursed with a lousy one, either.

"But what about the baby's birth date?" she asked. "I was engaged to Gavin until February, so he's going to know that he's the father."

"You can tell Gavin and other people that the baby came early. Or if it arrives weighing a whopping nine or ten pounds, we can say that you and I crossed paths at the end of last year. The old feelings we had for each other were hard to ignore, and we couldn't help ourselves. It just happened."

Miranda turned to face him, and as her gaze targeted his, a rush of desire swept over him. The explanation he'd just given her took on a life of its own, and he could see how a heated moment might occur when two old lovers met.

She didn't say anything, but she didn't have to. The emotion welling in her eyes told him all he needed to hear, all he needed to know.

Talk about old memories, sudden realizations and a burst of heat. He cupped her face, and her lips parted. As his fingers slipped along her jaw and around to the back of her neck, her glossy locks cascaded over his hand. Then he drew her mouth to his.

He hadn't planned to kiss her. If he had, he would've started out softly, tenderly, making the moment last. But the second their lips touched, his brain checked out completely and thoughts like *slow* and *easy* went right out the window.

Apparently, Miranda didn't mind things taking off like a blast from the past. She leaned into him, her hands re-exploring his body. Her lips parted, allowing his tongue to sweep into her mouth to mate with hers, dipping and twisting and tasting until he thought he'd explode.

But kissing Miranda senseless was one thing.

Taking her to bed was another.

Mustering every bit of strength and self-control he had, Matt ended the earthshaking kiss, but he didn't pull away. He continued to hold her close, savoring the chance to have her in his arms again, the faint scent of her floral shampoo, the warmth of her breath against his skin.

"See what I mean?" He rested his forehead against hers, and a slow smile curved his mouth. "Things like this happen when old lovers run into each other."

She didn't agree, but she didn't let go of him, either.

"Do you see how things could easily get out of control?"

At that, she drew back, and her passion-glazed eyes met his. "We shouldn't let that happen."

"We shouldn't?"

Her lips parted, as if she had a ready answer, but she didn't say another word.

Hell, she probably didn't dare to, because there was no way she'd convince him that a few bedroom thoughts hadn't crossed her mind as well. And there lay the problem.

Things were heading in a sexual direction, and as much as he'd taken the lead and enjoyed what they'd just done, he wasn't sure whether he should thank his lucky stars for that amazing kiss or run for the hills while he still had the chance.

The next day, after they'd eaten turkey sandwiches and apple slices for lunch, Matt continued to hang out at the kitchen table, hoping to find time to talk to Miranda alone. He had an idea he wanted to share with her, and this one wasn't as wild and crazy as the one he'd suggested last night.

Since she'd just asked Emily to help her clear the table, the chat he had planned to have with her would have to wait.

George, who'd left the table earlier, returned to the

kitchen with his hair damp and combed and wearing a different shirt than the one he'd had on before.

"Miranda," he said, "I've got a few errands to run in town. Would it be okay if I took the little munchkin with me?"

Emily cocked her head, furrowed her brow and looked at Matt. "What's a munchkin?"

"The munchkins are characters in *The Wizard of Oz*," he said. "Have you seen the movie?"

She shook her head no.

"That's too bad," he said, "It's a classic. I guess we'll have to schedule a movie night."

"That's a good idea," Miranda added. "We can make popcorn and root beer floats."

"That sounds fun." Emily leaned toward Matt, cupped a hand at the side of her mouth and lowered her voice. "But why did he call me that?"

"It's not always easy to know what your uncle is thinking." Matt winked at George.

"I like to keep some things to myself, but I'll tell you what I've got on my mind today." George lobbed a smile at Emily. "A big bowl of frozen yogurt. And maybe even a visit to the feed store to check out what kind of critters they've got on special today. If your mom says it's okay, I'd be happy to take you with me."

Emily clapped her hands and turned to Miranda. "Can I, Mommy? Please."

"Yes," Miranda said. "But don't bring home any animals. You have more than enough pets already."

George chuckled on the way out, while Emily trotted along behind him.

After the door closed, Matt studied Miranda, who'd turned back around to wipe down the kitchen counter. She wore a yellow sundress today, reminding him of the roses he'd once given her back in the day.

But it was the future he wanted to broach. So he opened by saying, "I've been thinking about something."

She turned around, her brow raised in apprehension. "About what?"

"About job opportunities. If your dad won't let you work remotely, I have an idea that might interest you."

The hesitation in her expression lightened. "What is it?"

"Have you heard of Kidville?"

"Yes, it's a local group home for abused and neglected kids. The Rocking Chair Rodeo is going to give it some of their proceeds."

"That's right. Jim Hoffman, one of the directors, is looking for someone, preferably a CPA, to handle the books. His wife, Donna, was doing it, but they're expanding Kidville, and she doesn't have the time. I'm not sure what they can afford to pay—or even if you'd be interested. But they're local."

"Thanks. If I end up needing to find another position, I'll definitely give them a call." She leaned against the kitchen counter. "I also had an idea of my own."

"Oh, yeah?" Matt asked. "What's that?"

"I have some money set aside for investments, and I thought about buying that pharmacy in town. I think the old-style soda fountain could really be a money-maker—if run properly. And if it also sold gifts and trinkets that would appeal to the tourists... Well, I think sales would increase."

"I like that idea." He also liked knowing that she was seriously planning to relocate to Brighton Valley. If she and Emily lived closer to the ranch, he'd be able to see them—and the baby, too—more often. Or at least every time he came home.

More importantly, though, she'd finally be pulling away from her father, which she'd needed to do for a long time.

"I'll have to talk it over with my dad first," she said. "A lot depends on whether I can work remotely for Contreras Farms. Either way, I'm moving to Brighton Valley."

"It'll be nice to have you living in town," he said.

She folded her arms across her chest, resting them on the top of her baby bump, and studied him for a couple of beats. "Okay, this is crazy."

"What is?"

"We've either ignored those two kisses or skated over them long enough."

She was right, although he'd still rather avoid having the conversation. He slowly got to his feet. He'd forgotten to wear the brace today, and that blasted tendon in his knee was already complaining. Maybe he ought to walk it off. Or else go back to his room and put the brace back on.

"Last night you implied that you were only kissing me to make a point," she said. "But I think there was a lot more to it than that."

As the accusation sunk in, so did the truth of it.

"You're right," he said.

"So what should we do about it?"

He shrugged. "Take it day by day, I guess."

"That makes sense."

"I won't deny that the chemistry is still there," he admitted. "But we probably shouldn't rush into anything sexual, even though that's a tempting idea."

"I agree."

"But that doesn't mean we can't do family stuff. I can always use more practice."

She smiled and leaned against the kitchen counter. "That day at the fair was awesome."

"And now we have a movie night to look forward to." Matt took a few steps, trying to shake the ache he'd gotten from sitting so long.

"I have a question for you," Miranda said.

"What's that?"

She placed a gentle, protective hand on her growing waistline, took a deep breath, bit down on her lower lip and lowered her gaze to the floor. After a couple of beats, she looked up again and blew out a sigh. "How will the baby fit into your idea of a family?"

Talk about cutting to the chase. But he really couldn't blame a mother for looking out for her child. In truth, she ought to be more concerned about how her father was going to fit into Matt's idea of a family.

"I don't see a problem." He crossed the kitchen, easing closer to Miranda, close enough to touch. He raised the palm of his hand toward her baby bump and asked, "Do you mind?"

She smiled, removed her hand and let her arm drop to her side. "No, not at all."

Matt had stroked the bellies of pregnant mares and heifers, but never an expectant mother. And as he felt a little bump move to the side of the womb—a foot, maybe?—his breath caught and his eyes opened in awe. "Wow. That's so cool."

And a miracle in the making.

He caught her gaze and smiled. "As far as I'm concerned, that little guy is my daughter's baby brother. And he'll always be a part of you. So I'll try my best to treat him as if he were my biological son."

She pressed her fingers against her lips, holding back either a sob or a response. Still, tears filled her eyes. "I'd hoped you would say that. But I was afraid that you might…"

"That I might not treat him fairly?" Matt reached out and, using his thumb, brushed a tear from her cheek. "I'll be damned if I'll ever show any favoritism to Emily over the baby. Or vice versa. And I'll do whatever it takes to make sure neither of them ever feels neglected or left out, the way I did when I was growing up."

"Does that mean you see a future for us? I mean as a family?"

"I guess that's what I'm saying."

The tears in Miranda's pretty caramel-colored eyes overflowed and spilled down her cheeks. This time, they flowed faster than he could wipe them away.

Matt had never felt comfortable around crying women, but this was different. Miranda was different.

"Don't worry," she said, sniffling. "I'm not sad or upset. These are happy tears."

He wrapped her in a warm embrace and drew her close. Happy or sad, he didn't like seeing her cry, so he stroked her back, offering whatever comfort he could. He wasn't sure how long they stood like that. A couple of minutes, maybe. He would have remained there for as long as she needed him to, but she was the first to pull away.

She looked up at him with a smile, and as their gazes met and locked in place, something passed between them, bonding them in an unexpected way.

He couldn't move, couldn't look away, couldn't think—until she ran the tip of her tongue along her lips, setting off a flurry of pheromones and hormones he hadn't experienced in a long, long time.

In spite of his resolve to take things one day at a time, his common sense and resolve dissipated in a rush of desire. And all he knew was that he didn't just want to kiss her again. He needed to.

As if reading his mind, she lifted her mouth to his, and they came together as if they'd never been apart.

Miranda was the last woman in the world Matt should be kissing, let alone making love with, but there wasn't much he could do about it now. Not when she was the only woman he'd ever really wanted.

So he took her by the hand. "Come here. I need to get off my feet."

When he led her away from the kitchen table and past the sofa in the living room, she asked, "Where are we going?"

He paused before reaching the hall. "Unless you have an objection, we're going to my bedroom."

Miranda continued to walk with Matt down the hall and into his room, her heart pounding, her blood racing. They stopped next to the bed, and he pulled her into his arms. She leaned into him, her baby bump pressing against him.

As their lips met, he swayed but quickly recovered.

"Are you sure you're okay?" she asked.

"My knee is messed up and hurts like hell most of the time. But don't worry. The other parts of me are in perfect working order. So I won't disappoint you."

At that, she laughed. "You never have."

"Good." He took a seat on the edge of the mattress, following through on the need to take the weight off his knee. "But what about you?"

"Me?"

He nodded at her growing belly. "Is it going to hurt anything if we make love?"

She smiled, appreciating his concern. "Between your knee and my baby bump, we might need to adjust our positions now and then."

"That's not going to be a problem." Matt drew her closer, bent his head and placed a kiss on her belly. When he looked up again, he blessed her with an old Matt grin. "I'll be careful with this little guy before and after he gets here."

Miranda didn't think she could ever love this man any more than she did right now. She brushed her lips against his forehead, and he drew her onto the bed, where he took her into his arms and placed his mouth on hers.

Their hands roamed each other's bodies, seeking, exploring, caressing. When Matt's hand worked its way to her breast, and his thumb skimmed across her nipple, she feared she would melt into a puddle on the bed if they didn't pull back the sheets and remove their clothes.

As a yearning emptiness settled deep in her core, she withdrew her lips from his. With a voice husky and laden with desire, she whispered, "I've really missed you, Matt. And I've missed this."

Matt had really missed her, too—more than he wanted to admit. He'd never ached for a woman this badly. And he doubted he ever would.

Unable and unwilling to prolong the foreplay any longer, he sat up in bed, unbuttoned his shirt, slipped it off and tossed it to the floor. Then he unbuckled his belt and undid the metal buttons on his jeans. As he peeled off his pants, he took care not to jar his knee.

When he'd removed his boxers, baring his body to her, she skimmed her nails across his chest, sending a heated shiver through his veins.

Her gaze never left his as she, too, sat up beside him. She lifted the hem of her yellow sundress, scooting and gathering the fabric until she could lift it over her head and toss it to the floor, next to his discarded clothes.

When she unhooked her bra, freeing her gorgeous breasts, much fuller now than before, he longed to take her in his arms. He wanted nothing more than to feel the heat of her skin on his, to sink deep into her, show-ing her that he'd missed her, too, and letting her know just how much.

Instead, he drank in the angelic sight he'd never thought he'd see again. "You're beautiful."

A slow smile stretched across her lips. "You are, too."

He didn't know about that, what with the few scars he'd added since the last time they'd been together.

Unable to ignore the tempting view of her breasts any longer, he took a nipple in his mouth, tonguing it, loving it, then moving to the other until she gasped in pleasure.

Taking mercy on them both, he laid her down and rolled to his side, thanking his lucky stars that he had her in his bed again, that he had the chance to savor the sight of those luscious dark curls splayed on his pillow, those expressive brown eyes glazed with pas-sion as they watched his every move.

An easy grin spread across her face. "This is the point where we used to need a condom."

He returned her smile. It would be nice to make love without a barrier between them for a change. At least that kind.

As he braced himself on an elbow, intending to rise over her, she placed her hand on his shoulder and pushed him back onto the mattress. "Under the circum-stances, it might be better if I get on top."

"Good idea."

She moved slowly at first, taking care not to bump his knee, but she soon settled onto his erection. His body responded to hers, up and down, in and out, the world-shaking tempo setting his soul on fire.

He closed his eyes, savoring the magic they'd always created in this room and on this bed.

Their lives might be heading in a complicated direction, one they probably should reconsider, but not when their hormones were spinning out of control. As it always had in the past when they'd made love, time stood still, and the only thing that mattered was the two of them and the love they made.

When Miranda reached a peak, she cried out, arched her back and let it go. He shuddered as she climaxed, releasing with her in a sexual explosion that gave him a glimpse of the heavens and a glittery night sky filled with shooting stars.

Matt had no idea what the future would hold, but at least for this afternoon, she was his.

Chapter Eleven

As they lay in the afterglow of an amazing climax, Miranda nuzzled into Matt, savoring his familiar, mountain-fresh scent and the velvet hard feel of the man she'd never stopped loving.

"How's your knee?" she asked.

"It's all right, I guess." An unreadable expression crossed his face. "I mean, making love didn't make it any worse."

She rose up on her elbow and stroked his chest, her fingers tracing a curved scar she didn't remember him having, reminding her even more of the danger he faced each time he climbed on a bull. "But it's still bad. Isn't it?"

"Yeah." He pursed his lips and frowned. "What's worse, I'm not going to be able to compete in the Rocking Chair Rodeo."

"There'll be others," she said, telling him what she suspected he wanted to hear.

"I hope you're right, but the jury's still out on that."

Miranda tried to conjure more sympathy for him than she actually had. Even when they'd dated before, she'd known how he felt about the rodeo. He'd loved the roar of the crowd, the thrill of the ride—maybe even more than he'd claimed to love her.

It might be selfish on her part, but if truth be told, she didn't want him to return to the circuit for safety reasons. And there were a few emotional reasons, too. She didn't want him to return to the buckle bunnies who were known to fawn over their rodeo hero.

In so many other ways, Matt was her hero, too, and she didn't want to share him.

"I'm going to Houston tomorrow to meet with the Rocking Chair Rodeo promoters."

"How long will you be gone?" she asked.

"A couple of days."

Now that they were back together, she wasn't ready to lose him, even for that short of a time. "Do you have to go?"

"I made a commitment to bring in more sponsorships and to help the Rocking Chair Rodeo draw a big crowd. And I plan to follow through on it, even if I can't actually ride."

Matt might be medically grounded, and he appeared to be back in the saddle again, so to speak. But there was a lot more going on under on the surface.

If he couldn't compete again, his heart would be

broken. And if he did go back out on the circuit, hers would probably break instead.

In spite of how special, how amazing their lovemaking had been, that bittersweet truth buffed the shine off the afterglow.

Her chest ached, and tears pricked her eyes. She had to get away before he asked her what was wrong. As she pondered the best way to escape, a familiar engine sounded, saving her from having to explain.

"I think George and Emily are back." She climbed over Matt and got out of bed. Then she picked up her dress and panties from the floor, slipped them on as quickly as she could and headed for the kitchen to make herself look busy—and guilt free.

She got as far as the living room, where she glanced at her reflection in the glass doors of the antique hutch against the wall and rolled her eyes. Talk about the walk of shame. She'd been in such a hurry to waylay George and Emily before they came inside and found her and Matt in bed, that she hadn't realized her appearance would pretty much shout out what they'd been doing.

Why hadn't she taken the time to run a brush through her hair? George was going to suspect that they'd...

Her shoulders slumped, and she blew out a sigh. For some reason, she suspected that the man already knew what would happen when he took Emily for the afternoon.

Either way, she hastily combed her fingers through

her hair, then went to the kitchen, where she planned to look busy until they opened the back door.

After she washed her hands and took out the hamburger she'd let defrost in the fridge, they still hadn't come in to the house.

Curiosity got the better of her, and she went outside, in her bare feet no less, to see what they were up to.

When she spotted George unloading lumber, chicken wire and a small blue plastic kiddie pool from the back of his pickup, she froze in her steps.

A few feet away Emily sat on the ground, smiling as she peered into a cardboard box. Before Miranda could cross the yard to look inside and see what held her daughter's apt attention, Emily pulled out a little yellow duckling and pressed it gently to her cheek.

Oh, for Pete's sake. Miranda slapped her hands on her hips. "Emily Jane, I told you not to bring any more animals home."

"But I *didn't*. Uncle George is the one who bought them. I'm just going to take care of them for him."

"That's a fact," the old man said, nodding sagely. "I've always wanted to have a flock of ducks. I just never got around to getting any."

Yeah, right. Once Emily got a look at those cute little yellow balls of fluff at the feed store, George clearly hadn't had the heart to object. And now he was claiming they were his. And they would be, once she and Emily moved to their new place, especially if they ended up living within Brighton Valley's city limits.

"Guess what else we bought." Emily placed the duckling back into the box, scrambled to her feet and ran to the passenger side of the old pickup. After opening the door and reaching inside, she hurried to Miranda, carrying a DVD. "We went to Shop-Smart and found this."

The Wizard of Oz.

"Cool," Miranda said with a smile, but her eyes remained on the confined ducklings, which had begun to quack and scurry around the box.

After the conscientious duck-sitter hurried back to her little charges and told them she was back, she looked up at Miranda and smiled. "Uncle George and I already picked out names for them. Dorothy, Toto and Scarecrow."

Miranda rolled her eyes and muttered, "Ponies and doggies and ducks. Oh, my."

When the back door squeaked open, Miranda looked over her shoulder and watched Matt hobble outside, fresh from the shower and wearing his brace. He looked good. Refreshed. As if he'd just taken a nap. On the other hand, she was a wreck.

She glanced down at her dusty bare feet and slowly shook her head. She must look worse than she'd thought. Before taking a step in either direction, she raked her fingers through her messy hair, only to snag a nail on a snarl.

Great. Just great. Too bad she couldn't click her heels and zoom off to Kansas.

She turned and tossed Matt a weary don't-even-say-it smile. Then she headed for the house—and to the shower—wondering what George must think.

Before she reached the back door, she scolded herself for falling back on a bad habit.

In the past, when she'd been an unwed, pregnant teen, she'd worried way too much about what others thought, which was probably due to her father's concerns at the time. But she wasn't going to fall back into that self-deprecating trap anymore.

The only opinions that really mattered to her were Emily's and Matt's. As for her daughter, Emily adored Matt and would be thrilled if he and Miranda were to have an intimate relationship, assuming things continued in that direction.

That only left Matt and his thoughts about the future. And so far, as troubling as it was, he hadn't said a word.

After taking a long shower and shampooing her hair, Miranda slipped on a pair of comfy black stretch pants and a pink top. Then she grabbed her cell phone and padded to the overstuffed chair in her bedroom.

She'd put off calling her father long enough. And now that she and Matt had reconciled—at least, that seemed like a fair assumption for her to make—she wanted Matt to know that she wasn't afraid to level with her dad. She'd tell him where she was staying and who was sleeping down the hall. After he blew a fuse, she'd admit that she was pregnant and that she planned to relocate to Brighton Valley. He'd be hurt and angry, of course. But experience told her that it would be best if he blew off a little steam. And then, as usual, he'd get over it.

When she dialed his number, the call rolled over to voice mail. So she left a message. "It's me, Papa. I'll try you at the office."

Less than a minute later, Carolina Sanchez, one of several secretaries, answered the phone. "Contreras Farms."

"Hi, Caroline. This is Miranda. Is my father available?"

"No, I'm afraid not. He flew to Los Mochis yesterday to meet with Gavin's father and two other investors. From what I understand, the cell phone reception is pretty sketchy. I've already got a list of messages to give him once he's back on the grid."

"When do you expect him to return?" she asked.

"Maybe tonight or early tomorrow morning. But since the company jet is having a maintenance check, he'll have to fly home commercially. Can I give him a message?"

"No, I'll wait until he gets back to the States and contact him then."

After ending the call, Miranda went to the kitchen to fix spaghetti for dinner. She really didn't mind cooking. And she hated to see both Matt and George pick up meals to bring home, even if they both insisted they were used to doing that.

Two hours later, after they'd eaten dinner and she'd put the dishes into the dishwasher, she pulled out a couple of microwave popcorn packets from the pantry, as well as a liter of root beer from the fridge and a gallon of vanilla ice cream from the freezer.

"Whatcha doin'?" Emily asked, as she entered the kitchen.

"Getting ready for movie night."

"Are you going to eat that sweet stuff, too?"

"Of course."

Emily joined Miranda at the kitchen counter, then lifted a cupped hand to her mouth and whispered, "I don't want to hurt your feelings, but you've been getting a little fat. And my teacher said that happens when you eat too much sugar. Want me to get you something healthy to eat, like a cracker or an apple or something?"

Miranda fought a smile. She hadn't wanted to tell Emily about the baby until after she'd told her father. But since that phone call was as good as made, she turned to her daughter, her eyes glistening in mirth.

"Uh-oh," Emily said. "You're crying. I'm sorry. I didn't mean to hurt your feelings. I don't care if you get big and fat. I just thought Daddy might like you better if…"

She didn't finish what she meant to say, but she didn't need to.

"First of all," Miranda said, "the look and shape of our bodies doesn't have anything to do with the people we are on the inside. So if your father doesn't like me just the way I am, he can move on to someone else."

Emily's eyes widened. "But we don't want that to happen, right?"

Miranda laughed. "No, we really don't. But do you want to know a secret?"

When Emily nodded, she bent down to her daughter,

cupped her own hands and whispered, "There's a reason my tummy is getting big. I'm going to have a baby."

Emily gasped and her eyes widened. "Really?"

"Yes, it's true. You're going to have a little brother by the end of the summer."

A smile slid across her sweet face. "Getting a baby is going to be even better than getting a litter of puppies!"

Without a doubt. Especially considering all the furry little mouths they already had to feed.

"Does Daddy know?" she asked.

Miranda nodded. "I told him first."

Emily let out a gleeful shriek, then turned back toward the living room, where Matt was setting up the DVD.

"Guess what," she called out as she hurried away, her decibel level high with excitement. "I know the secret, too, Daddy."

As happy as Miranda was to get such an enthusiastic response from her daughter, and as relieved as she was to have the announcement behind her, she still had one more confession to make.

In spite of her belief that her father, in time, would accept the news, a slither of apprehension swirled around her.

What if she was wrong?

Last night, after the movie ended and the house grew quiet, Matt had been tempted to slip into Miranda's room so they could make love again, but he'd remained in his own bed, pondering an uncertain future.

It wasn't just the possibility of ending his career and the subsequent hit it would take on his livelihood that kept him tossing and turning until dawn. Even before he came home and found Miranda and Emily staying at the Double G, he'd known that it wouldn't be easy for him to give up the rodeo—should it come to that. And now that he had Miranda and the kids to think about, giving it all up—not just fame, travel and the thrill of competition, but the money—was going to be even harder.

Sure, he could go to work with Drew Madison, his friend and the head promoter at Esteban Enterprises. The job would be a good fit. And he didn't mind having to hobnob with wealthy Texas businessmen. But no matter how good Matt was at charming folks with his soft southern drawl and his fun-loving style, he didn't feel comfortable dressed in fancy Western wear, which would be expected of him.

No, he'd rather ride in the rodeo than take on the responsibility of talking people into sponsoring them.

Of course, taking on a family and becoming a good role model for two kids was one hell of a responsibility. And when push came to shove, it was one that he wasn't quite sure he was qualified to assume.

Either way, he'd made a promise he meant to keep, and he figured it would all work out. Somehow. That is, as long as Miranda's father didn't interfere.

Not that Matt was afraid of the man. Hell, that had never been the case. The biggest problem he had with Carlos Contreras was that the guy refused to accept Matt's value as a human being. And he doubted the man's opinion would change whether Matt continued to compete, took on the job as a promoter or if, God forbid, he went to work as a ranch hand for his uncle. Actually, if truth be told, even Matt thought Miranda deserved better than that.

For now, he'd have to shake those troubling thoughts and focus on the stuff he'd packed to take with him.

When he was convinced that he had everything he'd need for the next two days, he grabbed the canvas handle of the carry-on bag and headed for the back door.

He paused in the living room, where Emily was sitting on the floor in front of the TV, watching a cartoon. Sweetie Pie lay beside her, taking a nap.

"I'm leaving now," he said.

The dog momentarily looked up from its snooze, but the little girl was so captivated by the story on the screen that she must not have heard him.

"Emily?"

She turned away from the television. "Huh?"

"I'm going to Houston for a few days. Do you have a hug for me?"

She tore her gaze away from the cartoon long enough to reluctantly get up from the sofa, cross the room and open her arms.

Matt set down his bag, scooped her up and kissed her cheek. "Be good for your mom."

"Okay," she said. "I'm going to miss you."

He was going to miss her, too. After setting her back on the floor, he picked up his bag and limped to the kitchen, where the warm, sweet aroma of something freshly baked filled the air.

Miranda had been busy this morning. Several dozen chocolate chip cookies cooled on the racks she'd spread out on the counter. Her back was to him as she took another batch out of the oven.

It was a homey sight and smell he'd rarely—if ever—experienced. And one he found surprisingly appealing.

"Something sure smells good," he said.

She set down the potholder she'd been using and turned around with a smile. "Doesn't it?"

He nodded toward the service porch and the back door. "I'm taking off now."

"All right, but don't leave yet. I want to send some cookies with you. I'll make sure you'll have some to snack on while you drive and enough to share with everyone at the meeting. It'll just take me a minute. Then I'll bring them out to the truck."

He wasn't sure what he expected from her. A little more emotion, he supposed. Maybe a hug or a kiss goodbye.

But then again, maybe she planned to do that when she brought the cookies outside. So he shook off the brief sense of disappointment and limped to the door.

He'd no more than taken two steps outside, when a black luxury sedan drove up and screeched to a stop. The driver's door opened up and Carlos Contreras got out, his face red and fists clenched at his sides.

"Where's Miranda?" he asked.

Matt blew out a sigh. "In the house. But she's on her way out."

Carlos folded his arms across his chest and chuffed. "I couldn't believe it when Gavin told me she was here."

Matt cocked his head to the side. "How'd Gavin know where she was?"

"He's the one who hired a private investigator this time." Carlos shook his gray head in disgust. "You always were a bad influence on her. And now, thanks to you, she's been lying to me again."

Matt's first impulse was to defend himself. Miranda and Emily had been at the ranch more than two months before he'd gotten there. And if anything, he'd encouraged her to tell her father the truth. But he wasn't going to throw her under the bus.

Besides, if they wanted the world to think that he was the father of her baby, that they'd reconnected last year, during the holidays, then her father's assumption would help their story hold up.

Carlos slowly shook his head. "I can't believe this. She's been here all along. With a *friend*, she'd said. But she wouldn't tell me who. And now I know why."

Matt wasn't up for a confrontation. Nor did he feel good about leaving Miranda to deal with it on her own. He dropped his bag on the ground, wishing he could ditch his human burden as easily.

Carlos shook his head in disgust. "I suppose she just made up that story about Gavin hitting Emily as an excuse to cancel the wedding."

It took all Matt had not to roll his eyes. "There's no way Miranda would make up something up like that."

"So where is she?" Carlos asked. "Hiding? Like she's done for the past three months? Tell her to come outside. *Now.*"

"I'm not telling her anything. In case you haven't

noticed, she's an adult now. And she can make her own decisions."

Before Carlos could respond, Miranda stepped out the back door holding a plastic tub of cookies. When she spotted her father, she froze.

Carlos started toward her, scanning the length of her from the shock splashed across her face to her baby bump. At that point, he stopped mid-step and slapped his hands on his hips. "*Dios mio.* No wonder you didn't come home."

He was right about that. Matt waited for Miranda to respond, but she just stood there. Stunned, it would seem.

Carlos turned his fiery gaze on Matt. "What kind of man are you? Getting her pregnant twice?"

Now it was Matt's turn to hold his tongue, but only because he wanted to get a grip on his anger before he blew a head gasket.

"I've heard all about *you.*" Carlos scrunched his face and let out a string of words in Spanish, most likely obscenities. "And I've read about your sexual exploits."

Matt had had several lovers over the years, and he'd heard the stories, too. But most of them were exaggerated. "You shouldn't believe everything you read."

"Have you no shame?" Carlos asked. "No honor? Where have you been for the past eight years?"

At that, Matt threw up his hands. Miranda's old man would never approve of him, no matter how many bulls he rode, how many buckles he won. And Matt wasn't going to stand here and argue with him. Besides, if he didn't leave now, he'd probably end up throttling the guy.

"I hate to run out on the family reunion," he said, "but I've had enough fun for the day."

As he turned toward his pickup, Miranda called out, "Matt! Wait up!"

He stopped, but only to say, "Don't bother, Miranda."

She set the cookies aside and started down the steps. "Just listen to me. I don't care what my father says or what he thinks. We're a family now."

"No," Matt said, "you're wrong. Your father and I will never be family. So choose me. Or choose him. But you can't have us both."

She pondered his ultimatum a beat too long.

"It's over," he said. "I'll never desert my daughter, but there's no way in hell things will ever work out for you and me."

As she started to cross the yard, he shook his head, silently telling her to back off. He needed space. And time to think.

What he didn't need was to hang around and take her dad's insults and then wait for her to acquiesce to the old man's demands, no matter how badly the rebel in him wanted to stand his ground. Or how badly his heart ached at her rejection.

As he limped toward his truck, he spotted George standing in the open doorway of the barn. He'd probably heard everything, but what the hell.

George followed him out to his pickup.

"You just gonna run off like a stubborn, broken-hearted fool?" his uncle asked.

Matt rolled his eyes. "Lay off me. I have a meeting in Houston. And my leaving has nothing to do with a broken heart. It just makes good sense. I'm not going to have a relationship with Miranda. Not while Carlos still has a hold on her."

"Men like him usually back down when challenged."

Matt would have stood up to him, but Carlos had a rapid-fire temper, and it wouldn't take much for Matt to double up his fists and let the old man have it. Besides, Emily's cartoon movie couldn't last forever. She'd come looking for cookies or something. And if she heard any commotion outside, she'd come out to see what was going on.

What would a confrontation between her father and grandfather do to her? Scar her for life, no doubt.

Matt reached into his pocket and whipped out his keys. "Since you enjoy having Miranda and Emily here, you're the one who should go back there and give him your two cents. I couldn't care less."

"I ain't the one who's lying." George narrowed his eyes as if making a silent accusation.

"Neither am I. Miranda's the one who hasn't been honest."

George folded his arms across his chest. "I beg to differ."

"When was I ever dishonest with her?" Certainly not nine years ago, when he'd worn his heart on his sleeve. And not this time around, either.

"I never said you lied to Miranda. You've been lying

to *yourself* for years about the feelings you've always had for her."

Matt merely shook his head and climbed into his pickup, his knee hurting, his heart heavy and his mind made up.

Tears stung Miranda's eyes as she watched Matt drive away. She wanted nothing more than to run to him and beg him to come back. But that wasn't going to solve anything. Not when what he'd said was true. Not when she already knew what she needed to do.

Choose me. Or choose him. But you can't have us both.

Only trouble was, she loved and wanted both men in her life. And there didn't seem to be an easy solution.

Her father shook his head in disgust. "There he goes. Ditching you and his responsibilities."

"What did you expect?" she launched back at him. "I don't blame him for leaving. Rather than ever giving him a chance, you've been mean and unreasonable."

He rolled his eyes. "You're just like your mother, ready to run off with the first man who says you're pretty."

She knew he'd apologize to her later, but the cruel accusation still lanced deep into her heart.

In typical cowboy fashion, George stepped up to defend her honor. "Listen," he said. "Miranda might be your daughter, but you'll speak to her with the utmost respect when I'm around and when you're on my property."

"If she'll get into my car, we'll take our troubles with us."

"I'm not going anywhere with you," Miranda said.

She wasn't a little girl anymore. Matt had been right about that, too.

"You belong in San Antonio. And so does Emily. She has everything she needs in the city."

"Emily is happy here," Miranda said. "I'm going to sell the condo and find a place in this area where she can raise her animals."

"You want to live on a ranch?" He clicked his tongue, then started toward her as if he could actually force her to do something against her will.

"Step away from her," George said. "Don't make me call the sheriff."

Miranda hoped and prayed that Emily would remain in the house watching TV. Because things were sure to escalate between the two stubborn old men.

But when George paled, clutched his chest and dropped to his knees, she forgot about her concern for her daughter and rushed to his side.

Chapter Twelve

Miranda's fingers trembled as she dialed 9-1-1.

"This can't be happening," she muttered as she waited for someone to answer.

Seconds later, the dispatcher did. "9-1-1, what's your emergency?"

"We need an ambulance at the Double G Ranch on Oakdale Road in Brighton Valley. George Grimes collapsed. I think he's having a heart attack."

Her father, who'd frozen in stunned silence, eased closer. "What can I...?"

Miranda waved him off, as she provided the information the dispatcher requested. "He's seventy-two. He's avoided doctors in the past, but he's seen one recently. I'm not sure who it was or why he went. He wouldn't talk to me about it."

Oh, God. Just send the ambulance. We can talk about this stuff later.

She glanced down at George, who lay on the ground, his eyes closed, his skin ashen and clammy, his chest rising and falling.

But too fast? Too slow?

"Is that ambulance on the way?" she asked.

"Yes," the dispatcher said. "Is he conscious and breathing?"

"Conscious? I'm not sure. But he's breathing."

"Do you know CPR?" the man asked.

"Yes. At least, I've had classes. And I know not to do it unless he stops breathing. But please tell the paramedics to hurry." She looked at George again, but this time his chest wasn't moving. "Oh, God. I think he stopped breathing."

"Don't hang up. I'll stay on the line while you begin CPR."

As instructed, Miranda set aside the phone without ending the call and began to pump George's chest, hoping that she remembered everything she'd learned during her health class in college. She swore she'd take a refresher first aid course as soon as she could find one.

Her father circled George, then dropped to his knees and looked at her with apologetic eyes. "What can I do to help?"

Seriously? He'd been enough help already.

Between the breaths she blew into George's mouth, and the two-handed pumps she pressed to his chest, she said, "You stay here. And watch Emily. I'm going to follow the paramedics to the hospital."

"Of course, *mija*. No problem."

Miranda returned her full attention to George, praying her efforts weren't in vain, that the paramedics would arrive in time and that George would be back to his sweet, gruff and rascally self in no time at all.

All the while, she continued to perform CPR until the ambulance arrived, lights flashing, siren blasting. It seemed as if it had taken them forever, but in reality, it was probably only five or ten minutes.

As she moved away from George, allowing the paramedics to take over, her father pulled her aside.

"I'm sorry," he said.

How typical. Blow up first, then think about the situation, realize he'd overreacted and apologize.

"You *should* be sorry," she said. "This didn't need to happen. Just look at that man. All he wanted to do was defend me."

"Mija." His brow furrowed. "You're looking at me like I'm a monster."

"Sometimes you act like one." She crossed her arms and lifted her chin. "You've never been physically abusive, but your anger, harsh words and knee-jerk reactions can be hurtful and, sometimes, that can be far more damaging than a smack in the face."

He blew out a sigh. "I love you, honey. And all I've ever tried to do was look out for you. And for Emily."

"That may be true, but you aren't looking out for me and my best interests when you try to control my thoughts, feelings and plans for my life. That's grossly unfair. You might call it love, but if you *truly* cared about me, you'd first ask me what I want, what I like, how I feel. But that never seems to matter."

His shoulders slumped.

Miranda didn't stand up to her father very often, but doing so today gave her a burst of confidence, a feeling of power.

She shot a glance at George, who still lay on the ground but seemed to be stirring. The CPR had stopped, and one of the paramedics was inserting an IV. Thank God. He was breathing again, but she suspected he wasn't out of the woods yet.

She left her father and hurried to George. Afraid to get in the way of the paramedics, she still managed to hover over him and say, "You gave us a good scare."

The old man attempted a half-hearted smile.

When one of the paramedics indicated that she should take a step back, she returned to her father's side and, with her eyes glued to the medical drama unfolding, spoke to her dad. "You probably don't know this or even care, but I didn't want to become a CPA. I would have rather gone into teaching. But I gave in to you out of appreciation for all you did for me when I was growing up. But what's wrong with me having my own dreams and following my heart? Wouldn't allowing me to choose my own path be a better way for you to show your love and respect for me?"

"I'm sorry," he said again.

"Sometimes being sorry doesn't help." She stood tall and held her head high.

"I'd like to make things better," he said. "I didn't realize how much you cared about Matt and his uncle."

"Papa, they're part of my family, too. George is the uncle I never had. And believe it or not, I love Matt Grimes even more today than I did nine years ago. You might have thought you were protecting me back then, by forcing me to break up with him, but it tore me up inside. Still, I went along with your demands when I should have run away from home and married him as soon as I turned eighteen."

Her father seemed to think on that. Finally, he said, "Why *didn't* you run away?"

"Maybe I just wanted to make up for the way my mom left you. But now I realize, at least in part, why she made the decision she did. Sometimes you can be a tyrant."

Her father lowered his head. "In some ways, you might be right. She left me for someone else, a man who could give her more than I could. I got over what she did to me, but I never forgave her for leaving you. And I tried to make up for it the only way I knew how."

"You need to put her rejection and the past behind you, like I've been able to do. That is, until you throw her in my face and tell me I'm just like her. But I'm not at all like her." Miranda placed her hand on her baby bump. "I'd never give up my children and let someone else raise them."

"I know you won't."

Miranda studied her father, noted his growing remorse. "I've always known how angry you are at my mother, and that you've let those bitter feelings take root inside you. So when you accuse me of being just like her, it hurts worse than you can ever imagine."

"I never meant to lash out at you like that," he said.

"But you did."

Miranda glanced at the paramedics, saw them loading George onto a gurney. Thank God the dear old man was stable enough to transport to the hospital.

"We can talk more later," she told her father. "I'm going to have to leave now. But there's something you need to know. Like it or not, I'm selling my condo and moving to Brighton Valley. And I'm going to marry Matt Grimes, unless you chased him off for good."

"Are you sure about that?" he asked.

"About my decisions? Absolutely."

"I mean about Matt leaving for good."

Her heart bent into itself, and she did her best to recover. "I guess that's left to be seen. Either way, if you don't seek therapy and get into some anger management classes, you won't see me or the kids very often. I love Emily and this new little boy with all my heart and soul. And I'll be damned if I'll let you talk to them the way you talk to me."

Then, while her father pondered her threat, she went into the house to get her purse and her car keys.

All the while, her heart ached and her gut clenched. Losing Matt for the second time threatened to be her undoing. But whether she and Matt reconciled or not, George would always be a part of her family, and she'd do whatever she could for him for as long as he lived.

As Matt barreled down the interstate on his way to Houston, he tightened his grip on the steering wheel and swore under his breath. He'd meant everything he'd said to Miranda back at the ranch. He'd had his fill of her father and never wanted to lay eyes on him again. And if that meant he had to sever ties with Miranda, then so be it.

Only trouble was, he'd never turn his back on Emily. That's why he planned to see an attorney while he was in Houston. He was going to need someone to help him get a court order granting him visitation and securing his legal rights as Emily's father.

Carlos would probably pitch a fit, and who knew what Miranda might think, but he didn't care.

His cell phone rang, and when Miranda's number flashed on the screen, he let it roll to voice mail. He was too raw to talk to her now, too angry.

Less than three minutes later, she called again. But he still wasn't ready to talk to her and just let it ring.

But that didn't stop her from calling again.

And again.

Dammit. He'd told her to back off. Maybe not in words, but he'd let her know he needed to put some distance between them. Apparently, she didn't care about giving him the space and time he needed.

He finally answered, just so she'd stop calling, but he didn't open with *Hello* or a cheery tone.

"There's nothing to talk about," he said. At least, not until after a process server handed her the documents from family court.

"George is headed to Brighton Valley Medical Center," she said. "He's in an ambulance, and I'm following behind it."

His heart sank, his anger fizzled and his foot eased off the gas pedal. "What happened?"

"I think he had a heart attack. I won't know for sure until I get a chance to talk to the doctors. I'll let you know what they say."

Did she think he was going to continue on to Houston after getting news like that? "I'm making a U-turn. I'll meet you at the hospital."

"Okay."

He expected her to end the call, but she didn't. And neither did he. For some reason, he wanted to keep the line open.

Because of his uncle, of course. Yet, as much as he hated to admit it, something else made him hang on. Because right this minute, he'd never felt so alone or so far away.

"Miranda?" he asked.

"Yes?"

"Thanks." He waited a couple of beats before he finally disconnected the line. He could call her back if he needed to. And he knew that she'd answer.

He spotted a safe place to turn around up ahead. Once he was back on the road and headed in the right direction, he drove as fast as the law would allow.

With each passing mile, thoughts began to plague him, each one coming at him in single images and in short phrases, snapping in his mind, the cadence like that of a Vegas dealer with a deck of cards, each one flashing before him face up.

George could die...

Or end up an invalid...

I could lose the only family I've ever had...

A family that almost included Miranda and the kids.

That is, until Matt had tossed her aside like a bad hand of cards, losing her all over again. And losing her for good.

Or had he? He'd just gotten off the phone with her. And she'd called him several times, pursuing him.

Of course, she'd only done that so she could tell him about George. She, more than anyone, knew how he felt about his uncle, and as a courtesy...

No, it was more than that.

Matt, wait up.

I don't care what my father says or what he thinks. We're a family now.

She was right. It'd begun years ago, when a lonely old rancher, a rebellious throwaway kid and the young girl who'd loved them all turned to each other, becoming a family of sorts.

They still were, he supposed. Some ties weren't easily severed, although Matt had taken a pretty good slice at them today.

And somehow, he had to make things right.

It wouldn't be easy, though. Not the way he'd gotten used to handling life's ups and downs. In the past, whenever faced with an awkward or trying situation, he'd just shake it off and go to the next rodeo. Bull riding and the cheer of the crowd had been his fix. And for the past eight or nine years, that fix had been the only thing that mattered to him.

However, that wasn't the case anymore. Making love

with Miranda had changed things. And as a result, it had changed *him*.

But had it changed him enough to challenge Miranda's father, to claim the family he wanted, the family that always should have been his?

All Matt knew was that he had to get to the hospital before it was too late.

Nearly twenty minutes later, Matt arrived at the Brighton Valley Medical Center. After parking his truck, he hurried to the Emergency Department entrance. Once inside the waiting room, he scanned the sea of people seated in chairs—a woman holding a bloodied towel to a child's head, a red-eyed man coughing into his sleeve.

This was no place for a pregnant woman to be waiting, but he figured Miranda would be here. The minute he spotted her, he let out a sigh of relief and headed toward the registration desk, where she stood, haggard with worry and grief. She was a welcome sight—and still the prettiest woman he'd ever seen.

His heart cramped, and as much as he'd have liked to hang onto his anger, his resentment, it all seemed to pale when compared to the things that really mattered.

"How's he doing?" Matt asked.

She tucked a strand of hair behind her ear. "I'm not sure. The doctor said he was conscious, but we can't see him yet. He told me where I could find the family waiting room. It's located near the cardiac unit, but I thought I should stay put until you got here. And now that you are, we can go together."

The hard facts began to snap like cards again.
Family...
Together.

He was tempted to reach for her hand, to bind them together, but he kept his arms at his sides and said, "Let's go."

As he limped down the corridor with her, following the signs and arrows pointing to the cardiac unit, he asked, "Where's Emily?"

"I left her with my dad."

Matt stiffened, and his fists began to clench, but he shook off the negative reaction that would undoubtedly set the clock back an hour earlier, to the time he'd confronted the old man. Besides, under the circumstances, that was Miranda's only option—other than staying at the ranch with their daughter or bringing Emily here.

Hospitals could be a scary place. And on top of that, if George didn't make it—*God, please don't take him yet*—Emily would be devastated.

No, she was better off at home.

"Just so you know," Miranda said, "my dad was pretty remorseful when I left."

Matt held back the retort that formed on the tip of his tongue.

"After you drove away, I told him that I was moving to Brighton Valley no matter what. And that you were going to be a big part of Emily's life." She paused, then added, "Mine, too—assuming that's okay with you."

A flood of emotions, relief only one of them, settled over him. He hadn't chased her away. And while she hadn't mentioned living together or anything legally binding, it'd be pretty darn hard to be a *big* part of her life if they didn't make some kind of commitment.

"It's more than okay," he said, as they continued down the corridor, "but if it's all the same to you, I'll make sure I'm gone whenever your dad comes to visit." He hoped she wouldn't object to his comment, but he wasn't about to roll over and accept her father's words and opinions as gospel.

"I don't think that'll be necessary. I also told my dad that he needed to get his anger under control because if he didn't get professional help, he wasn't going to be a very big part of our lives."

Matt blew out a sigh, glad she'd finally taken a stand. "How'd he take it?"

"Like I said, he was pretty contrite and quiet when I left."

As happy as Matt was to hear that, her father wasn't the only one who had to deal with his anger and hard feelings. "I'm sorry for blowing up and running off like I did. I wasn't up for a fight with your dad, especially since I was afraid Emily might come outside and witness a lot of yelling and harsh words. But I should have kept my cool, even if he didn't."

Miranda reached for his arm and pulled him to a halt in the middle of the hospital corridor. "And just for the record, I wrapped up my speech by letting my dad know that I choose *you*, Matt. I'll always put you first."

As their gazes met and locked, the love shining in her eyes chased away any lingering anger he might have been harboring and every painful memory he'd ever had.

"I choose you, too," he said. "I have no idea how things will work out—with George, my knee, the rodeo or your dad—but I love you, Miranda. I always have and always will. We've spent so many damned years apart, and now that we finally have a chance to be together, I'm not letting you go. Marry me, Miranda."

She tossed him a heart-strumming smile, her eyes bright and glistening with what could only be happy tears. "I'm definitely willing."

Before sweeping her into his arms and kissing her, he asked, "What are the chances of us pulling together a wedding before the baby comes? I want my name on his birth certificate. That way, there won't be any doubt about who his father is."

"I'd say the chances are excellent." A happy tear slid down her dimpled cheek. "Our son is going to be one lucky baby."

"And I'm one lucky guy." Matt brushed a kiss over her lips, then he continued to hold her close, to savor the feel of her in his arms and bask in the sweet smell of sugar, vanilla and chocolate that still clung to her hair and clothes.

If he'd ever wondered what a real home and family felt like, this was it. Miranda was it.

On those long hard days, when he felt broken and tired, the only place he wanted to be was wrapped in her arms, heart to heart.

"I could really get used to coming home to you," he said. "So much so, that I'm not sure I want to follow the rodeo circuit any more. Not if it means long absences."

"I hate to admit it," she said, "but I'd really miss you

when you're gone. And so would the kids But we can talk more about that later, after we find out how George is doing."

He took her by the hand, and they continued to the family waiting room, the soles of their shoes clicking upon the tile floor.

Just as they reached the door, a doctor met them in the hallway, and Miranda introduced them.

"Dr. Kipper," she said, "this is Matt Grimes, George's nephew."

As the men shook hands, Matt asked, "How's he doing?"

"Much better. We're still running tests, but there doesn't seem to be any long-term damage to his heart. We're going to keep him here for a few days, and it looks like he'll need a stent. But it's nothing we can't fix."

"When can we see him?" Miranda asked.

"Not for an hour or so. But I'm almost afraid to let him know you're here. He's been asking to go home, and he's giving the nursing staff a hard time, insisting they bring him his britches."

Matt laughed. "Sounds like he's going to be just fine. But don't worry. Once we get a chance to visit him, we'll insist that he stay here until he's on the mend."

"That's good to know," the doctor said.

"In the meantime," Miranda added, "you can tell him that Matt and I will let him help plan our wedding if he settles down and doesn't give the nurses any more trouble."

"Do you think that'll work?" the doctor asked.

"Without a doubt." Matt slipped his arm around Miranda, pulled her to his side and smiled. "He's been waiting years to hear news like that."

"Good," the doctor said. "There's nothing that makes my job easier than a happy patient."

As Dr. Kipper walked down the hall, Matt and Miranda made their way into the family waiting room.

"This may sound weird," he said, "but as bad as this day has been—the blowup with your dad, the news about George, the worry of it all—it's helped me to realize something important."

"What's that?"

"It's not blood ties that create a family. It's love. And as long as I have you and the kids, nothing else matters. Not a knee injury, not the rodeo and not even your dad."

She pulled him to another halt, threw her arms around his neck and drew his lips to hers, letting him know they were a team—friends and lovers for life.

George remained in the hospital for several days before coming home. Once he was settled in his own room, he'd told Miranda, "You don't need to take care of me. You already have your hands full, and I don't want to be a burden."

"But I want to be here," she'd told him, placing a kiss on his brow.

Since then, he'd been a real sweetheart. That is, until the opening day of the Rocking Chair Rodeo rolled around, and Miranda told him that she and Matt had hired a nurse from a home health care agency to stay with him at the ranch while she, Matt and Emily were gone.

"That was a damn fool thing to do," George said, grimacing as he tried to get out of bed. "And a complete waste of good money when I'm perfectly capable of taking care of myself."

Miranda placed a gentle hand on his shoulder, carefully pressing him back down on the mattress. "I know that, but we'd all feel better if we didn't leave you alone."

The tough old rancher grumbled and swore under his breath. "I'm not used to folks fussin' over me."

"You'd better get used to it," Miranda told him. "I'm going to need you fit as a fiddle by the time the baby comes. You're going to have to help me with little Georgie."

"Georgie?" he asked, his voice and his expression softening in unison.

At one time, she'd thought about naming the baby after her father, but she'd changed her mind the day Uncle George stood up to her dad.

"That's right," she said. "You have a namesake. We're going to call him George Matthew Grimes."

"No kidding?" The roughened old cowboy's eyes watered.

She nodded, as she rested her hand on her baby bump. "Since we'd rather not get married until the doctor says that you can attend, we'd all be disappointed if there was a setback in your recovery because you pushed yourself too hard."

George snorted. "All right. I'll stay home and take it easy. But I still don't need a nurse."

He continued to scowl and complain for the next couple of hours. That is, until he laid eyes on the nurse, an attractive forty-something brunette with big blue eyes and feminine curves that could rock a pair of pale green scrubs.

"My name is Jolene," the nurse said, extending a manicured hand to her patient.

"George Grimes," he said, offering her a big ol' smile and giving her hand a shake.

Miranda had to stifle a chuckle.

But she just about lost it when George said, "Now that Jolene's here, you guys had better get a move on. That rodeo is going to start soon, and they expect a big crowd. You don't want to be late."

Twenty minutes later, they arrived at the county fairgrounds and found the parking lot nearly full.

George had been right. People were already filling the grandstands and lining up at the concession booths.

"The bigshots at Esteban Enterprises have to be happy about this crowd," Miranda said to Matt, as Emily skipped beside them, her ponytail swishing across her back.

"I'm sure Drew Madison is thrilled. I haven't seen him yet, but he's here somewhere. And he's probably eager to talk to me."

Miranda knew why. When Drew learned that Matt had decided to end his bull-riding career, he offered him a job, and Matt told them he'd have to think about it.

"Have you made a decision yet?" she asked.

"Yes, but it's not what they're going to want to hear. Working for them would still require me to travel, and I'd rather stick closer to home. Besides, the doctor told George he'd better think about retirement. And I'd like to buy the ranch from him."

"I can't see that man sitting in a rocker all day. What would he do if he retired?"

Matt laughed. "Well, since he'd be a permanent resident at the Double G, I expect he'd follow me around all day and tell me what I should be doing differently."

"Do you really want to run cattle?" she asked. "Not that it would matter to me. But you never wanted to before."

"Actually, I'd rather raise rodeo stock. I have a lot of connections, and that would keep me in the thick of things, but I'd still be home for dinner most nights."

"Speaking of connections," she said, "it certainly looks as though your endorsement and personal promotional efforts were a success. Thanks in large part to you, both the Rocking Chair Ranch and Kidville will get sizable checks."

"I'm glad. They're both great charities and will put the money to good use."

"Emily," Miranda called to their daughter, who'd skipped a little too far ahead. "You'd better get back here before you lose us."

When she didn't respond, Matt released Miranda's hand and went after their daughter and brought her back.

"They're selling snacks," Emily said. "Can I have a popcorn? And a lemonade?"

"Okay," Matt said. "But first, I want to introduce

you both to Jim Hoffman, one of the directors of Kidville. I just spotted him on the grassy area near the front entrance."

A short walk and a minute later, Matt introduced Miranda to a round-faced heavyset man in his mid- to late-fifties.

"Jim," he said, "this is Miranda Contreras, my soon-to-be wife and the CPA I told you about. And this is our daughter, Emily."

Jim took Miranda's hand, his nearly swallowing hers up, and gave it a warm and gentle squeeze. "I'm so happy to meet you. If you have time next week, I'd like you to come to Kidville and talk to my wife and me about going to work for us. Matt says you might have something else lined up, but we could sure use someone to conduct an audit before long."

"I do have a couple of irons in the fire," Miranda admitted. "But I'd be happy to help with that audit. I'd also like to stop by and see you next week. I've heard wonderful things about Kidville and the work you two have done."

"That sounds like a plan," Jim said. "It was nice meeting you, but you'll have to excuse me. I need to look for my wife before she and the kids we brought with us find seats without me."

"And I have to find a seat before my knee gives out on me," Matt said. But he'd hardly turned toward the grandstand when he said, "Uh-oh. Getting off our feet will have to wait." He pointed toward a parade of senior citizens, all men wearing Western wear and cowboy hats. Several rode in wheelchairs, and a couple pushed walkers.

An older cowboy, who still stood tall and strong, pushed one of the wheelchairs, while an attractive redhead in her sixties pushed another.

"Looks like Sam and Joy, the couple who run the Rocking Chair Ranch, have brought some of the retired cowboys with them. I'd better say hello."

Miranda smiled to herself. One step forward, two steps back.

Moments later, Matt was introducing her to Sam and Joy.

"What'd you do?" Matt asked. "Rent a bus?"

"Just about," Sam said. "Joy and I both drove, but we wouldn't have been able to fit everyone who was able to attend into our cars. So some of the ladies from the Brighton Valley Women's Club offered to help out."

"Maybe, after you get the funds from the rodeo, you'll be able to afford to buy a van."

"That's the plan," Sam said.

"Hey, Sam!" one of the old men said. "If you don't quit your yappin', we're going to miss the opening ceremony."

Sam laughed. "I've got a rebellion on my hands. So I'd better go."

As he and the old cowboys headed toward the stands, Miranda gave Matt's hand a tug. "And you'd better sit down."

"You got that right."

But before they made any forward progress at all,

Matt paused and pointed toward the entrance with his free hand. "Look who's here."

When she spotted her dad, her breath caught. "I didn't expect to see him show up."

"Neither did I."

Her father headed toward them, looking solemn—but not angry.

"Abuelito!" Emily, who'd just realized her grandfather had arrived, darted toward him, clearly happy to see him. He stooped to greet her with a smile and a hug, followed by a kiss on the cheek.

When Emily took her grandfather by the hand and led him to her parents, he said, "I hoped I'd find you here."

"What's up?" Miranda asked.

"I need to apologize," he told Matt. "But under the circumstances, saying 'I'm sorry' doesn't seem adequate."

Maybe not, but it was a start.

"I also want you to know that I'm turning over a new leaf. It might not be easy. Old habits are hard to break, but I'm sure going to try. I've already met with an anger management counselor, and I like her. I'm going to see her again next week."

"Thank you," Miranda said, glad that he'd listened, that he'd followed through.

"I wasn't sure when you two were getting married," her dad added. "All Miranda said was *soon*, so I wanted to make sure I got an invitation."

"We're getting married at the Brighton Valley Community Church at two o'clock next Saturday," Matt said. "It'll be a small wedding, since we don't want to wait any longer than we have to."

"I hope you'll be there," Miranda said.

"I wouldn't miss it, *mija*."

"Good." Miranda gave her father a hug. He held onto her a bit longer than she'd expected, but she could sense his repentance in the embrace. When he finally let her go, he managed a sheepish smile.

Then he turned to Matt. "How's your uncle?"

"He's at home, recovering. But he looks good and says he feels better than he has in years. We would have gotten married already, but we both want him to be there."

"I'm not going to be a flower girl," Emily said. "I get to be a bridesmaid. And tomorrow, Mom and I are going shopping to buy my dress."

"I can't wait to see you wearing it," he said. "You're going to be as pretty as your mama."

Emily reached for her grandfather's hand, then looked at Matt. "Can we get the lemonade now? I've been waiting a long time."

"And patiently," Matt said. "So yes, let's go."

With her free hand, she reached for her daddy, joining the men with her love and innocence, rather than the animosity that had separated them for years.

"By the way," Miranda's father said. "I'm moving the main office back to Brighton Valley. I figure you'll probably want to stay home with the baby after he's born, but your job will be ready for you when he gets older."

"Thanks. I appreciate that. But we'll have to see what happens."

Her father tilted his head, no doubt surprised by her comment.

"Just so you aren't blindsided," she said, "I've been talking to Hazel Jorgenson, the owner of the Brighton Valley Pharmacy. I want to help her get the soda fountain up and running again. We think we can turn it into a local landmark."

Her father blinked, clearly surprised by her plan, but he didn't object. And after a couple of beats, he said, "I hope things work out for you."

As they neared the concession stand, Miranda's father surprised her yet again.

"Emily," he said, "college has always been important to me. I know it's still a long time off for you, but I've set up educational trusts for you and your little brother so the money will be there for you. But if either or both of you decide you'd rather take another career path, I'll support your decisions."

Miranda's eyes filled with tears, something that seemed to be happening a lot lately, and she mouthed a silent *Thank you* to the first man she'd ever loved.

"The trust is flexible," her father said. "That means you can use the money to buy a house or start a business instead."

"I'm *definitely* going to college," Emily said. "I have to because I'm going to be a veterinarian. So I can use the money for that. But if there's any left over, can I use it for my rescue center?"

"You bet you can, *mija*. I had no idea you liked animals so much, even when you introduced me to all the ones living on the ranch."

"I *love* them. And guess what? Tomorrow my daddy is taking me to buy another lamb. Remember when I showed you Bob and told you I wanted to get him a wife? Well, it's going to be a girl lamb, and I'm going to name her Betty. Then they can have babies."

Her grandfather laughed. "I guess it's a good thing that you live on a ranch and not in the city."

"Yep." Emily released both of the men's hands so she could get in line.

Miranda couldn't believe the way her life had finally fallen into place. Sure, there were bound to be trials and setbacks. But nothing that love and family couldn't overcome.

She eased toward Matt and slipped her hand in his. "Have I told you how much I love you?"

He pulled her into his arms. "A couple of times, but not nearly enough."

Then he kissed her—right then and there, for all the world to see.

Epilogue

On Saturday afternoon, Matt stood beside the altar at the Brighton Valley Community Church in black jeans, a white Western shirt and a bolo tie, waiting for his bride to walk down the aisle. His old high school buddies, Clay Masters and Adam Santiago, stood with him—best men in every sense of the words.

Uncle George took a seat of honor in the front row, across from the pew where Miranda's father would sit after giving his daughter to Matt.

George obviously couldn't be happier to see the two people he loved the most in the world finally tie the knot. In fact, last night, he'd surprised them both by giving them a quitclaim deed to the ranch—his wedding gift to them.

"The only thing I'm not deeding over to you is my

bedroom," George had said. "Because I aim to live on the Double G until I die—or until you move me to the Rocking Chair Ranch.

"That's a promise," Matt told him.

Matt had invited his father and stepmother to attend the wedding, something Miranda had encouraged him to do. It hadn't taken much prodding, though. After all, this was the time for family harmony, forgiveness and second chances. His dad actually seemed pleased to hear the news and congratulated him.

"We'd be happy to attend," his dad had said. "But we're leaving on a cruise the night before. Can I make it up to you by taking you and Miranda to dinner when we get back?"

"Sure," Matt told him.

Because of his father's absence, Clay's wife Erica sat beside George. Next to her was her sister Elena and Drew Madison, Elena's husband.

Adam's wife Julie, who was a music therapist and a whiz on just about any instrument imaginable, sat at the church piano. As she began to play the wedding march, signaling that the bride would soon walk down the aisle, Matt's heart soared in anticipation. It had been a long, nine year wait, but Miranda would soon be his wife.

Emily, who wore a pretty yellow dress and held a bouquet of daisies, began to walk toward the altar first. Her bright-eyed smile and dimpled grin just about turned Matt inside out. But when he spotted the pregnant brunette walking behind her, his breath caught. Miranda, the love of his life, the mother of his children.

His eyes grew misty. Damn. He wasn't a softy. He

never cried. But this was different. *Today* was different. He'd never felt so many powerful, nearly overwhelming emotions—love, happiness, pride, hope....

Carlos smiled as he handed over his daughter's hand, clearly—finally—accepting Matt into his family—and finding him to be a man worthy of his daughter.

As Matt and Miranda turned to face the minister, Matt squeezed Miranda's hand, letting her know that they were bound together.

Not just for this moment, but forever.

* * * * *

COMING SOON!

MILLS & BOON

Coming next month

A WEEK WITH THE BEST MAN
Ally Blake

Harper turned to Cormac and held his gaze, despite the fluttering inside her belly. 'Where *is* my sister?'

'Catering check. Wedding dress fitting. Final song choices. None of which could be moved despite how excited she was that you were finally coming home.'

Harper bristled, but managed to hold her tongue.

She was well aware of how many appointments she'd already missed. That video-chatting while wedding-dress-hunting wasn't the same as being in the room, sipping champagne, while Lola stood in front of a wall of mirrors and twirled. That with their parents long gone from their lives she was all Lola had.

Lola had assured her it was fine. That Gray was *such* a help. That she understood Harper's calendar was too congested for her to have committed to arriving any earlier.

After all, it was Harper's job in corporate mediation that had allowed Lola to stay on in the wealthy coastal playground of Blue Moon Bay, to finish high school with her friends, to be in a position to meet someone like Grayson Chadwick in the first place.

And yet as Cormac watched her, those deep brown eyes of his unexpectedly direct, the tiny fissure he'd opened in Harper's defences cracked wider.

If she was to get through the next five minutes, much less the next week, Cormac Wharton needed to know she wasn't the same bleeding-heart she'd been at school.

'You sure know a lot about planning a wedding, Cormac,' she crooned, watching for his reaction.

Harper played chicken for a living. And never flinched.

There! The tic of a muscle in his jaw. Though it was fast swallowed by a deep groove as he offered up a close-mouthed smile. 'They don't call me the Best Man around here for nothing. And since the Maid of Honour has been AWOL, it's been my honour to make sure Lola is looked after too.'

Oh, he was *good*.

But she was better.

She extended a smile of her own as she said, 'Then please accept my gratitude and thanks for playing cheerleader, leaning post, party planner, and girlfriend until I was able to take up the mantle in person.'

Cormac's mouth kicked into a deeper smile, the kind that came with eye crinkles.

That pesky little flutter flared in her belly. She clutched every muscle she could to suffocate it before it even had a chance to take a breath.

Continue reading
A WEEK WITH THE BEST MAN
Ally Blake

Available next month
www.millsandboon.co.uk